TO KILL IS NOT ENOUGH

CRUSADER VOLUME I

- A novel by -

CHRISTOPHER L. ANDERSON

iUniverse, Inc.
New York   Bloomington

To Kill is Not Enough
Crusader Volume 1

iUniverse books may be ordered through booksellers or by contacting:

iUniverse
1663 Liberty Drive
Bloomington, IN 47403
www.iuniverse.com
1-800-Authors (1-800-288-4677)

ISBN: 978-1-4401-9601-0 (pbk)
ISBN: 978-1-4401-9600-3 (cloth)
ISBN: 978-1-4401-9599-0 (ebook)

Printed in the United States of America

iUniverse rev. date: 12/18/09

To my wife, Jules, who made me sit down and write this novel. My dear, you are beyond my dreams as a friend, wife, lover and mother—how could I say no?

CHAPTER 1:   The Way Things Were

"September 10, 2001, the King County Court of the great state of Washington, the honorable Judge Brent presiding. The Court will now hear the case of Wolfe versus Wolfe."

Flint Wolfe stood up, guts churning in his six-foot frame. He took a deep breath, his wrestler's physique straining the shoulders of his tweed jacket. Wolfe's brows contracted, and his eyes narrowed to the point where he could have been blindfolded by a piece of dental floss. He had strong, Nordic features, but they were set in a tense mask. His dark brown hair had been drained of life, streaked with gray by the persecutions of an unnaturally red-headed vampire with an affinity for motorcycles and his money—his ex-wife, Vanessa. It wasn't the adultery, the draining of his hard-earned accounts, or the ruination of a marriage that scarred him—Wolfe was a big boy; he could take it. It was his kids. Wolfe was protective of his two little people; why their mother wasn't—who knew? His lawyer glanced at him; he read her thoughts.

"What's your problem—it's a slam dunk, relax."

I know, I know, he thought viciously. *I'm a pilot, and I'm supposed to be trained to handle stress. I've been shot, given up for dead, and even won the freaking Medal of Honor! Now some bull dyke judge is going to make me pee my pants!* He tried to pry his mind away from the uncertainty, thinking of concrete things under his control. *Get into uniform; get to the airport; I fly one leg to Boston, short layover, and tomorrow Boston,*

1

back home just in time for Alexander's soccer game. No problem, then four days off. It's the tenth today, September eleventh tomorrow; the family picnic is on Saturday, then I fly again Sunday—I'll have to go to Saturday mass. His lawyer gave him a dig in the ribs.

"Don't worry, Flint—we've got her dead to rights. You did everything right; she did everything wrong."

True, but still it all came down to the judge. He glanced up at the pink, pudgy face peering over gold-rimmed spectacles, her watery eyes glaring at him beneath bushy brows. She sported a crew cut of wiry, too-yellow-to-be-natural hair—man-hater, a truly virulent man-hater.

Flint took a deep, shuddering breath, trying to calm himself. *God, I'd rather be back in Iraq than to go through this!* He stole a glance at Vanessa. She wore a smug half-smile on her pallid, painted face, but she dressed like the proverbial church mouse. She wasn't stupid. She knew better than to wear her biker leathers to court. It was strange how he once thought she was beautiful.

The lawyers announced themselves, and then came the words, long streams of monotonous words. On and on, back and forth, without the drama reserved for TV law; it was torment to listen to. It was like watching his kids on the gallows, waiting for that trap door to open, and it was truly agonizing, far worse than anything he'd ever been through in Desert Storm. He had to stop thinking, just listen, dissect every word, every syllable, and calculate the case on the balance of facts. That settled him down. The law was on their side. As the evidence kept piling on Vanessa, crushing her, Wolfe felt an ease return to his chest. He could breathe again. Anything other than full custody was inconceivable. His kids would be home with him for dinner tomorrow night. September 11, 2001 was going to be the first day of their new life.

Vanessa's lawyer was almost finished. She tripped over her own words as if they were untied shoes, and she made no points—she babbled. A by-the-hour lawyer, hired from some mini-mall, she couldn't have made a worse impression. For an ex-military man who'd made presentations to generals, NASA, and congressmen, Flint could only mentally shake his head and wish her a quick, painless, professional death.

"I've got one last point to make, Your Honor, and that's what this is all about."

Flint's brows rose as he listened to her closing.

"Your Honor, despite Mr. Wolfe's façade of reason, it was Ms. Wolfe's right to end the relationship in any manner she chose within the law. This is a no-fault state, and yet Mr. Wolfe has found fault with Ms. Wolfe's behavior and that of her new partner. He's relayed that fault to the children, poisoning their minds against her partner, and indeed against her. He's said she cheated, lied, and broke the family up—so what? There's nothing illegal about adultery, and there's something very noble about a woman having the courage to leave her old life behind and pursue the opportunities of a new life; it's this new life that Mr. Wolfe is obstructing both for Ms. Wolfe, and more importantly, for the children."

Wolfe bit down so hard, his tooth chipped, and he stifled a venomous curse.

His lawyer held up a hand to calm him, but the judge cast a withering glance at him and hissed, "Tell your client he's not to speak unless I address him; anymore under-the-breath outbursts like that and I'll hold him in contempt!"

Wolfe clenched his jaw.

Vanessa snickered.

The judge glared at her and said, "And you, young lady, what were you thinking? You can't simply start a new life with your kids without regard to their father, especially a father who appears—despite his temper—to be a devoted parent."

Flint breathed again.

"However, the law is the law, and though I do not condone adultery, there's nothing illegal about it; in the broad sense of things, the children need to be close to their mother. I'm assigning Ms. Wolfe to be the Custodial Parent. Mr. Wolfe can have custody every other weekend."

Flint's breath caught in his lungs.

The gavel came down.

His lawyer ushered him out of the courtroom, her hand wrapped around his elbow. He could feel her nails digging through the tweed of his suit, but only in a detached, dead sort of way. Flint strode mechanically to the door, disemboweled, a husk, a shell, a dead thing.

Vanessa walked by him with a smug, crooked smile spreading beneath her wiry red hair. Her teeth showed like choppers biting at his will to live. She looked alien, not human; certainly, she was nothing like the woman he married fifteen years ago.

"Have a nice day, Flint," she cooed. Snickering, she trotted down the hall.

Flint stopped as if he'd been shot, his face twisting into a malevolent grimace.

"We'll re-file with another judge, Flint; don't do anything to aggravate the situation." She took his arm and told him, "This is a setback, nothing more. When you look back on this after a few years, it will seem like nothing. You haven't lost your children, Flint; you can still call them, see them, and go to their games. There are worse things that can happen."

"Really, that's what being a father has come to? What more can happen in my life?" He started walking again. His brain was in crisis mode—one disaster down, move on to the next. It was something that drove Vanessa out of her mind. Flint shook his head like a dog that had been struck on the nose. "Re-file if you want to. I don't have time to deal with it. I have to fly to Boston."

"Wait, you're flying an airplane after this? Can't you call in sick?"

Flint smiled mirthlessly, grinning like a death's-head. "I've used up all my sick time coming to court. If you and Vanessa want to get paid, I've got to fly."

"Well, don't take it out on the passengers, Flint."

"That all depends on whether they behave themselves," he growled, and left.

CHAPTER 2: A Fearful New World

After nine hours at the hotel in Boston, a few of which he actually slept, Wolfe boarded the bus from Chelsea to the airport. He hated the frenetic pace of early-morning travel, but at least he wasn't a passenger.

The line at security in Boston's Logan Airport was heinous. The surly, grumbling snake of humanity trudged forward one shuffling step at a time toward the hulking, silver-gray X-ray machines and metal detectors. Fortunately, Flint and his captain, Josh Bennigan, were able to go to the front of the line, but this perk didn't sit well with everyone.

"Excuse me," Flint said as politely as his bleary demeanor would allow; it was 3:00 AM at home. He cut in front of a smallish woman with bleach-blonde hair wearing an offensively pink suit and skirt.

"Why the hell do you get to go in front of me?" she protested. "I paid for this ticket—you get paid to flip the goddamned switch to 'autopilot' and check your stock trades."

Flint glanced back at her as he slung his bags onto the conveyor. *Too bad she was kind of a bitch,* he thought. She was in her thirties and despite the pink suit and the severe expression, she was really cute. The suit didn't hide her petite hourglass figure, and her well-toned calves spoke of hours on the stair climber. Her unfriendly glare did nothing to subvert her very lovely blue eyes. He asked politely, "Where are you going, ma'am?"

"Seattle," she said tersely.

"Good, I'm flying you there." Maybe she was just having a bad morning. Pretty women had bad days too. "Listen, miss, I'm sorry for cutting in line, but if you want to get to Seattle on time, I need to get to the airplane. I'll just be a second."

"A frigging monkey could do your job, buddy," she told him angrily. "You rake in a couple hundred grand to flip switches. I'm Dixie C. Dallas, and I'm *the* lawyer for the ACLU. I've got to be brilliant to earn my million; you just have to have the brains to wear a rubber when you're shagging flight attendants."

The effect of her pretty eyes disappeared, and his voice turned sharply sarcastic. "What's the matter, ma'am, couldn't get your last pedophile a community service award?"

"That shows what you know: my pedophiles get assigned community service at the playgrounds of their choice!"

Wolfe dragged his heavy flight bags from the conveyor belt and growled, "I could've used you in court a few hours ago!"

"You couldn't afford me, flyboy," she laughed, "but do something juicy like laying a sonic boom over the Crystal Cathedral or flying naked and I'll defend your right to express yourself."

Shaking his head, Wolfe started to walk away, but a group of men cut in front of him, coming from another security line. Both he and Bennigan came to an abrupt stop as the five men, moving in a tight-knit pack, hustled in front of them, jabbering away in what sounded like Arabic. One of them glanced his way and locked eyes with Flint. It was just for an instant, but the man's expression caused him to shudder.

"Rude bastards," Bennigan grumbled.

"Yeah," Wolfe said, a scowl settling on his face. He stopped. "Remember that story I told you about the two Arabs assaulting the crew in New York?"

Bennigan nodded. "The crew was in the middle of their preflight and the Arabs ran into the cockpit, slammed their heads down on the yokes, and then backed off. What do you think—these are the guys?"

"No, I don't recognize them," Wolfe said, walking again. "It just jogged my memory, that's all. Somehow, the two guys who assaulted the crew got off scot-free. They kicked them off the flight for the 'misunderstanding,' but the cops didn't do anything about it. The company thought about pressing charges until Pinky," he jerked his thumb at Dixie, who was arguing with the security screener, "and her ACLU buddies threatened to sue us for violating *their* civil rights! They weren't even U.S. citizens."

"Crazy world," Bennigan grumbled. "She reminds me of my second wife, the one who has my pension, my house, my car, and my dog—damn it, I loved that dog."

An hour later, they leveled off at thirty-five thousand feet. Flint was flying. He reached under the glare shield and pushed the center autopilot engage switch. "There, that should make that Dixie chick happy," he said caustically, changing the range of the electronic flight map from eighty miles to 320 miles. The magenta line of their flight path extended out into Pennsylvania and Ohio. Airports popped up along their flight path, their four-letter identifiers floating next to blue circles: KBOS for Boston; KJFK for Kennedy, which was southwest; up ahead, KBUF for Buffalo; and to the north, CYYZ, which somehow meant Toronto.

"The autopilot's on and we're still making money—it's a travesty."

The voice of the air traffic controller crackled over the radio. "United twenty-three cleared direct Albany Jet Sixteen, flight planned route. Maintain flight level three-five-zero."

Bennigan acknowledged, and he brought ALB to the top of the legs page on the CDU, the control display unit. The execute light came on, and he asked, "Does that look good?"

"Looks good," Flint said, cross-checking the navigation display with their clearance.

Bennigan executed the command and the jet turned toward Albany.

There was a knock at the door. Bennigan cocked his head and said, "Must be coffee, and about time, too." He hit the release for the lock and glanced at Flint. "Two more years and I'm done with these 3:00 AM shows. Thirty-two years of flying and three airlines—that's enough. It's time to kick back and watch the sun set from a condo on Maui."

"Aren't you going to miss it? Flying, that is," Flint asked, glancing back toward the door.

Bennigan opened his mouth to answer, but the door burst open with a crash. Instead of Tracy, the purser, a dark-haired man, a stranger, burst in. He threw himself on Bennigan, something bright flashing in his right hand.

"Hey, what the hell," Bennigan yelled, twisting to his right, an expression of surprise and anger in his watery blue eyes.

Flint erupted in fury—his great weakness—instinctively striking out with his left hand. Despite his anger, the angle was bad and the lap belt restricted his movement—he struck the attacker on the shoulder. Flint hit him hard, but it didn't knock him off the captain. The man grabbed Bennigan around the head with his left arm and punched him in the throat with whatever he was holding. Bennigan cried out.

A fountain of blood spurted from Bennigan's neck and splashed in Flint's face. Flint reached for the release of his lap belt, half turned, his legs gathering to leap upon the attacker as soon as he was free. Yet as he turned, he saw the blur of another man forcing his way into the cockpit behind Bennigan's attacker. Only one thing came into focus— a set of dark, soulless eyes, like pits filled with black water from the ocean abyss.

At that moment, a cold fury enveloped him, and everything slowed for Wolfe. His vision became sharp, almost painful in its detail, but it blurred beyond the object of his focus. Sounds blended into a drone of monochromatic voices fighting against a background of hollow static. Fear flashed in his mind, fear that he would move too slow, that terror would render him immobile. A hand touched him, the dark palm striking at his head, the fingers trying to grasp his hair. All vestiges of fear fled, leaving him in a roiling pool of frigid ferocity.

The hijacker had momentum, but the shock of his advance was born by the steel pilot's seat and not by Wolfe. The hijacker tried to grasp, claw, and punch Wolfe. Wolfe leaned away from him, striking backward with his elbow across the dark, stubbly, sweating face. He sent the hijacker's face twisting to the left, but he was trapped, still confined by the now life-threatening lap belt. While he pushed, struck, and punched with his left hand, he groped desperately at the release— now jammed with his full weight on the belt.

The hijacker was on him, sweat flying from his dark face and landing on Flint's skin. He felt the warmth of the droplets; he smelled the heavy mix of oil from the man's hair, rancid sweat, and pungent perfume. The hijacker wormed his way behind the seat, reaching around

Wolfe's head with his right arm; in the right hand, something metallic flashed in the morning sunlight, then it disappeared beyond his vision. Flint twisted, tucking his chin to his chest. A triangular metal blade glinted next to his left eye; in an instinctive spasm of pure rage, Flint ripped his left elbow back and forth like the rocker arm of a locomotive wheel. The attacker fell back with an inarticulate cry, but the blade of his knife stabbed down at Flint's eye. The blade buried itself in his brow and ripped downward.

His eye watched the stained blade as if he saw it on a movie screen—in perfect focus, seeming like it was fifteen feet high, moving frame by frame. The edge cut a channel through his brow, parted two eyelashes, skipped over his eyeball, and disappeared into his cheek. From there, he felt the flesh of his cheek and jaw part, not painfully, just in a cold, sharp, detached way; the most irritating thing was the way it grated against his bone—as if it were chalk scraping over the concrete of a sidewalk. The worst part of it for Wolfe was the degrading way he was allowing this attacker, this idiot, this son of a bitch, to get the better of him.

That was enough. The years of wrestling, the martial arts, his time with the SEALs, all of it took over. Conscious thought fled; instinct took over. Instinct and bloody, deadly training. In that split second, Wolfe transformed from a rational being to a machine whose only programming was to kill and to survive.

The attacker lunged in to grapple him, to pin him to his seat and finish him. Wolfe threw all of his weight into a back elbow strike, coiling from his hips and shoulders, unloading all of his rage into the attacker's jaw. This time, he hit home. A heavy, dull force came from his left elbow as it thudded mechanically into the attacker's face. Wolfe watched the stubbly jaw swing oddly back and forth amidst a spray of spit and blood—broken. The hijacker reeled back into the maintenance panel behind and to the right of Wolfe's seat. Wolfe turned the other way and grabbed the attacker's head in the crook of his right arm, pulling him down between the seat and the maintenance panel. Turning the attacker's head in his arm, Wolfe pummeled the bloody face with his left fist. The hijacker stopped fighting and began to curl up, sliding down until he was wedged between Wolfe's seat and the panel. Wolfe clutched a handful of oily hair in his left hand and smashed his

9

right elbow down on his skull again and again, trying to kill—not trying to stop or to knock out—he was trying to kill.

How many times he struck, Wolfe couldn't say, but he saw the hijacker's sweat fly, his face deform, his eyes close tightly with every strike—like the slow-motion images of a boxer being hit in the ring. The hijacker's eyes fluttered. Wolfe's vision honed in on the flat, triangular patch of the hijacker's temple. His arm swung back and he twisted as much as he could, coiling his hips and unleashing his blow in a flash of violent motion. The point of his elbow smashed into the temple. The hijacker's head turned with a hard snap and hung limp, dripping blood, sweat, and saliva. His body crumpled.

Free from attack, Flint reached down on the right-hand side of his seat and yanked on the release lever. He kicked his seat back and toward the outside of the cockpit. There was a dull crunch as the steel seat pinned the terrorist's head to the corner of the maintenance panel. He didn't even whimper.

Wolfe had a clear path from his seat now. Reaching blindly into his flight case, he grabbed the three D-cell flashlight by the bulbous end and pulled it free. With his left, he fumbled for the release on his lap belt.

Bennigan's attacker stared at him, wide-eyed, his hands awash in Bennigan's blood. Bennigan sat slumped over his left side, gray, with his glazed blue eyes staring lifelessly at the sky. A third hijacker entered the cockpit next to Bennigan's attacker, and another stood behind him in the narrow doorway. The third hijacker howled something at Flint, and everyone simply froze, glaring at each other for that moment in time. The incomprehensible drone of sound formed words, and in a flash of sanity, Flint actually heard the hijacker shout, in slurred English, "You defy Allah, infidel! This is Allah's will!"

Flint almost laughed, but all became clear. This was no hijacking. There would be no demands to fly to Cuba. These were terrorists.

As if spurred on by the remark, all three terrorists leapt at him, seeking to crush him under their flailing mass. Wolfe desperately turned the latch of the belt, but it wouldn't come free. They were on top of him, and he met them with the heavy flashlight. He felt it thud home. His left fist abandoned the lap belt and jammed viciously upward through the tangle of limbs, trying to fend off the crushing rush of men. He felt the soft, stubbly flesh of a throat and squeezed. Someone grunted in reply. Wolfe swung blindly, and his flashlight thudded repeatedly into the mass of attackers. The weight felt powerful in his hands, and suddenly he felt a wrathful joy. The flashlight crunched into skulls, shoulders, arms, and faces with a gleeful thump—wham, wham, wham, wham! Blood splattered the cockpit, and the terrorists looked stunned.

"You cannot resist Allah's will!" one of them cried out, his voice almost a scream.

"Fucking bastards, how do you like that? Do you want more? Are you ready to die, you fucking sons of bitches?" Despite his fury, the seething, flailing terrorist monster enveloped him. He wasn't fighting a single man, or even a group of men; it was an inhuman mass of arms, torsos, heads, and darkly insane eyes. The monster pinned him back against his window, making his gore-stained flashlight useless. His head thumped against the Plexiglas. The window handle dug into his shoulder blade. He was racked, his torso trapped by the lap belt and the weight of three men stretching him back over the arm of his seat and into the window. The face of one of the terrorists touched his, eyes mad, teeth bared in an evil grin, and sweat popping from his swarthy flesh. He was suffocating in that press of bodies.

"Die, crusader dog!" a terrorist spat, sending foul-smelling saliva into his eyes.

"Not today, you fucking bastard!" Wolfe seethed through clenched teeth. He reached for a terrorist's face, forgetting all else. Wolfe's nails dug into the terrorist's cheek, then clawed upward and found the soft flesh of his eye. The terrorist screamed. Flint felt the flesh give way, and warm fluid doused his hand.

"Kill him! Kill him!" the terrorist screamed, clutching at his face and trying to get away. Some of the weight shifted off Wolfe's right side.

The other two terrorists flailed wildly with their knives, and Wolfe knew it was only a matter of seconds before they shredded him. Desperately, pushing sideways with the knee of his right leg and the back of his right elbow, Wolfe shoved the control column forward. The autopilot disengaged; the plane lurched; and the warning horn began to blow. The plane nosed over suddenly, and the three attackers flew up into the overhead panel on the cockpit roof. Wolfe flew upward with them, but the lap belt yanked him back into his seat.

The airplane groaned, and Wolfe prayed, "Papa Boeing, don't fail me now!"

Wolfe squirmed around and grabbed the controls. The terrorists shrieked like frightened girls, and Wolfe grinned with wicked glee as he pulled back on the yoke. All three terrorists came crashing down, grunting in pain as they smashed hard into the communications panel and its protruding toggles and switches. He pushed over again, and up they flew. When he pulled back again, they came down in a thudding mass of bodies. Wolfe centered the controls and punched the autopilot back on.

"Papa Boeing, you and God have the aircraft!"

Finally, he released his lap belt and turned his full attention on the terrorists. He grabbed the closest terrorist by the hair and slammed his ravaged face down on the ACARS screen, a small, six-inch plate of glass surrounded by a heavy metal frame. The glass shattered on the second hit, and the terrorist's screeching climbed higher and higher in pitch. Blood whipped across Wolfe's instrument panel every time he lifted the terrorist's head, but he didn't care; he kept it up, like the staccato crunch of an assembly-line wrecker.

At first, the terrorist screamed; then he cried; then he whimpered; and finally, he went silent. The other two terrorists scrambled back to their feet. Another dark-haired man appeared at the door.

Wolfe let the terrorist on the panel go and leapt into their midst like a starving lion.

Whoomp! The flashlight buried itself in the forehead of a terrorist. Flint watched the round steel embed itself halfway into the skull. There was the crunch of bone, and the terrorist collapsed in a heap to the floor. The two remaining terrorists stumbled back, trying to flee his rage, spilling out of the cockpit like rats out of a burning window. He followed them, retrieving the crash axe from its cradle beneath the second observer's seat. As he was about to exit, the terrorist behind his seat began to struggle up. Wolfe didn't let him get to his feet. He buried the pick of the axe in the back of the terrorist's skull. Blood and brains splattered over the floor. Flint wrenched the axe out of the quivering mass, gray brains glopping onto the dark blue of his trousers, and stormed out of the cockpit. With the gory flashlight in one hand and the dripping axe in the other, Wolfe felt like some nightmare warrior emerging from a Frazetta painting.

The rearmost terrorist was in first class trying to pull the obnoxious woman in pink out of her seat and use her as a shield.

"You damned coward!" Wolfe fumed, striking through the terrorist's desperately raised arm with the flashlight. The terrorist clutched at his broken arm instinctively, half turned to face Wolfe. His mouth was wide in a silent scream as the axe clove through his forehead and into his brain. Dixie C. Dallas screamed as he fell on her, collapsing with his mangled head in her lap.

"Excuse me, Dixie!" Wolfe growled, placing his bloody boot on the corpse and prying the axe free. A fountain of blood gushed out of the wound and all over Dixie C. Dallas.

She screamed something incoherent at Wolfe, but he hadn't the time for her protestations. The last hijacker was wrestling a flight attendant, but she smashed a coffee pot into his face and beat him off. He turned toward the front of the airplane—then he saw Wolfe. Not being able to flee any farther, he held out his hands, as if asking Wolfe to stop. It was too late. Whatever link Wolfe might have had to rationality and sanity was severed. He was a beast. Wolfe de-evolved into the animal in his desperate struggle to survive. He was vicious; he was cruel; he was incapable of guilt, mercy, or negotiation. They'd torn the mantle of civilization from his back when they themselves deserted it; he couldn't replace it in that bloody moment even if he wanted to.

Wolfe swung with one arm and then the other, wading into the terrorist like a threshing machine. Blood flew wildly as he ignored the cries. The terrorist fell, but he fell against the seats. They held him up, so Wolfe kept striking him. Finally, the lifeless lump of quivering flesh slid to the floor.

Suddenly, to Flint, there was no movement, no sound, nothing. Flint lifted his head and looked around. Scores of wide, fearful eyes stared back at him. He stood panting for a long, seemingly endless moment, but there was only the constant, steady droning of the engines and the sharp hiss of the air-conditioning system. Flint straightened up.

"Is there anyone else who wants to try and take my airplane?"

A tawny-skinned woman in a gray suit stood up. She had a business-class seat and was obviously of Middle Eastern descent.

"I think that's all of them, Captain," she said.

Wolfe approached her, tapping her on the shoulder with the bloody flashlight, and asked, "Are you sure?"

"My name is Orani," she said, carefully opening a slim billfold.

Wolfe squinted at it through bloodstained eyes. Inside was a picture of her. She was quite good-looking, strikingly so. Next to her photo was a holographic seal that read, "Central Intelligence Agency."

He glared at her and asked, "Aren't you armed?"

Orani shook her head and said, "I'm an analyst, not a field agent."

"You're a field agent today, ma'am, help out back here."

"Not much to do except clean up," Orani said flatly. "It looks as though you took care of all of them."

The plane lurched and began to dive.

"Not all of them!" cried Wolfe, and he laboriously climbed back up the aisle toward the cockpit. He reached the door and forced his way over the prone bodies. The one-eyed terrorist was in his seat.

"Not dead yet, eh?"

"Allahu Akbar!"

"Tell him in person!" Flint growled, and he buried the pick of his axe in the back of the terrorist's skull.

The terrorist went into spasms.

Wolfe couldn't wait. The sound of the air outside the cockpit was deafening. The airspeed warning clacker went off—screaming that the aircraft was exceeding its maximum design speed. The heavily forested landscape of New York State filled the windscreen. He grabbed the terrorist by the collar and dragged him out of the seat.

Wolfe jumped in and leveled the wings, pulled the throttles to idle. Gingerly, he pulled back on the yoke because if he pulled too hard, the wings or the tail would come off. The air buffeted the plane, but the nose slowly began to come up.

A piercing, Stuka-like yell sounded behind him.

He twisted around to see someone at the door, a fist raised threateningly.

CHAPTER 3: Nobody's Hero

"I saw you execute that man!" a blood-drenched Dixie C. Dallas screamed at him. "How dare you endanger our lives and then murder a man in cold blood!"

"No time to explain, Dixie!" Wolfe growled, easing the big airplane back under control. The buffeting was still racking the fuselage, making the metal tube sound like the inside of a kettle drum, but the speed was coming back. "I'm too busy saving your ass!"

"Saving my ass! Look what you did to my suit!" she screamed. She staggered into the cockpit and grabbed his shoulder, ignoring the vivid, gray corpse of Captain Bennigan, staring up at her in disbelief with his dead eyes. "Do you have any idea what I'm going to have to pay in therapy after this? It'll take years to get the image of man's open skull off my lap! Believe me, that's not what men do in my lap!"

"Dixie, get out of here!" he ordered.

"What are you going to do about it?"

A woman's shout interrupted Dixie's tirade, and Flint glanced back to see two of the flight attendants dragging her away.

Finally, it was just the dull roar of the atmosphere over the fuselage. Wolfe sighed, and for the first time that morning, he worried about flying the plane.

"Well, at least that's something I normally do!" he said. It took another few moments to ease the plane level at twenty-one thousand feet. The airspeed was coming back, and back, and back. It was dropping through 250 knots when it struck Wolfe that it was growing surprisingly quiet in the airplane. He glanced at the instrument display. Both engines were dead.

"Great, we're a glider now," he said.

Wolfe set the airplane in a shallow dive to maintain 250 knots. Then he turned the air-conditioning packs off, switched both starter switches to the "FLT" position, and brought the fuel control switches to "RUN."

Nothing.

"What the hell?"

"Flint, are you alright; how are we doing?" the purser asked, poking her head in the cockpit.

"Sorry, kind of busy right now," he said, fighting a rising feeling of nausea. "You're not going to win, Abdul. Now what did you do to my airplane? Why aren't the engines starting?" Wolfe took a deep breath to clear his head. What was he missing? It was almost always something simple, something stupid. With forced calm, he scanned everything again. The engines were rotating as they should be. The starters were on. The fuel-control switches were on—he checked the fuel-flow displays. They read zero. His eyes snapped to the fire handles. Someone had pulled them and rotated them.

"Abdul, you bloody bastard, you did your homework. You shut down the fuel-control switches and fired the extinguishers." Wolfe reset the handles, opening the fuel valves. The fuel flow jumped to six hundred pounds an hour. The left engine started to wind up. The right one followed, but then it sputtered and flamed out. Wolfe tried it again, but nothing he could do would bring it back to life.

"One is better than none," Wolfe sighed, and he trimmed the plane up, moving the electric trim tabs on the elevators and rudder to ease the forces on the control column. He glanced back at the purser. She was still waiting, white-faced and trembling. He sympathized, but he needed her help. He said, "See if you can help Larry. I've got to get this thing on the ground."

She stepped over the twisted forms of the terrorists and bent over the captain. "I think he's dead, Flint," she said, her voice trembling.

"Alright, sit him up and lock his shoulder harness, will you—that lever there, that's it; I can't have him draped over the controls when we land."

The purser grabbed Bennigan's shoulders and pulled him back. Blood got all over her hands and blouse. She threw up, but fortunately, she had enough presence of mind to turn her head. She missed Bennigan and hurled on the corpses of the terrorists. The she sat Bennigan up and locked his harness.

"Good girl," he said, reaching for his headset. "Now get some help in getting these bodies out of here. Then close the door. See if we have some cops or army boys back there and post a guard. I'll get us on the deck as quick as I can."

He turned to give her a reassuring smile, but her expression turned to horror.

"Flint, oh my God; you're all cut up!"

He felt his face. There was a slice in his flesh beginning at left brow, jumping over his eye, and running through the middle of his cheek to his jaw. The cut felt sticky and warm, but there didn't seem to be any fresh blood.

"I'm alright, for now," he said. "Just button up the cockpit and get the cabin ready for landing."

She ducked out of the cockpit to get some help, and Wolfe plugged his ear bud in. Almost at once, he heard his call sign.

"United twenty-three, United twenty-three, do you read New York Center?"

"New York, United twenty-three here," Wolfe said. "We are now level flight level one-nine-zero. I'm declaring an emergency. We've had an attempted hijacking. One pilot is dead, and we have multiple casualties. I need vectors present position to JFK, LaGuardia, or Newark."

"Roger, United twenty-three, turn left heading zero-six-five and descend to one-three-thousand, altimeter two-niner-eight-seven," said the controller. "When able, state souls on board, fuel remaining, and status of aircraft; FAA request, do the hijackers have control of your aircraft?"

"Negative," Wolfe told them as he turned the plane east and descended. Wolfe craned his neck and saw Manhattan in the morning sun only forty miles away. A dark pyre of smoke rose from the skyline. Something cold settled in the pit of his stomach. It was then that he noticed the chatter on the radio. Aircraft were being vectored every-where and asked to report their security status.

"United twenty-three, can you talk in the clear?" asked the control-ler.

"United twenty-three, New York Center, that's affirmative," Wolfe said. "The hijackers are all dead, and I have a guard posted at the cock-pit door. What's going on in the city?"

"We've lost contact with two other United aircraft and two Ameri-can aircraft," the controller said, and even with the radio static, Wolfe could hear the emotion straining his voice. "Moments ago, two aircraft hit the World Trade Center towers. Apparently, this is a concerted ef-fort, but we have no idea how many aircraft are involved." There was a pause, and then the controller added, "Air Defense Command informs me that they have two fighters en route to your position. Continue descent to one-three-thousand and hold present position, right-hand turns, until they join up on you. Be advised that deviation from course or altitude, or loss of transponder, will be considered a hostile act. The fighters will have authorization to engage and shoot. Is that under-stood?"

"Perfectly," Wolfe said. "Well, then, we're at war."

The plane was heavy, and he had to wipe the congealing blood clear of the displays to see anything. After a few minutes, he heard the unmistakable sound of a voice talking through an oxygen mask.

"United two-three, this is Eagle zero-one, how copy?"

"Loud and clear, Eagle zero-one, where are you?"

"I'm joining up on your left wing."

"Sorry, I'm in the other seat, I can't see you. You got a heading for me?"

"Roll out heading zero-seven-zero, United two-three."

Wolfe did so and after a moment, a gray F-15 pulled up alongside him. It would've been a beautiful sight if he didn't have to look over Bennigan's lifeless body.

The F-15 pulled up close enough for Wolfe to see the pilot's eyes. The fighter pilot could see him too.

"You're a mess, buddy; you going to be okay to land this thing?"

"I've got no choice, pal, just get me to the runway."

"Follow me."

The F-15 led Wolfe's stricken aircraft to runway 31R at JFK. He had them on the radio, informed them of his approach speed, and configured the aircraft for landing. The lead F-15 swapped over to his right side, watching him from the wing. The wingman flew behind the 767, ready to shoot him down if he strayed from the approach path. Wolfe understood why. Looking out the cockpit window, he had a wonderful view of the Brooklyn Bridge, but beyond the masonry towers, the smoke over Manhattan rose in a tragic gray pyre.

But there was something else, something strange about the skyline, something he, as busy as he was, couldn't put his finger on. Then he understood. The smoke was coming from only one of the towers. Where was the other one?

He shook his head, bringing himself back to the task at hand. A thousand feet, he cross-checked everything: gear, flaps, approach course, and glide path. Five hundred feet—he sank low on the glide-slope, so he added power and rudder and pulled up slightly. Flaps at twenty, gear down, airspeed good, and the runway was clear. Shit, the APU; he'd need it when they landed. He reached over with his left hand and turned the rotary switch clockwise to the first stop, then all the way over to the two o'clock position. It fired up, and he turned back to the approach. Fire trucks waited alongside the runway, their lights flashing red in the morning air. There was a movement on the horizon. He pulled back on the yoke, rotating the aircraft a few degrees nose-up. He glanced at the movement. As his main gear touched down, Wolfe saw the second tower collapse.

He lowered the nose gear to the runway, and his heart sank with it, coming to a shuddering thump on the concrete. Wolfe didn't mess with taxiing. He brought the plane to a halt at the end of the runway and got on the PA.

"Remain seated, ladies and gentleman, please remain seated."

Wolfe shut down the engine, slumped back in his seat, and closed his eyes.

"They don't pay me enough for this."

He almost lapsed into sleep, but a bullhorn sounded through the cabin. "Everyone, head down; put your hands on the seat in front of you! Head down; put your hands on the seat in front of you! Now! Head down; put your hands on the seat in front of you!"

The cockpit door burst in. A man in black turned his M-16 on Wolfe's head. He put his hands up.

"Get on the floor, now!" the officer ordered.

Not wanting to get shot after all he'd been through, Wolfe complied, but not everyone in the airplane was as willing to cooperate. An irritatingly familiar female voice shouted above the barked orders.

"Look what they did to me! What are you doing, you jackass, put that bazooka down and cut this tape off. I'm with the ACLU. I'll sue your ass off if you don't do it now! Goddamn it, what are you waiting for? Do what I say; I'm a lawyer, damn it!"

Wolfe lay on the floor, his cheek on the gooey carpet. He had a perfect view of the terrorists, who lay stacked like cordwood in the galley, and of Dixie C. Dallas as she assaulted the SWAT team.

Oh, please, someone shoot her, he thought.

Unfortunately, somehow, SWAT showed monumental professionalism and restraint. Wolfe was certain they'd regret it, just as he did now.

"Mr. Wolfe?" asked a voice.

He looked up to see a SWAT lieutenant kneeling in front of him, his M-16 pointing away.

"That's me, or what's left of me," Wolfe said.

The man checked a photo in his hand, selected the mike at his shoulder, and said, "I've got the first officer; he's pretty badly cut up. Send a doctor up here. It looks like the captain is dead."

"Keep him on board for now," said a voice. "The passengers and crew are being deplaned. The paramedics are on the way."

"Roger. What do you want us to do with the hijackers? All five are in the galley and appear to be dead."

"We'll sort them out later," said the voice.

"You can get up now, sir," the lieutenant said, reaching down with his free hand to help Flint up. He yelled back, "Hey, get me some towels or something with some water on it, will you?" Another SWAT officer came forward and handed a white towel to the man. He folded it up and placed it, himself, over the left side of Wolfe's face. "Hold it there, sir," he said with a grimace. "Sorry, but it'll have to do until we get a doc up here."

"Thanks," Flint said. "It's better than what those bastards planned for me or my passengers." He gave one of the cold, gray faces a dig with the toe of his boot.

"You do all this yourself?" the officer asked, nodding toward the stacked bodies.

"I didn't have much choice; they didn't seem to want to talk," Wolfe said sarcastically. "Of course, I'll probably get sued by that wacko from the ACLU—you know, for violating their right to express themselves or something."

The officer suppressed a chuckle and led Wolfe back to first class. Orani was there with a couple other SWAT officers, giving a statement. Wolfe sat down in 2B. A pair of paramedics came up the jet stairs through the main door, one-left, to Wolfe's left. The officer waved them to Flint. One of them took the towel off his face and grimaced.

"They sliced you up pretty bad, sir," he said as his partner put a blood pressure cuff on his arm. "It's clean, though; I can go ahead and stitch you up here. You won't feel a thing."

"Just like hockey," Wolfe muttered, remembering how they stitched him up on the bench after taking a puck in the cheek. It was something about shock deadening the pain—was that it, was he in shock? He felt suddenly very tired, like he wanted to nod off for a moment. A pat on his shoulder woke him up.

"You're good to go!" the medic told him.

His phone rang. Damn, he'd forgotten to turn it off before takeoff! Before thinking about it, he retrieved the cell phone from his pocket and said, "Wolfe!"

"Where's the check?"

"Excuse me?" he said, and his eyes refocused on the scene in the first-class cabin. The paramedics were packing up. SWAT officers loitered around, searching the bodies and talking on their radios. Orani was talking on her cell phone.

"This is Vanessa, your ex-wife, remember? Where's the check?"

Everyone turned and looked at him.

He swallowed hard, embarrassed. Reality hit him. Embarrassed, after what he'd just been through? Good God, what a thought! "Are the kids okay?"

"Yes, but they've been freaking out all morning—have you seen the news?"

"I'm part of the news," he growled, getting irritated. Funny how she affected him that way.

"Great for you; so where's the check?"

The SWAT officers and Orani looked at him with stares of disbelief.

"I'm alright; thanks for asking."

"Good, so where the hell is my money?"

"Aren't you the one who had the affair and left me, or am I remembering things wrong?" he asked with a spasmodic burst of anger.

"The state doesn't give a damn, Flint! We're divorced—that means you pay alimony," she replied in a self-righteous voice. "I've got a life now, understand? So, where's the goddamned check?" Her voice grew shriller. "If you can't live up to your end of the bargain, I'll take you to court again and rape you for every penny—that's what my lawyers want me to do anyway. Is that what you want?"

The SWAT officers all rolled their eyes.

Orani got up and reached for the phone. "May I?"

Wolfe was about to explode, but instead he gave the phone to Orani.

"Ms. Wolfe—I assume you still go by Ms. Wolfe?" she asked.

"Who are you, some slut flight attendant? I knew Flint wasn't as chaste as he claimed," Vanessa started. Orani interrupted.

"No, I work for the CIA, Ms. Wolfe, and we're debriefing Mr. Wolfe right now," she said calmly. It was the calm demeanor he liked; it was so different than Vanessa's volcanic temper. Orani was the exact opposite of Vanessa. She was tall, elegant, and self-assured. Her large, dark, almond eyes were so different than Vanessa's severe, staring orbs. He smiled, pleased with something for the first time that morning. Orani was firm, but surprisingly insightful. "Mr. Wolfe will be unavailable for some time, but if the children are there, I'm certain he'd like to allay their fears. They must've seen the news, and I'm certain they're worried about their father. Can you put them on, please?"

"As soon as he tells me where my money is!" she replied venomously.

Orani looked at Wolfe.

"That's up to the state, they took it out of my account two days ago," he replied with more control.

Orani nodded and said, "I suggest you call the department of child services, Ms. Wolfe. Now can he talk to the kids?"

Orani gave him back the phone.

"Thanks, I needed that," he told her. A moment passed, and Conner, his six-year-old, came on the line. "Hi, Dad," he said. "Are you alright?"

"Sure, son," he answered. "Why do you ask?"

"I saw an airplane fly; it flew into a building," he said. "I thought you were on it. That scared me."

"I'm fine, son," Wolfe said. "Hey, I love you, but I have to go. Is your sister there?"

"Yeah, love you too, bye!" he said.

There was some shuffling of the phone, and his daughter's voice came on. "Hi, Daddy, are you okay? Did you fly into a building?"

"No, I'm fine, honey, don't worry about me," Wolfe said. The SWAT officers were stuffing the terrorists in body bags and then dragging them unceremoniously down the jet stairs. By the sound of it, they took the bodies feet first, because the heads were clomping on the steps like old melons.

"Hey, you there, you idiots!" called the unmistakable voice of Dixie C. Dallas—it reminded him of Vanessa. "Be careful with those corpses; those are evidence! He murdered those poor men! Hey you, are you listening to me?"

"Hey, honey, I have to go," Wolfe said with a sigh. Orani was giving him the cut-off sign, a finger across the throat. Wolfe thought of Bennigan and clenched his teeth, feeling suddenly ill. "Some people want to talk to me. I love you, and I'll call you tonight."

"Bye, Daddy," she said in a plaintive voice.

Vanessa's voice came on immediately, saying, "When are you going to be back? I'm going on a motorcycle trip this weekend, so I can't watch the kids."

"I'll call tonight before the kids go to bed," he said and hung up.

"Sounds like a very sensitive woman," Orani said.

"Oh, yeah, you're as good a judge of character as I am," Wolfe laughed. His face started to ache. Instead of asking for anything, he got up, went to the galley, straddled the two dead terrorists still there, and filled a plastic bag with ice.

"Oh, sorry," said a paramedic. He took out a bottle of Tylenol. "Here, take four, that's going to get pretty bad until we get you to the hospital and get you something stronger."

"No need for that, it's just a cut and you got it all stitched up." Wolfe shrugged, but he took the pills anyway. Then he rummaged through the galley and got out two single-serving bottles of Tanqueray gin.

"I'd rather have Bombay Sapphire for the occasion, but the company's cheap; I'll have to make do," he said, pouring the gin over ice. He carried the drink and the bag back to his seat, sat down, took a swig, and slapped the ice bag on his face.

"Now, Ms. Orani, I sense you want to debrief me, or whatever it is you people do," Wolfe said. "Fine, since the company has undoubtedly not gotten around to getting me a hotel, I'll wait here where I have a full bar at my disposal."

"I hope you're not planning on getting drunk, Mr. Wolfe," Orani told him.

"Ms. Orani, I doubt there's enough liquor on this jet to get me drunk—not after today," Flint replied, taking another measured gulp of gin.

Orani smiled and seemed about to reply when there was a flurry of sharp footsteps coming up the metal stairs. Two SWAT officers rushed to the doorway, M-16s drawn. They barred entry to the jet, but by craning his neck, Wolfe could see a flash of pink at the door.

"She doesn't give up, does she?" he grimaced, taking another drink.

Dixie pointed her pink-nailed finger at the two remaining corpses. "You need to document those bodies!" she shrieked. "You've already compromised the other bodies; do you have any idea how to do your fucking jobs? Have you ever seen *CSI?*"

"Ma'am, you can't be up here; this is crime scene," a SWAT officer informed her, barring her physically with his rifle.

"You're damn right it's a crime scene," she yelled, and she saw Wolfe. Pointing at him, finger trembling, eyes wide, she tried to force her way past the officer. "He's the criminal! Why don't you arrest him; instead you're serving him drinks. What kind of country is this?"

"It's a country where we kill terrorists and recognize the heroes who saved your ass!" the SWAT officer told her. "Get her out of here before I shoot her!"

Another SWAT officer picked her up, much to her displeasure, and carried her out of the jet. Her complaints faded mercifully away.

"Sorry about that, sir," the officer said.

"Thank you, officer," Wolfe smiled. "I'd pour you a drink, but you're on duty. Therefore, I'll drink for you, and to you and your men." He downed the rest of the gin.

A man and a woman appeared at the entrance, dressed in gray suits. The SWAT officer turned on them, and they flashed a pair of badges. He let them by. They entered the first-class section and presented their credentials to Wolfe.

"First Officer Wolfe, I presume?" the woman said, showing him her badge rather too quickly for him to read it and then tucking it in her blazer. "We're with the FBI. I'm Special Agent Figura, and this is Special Agent Hoskin. We have some questions we'd like to ask you."

Orani showed them her ID and identified herself, adding, "The CIA is taking charge of his debriefing, but if you'd like to sit in on it, you're more than welcome."

Figura looked put out and said, "The attack occurred on United States soil—this is our jurisdiction."

"We believe the attackers to be foreign nationals, possibly with al-Qaeda connections or backing by Syria, Saudi Arabia, or Iran," she said forcefully. "That makes it the CIA's jurisdiction."

The FBI agent was about to retort when Wolfe noticed two men were removing Bennigan from the cockpit. He got up and moved toward them. The FBI man held his hand out to stop him.

"Mr. Wolfe, we need to talk," the FBI man told him.

"Excuse me, but if you don't move I'll go right through you."

The FBI man stepped aside.

Wolfe went to the cockpit.

The men carefully lifted Larry out of his seat and backed out of the cramped space. They laid him down on a body bag placed in the galley. As they zipped him up, Wolfe toasted him.

"Sorry I wasn't quicker. You deserved a better retirement; happy contrails, Larry."

They took Larry out.

Wolfe rummaged in his pocket, found the second bottle of gin, and poured it in his drink. He returned to his seat and said, "Folks, I don't really give a damn who has jurisdiction. In an hour, my face will be so swelled up I won't be able to talk. So if you have questions, ask them now."

"Perhaps we could start by you telling us what happened, from your point of view," Orani said quickly. The FBI people nodded.

Wolfe related the story without interruption. Then they had him go through it again, but this time, they questioned him at various points. By this time, his face was beginning to ache.

One of the paramedics said, "Hey guys, we need to get the pilot to the hospital. A surgeon needs to take a look at his face; otherwise, he's going to have one nasty scar."

Wolfe grimaced but got up to grab another drink.

Special Agent Figura said, "We'd really rather you didn't do that."

In a surly voice, Wolfe told her, "I'd love to have you try and stop me." He walked past her, shaking his head, adding, "You guys got to get your priorities straight. When was the last time you had to cash five terrorists out with your bare hands?"

"Never," Figura admitted.

"You ever *cash anyone out* before this, Mr. Wolfe?" Orani asked, a slight smile on her face.

Wolfe growled, "Who have you been talking to?"

"Did you ever work with the Company?"

Wolfe ignored her.

The SWAT officer, himself, poured another gin.

"Thank you, sir."

"You earned it, sir. I do the same thing after a tough day."

"You ever get used to it?" Wolfe asked.

The SWAT officer grimaced and shook his head. He added, "When I do, I'll know it's time to retire."

"Yeah, I thought I did that ten years ago," Wolfe murmured. He turned back toward the door, and unexpectedly, he saw himself in the mirror—he was a bloody mess. Maybe having a doctor check him out wasn't such a bad idea—at least his kids wouldn't call him Frankenstein. Besides, he'd had enough of the jet—the smell of blood permeating the cabin was getting to him. He tossed the rest of his drink, stepped out, and asked, "Can we continue this on the way to the hospital?"

Sirens and horns drowned out their answer.

For a split second, Flint worried about the future of his nation, his people, and his civilization. He knew what this was—a jihad, a holy war. It had been brewing ever since the hostage crisis in Iran, the slaughter at Munich, the Battle of Lepanto—damn—even before the Crusades. He swallowed hard again. They'd get through this. There would be a world for his children. He had to have faith.

CHAPTER 4: From the Inside Looking Out

The only man in the al-Zhi'theri mosque not cheering the onslaught replayed over and over again on the television was Marwan Hamdi, originally from Kuwait. He was spare and lithe, with a closely shaved beard, narrow face, and an aquiline nose that he thought far too Western for his taste. He wore his hair long so as better to blend in with the Americans of New York. It made him appear much younger than his mid-thirties, and he didn't like that either. He sipped his tea quietly in the corner of the prayer room as the two dozen other men watched the events of 9/11 unfold with unbridled glee. Eventually, Imam al-Bashri joined him.

"Why don't you celebrate, Hamdi, this is a great day," he asked, beneath grizzled gray brows.

"It should've been me," Hamdi said flatly. "I should be in paradise now."

The imam sighed, saying, "And so you would be, but for that engineering degree from Yale University. You are the best and brightest among us, Hamdi; we could not waste you on this operation. We have a long war ahead of us. Your success must build on this great success."

"And yet, only three of our six operations reached their targets," Hamdi mused. He lit a cigarette before moving over to the kitchen and pouring himself some more tea. "One of our planes crashed in a field, another never took off, and I've no idea what happened to the last—strange. For all of our efforts, the White House, the Capitol, and the Supreme Court are still standing. We missed the biggest of the six targets; how that is possible, in Allah's grace, I don't know."

"Hamdi, you are too hard on yourself and our cause; steel your mind to the struggle," the imam said, laying his hand on Hamdi's shoulder. "You're tired. Go home and get some rest; no one has paid closer attention to this than you. Certainly, no one has been more instrumental in our success than you. Allah will reward your efforts as well as your patience."

The imam sent Hamdi on his way, insisting that he go home, and cutting off Hamdi's protestations. Marwan got the distinct impression that the imam didn't want him dampening the spirits of the celebrants. Obediently, he left the mosque and walked down the oak-lined suburban street. The sun showed through the trees, dappling the sidewalk. He passed several people hurrying down the sidewalk. They looked at him fearfully.

"Yes, they're afraid now," he said to himself. "Soon, that fear will turn to anger. We didn't strike hard enough, nor are we ready to strike again soon enough." He stopped in the middle of the sidewalk and berated himself for such pessimism. "The imam is right; we've won a great victory. We have many more victories to look forward to. One day, I'll walk in the White House or the Capitol and see that they are made grand mosques to the glory of Allah. That must be why they were spared. Allah be praised! I have to have faith."

His pace quickened, and in fifteen minutes, he was at the front door of a neat, basement-level apartment. He went down the steps past planters full of autumn mums, his father's favorites. Hamdi's father always kept flowers according to the season or the holiday. He even put an evergreen wreath and holly on the door for the infidels' Christmas.

When Marwan would invariably complain, Father said, "The Prophet considered the Bible a holy book as well, my son."

Such drivel!

He got to the door, but for some reason, it was locked. Marwan hadn't brought his key. A knock brought his father to the door. The old man opened it and ushered Marwan in, peering furtively this way and that.

"What, are you mad, walking out of doors and in the open on such a day?" he asked excitedly, which was unusual for his father. The man was always extraordinarily calm. "Haven't you seen the news? Don't you know they're already saying this was our doing?"

"What of it, Papa?" he said, enjoying his father's dread more because it emanated from the fear of the Americans, not his own. He stepped in as his father slammed the door shut behind him and turned the latch. "Let them say what they want. Allah will have his revenge!"

"What talk is this?" his father asked, following Marwan through the small but tidy living room and into the spotless white kitchen.

Marwan poured himself tea and explained. "Simply put, they're getting what they deserve. Why should we care? The wrath of Allah isn't directed at us, Papa, but at the infidel, where it belongs."

"The infidel who gave you and your father this house over our head, an education, and my pride back!" the old man replied vehemently. Then he sighed and calmed himself. His father didn't like being angry. "God didn't create us to be angry men, but godly men," he would always say. His father continued in a more tempered voice. "You and your friends at the mosque, have you ever stopped to think where we'd be if it weren't for the infidel, as you so like to call them?"

"That's what they are," Marwan replied, putting sugar in his tea. He had to admit, the tea and sugar of the infidel was of much better quality than that he had in Afghanistan. It was nice to have a stove too, instead of heating tea over a burning pile of dung. "Father, why should you care? They're beneath our contempt."

"You know what I have contempt for—ingratitude!" the old man said, wagging the one boney finger he had left on his right hand at his son.

Oh, no, here it comes, thought Marwan, *the oil field story again. Please, God, not again.*

"When I lost my hand in the oil fields of our home in Kuwait, what did I get for thirty years of service?" he asked, holding up the claw of his right hand. Marwan rolled his eyes. "Go ahead, turn away, Marwan. You turn away because you have no words to refute my fact. In our country, our home, with people of our faith, there was no pity. The Sheik had only enough time to get off his gold-plated toilet to tell me to go begging, as he had no more use for me!" The old man grabbed

Marwan by the shoulder and spun him around, looking him straight in the eye. "We came here and your infidel helped us to a home and found me a job; Allah be praised, they gave me back my life."

"Yes, Papa, I've heard it all before." Marwan smiled. "The Sheik succumbed to Western greed; he acted as a Western despot—and he paid. When Saddam Hussein invaded Kuwait, he paid; they all paid."

"Oh, yes, glorious Saddam," the old man chuckled grimly. "Ask the Shia how much they loved old Saddam!"

"The Shiites are pigs!" Marwan spat, throwing himself down in the La-Z-Boy and turning on the television. Every channel had the day's operations playing over and over. It was very gratifying, but he couldn't help but wonder what happened on the other aircraft. "They'll rot in the same hell as the Christians and Zionists."

"I never taught you that," the old man said sadly. "Your mother never taught you that."

"Leave her out of this," Marwan warned.

"Daddy, why do you hate those people so much?" said a little voice. Marwan turned to see his daughter, Lufti, now eleven years old and, much to his chagrin, very much her mother's daughter—meaning she was her own girl.

"Lufti, go to your room; it's not right for you to think of such things," he told her sternly.

"Meaning it's not right for her to use her God-given brain," the old man retorted.

"You overstep your bounds, old man," Marwan said.

"But all the girls in the old school were nice and they liked me," Lufti observed. "I don't want them to go to hell, and I don't see any reason for Allah to send them there. Hell is for bad people, evil people, and they were my friends."

"I never should've let your mother send you to the public schools here; they poisoned you!" Marwan growled. "At least you're going to a proper school at the mosque now where you can forget all the lies you were told."

"They're not lies, not like the ones they're telling me now!" she protested. "I hate this school. The teachers are mean, and all they ever do is teach the Koran. I like math! I was doing multiplication and long division last year, but we haven't done any math this year—none! I'm falling behind all my friends."

"Enough!" Marwan exclaimed, jumping out of his chair and raising his hand as if to strike her. Lufti scooted across the room for the protection of her grandfather, who hugged her close. "I don't want to hear another word about the school of the infidels! You are going to learn to be a proper, modest Muslim woman, and that's final! Now go to your room!"

"Go, child, we'll talk later," her grandfather told her soothingly.

She wiped the tears from her cheeks and ran from the room, but before she closed the door behind her, Lufti turned and glared at her father. "I hate you!" she told him. "Why did Allah take mother instead of you? It's all your fault!" Then she slammed the door.

Marwan shook his fist at the old man, shouting, "You encouraged her! What kind of thinking is that? Where does she get such ideas? From you, old man, that's where she gets them!"

"Not at all," the old man smiled. "She gets them from your mother and your wife, not from me." He sighed, holding out his hand to reconcile. Soothingly, he told Marwan, "She is her own woman, like the women of our family before her. Don't try and fight it; I can tell you from experience, it won't work." Marwan ignored the gesture and turned away.

"You've turned her against me; you've turned her against God!"

"Allah gave her a quick mind and a curious spirit," the old man told him, laying his gnarled hand on his son's shoulder. "It is not for us mere men to waylay the gifts of Allah but to cherish them. She doesn't hate you, Marwan, but she wants you to reach out to her and to respect her."

"She's a child!" he insisted.

"She's growing up," his father reminded him painfully. "You don't want her to grow up to be one of those virgins your friends are so fond of talking about, do you?"

Marwan whirled on the old man, striking his hand from his shoulder and shouting, "How dare you blaspheme the scriptures! Who are you, old man, to know what's blessed and what is depraved? I am her father, and I will raise her in the righteous manner of our faith!"

"I never said anything against raising her in our faith, Marwan," Father told him, trying to calm him.

"You lie! You've lied to her ever since we got here. Because of a few handouts, you've put your faith in the infidel and abandoned Allah!"

"Do you not see me pray every day?" he asked in agitation. "Do I not go to the mosque? Hear what you are saying, my son, you make no sense!"

Marwan shook as if he had a fever. He brushed his long, lank hair back with a trembling hand and said in an unsteady voice, "The day of reckoning is upon us, old man. You'd best remember where your faith and your loyalties lie!" Then he turned on his heel and stormed out of the house.

Thirty minutes later, Marwan was at the nightclub. It was early and the place was nearly empty, but a waitress was there to serve him whiskey. He took a long sip from the first of six shots lined up in front of him, finishing it when the first dancer came out. She spun around the pole and smiled at him, or rather the wad of bills he pulled from his pocket. He tossed a few her way and she stuffed them into her g-string.

As the music, smoke, and alcohol rolled over him, Marwan smiled up at her and thought, *Soon, I will have you in paradise.* Then, as she began to strip, he thought again, *No, not you, but your daughter and your son—definitely.*

CHAPTER 5: Stand in Line

It turned out to be a motorcade, and all for him. They took Flint to a hospital, he didn't know which one, and then to a hotel via the rear entrance. It was all very secretive, and for once he was glad. The thought of facing the press after this was already grating on his nerves. He stayed in the hotel for several days, and they allowed him one phone call a day to his kids, but they wouldn't even let him go to the weight room. He was a prisoner, but he soon realized it was because he was the government's best living witness to what went on that terrible day.

After four days of confinement, Flint's face was stiff and sore, more from the constant reiteration of his story than from the wound, and he was getting irritable. He wanted to see his kids, but the Feds shut down the air transportation system, and Flint learned that he was becoming something of a sensitive topic.

Orani and the CIA won jurisdiction over him, and the analyst was his de facto handler. That wasn't all bad. She was a tall, elegant, busty, and intelligent woman who, Wolfe was almost ashamed to admit, was distractingly nice to look at. He found himself wondering what she might look like in something other than a suit, or with her hair long, falling over her shoulders in a cascade of raven folds—he stopped himself. He couldn't, more to the point, he didn't want to think of her that way. It wasn't because of her nationality. He didn't have a problem with her Iranian heritage. She was a U.S. citizen and fiercely proud of it. He didn't even have a problem with her religion. No, it was him. Wolfe had trouble admitting it to himself, but it was all him.

Orani's singular vice was cigarettes. She smoked Camels without filters, and right now, she'd smoked enough to leave a thick, blue haze in the air as she paced the room. She was trying to explain the present situation to an increasingly impatient Wolfe. He was feeling cooped up, trapped, and volcanically restless. That made his naturally sarcastic demeanor sharper and increasingly less diplomatic. What made it worse was that Orani really didn't seem to give a damn.

"The fact is, Wolfe, we're still not sure what to do with you," she said, seemingly as indifferent as he was frustrated. "The higher ups are debating this as we speak. Some want to make you a hero. To a layman, that makes sense; I mean, we're at war, right?"

"It sure looks that way," Wolfe said cautiously, knowing she was in fact taking a swipe at him. He left the bait alone, puffing away at his pipe to cover the smell of the Camels and soothe his temper.

"Well, others don't want to admit your flight was even hijacked—at least not the particulars of it." She flicked the stub of the Camel expertly through the air. It landed on a heap of other butts amidst the remains of his half-eaten room service pot roast. Automatically, she retrieved a fresh pack, tore it open, and lit another.

"You're going to ruin those pearly whites," Flint observed, throwing out his own bait.

"What's that to you, Mr. Wolfe?" she asked with a dark, insistent glare. Over the last four days, Wolfe found that Orani's brown, almond-shaped eyes could be stunningly beautiful in her unguarded moments, and he caught himself looking at her, admiring her. He had no thought of that now, for they seemed quite dangerous. She approached him and stopped in front of his chair, so close he couldn't have gotten up without running into her. "What's going on in that strange mind of yours, Mr. Wolfe?"

"What do you mean by that?" She'd turned the tables on him. He was on the defensive suddenly. How did that happen? He moved to get up, but she was in the way. "Do you mind? Your pacing has got me wound up, but it seems to work for you. I'd like to give it a try."

"You always try humor when threatened," she said, stepping even closer. "What's the matter, Wolfe? You've done ten miles in this room, or don't you remember? I've been watching you all this time." She bent over, putting her slender hands on the arms of his chair, just brushing against his arms. Despite the full blouse beneath her suit coat, Orani couldn't hide the strain of her chest against the white silk, contained by the gray material of her jacket—or maybe she wasn't trying to hide it. She smiled, but it wasn't pleasant; it was a conspiratorial smile. "Don't think I don't know about you, Mr. Wolfe."

Wolfe flushed, his eyes narrowing.

"You put up a good front, the alpha male, the silent hero, and the martyr dad," she said smoothly, like some incredibly beautiful and evil snake. She leaned closer to him and whispered into his ear. "I know all about you. I know what you like, who you like, and how you like it!"

"What does that have to do with anything?" Wolfe growled with ill-concealed venom.

"Why do you think I felt so safe here?" She smiled. It was a completely female, feral smile. Teeth bared, lips drawn back in a slight pout, Orani couldn't be any more wicked. "Four days with you, Mr. Wolfe, all locked up with no place to go, and you've got all that pent-up energy. Why can't you let it out, Mr. Wolfe? Why is that?"

He simply glared at her.

"There's that stare, daring me to step over the line. Is that what you want? Do you want me to tell you what it's all about—your dirty little secret?"

"If you're about to tell me I'm impotent or gay, save your breath, Orani," Wolfe said evenly. He stood up, grabbing her arms and lifting her slowly but irresistibly out of the way. Every move was calculated, emotionless, cold, and driven by nothing but his angst, but somehow, he couldn't explain how, his hand brushed her breast as he let her go. He turned away from her and walked quickly to the window. "You don't know me, Orani; you don't know anything about me."

"You've got more self-control than any man I've ever met," she laughed, her mannerism changing. "You're emotionally charged up, cooped up with a woman you find attractive, and horny as a rutting bull." She walked across the room and stood next to him. "You'd probably be willing to screw a roller derby queen right now just to get some release, but you haven't even made an advance on me. What is it, Wolfe? Who do you think you're cheating on if we do it?"

"Is that an offer?"

"It's a rhetorical question," she corrected him. She took another drag at her cigarette and sent a smoke ring at him, her lips making a large, succulent *O*.

Wolfe shuddered and looked away. "I don't take advantage of women."

"The question is why, Wolfe." She smiled. "Even when you have an offer, or an excuse, what is this need to be so damnably virtuous? Is that what you think women want, or is it fear of rejection, fear of failure?" She turned toward him but backed herself against the wall. She undid the buttons to her suit and raised her arms against the wall, allowing her breasts to part the lapels of her suit, standing out round and firm beneath the white silk blouse. "Don't you know women? Sometimes we just want to be taken."

Wolfe stared at her, two competing facets of his mind butting heads. Of course he wanted her, who wouldn't, but his rational side knew this was just a game. It didn't mean anything, she didn't mean anything by it other than to coerce him into something—what? He stepped up to her, taking her slim hips in his hands and pulling her toward him. By that action alone, he almost gave in, pressing himself against her. He meant to stop there, to confront her about this little game she was playing, but somehow his hands slipped from her hips to her cheeks, and he found himself squeezing, forcing her back against the wall.

"That's it, Wolfe," she told him viciously, wrapping her arms around him and digging her claws in his back. "You want it, so take me. Let loose and take me!"

She closed her lips to kiss him, and Wolfe felt himself dissolving into a warm, red fog. He was losing it. Alarm bells rang, and with them, desire turned into anger. He tore himself away from her and backed away, glaring. "What the hell are you up to? What's your game?"

Wolfe's anger evaporated into stunned silence as Orani's expression changed from seductive passion to a calm mask of contemplation—a scientist watching the very interesting antics of a new rat.

"This is a session to you," he said, letting his guard down. Then revulsion at his own weakness rescued him. He shook his head and turned around, striding to the bar to mix a drink. As he put ice in the tumbler, he asked in a tense but even voice, "You want a drink?"

"The shields are up again," she said from behind. He glanced back to see her picking up her cigarette. "I almost got through, but not quite. Interesting, and not what I expected. You're a control freak, Wolfe, but it's not people, things, or situations you want to control—it's you. We don't run into that very often."

"What does that tell you?"

"It tells me you're disciplined and very, very unhappy."

Wolfe poured Amaretto into one tumbler and added a twist of lemon. After four days, he knew what Orani drank. He handed it to her and said, "You're lucky I've got such self-control. If I didn't, you'd be getting laid by now. Where would that leave you?"

"Oh, I've come to grips with the necessity of sex on the job," she said coolly, taking the drink. She sipped it and let her glance linger on him. "Rest assured, I would have allowed myself to enjoy it." She smiled and returned to her chair. The moment of seduction was over and she was calm and businesslike again. "So there you have it. You're still swimming in a sea of pent-up emotion, ready to boil over. You've got your self-control, but you didn't get laid; how's that working for you?"

"Not very well," Wolfe admitted, and he had to laugh. He poured the gin in his glass and walked back over to his chair, sitting down heavily. "So what's this all about, Orani? Why did you need to seduce and deny me; where does that get you; and where does that leave me?"

"We're interested in you again; by we, I mean the CIA. The Company is in the middle of reevaluating everything in the counterterrorism business. We're even re-thinking the necessity of a more aggressive covert campaign against al-Qaeda and their contemporaries; it's a level of operation we haven't seen since the height of the Cold War."

"What do I have to do with any of that?" He didn't like the direction this was heading, but right now Wolfe didn't control his own actions. Thinking back to his one brief experience working with "the Company," he still didn't know what they wanted with him. "Listen, I'm sure you know my record. I wasn't a Company man in Iraq. My association with your people was purely accidental."

"You earned the Medal of Honor during that association."

"I also became an honorary SEAL, but I don't see them knocking on my door or sending gorgeous operatives to screw with my testosterone levels."

She smiled and put out her cigarette. "Your resistance was the only successful one, although it appears that the passengers of flight 93 prevented that aircraft from reaching its target—presumably the Capitol or the White House." Orani sipped her drink. "They're going to be lionized, naturally, and rightfully so. Another flight never got off the ground. We have those five. We spirited them away as soon as the jet returned to the gate, and the public will never know a thing about them."

"That way you can do what you want with them," Wolfe interjected, making it plain that didn't bother him.

"Exactly," Orani said. "No one knows they exist, and I doubt al-Qaeda will ask us to account for them. But then there's you, and flight 23."

"I don't understand the problem," Wolfe said, getting up and looking out the window. New York City was by and large back to normal. The day was bright, clear, and cold—the brown haze from the Twin Towers was gone. "Why should it matter? I'm not looking for notoriety, leave me out of it for all I care, but what's the big deal?"

"Allies," Orani said. "We're already lining up allies in this war, and make no mistake about it, this war's going to be long and ugly—religious wars always are."

"That doesn't answer my question."

Orani got up and joined him. She cradled her chin and said, "Think of it this way—if we play up your heroics on flight 23, and we wouldn't need to do much, do you have any idea what kind of effect it will have on the Arab world?"

"Ask me if I care."

"You'd better care!" Her voice became sharp, and her eyes flashed with a tinge of that dark anger that was somehow beyond his naivety; it came from somewhere else, somewhere deeper. "There are a billion Muslims out there, and a significant number of them are calling for jihad. The small numbers of Muslims actively engaged in jihad, specifically al-Qaeda, have accomplished something of a shocking success. That shock isn't limited to the United States and Europe. The Muslim world feels it too, especially the Muslim world already engaged in keeping fundamentalist Islam at bay. Ask anyone from Egypt, Jordan, Lebanon, or Pakistan. This war started thirteen hundred years ago and flared up again in 1979 with the fall of the Shah of Iran."

"Go on," Wolfe said, pacing up and down the room.

"Well, let's just say we release what happened on flight 23." Orani's voice turned gravely serious. "The networks will grab it, and why not? People are scared, and they'll latch on to any bit of good news they can find. Now we actually have film of you in the cabin—camera phones are wonderful things for the media. The networks will show you beating off the attack again and again and again until it actually looks like we won the 9/11 battle."

"When in actuality, this is worse than we ever imagined."

"Short of a nuclear attack—yes," Orani said, nodding her head. "Right now, we have the sympathy of the world. Everyone is offering to help. Pakistan is even offering us bases for use in hunting down Bin Laden. The Saudis are giving us the green light to go after the Taliban."

"That sympathy will evaporate if we turn this into a victory of any kind," Wolfe sighed. "We won't get any cooperation in hunting down the people who did this."

"Worse, it will galvanize the public opinion of the Arab world, and we won't be prepared for the attacks that follow."

"Why get ready for more attacks if it appears you've already won?" Wolfe grimaced. "It would be like trying to get the nation to mobilize against the Japanese if we'd won Pearl Harbor." He rubbed his temples. "The politicians need to milk this defeat so they can ready us for war."

"The war's already here, Wolfe," Orani said. "The history books will say that World War III, the war of fundamentalist radical Islam against the West, began in 1979 with the Iranian revolution. We're already late in preparing for it."

"And where do you stand, Orani?" Wolfe asked. "You're Muslim, aren't you? Why should you want us to win?"

"Don't be a fool, Wolfe!" Orani took out her cigarettes, her lovely dark eyes turning hard like obsidian. "Do I look like one of those Muslims who want sharia, to go back to the ignorance of the seventh century? Those Muslims are the minority, albeit a dangerous minority. Islam has a place in the twenty-first century and beyond. These jihadists view me and my contemporaries as infidels just as they do Christians and Zionists."

Orani's phone rang. She answered, said a few curt words, and ended with, "Alright, I'll show it to him and see what he says."

She flipped the phone closed and went to her laptop.

"Take a look at this," she said, downloading a message. "It's a video of a cleric named al Zawahiri. He's an Egyptian, and supposedly second in command at al-Qaeda. He made a video, and he mentions you, though not by name, not yet."

Wolfe felt a chill of surprise but watched as a bearded man began an animated speech. He could hear the man's voice emoting in Arabic, but the voice-over was in English.

"We pray Allah accepts our martyred brothers, and we curse all responsible for thwarting Allah's will. In particular, we damn the CIA crusader masquerading as a flight officer on the operation appointed by Allah. He shall feel our vengeance. I declare a fatwa upon him."

Orani stopped the video and turned to Wolfe. "There it is; you're right in the middle of it all whether you want to be or not. The story is in the papers, but we've reported it as a rumor—nothing more." Orani closed the laptop. "With everything else that's going on, your story hasn't taken off yet, but the enemy knows about it, and Dixie isn't helping."

Flint groaned, having mercifully forgotten about the lawyer for the ACLU. He went to the mini-bar and refilled his drink. "What's her agenda, or is she just automatically pissed off every time she's inconvenienced?"

"I don't know, it's a thing with those people, the ACLU, I mean; I don't try and make sense of it." Orani lit up another cigarette. "Right now, she's being held on suspicion of complicity. It's pure fabrication, of course, but not so farfetched considering her attitude. Good God, I was born in Iran in the middle of the Muslim world, and I'm more of a patriot than she is."

"Those people don't stand for American values," Wolfe growled. "In fact, I'm not sure what they stand for. They defend pedophiles, cop killers, flag burners, you name it—apparently anything or anyone that will bring down society."

Wolfe turned, sipped his drink, and eyed Orani beneath constricted brows.

"Still, I understand them in a way," he said, his voice sinking to a growl of displeasure. "They have too much freedom and too little appreciation for the cost. They never bled for this country—they take it and its freedoms for granted. You, on the other hand, I don't understand. From what I've heard, Muslims are for Muslims and to hell with everyone else. Isn't Bin Laden's message convert or die?"

"You have the common, ignorant Western view of Islam," Orani said, smiling mirthlessly, her full lips pulling tightly against her white teeth.

"Please enlighten me." He sat down.

"I came out here in '80, right after the revolution," Orani sighed. She returned to the chair and sank into it, leaning back and covering her eyes with the hand holding the cigarette. The smoke wreathed her in a heavy fog. "That's not to say I loved the Shah, but we lived a comfortable life. I was going to college the next year—I wanted to go into international studies, but the Revolution got in the way. In the blink of an eye, my world disappeared.

"You have no idea how things changed, because that can't happen here—not yet. One day, I attend prayers at the mosque, and my imam speaks calmly with measured, rational, and tolerant dialogue. Overnight, literally, that same cleric is waving a sword over his head, quoting the Koran in some insane fervor. I didn't recognize him. He was saying things that didn't make sense—words of hate, ideas that had no basis in reality. My uncle raised his hands and objected.

"The imam, who a few days ago consoled my uncle on the loss of his father, whipped the crowd against him. He ordered the men to drag my uncle outside and had him hanged from a lamppost. My aunt tried to stop them. The imam himself dragged her by the hair to a corner behind the mosque and ordered the crowd to stone her. They did."

Orani shook her head and took a long drag from the cigarette. Her almond eyes opened and looked directly at Wolfe. "I spent that night awake, looking out of my bedroom window at the body of my uncle as it slowly turned in the desert breeze, his features lit up under the street light. We snuck out through Turkey the next night—so much for three thousand years of civilization."

"You're right, I'm sorry; I can't imagine that—it makes my little adventure just that—little," Wolfe said.

"Don't worry about it," Orani said, looking at him through the smoke. She pointed the cigarette at Wolfe and told him, "You've a decision to make, my friend. You can be an active part of this war, as you already are, or you can let it run over you."

"What do you mean?"

"I mean there's a vendetta out on you already; we can help."

"How?"

"Work for us," Orani told him. "You're safer on the inside than outside. You can't go back to your old life—not anymore. We're all in a brave new world. We have a new war to fight and win."

"I fought my war," Wolfe said evenly. "Now I have a couple of kids to worry about."

"All the more reason to join now; everyone's going to be in this one—everyone."

Wolfe was silent for a long time.

"What part do you see me playing?"

Orani got up and went to the window. Opening the curtain, she looked out at the bright skyline and said, "We'd like to take advantage of your unique situation. You've an interesting military record, which you've already put to good use. As an airline pilot, you can fly all over the world without attracting attention. We can use that in the Middle East and Asia—but you offer us the same value here at home."

"I won't be much use with a fatwa on my head and a wanted poster in every mosque."

"We've got a lid on it, for now," Orani told him. "Your name and actions will remain hidden until such a time that it doesn't matter."

"And what is it you want me to do?"

"We need a fireman—someone who can travel anywhere, whether it be across the country or internationally, unobtrusively, and take care of specific problems."

"What kind of problems?"

"People problems," Orani said flatly. "These are dangerous times, but they are also delicate times. We can't go around arresting certain types of people without causing a public outcry—at least not yet. However, as 9/11 demonstrated, we can no longer afford to sit on the sidelines. We need an active and aggressive defense against terrorism. People need to disappear before they cause problems."

"Are you asking me to be an assassin?" Her request stunned him.

"You've already shown the required skills and the requisite emotional detachment," Orani said with a very unpleasant smile.

"I killed those terrorists because I had no choice!"

"Just because the knife is no longer at your throat doesn't make it any less dangerous," Orani said, got up, and walked right up to Wolfe. Her face was a cold, unfeeling mask. "Make no mistake about it, Wolfe, they're not done yet. This is jihad, a holy war, and they won't stop until the West falls and you, me, and our kids are either dead or worship Islam the way they preach it. There's no middle ground with these people—there's no such thing as negotiation."

"What you're asking is …" Wolfe couldn't finish his sentence; he didn't know what to think. The concept kicked him in the gut. How could he face his kids? How could he face God? Yet, in a war, how could he sit by and not do anything?

"Wolfe, there are jihadist cells in every major mosque in this country, Canada, and Western Europe," Orani said. "These groups have operational taskings already. We need your help—don't worry; you've already got military training. We'll fill in the blanks for whatever else you may need."

"Orani, I'll be a courier, a spy, whatever you want—but I can't be an assassin," Wolfe said firmly. "My kids lost their mother. I can't afford to leave them without a father."

"You have special talents, Wolfe; let us be the judge of how best to use you in this war."

"I've done my killing for king and country," Wolfe said. "If it's all the same to you, I'll just remain an anonymous airline pilot and watch over my kids," Wolfe said. "That is, unless you plan on tipping the bad guys off."

"Not me, or the Company," Orani smiled. "You needn't worry about that, but they may already know who you are. If they do, then you can bet they're going to come looking for you. You can't depend on our help if you're not on the inside."

"You have no idea what you're asking," Wolfe said, his voice sinking to a whisper.

"You're a Catholic, aren't you?" Orani asked, taking a drag from her cigarette and staring at Wolfe with her thick lashes veiling her narrowed eyes.

"What does that have to do with anything?"

"Thou shalt not kill, is that it?" Orani smiled. "It's convenient, but it doesn't wash. You've killed before, so what's the problem?"

Wolfe turned away and walked to the window.

Orani followed him and again confronted him. "What is it, Wolfe? I saw that look in your eyes when you killed those terrorists. You sunk into barbarism; you relished it; and you ate it like candy. You're not afraid of killing, are you?"

Wolfe stared at Orani, hating her with a slow, burning fury, and wanting desperately to punch her. The CIA analyst smiled and blew smoke in his face.

"So that's it—it's fear again. This time you're not afraid of failure, you're not afraid of doing it; you're afraid of liking it." She grinned as if she'd finally picked a particularly difficult lock. The lid to Wolfe was now open, exposing him to her prying eyes.

"Get out," Wolfe told her in a dangerous voice.

"You don't want to be the crusader gone bad," Orani said evenly. "You don't want to be the man who left the path of God in God's name, the man who risked all for the ideal and then got swallowed up in the act. You're afraid."

Wolfe picked up Orani and carried her across the room to the door. He jerked it open and said, "I saved your life once, and now I'm saving it again—you owe me twice!"

He dropped Orani in the hall and slammed the door shut, steaming in fury.

A small, white card slid under the door. He picked it up.

It was Orani's business card. The logo for the CIA was in the upper left corner.

CHAPTER 6: Guided Blonde Missile

"What do you mean it never happened; I was there!" Dixie C. Dallas exclaimed. Her voice made everyone in the Washington DC offices of the ACLU jump as if they'd suddenly had a car battery connected to their privates.

"Sorry, Dixie, both the State Department and United Airlines deny there ever was a flight 23 out of Boston on 9/11," her assistant legal counsel told her. He was too young and idealistic to be afraid of her. She was a goddess in the pursuit of righteousness. "They say flight 23 cancelled due to a maintenance issue and the passengers were rerouted to other flights."

"The maintenance issue was a hijacking gone awry—a hijacking turned deadly by a John Wayne in the cockpit!"

"Didn't the other four jets that were hijacked run into buildings?" he asked.

"Only three of them ran into buildings," she said, storming down the hall in idealistic fury. She wasn't going anywhere; she just felt the need to move and wreak havoc on everybody's morning. Wagging her pink-nailed finger at the young man, she announced, "He didn't know their intentions when he flagrantly put our lives in danger—whether they were going to kill us or not is immaterial."

"Okay," he said, following awkwardly and apparently a little slow on the uptake. "So he saved your life but you're torqued at him. The terrorists wanted to kill you, and who knows how many other people, but you're not torqued at them."

"They intended to kill everyone," she corrected him; drawing out the word *intended* like it was a long, luxurious lick on a pink lollipop. "That doesn't mean they would've done it."

"But the other airplanes—" he began, obviously trying to be logical.

"Honey, the other airplanes didn't have me on board." She planted herself under his lanky frame, hands on hips, and cocked her head to the side as if amused. "What's the matter, did we not have our coffee this morning? Are your synapses not firing? Excuse me, I don't care what their intentions were, this here," she pointed to her mouth, "this is a golden tongue. I can talk a scorpion out of its venom, rust off a nail, and Christ off the cross!" She poked him with her finger. He shuddered and backed up a few steps. She stalked him. "You're happily married to your high school sweetheart with three kids," she told him.

"Two kids, Dixie."

"Whatever," she sneered, putting herself within inches of his face. "If I unleash this golden tongue on you, there won't be any wife, any kids, or any home to go to. You'll forget about them before lunch, and you'll do as I say. Intentions? Honey, I don't care what intentions those terrorists had, because once I got through with them they'd be shaved, bathed, and Catholic!"

"But what about the people who died?" he asked. "We're not going to look very good defending a bunch of terrorists and prosecuting a man who saved thousands of lives!"

"Emotional engagement is baggage, honey," she told him firmly. "We do what's right, whether it's for the good of everyone or not, and what's right is to protect their rights whether they mean us harm or not. Got it?"

"I'm working on it," he said, seemingly hanging on by pure faith alone.

"Listen, honey," she said, changing her tone from dismissive to syrupy sweet. She put her arm around the younger man's shoulders so that he positively glowed under the attention. "When we defended those perverts from NAMBLA, we did it because everybody has the right to pursue happiness in their own way. Forget the fact that we endangered millions of innocent children. Forget the fact that the Founding Fathers never intended the Constitution to protect such sickos. We have an obligation to protect the letter of the law. We can't allow Big Brother to use judgments from cases that are morally justified but structurally unsound against cases that are not morally justified, sound or not."

"I don't follow."

"If we didn't defend NAMBLA's right to free speech and allow the Internet to become a tool for child predators, that precedent could be used to deny *Betty Crocker* the right to spread her Thanksgiving turkey recipe throughout the country—how un-American is that?"

The boy beamed. The light of the goddess once more illuminated his world.

"We've got to nail this guy before the newspapers make it heroic to fight back against terrorists!" she mused. "First it's the Muslims, next it'll be the liberals, and then the lawyers. We could be lined up against the wall by the end of the year! We have to nip this in the bud. Get me those passenger lists!"

The boy lawyer ran off as if Lady Justice herself stepped off her marble pedestal and kicked him in the ass. He returned in a few minutes with a sheaf of papers. While he was gone, lunch came. One of the other lawyers had just returned from Paris, and he was eager to share the latest delicacy.

"You've got to try this," he told her, placing the cardboard box on her desk.

"What is it? Not that I really care, damn it; if it's European, it's got to be better than what we have here. I mean, really, what good's the best health care system in the world if you can't give it to illegal aliens." Her tirade came to an abrupt end when she opened the box and stared at the contents.

Her assistant returned, putting a sheaf of papers on her desk next to the lunch. "This is the passenger manifest, but it's not an official document; that is, we can't get anything on letterhead—what is it?" The expression on Dixie's face stopped him.

"That's what I want to know; what is this?"

"Finance and accounting documents."

"No, I want to know, what this is?" she demanded, one pink fingernail quivering over the boxed lunch.

"Like I said, it's the latest rage in Paris," the lawyer told her excitedly. "It's sheep's brains on toast."

"Brains! I had brains on my lap the other day!" she screamed, puking on the papers her assistant brought. The two men leapt to get out of the way, but the vomit splashed all over the office, and especially on Dixie's white suit with pink lapels. Her morning breakfast, some kind of latte mixed with some form of bran something or other, clashed violently with the suit. The smell of acidic soy permeated the office.

"Oh, God, he did it to me again! That bastard Flint Wolfe did it to me again! He owes me a new suit! He owes me a new appetite! Good God, he's ruined Paris for me!" Dixie began running around the office, and then into the halls, throwing papers off desks, tearing down bulletin boards, and waving her arms. "What are you doing? What the hell are all of you looking at? Find him! I want to know where Flint Wolfe, the airline pilot, lives! As God is my witness, he'll pay for this!"

Behind Dixie, staying safely in her office, the lawyer who brought the sheep brains brushed a glob of vomit from his shoes. He finished and stood up, straightening his tie. Looking after her, he raised his eyebrows. "I didn't know Dixie believed in God."

"I didn't know we were allowed to in the ACLU," the assistant admitted.

"You just can't say it very loudly," the lawyer said, and he slipped out of the office before Dixie returned.

The assistant knew better than to leave before Dixie's office was completely bereft of vomit and brains. When she did return, it was as if nothing happened, other than her suit being covered with vomit stains. She disappeared into her private bathroom and re-emerged fifteen minutes later in a fresh suit.

"Have the old suit burned, will you, dear?"

"Yes, Dixie!"

She sat at her desk, expecting to see the papers laid out before her with no hint of previous problems, and that's what she got. Besides getting new copies of his original documents, the staff had somehow found the records of one Flint Wolfe, airline pilot.

"They're purchase orders; basically, they don't prove the flight ever left the ground. We do, however, have Mr. Wolfe's company records. They're here." He tapped a manila folder next to the other papers.

Dixie's face twisted unpleasantly when she opened the folder and saw Wolfe's photo. She turned the picture over and returned to her bright, boisterous self, except for the slight tinge of hysterical evil in her voice. "No problem, we'll file suit anyway. We know who Mr. Flint Wolfe is and where he lives. If all we can do is spend his money and give him ulcers, well, that'll have to do, won't it?" She looked down the list of names and tapped her finger on one of them, then another, and then three more. "Well, looky here, these must be our five enthusiastic missionaries. They all have the same address: Zhi'theri Mosque, New York, New York. Hey, I'm sure they're not going to be too happy about Flint Wolfe's cowboy diplomacy. I'm sure we could get some juicy sympathetic testimony from their priests or witch doctors."

"I think they're called clerics, Dixie."

"Whatever," she said, waving the courtesy aside as easily as she ignored reality. She plugged in her earpiece.

"Four-one-one," she said, mouthing the word *coffee* silently. Her assistant ran out and brought back a one-quarter coffee, one-quarter hazelnut soy, one-quarter vanilla soy, one-quarter caramel soy, and three saccharin cubes. He laid it down by her left hand. Dixie whispered an exaggerated, "Thank you!" and stirred it vigorously.

"Operator, I want the number to the Zhi'theri Mosque, New York, New York. Thank you. Hello?" Dixie's face lit up as if she'd seen an angel. She covered the microphone and said excitedly, "Hey they have an Arab accent and everything!"

Uncovering the mike, she said in an excited voice, "Can I speak to your head cleric? This is him? Great! I'm Dixie C. Dallas with the ACLU. The American Civil Liberties Union, but that means you guys too. I mean, what's the use of having civil liberties if you can't give them to everybody, right? Anyway, we have a mutual thorn in the heel. His name is Flint Wolfe."

She listened for a moment, her mouth hanging open.

"What do you mean you never heard of him? Well, have you heard of these guys?" She read the five names from the manifest, butchering them in English with the same brutality Wolfe used with his hands. An evil look of glee spread over her face. "Yeah, now we're getting somewhere, because this Wolfe guy is the one who murdered your boys— that's right, murdered! I saw it all. Now the government's trying to cover it up, but I think if we work together, we can nail this guy to the proverbial cross! So what do you think? Are you interested in swapping notes?"

CHAPTER 7: Surrealism

He was home, and yet he wasn't.

When Flint picked up the kids from Vanessa, he took them to see their grandparents. They thought his fresh scars were cool—his kids, that is. As far as his mom needed to know, they were from a botched mugging, but Flint told his father the truth over a martini. Dad was a corporate consultant; he knew all about how brutal and ruthless the world could be.

The elder Wolfe leaned against the rail of the back deck, looking into the woods with furrowed eyes. He took a gulp of his scotch and said, "Are you going back into that world?"

"I was never in that world, Dad, not in this way," Flint sighed, swirling the gin in the glass, watching the twist of ginger dance amidst the ice, and feeling for all the world like a trapped animal. "This is different, Dad; this would make me a professional. Necessity is one thing; premeditation is another."

"We're at war, son, even your mom sees that much. As much as I hate the idea of you being in this mess again, I'd understand if you did. You always said if someone had to take care of these things; it might as well be you."

Flint sipped the martini. It was cold: shaken, poured in a chilled glass, and then bombarded with ice. The shaving of ginger gave it an extra bite. He needed it. "Damn it!" he growled as he stood up from the rail. A snapping branch and laughter caused him to look to the right, beyond his father. What were the kids up to now?

Conner and Kathy ran around the back corner—the path around the house and through the woods was their own personal racecourse. Flint smiled, but then his blood turned to ice.

Behind them appeared a man in jeans, a green shirt, and a red jacket. He wore a Kufi cap and a long, wiry beard. The man reached into the breast pocket of his jacket.

Flint leapt past his dad, shouting, "Kids!"

The man's eyes grew wide with alarm, and he jerked his hand from the jacket. A pen and notebook clattered to the gravel path. He raised his hands and stared open-mouthed at Flint.

"I'm here to read the meter!"

Flint slid to a stop, glaring at the man with angry embarrassment. He fought with himself for a moment and then waved at Conner and Kathy, saying more sharply than he intended, "Time to go in, kids; let the man do his job!"

They scuttled by him, their expressions clearly reflecting their confusion, but he patted their heads and said, "I'll be there in a second and we can play a game or watch a movie."

"*Beauty and the Beast!*" they cried together.

"*Beauty and the Beast.*" He smiled, turning back toward the meter man. He glared at the man, who nervously gathered up his pencil and notebook and wrote down his numbers.

"Flint, don't hold him accountable. He had nothing to do with 9/11," Dad said, laying a hand on Flint's shoulder.

"We have a mosque on the island, don't we?" Flint asked, loud enough for the meter man to hear, knowing the answer as well as his father.

"What's that got to do with it?"

"Has the mosque issued an apology, a condemnation, or anything along those lines? No!" Flint continued to stare at the meter man. "If the terrorists were Norwegians and Scots, we'd be the first to condemn them, but all I've heard thus far is American clerics insisting we have to understand how angry they are, that they were forced to do this—bullshit!"

His father looked at him sadly and said, "This has hit you hard,

Flint. I understand that. But we don't have any reason to hold them accountable."

Flint shook his head and said, "A Muslim friend of mine told me that we needed to bug every single mosque in the Western world, for the sake of Islam as well as the West. I'm beginning to think she was right."

The meter man stiffened perceptibly and seemed about to retort, but he thought better of it and left.

Flint sighed and said, "I wonder how long I can stay out of it and at what cost?"

"Then why wait?" his father asked bitterly. "Why not start now and shoot the meter man?"

His dad didn't mean it as a joke, and Flint didn't find it funny at all.

After dinner, Wolfe and the kids went home. He couldn't get the Muslim meter man out of his mind. Was he overreacting? Were Orani's warnings getting to him?

He pulled into the driveway, leaving the neighboring houses out of sight behind the cedar trees. It was dark, and so was the small mountain chalet nestled in the woods.

Flint always left a light on.

The kids scrambled out of the car, eager to get inside.

"Hold it! Stay in the car!" he told them, but so sharply they obeyed instantly with eyes wide with surprise.

"Sorry, I didn't mean to snap at you; please, guys, just stay in the car for a minute."

"Why?" they returned with the obvious question.

"I need to turn on some lights. You just stay put for a second."

"But, Dad, it'll be dark in the car."

"I'll leave the light on," he said, turning the overhead light on. He took the keys out of the ignition and stepped out of the car. Wolfe locked the door and took a few steps toward the house. He stopped and looked back at his kids, suddenly indecisive.

The wind sighed in the trees, carrying the innocent scent of cedar with it. Fat raindrops began to fall onto Flint, feeling cold and wet on his neck. Still he stood there, like a deer in the headlights. Is this what they wanted? Were they waiting to ambush him in the dark house, or were they waiting for him to get far enough away so they could snatch the kids?

"Well, which is it, or is it nothing?" Wolfe asked himself.

He couldn't decide.

"Damn, they've won any way you look at it."

Wolfe went back and opened the car. "C'mon, guys, you're with me, but let me go first."

He took their little hands in his fists and walked up the gravel path to the front door, his heart beating painfully. He fumbled for the keys and opened the door, putting a hand out to hold Conner and Kathy back. They squealed, wriggled, and ducked under Wolfe's outstretched arm to rush into the dark house.

"Conner, Kathy, damn it!"

Wolfe plunged in after them, throwing the lights on. The main lights came on, illuminating the living room, dining room, and kitchen area. There was nothing there.

Conner and Kathy were already running up the stairs to their bedroom. He leapt after them, but somehow they were quicker than he was, skittering and laughing ahead of him. He bit back a curse and stormed up behind them. Wolfe caught them just before they got to the door of their room, scooping them up in his arms. They giggled and wriggled, thinking it was a game, and Wolfe gave up trying to quiet them down.

He put them down and said, "Let me go in first, just in case there are monsters!"

"But, Dad, you told us there were no monsters!" they laughed.

"Dad was wrong," he said lowly. "Monsters gave Dad this scar—we have to be careful."

"Did you kill the monsters?" Kathy asked, eyes growing wide with wonder.

"I did, but there are more, and we can never tell where they are," he said, and he shoved the door open. The light from the hall flooded in. He turned on the switches and checked the room.

"Can we go in now?"

"Sure, get your jammies on and get ready for bed. I'll be up in a few minutes to read you a story."

While the kids got ready for bed, Wolfe checked the house. It was empty. The lamp on the game table, the one he normally left on, had a burned-out bulb. Sighing with relief, Wolfe went upstairs and read the kids their bedtime story, kissed them with a greater appreciation than ever before, and chastised himself for his paranoia.

"Really, Wolfe, you can't spend the rest of your life looking over your shoulder!" he told himself as he came down the stairs. Then he noticed lights shining on the front windows.

"What the hell?"

He went to the window and drew back the corner of the curtain. A car sat in the driveway, its lights shining on the front of the house. Anger swept over Wolfe and he stormed through the front door and onto the porch.

"Damn it, Orani, the answer is no!" he shouted.

Silence.

Wolfe froze. If it wasn't Orani—he was standing in the glare of the headlights, the perfect target.

Nothing.

He walked to the car. It was his. He'd left the lights on in order to get to the front door, just like he always did when he came back home from a trip.

The next morning, Flint adopted a pair of Great Danes from the rescue organization. He retrieved his two guns from storage, sharpened his military knives, called a security service, and filed the necessary paperwork to carry a concealed weapon.

After church, he took them out for pizza, and they played soccer in the yard until Vanessa came to pick them up—just like in the old days. Those days seemed an age past.

The Danes barked. Vanessa pulled into the driveway in her white SUV—the one he paid for. The kids ignored their mom and kept playing, so the Danes returned to chasing the soccer ball and slobbering on it.

Flint scowled to see a frog-faced mustachioed man sitting next to her. His name was Clarence, but Flint could see where he got his nickname: Toad. He was a parking attendant who liked to ride Harley's and date skanky women. Flint gritted his teeth. *How the hell could I get traded in for a parking attendant named Toad?* Flint's scowl turned into a leering grin as he approached the car. Vanessa shouted for the kids.

They ignored her and kept playing; they hated Toad more than Flint did, if that was possible.

"Oh my God, what happened to you?" Vanessa exclaimed, seeing the still-red scar lining his face.

"Rough day at work," Wolfe said evenly.

"What do you mean?" She turned so white at his insinuation the rouge on her cheeks looked like clown paint.

"What do you think I mean?" He was instantly angry, and she knew it.

"Bullshit!" Toad exclaimed.

"You want to test the waters out, parking attendant?" he smiled.

Toad didn't seem to know what to do—Wolfe's physique didn't give any doubt as to who would win any altercation, but his expression turned positively frightening.

Vanessa got out of the car, telling her boyfriend to stay where he was. Toad looked put out, but he didn't argue. Wolfe's ex-wife took his arm and walked him to the porch. Then she stopped, and for a moment, she looked almost recognizable. "Flint, what in God's name happened to you?"

"I don't think I'm allowed to tell you, Vanessa, but I think you can guess." Vanessa knew about the Medal of Honor, the rifle in storage—the one with all the notches carved in the stock. She never knew the details, though; she never wanted to know, and she didn't want to know now. What she did know was that after he got out of the air force, the CIA offered him a job. She vetoed that, had their kids, ran off with Toad, and ruined him financially as well as emotionally. Thank God he had the kids, though, at least until she rode back on her Harley and took them back as well.

That's what went through Flint's mind, and it turned his frown into a scowl. Vanessa never got beyond the scars. "I can't believe it. Was anyone else hurt?"

"Larry's dead," Flint told her. Seattle was a small domicile. Everyone knew everyone. They'd had Larry and his wife over to barbecues a dozen times.

"Oh my God! Flint, what are you going to do?" Her voice was almost sincere, or maybe it was sincere, and he simply hadn't heard that tone in so long—what, three, four, no, five years.

He shrugged, "I'm going to keep doing what I'm doing. Bills need to be paid; the children need to be raised. I can't stop the world because of this." He traced the scar.

Vanessa put her hand on his chest and closed her eyes. Flint had no idea what that meant, but there was a flutter in his breast. What was that? He couldn't tell whether it was revulsion, desire, or nostalgia. Vanessa opened her mouth to say something. It started to come out like, "I'm sorry," but a black Suburban pulled into the driveway. Flint couldn't see who it was through the tinted windows.

"What's going on; who the hell is that?"

The SUV rolled up behind Vanessa's SUV and nudged it with its bumper.

"Goddamn it!" Vanessa exclaimed, ignoring Flint and flying toward her truck.

Flint strode quickly to the driver's side door of the Suburban. As he reached the car, the two front doors opened. A tall black man in a black suit and tie wearing black sunglasses got out of the passenger side. A tall, elegant woman in a gray dress suit got out of the driver's side.

"Are we a little edgy, Mr. Wolfe?" Orani asked, taking off her sunglasses.

"What are you doing here?" Flint asked, but before Orani could answer, Vanessa stormed her, getting into the taller woman's face.

"What the hell do you mean bumping my car, you bitch?"

Orani smiled and said, "Do you always curse in front of your children?"

Vanessa took a swing at her.

Orani easily sidestepped it, grabbed Vanessa's wrist, and put her in an arm bar. She forced Vanessa up against the side of the SUV.

"Flint, do something!"

The new Vanessa was back, and Flint had no great desire to do her any favors. "Hey, you took the first swing!"

"Do something now!"

Toad was getting out. The other agent drew his gun. Toad got back in.

"If you can be civil, I'll let you go, Vanessa, but I'll feel guilty sending you away with that poor excuse for a man. I mean really, girl, look what you had. What were you thinking?"

"Shut up, you bitch!"

"Was she always like this?" Orani looked at Flint, seemingly sincere.

He shook his head, but as the kids were coming up, concerned about their mom, he went to meet them. "Don't worry guys; Mom and Ms. Orani are just playing. Ms. Orani was showing her some karate moves."

"Can she teach me?" Conner asked excitedly. He really wanted to learn karate.

Orani laughed and let Vanessa go, saying, "Your daddy can teach you more. He's much better than I am."

Vanessa glared at her and gathered the kids up. When the doors closed, she stomped over to Orani and demanded she move her car.

"Certainly," she smiled, "I'm just here to deliver something to Mr. Wolfe."

"What?" Vanessa asked.

"It's really none of your business," Orani said with a bright smile. Her partner took a long, black case out of the back. He brought it to Flint. He took it, but didn't open it—he already knew what it was. Orani handed him a folded paper with a certificate stapled to the corner.

"My concealed carry permit, but I just filled it out this morning."

"We put a rush on it—now, about the job."

"Are you finally going to stop flying?" Vanessa interrupted.

"No!" Orani insisted. "We want Mr. Wolfe to keep flying—and perhaps be more selective with his routes."

"What's going on, Flint?"

"That's not your business anymore, Vanessa."

"Who are you?" she asked Orani.

"I work for the government."

Vanessa's eyes grew suddenly wide with alarm. Her nostrils flared like some red-headed demon, and she screamed, "You're not going to work for them, are you? I told you after you left the air force you were through with that! I told you!"

"You lost the right to make decisions for me when you left with your parking attendant there!" Flint said harshly. "This is none of your concern, Vanessa."

"Bullshit!" she said, her voice rising in indignation.

"Listen, I have no intention of working for them, but that's my decision, not yours."

"Are you sure you two aren't still married?" Orani asked.

Flint shot her a withering gaze, but before he could answer, another car pulled up. Orani's partner melted to the flank, just in case. Orani turned and stood next to Flint. A white man in a gray suit jumped out of the car.

CHAPTER 8: Anything but Home

The newcomer looked hesitantly at the people gathered around Flint, but finally he approached. "Are you Mr. Flint Wolfe?"

"Yes."

He reached into his breast pocket.

Orani pulled her gun and held it on his breast. Her partner leveled his weapon at him from behind.

He put his hands up, a fearful look in his eyes.

"What do you want with Mr. Wolfe?" Orani asked.

"I have a letter for him," he stammered.

Orani opened his coat and took a manila envelope from his breast pocket. She holstered her gun and opened it. A grimace crossed her face.

"You've been served."

Flint took the envelope and read aloud, "Dixie C. Dallas is suing me for reckless endangerment." He shook his head and muttered, "A fine thank you for saving her life—only in America."

"You better be nice to me, Wolfe, if you want me to testify on your behalf," Orani said with a smile.

"What's this all about?" Vanessa asked. "Guns, lawsuits, secret agents—Flint, what have you gotten yourself into?"

Orani stepped up to Vanessa and stared down at the woman. With one sharp finger, she poked Vanessa in the chest, right between her sagging boobs. "Listen, you little," she said something in Arabic, "he saved the lives of a hundred people on his airplane, and the lives of thousands of people on the ground, including the President of the United States."

Vanessa backed down, almost. "And what do you have to do with him?"

"I'm here to make sure that nothing bad happens to Mr. Wolfe because of his heroism." She crossed her arms and glared at Vanessa.

"Excuse me, but you seem to have a personal stake in this. I can see it in your eyes," Vanessa said in a snide voice.

Orani put on her sunglasses. "Why should you care; you've got Mr. Parking Attendant. Who could resist a man with sixth-grade education and a ponytail?" She leaned in close to Vanessa and whispered in her ear, her voice laced with so much scorn it made Flint cringe. "Actually, I do have a personal stake in him—I was on the airplane. He saved my life, sweetie, and unlike you, I appreciate him tremendously."

Vanessa turned on her heel in a huff and got in her SUV.

Orani released the messenger, and her partner moved the Suburban. Wolfe waved at the kids as they backed out. Then they were gone.

"So are you going to invite me inside for a drink?" Orani asked.

"What did you call her, that Arabic word you used?"

"It was Persian, and loosely translated, it means troll."

Flint laughed. "She does kind of look like one of those troll dolls when she's mad." Then he sighed. "She wasn't like that when I married her. Come on in."

He trudged to the house, followed by two bouncing Danes and the CIA. His only consolation was that Vanessa was furious.

The dogs burst inside and flopped onto the bearskin carpet in front of the fireplace. Flint dropped the case at the door and walked to the fridge. He withdrew his Bombay Sapphire from the freezer and took out a martini glass.

"Make yourselves at home; do you want your usual?"

"No," Orani said, rooting through the kitchen and taking out a bottle of wine. She rummaged through his silverware until she found a corkscrew. As she opened the bottle, she said, "This isn't just business; it's a social call, if you want. We're interested in how you're doing."

Flint shrugged as he poured his gin. "I'm fine, except for a bit of stiffness in the face. I can't complain."

"No nightmares?"

"No."

"No cold sweats?"

"Wish I could say yes, but no."

"How much have you been drinking?"

"One a day whether I need it or not—for medicinal purposes, of course," he said, taking a long sip at the martini.

Orani poured herself some wine, swirled it in the glass, and sipped it. "Excellent wine! You haven't been looking over your shoulder, have you?"

"Should I be?"

The other agent approached Orani and said matter-of-factly, "The cameras are in place at the front, back, and stairwell." He put a black router on the kitchen counter and turned to Wolfe. "Your laptop can receive the signals from the cameras." He held up a disk. "Load the software and you're set to go."

"Thanks," Orani said. "I'll check in with you back at the hotel."

The agent nodded and left.

Wolfe looked at her. "Are you spending the night?"

She smiled. "Roger runs five miles a day. He's leaving me the car."

Wolfe walked out of the kitchen and through the back hall. He entered the bathroom and closed the door. Putting his drink on the windowsill, he began to undress. "Well, should I be looking over my shoulder or not?"

"No, not yet at least," came Orani's voice. "You're not quite free and clear. There's a cleric in New York who mentioned your actions, if not your name."

"What'd he say?" asked Flint, stripping naked and shrugging on a robe.

"I thought I'd let you see for yourself."

Flint swept up his drink and opened the door. "Why not take me back to New York; I'll rub him out. Isn't that what you want me for anyway?" He strode by her and walked out the back door and onto the deck. Flint put his drink on the rail, opened the cover to the hot tub, hung up his robe, and slipped into the warm water.

"So that's what shrapnel in the ass looks like," she said. "I assume that's from your adventures during Desert Storm I?"

63

Flint sank down in the warm water and turned on the jets. It always felt good against the old wounds.

"You took the shrapnel while you were still in the air—that's how you earned the Medal of Honor."

"Yes, that's what the commendation says," he said evenly, trying to relax. He listened to the bubbles, trying to ignore the drone of Orani's voice.

"A marine corps reconnaissance force was surrounded in the Iraqi desert. They diverted your B-52 from the original target and you dropped down low to deliver your cluster bombs."

"If we'd dropped higher up, we'd have blasted the marines as well—wouldn't have been much point to saving them then, would there?"

Orani began to pace the deck, crossing her arms and sipping at the wine. Wolfe watched her under hooded lids. He had to admit, she'd look really good in the hot tub. He wondered if she was really interested, or if it was all part of the secret-agent game of hers. He started to make the suggestion, but she began to talk about the past again—a past he'd just as soon forget. He wasn't that person anymore, and he didn't want to go back.

Orani gazed out into the woods as if the words of her litany floated in fiery letters in the deepening dusk under the trees. "You made four passes, flying a box around the marines, dropping the cluster munitions from one wing, then the other, then half the bomb-bay, and finally the other half."

Flint was unimpressed. "That was the radar nav's magic, not mine."

"After the first pass, your aircraft was hit by two SA9 IR missiles. The first hit your number-four engine nacelle from below and behind, and the warhead skipped off and detonated right outside the cockpit. It blew out the windows and peeled away the aircraft skin, leaving you wholly exposed. You and your co-pilot suffered shrapnel wounds from the warhead and glass, but you took the brunt of it—in the left cheek."

"And yet I still have this delightful smile," he smirked, downing the rest of his martini. He got up and stomped into the kitchen to make himself another, ignoring the watery tracks he left behind and his nakedness.

Flint finished making his drink and went back outside.

Orani was in the hot tub. Her hair was down and it fell over her naked shoulders in a cascade of raven waves. Her clothes were draped over the deck rail—all of them. She looked amazingly like a beautiful woman, and not a secret agent.

"If you're going to rehash this whole thing," he stopped, staring at her through the swirling waters.

"Yes?"

Flint took a deep breath and climbed back into the water. "Oh, I was just going to let you know, just in case you didn't know, well, I'm aware of how the story ends."

"Is my nudity bothering you?" Orani refilled her wine, blinking at him like a cat.

"I would say not." Flint sipped his gin and decided to enjoy the show. Then, much to his chagrin, she continued.

"The second SAM hit the number-one engine and started a fire, but you kept at it and laid three more tracks of bombs before you tried to get out of there. Unfortunately, the fire spread and you were forced to bail out in enemy territory."

"Your point?"

"If the story ended there, I might not have a point, Wolfe, but after you and your crew bailed out, you began your new career—that's why I'm still hanging around."

"I was beginning to think you took a fancy to me." He sank neck-deep into the swirling water and he growled, "You're making it hard to relax; why don't you just enjoy the water, or aren't you allowed to enjoy yourself in the CIA?"

"Am I cramping your style? I didn't want to interrupt your fascinating social life. I can leave if you want."

"Hey, you're the one who said it was a social visit—I'm trying to be sociable."

"You need some work, then," she smiled, nudging him with her foot. "After you were shot down, you got your crew out on a helo but were stranded behind enemy lines. You evaded capture for several days, and that's where we came in …"

Flint sighed and closed his eyes. The wild melee of rescue and abandonment came flooding back. His crew scrambled ahead of him, running for the two rescue choppers. The EWO, the gunner, and the radar nav made the first chopper and it lifted off. The EWO, Steve, pulled out his 9mm and his .44 and stood on the skid, guns blazing to cover the second chopper. His navigator and co-pilot piled into the second one. Flint was only ten yards away when it took a direct hit and burst into flames.

The first chopper bugged out along with the A-10s.

No one knew Wolfe survived.

He couldn't get on the radio because the place was crawling with Iraqis who were just dying to take out their defeat on a bumbling pilot. He melted into the desert, burying himself in the sand for an entire night while the enemy combed the area for survivors. He spent the time digging shrapnel out of his ass and staying quiet. The next day, an Iraqi battalion set itself up in a series of bunkers and trenches not twenty yards from his hiding place and between Flint and the border. He escaped the next night, fleeing deeper into the desert with only a captured AK-47, his 9mm, three clips of ammo, a knife, a Snickers bar, and a half-filled Iraqi canteen.

Flint didn't really remember the fear as much as he remembered how his ass hurt from the shrapnel, how thirsty he was, and how much he needed to take a dump while hiding from Iraqis only a few yards away. Still, he got away, and that's when his life really changed.

"Rescue had you hook up with a SEAL team on a deep-strike mission. There was a cache of chemical weapons under Republican Guard control. Their mission was to kill the guards and seal up the cache so it couldn't be used. You linked up with the SEAL team."

"Yeah, they were really happy to see me limping along," Flint recalled. "Talk about being the square wheel! A wounded bomber pilot and two young, gung-ho SEALs."

"They left you behind to hit their target," she said, and then to his delight and surprise, Orani got up and climbed out of the tub, naked and dripping. She walked into the house and a moment later came back out, still naked, but now she held the black case.

She opened it, saying, "The SEALs went on without you, but something went wrong, and that's when this came into your life."

A naked, dripping Orani held up a battered desert camouflage

Remington 700 rifle with a large telescopic sight—a SEAL sniper rifle. The stock had notch after notch carved in it.

It should have been the ultimate in erotic images, the exotically beautiful, naked woman holding a rifle, but all Wolfe felt was a freezing flash of pain behind his eyes.

CHAPTER 9: Mr. Wolfe, Meet Mr. Remington

Wolfe saw it all again.

Huddling beneath the thorny branches of a bush, he watched the green images of the two-man SEAL team through a night-vision scope. They set up a few hundred yards from his hiding place at the end of a craggy ridge overlooking a cave. Inside the cave were the chemicals. He could see a dark slash beneath the speckled green rock and two small, thin bright spots that must be guards. They stood out in the open. There was a slight, but noticeable, twinkle near the top of the tiny forms. It passed from one to the other. They were lighting cigarettes.

He waited.

There was a flash that blanked his scope—a five hundred-pound laser-guided bomb brought in by the SEAL team. When his scope cleared, Wolfe looked to see if the entrance was sealed, but through the dust and smoke, he could still make it out—a dark shadow against the faint green rock. Then he saw movement. It was the two Iraqi guards picking themselves up from the ground.

Where were the SEALs? He couldn't find them with the night-vision scope. He knew where they should be, but all he could see was a light veil of smoke and shattered rock. His stomach turned to ice as he realized what must have happened.

Painfully but carefully, Wolfe worked his way to their sniper's nest only to find one SEAL dead and the other nearly so—the bomb somehow went astray and struck them. All that was left was a scratched-up sniper's rifle, his ammo, and some odds and ends. He collected the dead SEAL's dog tags and bound up the other man as best he could. Then he made ready to leave. Before he began the arduous task of carrying the other SEAL out, Wolfe plugged the SEAL's ear bud in and called the Operations Center.

"Your boys got hit by the damned bomb!" he whispered harshly.

"Was the objective sealed?"

"Negative. The bomb missed the target."

"Is the laser gear still intact?"

Wolfe looked through the smashed gear and found the laser. It was cut in two. "Negative. All I've got is an AK-47 and their sniper rifle."

"Listen, Captain Wolfe, it's essential that weapons cache is sealed. We don't have time to send another team. We can't carpet-bomb the place without detonating the munitions and the chemicals."

"So detonate them," Wolfe said tersely.

"We can't," said the voice. "About a half-kilometer down the valley from the cave entrance is the city of Najaf. There's enough gas in that cache to kill all fifty thousand inhabitants. Naturally, we don't want to do that."

"Naturally."

"I can't order you to do what I'm about to ask."

"Actually, I'm sure you can," Wolfe sighed.

"I'm not military, Captain Wolfe, I'm a Company man. Do you know what that means?"

"Of course, I've watched my share of spy movies," Wolfe retorted. "What about my SEAL here? He needs medical help pronto, and I'm not in much better shape."

"I appreciate the difficulty of your decision, Captain Wolfe," replied the voice. "We're not expecting you to extricate the SEAL. Nevertheless, I'm asking you to neutralize the guards and complete the mission, but you'll have to be fast. I expect reinforcements are already on their way from Najaf to investigate the blast."

"And how am I supposed to seal up the cave?"

"They must have grenades, mortars, or even C-4 in the cave—it's a Republican Guard ammo cache. Hopefully, you've seen enough war movies to get some ideas."

"Right, thanks for the help."

Wolfe recalled the first shot with the sniper rifle. He'd never killed a target he could see, not a human one, at least. The Iraqi guards were just standing there like dolls in his scope. He shot the first one. The guard didn't look or act like a man, Flint thought, just a marionette jerked off his feet and allowed to collapse in a disjointed heap as his buddy looked on in disbelief. His buddy dropped his AK-47 to the ground and ran. Wolfe shot him in the back. Even at a hundred yards, he could see the blood splash in the night scope.

He felt sick.

Iraqis swarmed out of the cave entrance like cockroaches. He shot them down one after another. The breech of his rifle was getting hot. After a moment, there weren't any more. He waited. He counted to sixty and then limped down the slope toward the cave.

The cave entrance was about twenty-by-twenty; it was large enough for a truck. About twenty paces inside were boxes stacked to the ceiling. He didn't bother checking them, but rooted around the station where the guards camped out. Wolfe found a box of grenades and a shoulder-mounted rocket launcher with a crate of rockets. He dragged the weapons outside.

Climbing the rock was painful, especially dragging and carrying the heavy crates, but he did it. Wolfe wedged the box of grenades above the overhang, taking four out and shoving them inside his survival vest. He put the crate of rockets in front of them, but took four and shoved them in his vest next to the grenades. Then he climbed down.

Halfway down, he heard the sound of trucks from down in the valley.

"Damn!" Wolfe scrambled the rest of the way down and retrieved his AK-47 and the rocket launcher. Running with a horrible limp that made him feel like Quasimodo, he made his way back to the sniper's nest. Luck was with him. It was dark, and the headlights from the trucks had blinders. Despite his wounded gait, he made it to the cover of the nest just as three trucks were parking in front of the cave.

Picking up the sniper rifle, Wolfe took in the scene through the night scope. The three trucks were loaded with Iraqis, some in uniform and some in civilian garb, but all armed. One truck drove right up to the cave, only stopping when there were too many bodies in the way. Men piled out of that truck, and he could hear angry shouts and curses in Arabic. One man, apparently an officer, waved several men into the cave and sent the rest along the ridge toward Wolfe.

Wolfe squeezed the trigger. The Remington bucked sharply but smoothly, and the officer threw his hands into the air and fell hard onto his back. There was instant pandemonium amongst the Iraqis and they fired indiscriminately into the hills.

He ducked behind the cover of the rock and picked up the rocket launcher. The rocket fit neatly on the front of the tube; he flipped the arming lever down, and he was ready to go. There was no need to use the night scope, the Iraqi trucks illuminated the cave mouth well enough for him to see where he put the grenades and rockets—so well, in fact, that an Iraqi in civilian garb was climbing the rock face toward the boxes.

The rocks and earth began to pop and ping around him as one or two of the Iraqis fired in his general direction. Wolfe ignored it and squeezed the trigger. He expected the rocket to fail—after all, he was guessing at its operation—but to his surprise, there was blinding flash and slight recoil. The white-yellow plume streaked toward the cave. He saw the Iraqi on the rocks turn at the sound, and the cliff-face erupted.

There were a number of explosions along with the sounds of rocks whistling through the air and landing with a clatter amongst other rocks, or hitting with a dull thud into the earth. A dull rumble followed.

He ducked down and fumbled for another rocket. Snick! It slid into the muzzle. Wolfe rose, gazing through the darkness. Smoke and dust obscured the area, but he could make out the three sets of headlights. He aimed at the last one, as the last two trucks hadn't yet disgorged their troops. Wolfe squeezed the trigger. The rocket sped like a flare into the night, and boom! There was a bright, orange explosion.

He loaded another rocket and fired at the second pair of lights; he did the same with the last. Each truck took a rocket, and each burned fiercely. The only problem was the fires from the fuel tanks; they lit up the night in a hellish but revealing way, and the surviving Iraqis knew exactly where to find Wolfe.

A flurry of bullets hit the rocks. Wolfe ducked, laid the rocket launcher under the arm of the dead SEAL, slung his AK-47 and the sniper rifle over his shoulder, and grabbed the living SEAL by his vest. He couldn't carry the man, so he dragged him backward into the night. Wolfe couldn't drag that much weight up the slope, so he followed the ridge, working his way as best he could along the military crest, about three-quarters of the way up. Within moments, he was sweating profusely and his breathing became labored. The Iraqi fire was getting closer and that gave him a second wind.

"Buddy, you better still be alive when we get out of this!"

The terrain was rough, and he was going backward in the dark. He tripped and fell, landing on his already wounded ass. It felt like someone peppered him with shards of white-hot metal; it was all he could do to stifle the screams of pain. He lay there, clenching his teeth, waiting for the waves of agony to subside. When they eventually died down, Wolfe squirmed out from under the dead weight of the SEAL and began again. This time, he went all of three steps before he tripped and fell again. He was certain the Iraqis could hear him; they must. Tears streamed down his face, but in a few moments, he was up again. Wolfe kept going and fell twice more before the burning in his back muscles told him he had to stop.

There was a clump of small boulders and scrub just above him. Wolfe pulled the wounded SEAL into the brush as far as he could. Then, gasping for air, he settled in between two rocks and got out the sniper rifle with the night scope. By the scope, he was still only two hundred yards or so from the cave, but there was no way he could go any further with the SEAL. At this range, the Iraqi fire was wild and didn't seem directed at anything in particular. He didn't know how many of them there might be, but one thing was certain: there was more than one.

The shouting gained on him, and he could hear booted feet running below on the rocky road. Wolfe got out the AK-47. They were all around him now. The wounded SEAL let out a slight groan.

A fine time to wake up! He thought savagely, but then there was a shout down the valley back from where he came. The Iraqis around him seemed very excited at the discovery, for they ran toward the shouting. There was some scattered gunfire, but from what Wolfe could see, it was celebratory. The Iraqis were firing in the air. At first he was dumbfounded, but then he realized they must've found the nest and the dead SEAL.

In the space of a few moments, the Iraqis gathered at the sniper's nest. Wolfe shook his head. Sooner or later, someone was going to realize this was just a single man—there must be more. The hunt would begin again.

Without hesitation, Wolfe left the wounded SEAL secreted in the darkness and worked his way back to the sniper's nest. The Iraqis gathered there, illuminated in the flickering red light about thirty yards below. It was a group of around two dozen men. One man held up a lighter, illuminating another man who, from his gestures, was organizing the search. Wolfe laid the AK-47 down and reached into his vest for a grenade. With great care, he pulled the pin—this was his first grenade. Thirty yards, it was an easy throw, so he told himself, and they were all bunched up. Even in the movies, it was never this easy. He took a deep breath and tossed the grenade in a high, lazy arc, hoping to land it in the middle of the circle. Wolfe was so eager to see whether he'd screwed up the throw or not, he almost forgot to duck. At the last second, he remembered that he probably shouldn't be watching a grenade explode from so close. He hunkered down behind the rock just as the grenade exploded. There was a flash, a number of screams, and the deadly clatter of shrapnel against the stone just inches from his head.

Anxiously, Wolfe peered over the rock. The sniper's nest was awhirl with smoke and several small fires. The fires revealed a shadowy, flickering montage—a tangle of bodies lying all over the ridge. There were a number of men running or lurching down the slope. Wolfe sprayed the area with the AK-47; then he brought up the sniper rifle and shot down everything that still moved.

That's when he snapped out of it, shaking like a sleeper awakening from a nightmare.

He focused on Orani, who stroked the stock of the Remington, lingering on the scratches and gouges made by shrapnel. She ran her nail along the series of notches cut in the top of the stock. She shouldered the weapon, standing like some pagan goddess of war under the growing moonlight. "Why up here?" she asked. "Why cut the notches up here; I can feel them on my cheek. Why not put them down on the bottom?"

"I wanted to feel them, to remind me of what I was doing every time I lifted that damn rifle," Wolfe sighed, closing his eyes again and taking a drink.

Orani put the rifle gently on the sill next to Wolfe and climbed into the tub again.

"Some of the notches are shorter than others; what's that all about?"

Wolfe's chin dropped to his breast and his eyes opened. "The half notches are the ones I shot in the back the next morning. They found me and came after me. After I shot two, the rest turned tail and ran. I shot them down anyway; it was like an arcade game. I could've let them go; they were beaten—but I lost it, I mean, completely lost it. The ones I didn't get, the Hogs got. They chased single men down. You ever see what a uranium-tipped thirty-mike-mike does to a man?"

"You did your job, Wolfe, but the job's not done."

Wolfe's brows drew tight together and he felt the old red rage building in him again. "I'm past retirement—count the notches. After twenty-five, you're through. I got more than twenty-five. I had three shells left, Orani—three." He closed his eyes again. "You're done after twenty-five, that's the policy. They don't want you needing it, or worse, wanting it."

"I can see why you're afraid, but you're not done yet, Flint."

"Are you through, because I am?"

"I have one more thing to show you," she said. Orani put down the rifle and drew a small, silver case from her purse. She opened it and set it next to Wolfe.

It was a DVD player.

"Mission impossible!" Wolfe laughed without any humor whatsoever.

Orani started the disk.

CHAPTER 10: Unfinished Business

The DVD showed a bearded cleric at a podium.

Wolfe listened, watching the man as he stared with watery gray eyes directly at the camera, and him.

"America, are you listening? The events of 9/11 were a wake-up call, a wake-up call to a new world and a new reality. Islam is the one and only true path, and those who choose not to take it will walk the path of the infidel—like those infidels who died in the skies and on the ground. There is no escaping our fury, our righteous indignation, or our revenge. Allah has spoken. The infidels must die; the sword of Allah will sever their heads, and the righteous will bathe in their blood, the blood of the true jihad. The jihad is upon you. For those who seek to prevent the will of Allah, as the captain of the anointed aircraft did, a special hell awaits you. We know who you are. You have desecrated the sacred mission of our jihadists, and we will find you. I declare a fatwa on you. You will die. A bed in hell awaits you."

"That was the cleric al-Bashri, the imam of the largest mosque in New York," Orani told him.

"A charming man."

"He's a big fan of yours. Think it over, Wolfe. We can protect you and your family much better from the inside than the outside."

"Your point and your threat are taken."

"I'm not the one threatening you, Flint," she said softly, using his given name for the first time. "I owe you. I sincerely want to see you get through this in one piece—but there's a price. I'm sorry, but that's the way it is." She sank into the water and soaked silently for a while. At length, she smiled and said, "Besides, think how much better the imam would look in your sights than on TV crowing about your assassination. Think about which way your kids would rather see him."

Flint didn't answer for a long time, but when he did, it was with a question—a different question. "Are you going to stay the night?"

"Do you want me to?"

Flint took a deep breath. "Yes."

Orani reached out and touched his shoulder, but she said, "I'm actually tempted, Mr. Wolfe, but I'm afraid this is good night."

She climbed out of the hot tub, toweled off, and dressed. Then she was gone.

Wolfe watched Orani leave, unable to decide whether he hated her even more or if he was actually beginning to like her.

***

Twenty-five hundred miles away in his office at the Zhi'theri Mosque, mullah al-Bashri of Saudi Arabia sat with Hamdi in his office. The cleric, a short, bent, bearded man with baggy eyes and an outthrust jaw, started a conference call on speakerphone.

"America is ripe for jihad," he said in Arabic. "Already they quake before our words and fear the next wave of jihad."

"Allahu Akbar!" said the voice on the line.

Hamdi leaned over the speaker, saying, "The Americans are stupid, but we must move fast. I will take Khallida with me. We'll see to the operation in the West and have our final meeting with the doctor. However, we need the next group of operatives. They are instrumental to the Wave of Allah. We need as many operatives as we can get to take advantage of the chaos that will follow."

"It will be difficult," replied the voice on the other end. "How are we to get them there? Travel restrictions will be imposed, and I must send them without weapons."

"Don't worry, the American ACLU will ensure that we have more right to travel than any American citizen," al-Bashri laughed. "I already have a contact at their Washington office. She will pave the way. We will use religious visas, as we already have. The Americans are so frightened of offending us they won't dare scrutinize our people."

"And the weapons?"

"This is America," Hamdi replied with a shrug. "I can buy anything. Our people will be more heavily armed than their police. Be at peace, brother, America is falling into our laps. Soon, every cathedral will be like the Hagia Sophia, a holy mosque built from an infidel's church. We will raze every synagogue to the ground. The Western man will convert or fall under the sword, and the Western woman will enter our harems."

"Allah be praised; we will start the operation with this infidel who thwarted our holy mission. I know just the jihadists for it."

"Send them as soon as can be."

"You know his whereabouts?"

"We have holy warriors working within his company."

"And his name—we know the infidel?"

"Yes, by the grace of Allah, my contact at the ACLU, Ms. Dallas, knows who the infidel is and she hates him as much as we do!"

"Allah be praised!" said the voice. "Can you give me his name so that we may broadcast it throughout the world? The High Mullah is greatly interested in this infidel."

al-Bashri leaned forward to tell them, but Hamdi put a finger to his lips and said, "We would prefer to keep this quiet. If we warn him by name, he will disappear. These Americans are cowards; he'll hide in Alaska or some such wilderness and we'll never have our revenge." Hamdi thought for a moment and added. "Tell the High Mullah that I'll see to this personally. Send me your two best assassins, and we'll pick the time and the place for Allah's vengeance."

"It will be done. God be with you."

"And with you."

The call ended, and al-Bashri looked quizzically at Hamdi.

"This is personal," Hamdi explained. "That was supposed to be my operation. I want to finish what was started. I want to see his dead body before I leave for the West."

"Is it worth delaying the Wave of Allah for your revenge?"

"It is not my revenge!" Hamdi snapped. He caught himself, reminding his fevered brain that this wasn't his father chastising him; it was his imam, who was as fervent a jihadist as he. "No, we've decided to push the Wave of Allah to the summer. The East Coast will have many millions of visitors then, and the chaos will be all that greater."

"A blessed time that will be, my son, a blessed time!" al-Bashri beamed, taking Hamdi's hands in his.

***

Flint dropped the kids off at school; he'd convinced Vanessa to allow him to take care of the kids before and after school on his days off. She was amenable because he was free, so long as he didn't join with the Company. He headed back home via the back roads, as he usually did, thinking long and hard about everything Orani said. He'd hired another lawyer on the advice of his divorce lawyer, who didn't feel up to a civil case against the ACLU. The prospective cost was staggering, and nearly reason in and of itself to give in to Orani and the Company.

"The kids better get good grades in high school, because there's no college I'm going to be able to afford!" It was so grim; he wondered how much longer he could hold on to the minivan with all its bells and whistles before that had to be sold for legal fees—not that it was worth much. Oh, well, he had it now. Opening the sunroof allowed a cool breath of autumn air into the car. He tried to relax and empty his mind. Turning onto Cemetery Road, he followed it until it made a sharp left and started to meander. That's when he noticed a group of motorcycles closing in on him.

"A bit early isn't it?" he said aloud. Motorcyclists often rode the island because of its well-maintained but empty roads, but not usually this early in the day.

They approached him, half a dozen bikes, and Flint slowed to allow them to pass on the short stretch of straight road ahead. Two bikers pulled alongside to pass. The rest lagged behind. He glanced in the rearview mirror. One of the two bikers alongside caught his eye. He wore leather like all the others, but his complexion was excessively pasty and he had a handlebar mustache. It looked like Toad. He pulled something short and black from his jacket.

It was a sawed-off shotgun, and Toad leveled it at his rear tire. Wolfe gunned the engine, but it wasn't enough. The tire shredded and the van swerved hard. Wolfe eased off the gas, but when he saw a biker close behind, he slammed on the brakes. The biker smashed into the back of the van, bouncing off the rear window and onto the pavement. Wolfe leapt out of the van. Toad and the other bikers skidded to a stop ahead of him.

Wolfe didn't have his gun—he was home on the island; surely, he wouldn't need it here! He dragged the fallen biker from the ground and wrapped his arm around his throat. The other bikers closed in. Toad still held the sawed-off shotgun.

"What the hell, Toad? You've got my wife and she's got my kids; what more do you want?"

Toad and the bikers laughed. "Not so brave without your secret agent friends are you?"

"Back off, Toad, or I'll hand your friend's head to you on a platter!"

They surrounded him, taking out chains and nightsticks and laughing. Toad waited for them get into position. "What, the secret agent man is afraid of a few chains, sticks, and a little rock salt?" He lowered the gun at Wolfe's legs and shot, not caring that his friend was in the way.

The man cried out in agony, and Wolfe felt the hot sting of salt pellets against his legs. He let go of the writhing biker and attacked the nearest man. The man had a chain whirling over his head. He snapped it at Wolfe, but he ducked under the whistling chain and threw a short, sharp punch into the man's midsection. The biker grunted, but he didn't go down. Wolfe stepped in, reaching around and grabbing the man's chin as he placed his right leg behind the man's right thigh. Wolfe heaved, throwing the biker up and backward, and then slamming the man to the pavement. He followed through, his hand cradling the biker's chin, driving the back of the man's head hard into the pavement. It hit with a loud crack. Wolfe didn't stay put, but leapt blindly to the side. The shotgun barked again, and a handful of rock salt whipped him in the back. The rest hit the downed biker full in the face.

"Goddamn it!" Toad cursed.

Wolfe snatched the downed biker's chain from the ground and faced another biker with a nightstick. The chain won. Wolfe lashed him across the arm and then across the shoulder.

The nightstick flew out of the biker's hand; he cursed and ran for his machine.

Toad fumbled with his weapon, trying desperately to reload.

Wolfe rushed him, knocking him sprawling with his shoulder. Two other bikers were right there, so Wolfe didn't have the time Toad deserved, but he stomped him in the groin for good measure.

The wail of a screaming girl echoed down the deserted road.

Two bikers were still up. One had a chain, but the other drew a long knife. Wolfe whirled the chain in quick figure eights and lashed out. The chain wrapped around the knife wielder's arm, and Wolfe wrenched it toward him. He caught the biker in the solar plexus with a knee. The man stumbled face-first to the ground, and Wolfe wrenched at the chain again, forcing the biker's arm behind his back. With a merciless lunge, he caught the arm and forced it upward. The shoulder popped out with a crunching sound; the biker howled; and the knife clattered to the asphalt.

The other biker was on him. Wolfe had no time for anything fancy. He took the chain in both hands, flailing it back and forth like a machine. He reveled in the thud of the heavy steel links on leather and flesh and the short, sharp barks of pain emitted by the biker.

The biker connected as well, but Wolfe was in that hazy red world of blood lust and survival—there would be time enough to feel the pain later.

The biker collapsed under the onslaught, groveling on the ground with battered limbs and a face like hamburger. The knife wielder was still beneath him, clutching his shoulder. Behind him, the biker Toad shot was moaning in agony on top of the still form of his biker buddy. Wolfe turned. Toad was on his feet, injecting a red-cased shell into the shotgun—it looked like a normal, and lethal, pellet-loaded shotgun shell.

"This is the last time you bother me, asshole!"

CHAPTER 11: Complications

Wolfe whipped the chain at Toad's head and let it fly.

Toad fired instinctively at the chain, but it caught him in the face regardless. Wolfe followed, kicking the coward in the chest and knocking him on his back. He wrenched the shotgun away from Toad's fat fingers and stomped him in the groin again.

"Next time, be careful whose bed you violate, you fucking worm!" he growled, adding a few more heel marks to Toad's balls, just for good measure.

That was it.

Wolfe got out his cell phone and dialed 911.

The cops arrived in a few minutes, both of them—there were only two on the island. The ambulance came a few minutes later. In short order, all the bikers were face-down on the pavement, cuffed and waiting for their turn in the squad car—all but two. One got away; the other still lay on the road where Toad shot him. As Flint gave his statement to the officers, the paramedic came up to them.

"Officer, the one guy over there's dead. It looks like his neck is broken."

"Jesus!" exclaimed the officer.

"Just what I need!" mumbled Flint to himself.

The officer must have seen the look on his face, as he said, "Don't worry, sir, this is about as clear a case of self-defense as I can imagine. Come on down to the detachment and we'll get your statement, and then you're free to go. These bastards, we'll put on ice for a while—at least until we file attempted-murder charges against them."

Wolfe called his lawyer, more concerned over how this might affect his residential rights to the kids than anything else. The lawyer came down to the station with his new criminal defense lawyer, and they hung around cashing in on his time while Flint made his statement. That being done, Flint was released for a medical checkup at the clinic. Legally, everything seemed to be under control, other than the pending bill, so other than a beating by chains, nightsticks, and rock salt, Flint had no worries.

"In fact, this is a stroke of good luck," his lawyer said. "You can file for sole custody. We can get a restraining order on Vanessa today."

"What do you mean?"

"Hey, biker-boy will make bail—he's pleading not guilty; if she keeps seeing him, he'll have access to the kids. You don't want that, do you?"

"How's he going to make bail?"

"It's just attempted murder, and he'll claim you threatened him," the other lawyer said. "Trust me, he'll make bail. I'll go ahead and file a restraining order on him that includes the children. The court won't fight that, considering your case."

Flint's expression must've looked dubious.

"Mark my words, Vanessa's going to blame you for all this," they told him. "She may even file papers of her own. It'd be better for you and the kids if you beat her to the punch."

"That's for sure," Flint sighed. "Alright, go ahead and file the papers."

Flint left the clinic filled with Advil and took out his phone. Dialing the number for the small rectory on the island, he waited patiently. The phone rang three times before Father Richard picked up. Flint's heart was racing.

"Father, it's Flint Wolfe," he said quickly, too quickly.

"Flint, what can I do for you?" asked the Father.

"I need confession, and guidance," he said.

"So soon?" the Father asked, surprised. After all, it had been only a week. "Never mind, I'll meet you at the church."

The cops helped Flint put on the spare, and then he drove to the church. On the way, it began to rain. Flint pulled into the church. He got out of the van, glancing dismally at the pock-marked quarter-panel. Putting it out of his mind, he entered the sanctuary. Calming himself, Wolfe dipped his hand in the basin of holy water. The water turned red. Flint snatched it out. The blood from the fight ran down his hands and arms. Hurriedly, he dried them off and walked to the confessional, more troubled than ever.

There was a cold, queasy lump in his gut. He couldn't say why, but he felt unnaturally detached, and as he entered the confessional, his hands shook. Flint sat down and closed his eyes, waiting. His heart sounded like a drum in his ears; his breath turned ragged; and he fought the sudden thought that this wasn't a confessional—it was a coffin. The panel slid to the side, and a voice entered the booth.

Almost automatically, Wolfe mumbled, "In the name of the Father, and of the Son, and of the Holy Spirit. Bless me, Father, for I have sinned; it's been seven days since my last confession."

"Yes, I know, my son," said the voice. "How are the kids holding up; do they know yet?"

"Not yet, Father, but it's only a matter of time. Vanessa knows. Still, they're adapting."

"Confess your sins, my son."

"Father, forgive me. I've taken the Lord's name in vain countless times."

"Countless times? That's a lot. Is there a reason for these outbursts beyond your domestic situation and the obvious event of last month?"

"I killed another man this morning, Father."

There was a moment of silence from the other side of the screen, and then a heavy sigh. "So your work's begun again, has it?"

"Yes and no," Flint said, his mind whirling. "You're familiar with the terrorist attack I was involved in."

"Of course, we've been over that. You're absolved of any sins of self-defense, my son. Certainly the Lord would not wish you to be the lamb led to slaughter any more than he wished so horrible a fate on your passengers. In action, you committed sin, but not so great a sin as with inaction. Was this morning related to your previous trials?"

"No, Father, though it was an attack all the same."

"May the Lord have mercy on you, my son. Tell me of your trials."

The story tumbled out of Wolfe in a torrent of rapid fire words, but when he finished, he realized he still didn't feel absolved at all.

"You still feel guilty over your actions," the Father said evenly.

"Father, I was a soldier in my former life," Wolfe said. "I came to grips with the necessity of killing before. I thought that life was behind me. I thought I could live quietly and make amends. I thought that was over."

"So that is what distresses you," the Father sighed, stirring uncomfortably in his seat. "It's understandable, and laudable, that you should wish to leave violence behind you."

Wolfe took a deep breath and said, "Is that all I'm good for, Father? Is my sole purpose in this world to destroy? I've been asked to return to that world. The government wants me back, but this time it's far more personal. They want me to be an assassin."

Wolfe waited.

There was a sigh from the panel, and the words, "Go on, my son."

"I'm conflicted," Wolfe said.

"You should be," replied the priest. "Did you refuse them?"

"Yes."

"Why?"

The question caught Flint off guard. He felt like he was back at school trying to answer the question of a demanding teacher; he knew the answer, but he couldn't shed the fear that it was a trick question.

"I can't just go around killing people and then come home and watch cartoons with the kids!" he exclaimed under his breath. "That sounds too much like Eichmann or Attila."

"I cannot imagine the two situations are comparable," the priest said. "Tell me everything about this."

Wolfe relayed the entire encounter with Orani. When he finished, the priest's voice was calm but sad, and he said, "My son, God does not give us a world of black and white, nor does he give us a guarantee that our appointed path is free of sin. Men kill in times of war, and though that act can never be without sin, we are sometimes placed in situations where we must choose the lesser of two evils in order to prevent greater sin."

"How can I do what these people want and face my kids, not to mention God?"

"In your former vocation, you were asked to drop weapons that would kill millions, yet you agreed to take that sin upon your brow, and sin it was, even in the intent. You did so because inaction would have been the greater sin. When the shepherd kills the wolf, he kills one of God's creatures. Yet should he spare the wolf, his flock is destroyed, and not only is the sheep killed, but those who depend on the sheep for sustenance then face cold and starvation. Which sin is greater?

"For you, the task is stern. I cannot advise you to take on this mantle of sin, unless you consider that by inaction, your sin is greater. In this endeavor, are you staining your soul by crime, or by self-sacrifice in the saving of innocent lives? Only God can say."

"Yet by saying yes to them, I give them the power of using me for purposes I do not control."

"Christ said, 'Render onto Caesar what is Caesar's; render onto God what is God's.' Your body may be a tool, but your soul is your own—Henry the V."

"*Each man's duty is to the king, but each man's soul is his own,*" Wolfe whispered.

"Hail Mary's cannot absolve the loss of a man's life," the priest said. "Beware! This is the devil's playground. We are mortal, and it is as easy to corrupt the mortal soul through violence—even with the most honorable intentions. This is a slippery slope, my son."

"How can I navigate it so that I can look myself in the mirror, or more importantly, look my kids in the eye?"

"Never take another man's life with God's name or blessing on your breath," Father Richard said. "God does not glorify slaughter, but he is wise enough to accept necessity with mercy. Remember, your perceived enemies are people of faith as well. Whether we be the followers of Christ, Moses, or Muhammad, we are all children of God."

Wolfe left the confessional feeling as if he stepped out of a Salvador Dali painting; after all, how often did you talk with a priest about becoming an assassin?

He picked up the kids from school and took them home. They were sitting down to dinner in the living room, watching Disney's *Fantasia*, and Conner was standing up to conduct Bach's Toccata and Fugue in

D minor alongside Leopold Stokowski when the sound of tires sliding to a stop came from the gravel drive.

Wolfe leapt up, but to his relief, it was only Vanessa. She jumped from her bike and stormed through a cloud of dust.

"Kids, you stay in here and watch the movie. Mommy is going to yell at Daddy for a while. Don't worry; everything is going to be alright. This is adult stuff, and it doesn't have anything to do with you. It's about Toad."

"I hate Toad; he's a liar and a cheater!" Conner said emphatically.

"He looks like a frog with a mustache," Kathy said sourly.

"Watch the movie, guys," he said, and he stepped outside on the porch.

Vanessa tore open the gate and stomped onto the porch. She wore her black leather pants and boots. Above that was a black vest with seemingly nothing underneath. Her breasts looked as though they were ready to explode.

Flint shook his head absently at the level to which she'd fallen.

Vanessa's skin was paler than normal, and her nest of red hair, once her pride and joy, was dry, wiry, and everywhere. Yelling and waving a piece of paper, she accosted him, "What's this, Flint? What the hell is this? It's not enough to try and murder my boyfriend; now you're trying to take my kids away?"

"Keep your voice down; the kids are inside!"

"Fuck you! You son of a bitch, you're trying to ruin my life!"

"How, by staying alive?" Flint retorted. "In case you didn't notice, Toad was the one arrested for attempted murder, not me."

"Yeah, right, I know you attacked him!" Vanessa used her finger like a dagger, stabbing him repeatedly in the chest.

"You're right, you got me, it was rather clever of me to force him to shoot out the tires of the van and then make sure he had five of his buddies around him, all armed with chains, batons, knives, and guns, before I settled the score with him." Flint's voice sank to a harsh whisper, dripping with sarcasm. "I had it all planned: drop the kids off at school, ambush Toad and his motorcycle gang on the way home, and beat the shit out of them after getting shot, whipped, and almost knifed."

He loomed over her, putting his face inches from hers. "What's the matter, Vanessa, would you rather Toad shot me dead? Would you rather the kids grew up knowing their father was murdered by your boyfriend?" Flint's voice began to growl—a sign Vanessa would recognize as absolute fury. "What the hell is wrong with you? Everything's a plot on your life; it's all about you, not about the kids, not about me, and not even about Toad. It's about you! You want to be the victim so everyone can feel sorry for you; well, give it a fucking rest and use that red head of yours!"

Flint threw himself in one of the porch chairs, an expression of extreme exasperation clouding his face. Vanessa was steaming, but she stood silently with her arms folded, momentarily at a loss for words.

"Vanessa, there are more important things on our plate right now," he said in a calmer voice. "I didn't ask for Toad to attack me, but I'll be damned if I'm going to allow that bastard to come into my bed, into my family, and then murder me. He's lucky I let him live—I'm serious about that. Now, will you get off it and address the real issue: the kids?"

Vanessa sat down in the chair opposite him with a deep scowl on her face. For the moment, her anger seemed replaced by something that resembled hurt. "How could you try and take the kids from me?"

"The order depends on you—so long as you stop seeing Toad."

"I love him."

"I don't give a damn whether you think he's the pope; he tried to murder their father. Do you think it's safe for them to be around him?"

"You don't know him!" She stomped her leather boots and balled her fists.

"Vanessa, I know as much about him as I need to know. Forget the attempted murder charge; he had an affair with a married woman who had two young children at home. That's outright despicable. He has no morals. He's a philanderer. He's an adulterer."

"And what does that make me?" she asked in a shrill voice, as if she couldn't believe what Flint insinuated.

"What do you think? Vanessa, you had the affair; that's adultery." Flint rubbed his temples. He still couldn't grasp how this woman's mind worked. He reached for a drink, but there was nothing there. A shiver went down his spine. Did he need the drink that bad? Flint instinctively closed his eyes and cleared his mind; his need for complete self-control didn't allow for crutches—the thought of needing a drink scared him more than terrorists, Toad, Vanessa, and anyone else except—well, at least she wasn't in the equation.

He sighed and said, "Listen, Vanessa, at the time, I would've forgiven you for the sake of the family. The truth of the matter is that your life is more important than your family. Well, you got what you wanted."

Vanessa actually jumped in anger, her tiny hands waving in the air like a two-year-old. "I did what I had to do! It's my life!"

Flint reclined, now more at ease, and reached for his pipe. With slow deliberation, he lit it and puffed out a cloud of blue smoke. Finally, he said in as reasonable a voice as he could, "Vanessa, it's your life, but my concern is the kids, not you. I think it's more important for me to be their father and not be Flint Wolfe. If you can't do that, it's your business. Understand me; I think it's important for them to have time with you, but I can't do that at the expense of the kids' safety."

"He's not a threat to the kids."

Wolfe shook his head and drew in the smoke with relish. "I respectfully disagree. He's got it in for me; who knows what he'll do to get at me. He's a scumbag. It's no great leap of faith to see him getting back at me through the kids, and no judge is going to give a damn what your opinion of him is. Face it, Vanessa, as far as Toad is concerned, you're blind."

Vanessa stood there vacillating. Her face waffled between expressions of hate, rage, guilt, and confusion.

"Get some help, Vanessa; get someone to talk to."

"I can guarantee he won't do anything to them, Flint," she said in a tightly controlled voice, as if trying to sound convincing. "He cares about them. He's even trying to be Nathan's friend, although that's tough considering how you've poisoned your son's mind."

"Are you kidding?" Flint laughed. "Vanessa, you're the one who told me he didn't want anything to do with your 'damn' kids. That doesn't show very much consideration for our kids, or you for that matter. Sorry, that's not much of a guarantee."

Vanessa grimaced as if he struck her. "You wrote that down, didn't you; you've been writing down everything I say!"

"You've threatened to haul me into court and take me to the cleaners on six occasions, Vanessa; of course I wrote it down."

"I love him, Flint, and I want to keep seeing him, but I'll agree to insulate the kids from him," Vanessa said, her voice sounding almost rational.

Flint had a moment of hope.

She took a deep breath. "What if I brought the kids over here when he comes over?"

"You want me to babysit so that you can pork the man who violated my bed, my home, and my family, and then tried to kill me?" Flint stood up and walked around her like a stalking wolf, not allowing her to shrink back and escape. Again, his voice sank into that vicious growl. "That's just plain sick, Vanessa! Damn it, when are you going to wake up? Cut your losses! This guy cost you your marriage, your financial stability, and your reputation. Don't let him cost you the kids!" He stopped in front of her and crossed his arms over his chest, standing like an immovable stone. "I will not have him anywhere near my kids—that's final! If you insist on seeing him, then that's your choice, not mine. You need to decide who's more important: Toad or the kids. For once, make the smart choice!"

Vanessa's face was a changing mask of conflicting emotion. Fury fought with shame. Vanessa's mouth opened to speak, but before she could say a word, a truck drove into the driveway. They looked at it, and Vanessa queried Wolfe. He didn't recognize it and scowled. A woman stepped out, her white smile flashing across the evening gloom like a beacon.

Flint stared at her—dumbstruck.

CHAPTER 12: The Link Is Forged

"I will leave this to you, brother Hamdi," al-Bashri told him. "These matters are for the fires of young hearts, not the even temper of an old cleric."

Hamdi took the proffered folder. It had the company file photo of Flint Wolfe inside, along with the narrative of the thwarted 9/11 attack. "So this is the Crusader; he fought in the first invasion of Iraq with the American Special Forces. So that is why our brothers were defeated."

"You will have to handle him with care," al-Bashri told him.

Hamdi's brows contracted. He was about to say something, but then thought better of it.

al-Bashri must have noticed his expression. "What is it, my son?"

"Forgive me, but I couldn't help but wonder why, after all our devotion to the cause, Allah would put this man in our way at such a time?" Hamdi voiced his doubt, first born when only half of the 9/11 operations actually hit their targets, leaving the greatest targets of American government unscathed.

"Perhaps it is to give the infidels hope," al-Bashri replied. "Americans and Westerners in general feed off hope, but their will is easily broken when that hope is dashed. They've raised a generation of spoiled braggarts. Do you think 9/11 had a great effect on their psyche? Wait until this Crusader is slaughtered and the wave of Allah's wrath washes over them again. Their fall will be that much greater."

Hamdi shook his head and said, "Didn't the Japanese think that way before Pearl Harbor?"

al-Bashri smiled and replied, "That was their greatest generation, or so they say, but they have no one of that character now. Sloth and lechery have bled the Westerners of their strength. They cannot but fall."

The cleric's words mollified Hamdi's doubt. After all, he thought, what kind of strength or courage could be found in a people who sat home at night watching television shows about gay couples, singers, and bratty heiresses? As in the fading days of Rome, America was rotting from within. Give her a big enough shove, and she would topple before she could recover.

CHAPTER 13: A Twist from the Past

"Wolfy!" cried the buxom blonde with a Teri Garr-like German accent, making the *W* sound like a *V*. She bounded like a lady Tigger down the driveway and burst through the gate. Flying into his arms, completely ignoring the shell-shocked Vanessa, she cooed his name again and kissed him.

"It's her! It's her! It's the bitch, isn't it?" Vanessa's eyes grew wide and round. Her mouth opened like a big, red sucker, and she pointed at the woman as if she were the Antichrist.

"C. J.!" Flint coughed when she finally pulled away, equally as surprised as Vanessa, but in a different, visceral way. The sudden, unexpected appearance of Flint's high school best friend, assumed sweetheart, old flame, confident, ex-fiancée—twice—best friend always, caught him completely off guard.

C. J. was actually Jane, which was short of the mark and made more appropriate by the addition of Calamity before her given name. Although Calamity Jane was wonderfully descriptive of Jane's over-exuberant personality, it was all too flowery for her everyday use, so C. J. it was. She threw herself on him and Flint returned the embrace, wondering how she got there and not giving a damn what Vanessa thought.

"What's it been, twelve years?" she asked, throwing a bright smile at Vanessa. "You put me on the shelf when you married what's-her-name. This must be her," C. J. cocked her head to the side and grinned in a way the Wicked Witch of the West would've positively envied. "You must be the *new* bitch, the one that left my Flint here for a parking attendant. That's something to put on the resume of life: left a great guy and two young kids for a parking attendant who rides a hog. All I can say is he must have a big dick, honey."

Flint rolled his eyes, waiting for the storm, but Vanessa just stood there in amazement. Her mouth twisted and champed as her brain worked on some particularly venomous response.

C. J. beat her to it.

"I understand; I'm not the mothering type either—don't worry, your reputation's safe; no one's going to mistake you for a mom when you're dressed in leathers. Hey, you got a bra under that vest? Those things look like they're about to explode!"

Vanessa blushed as red as her hair, turned on her heel, and stomped off to her bike. In a flurry of gravel, she sprinted out of the driveway, nearly losing it as the bike fishtailed.

"You've got to be kidding," C. J. said, shaking her head. "You were married to that?"

"That's who she is, C. J., but that's not who I married."

"What were you thinking? You were in love with me; you've always been in love with me." She reached up, kissed him, smiled, and patted him on the chest. "You'll always be in love with me, too; it's the one thing in the world I can count on."

Flint replied with a wry smile and let her go. "If I remember correctly—and I'm almost certain I do—we were talking engagement and the next week you were off in Ohio living with Gabriel, Garret—"

"Gary."

"Ah, yes, Gary," Flint sighed in a dramatically flippant manner. "Isn't he the one who threw the vacuum cleaner at you?"

"And you told me to leave him," C. J. nodded.

"But I love him!" they said in unison, laughing.

"What can I say; I was screwed up."

"Are you all better now?" Flint asked, picking up his pipe and relighting it. He put up his defensive screens; puffing violently on his pipe, Flint wreathed himself in the blue smoke. He needed all his defenses when C. J. was around: smoke, fire, a beating bass drum, anything to keep her from hearing or feeling the thumping of his heart. "You look great, C. J., just like you did in high school."

"Meaning you still got the hots for me, don't you?" she grinned, sashaying her round hips back and forth and squeezing her boobs. Then her face fell and took a more serious look. C. J. reached up and traced his new scar. "What in the world have you been up to, Flint? You look like a truck ran over you."

"Come on in; a lot's happened," Flint said, and he opened the door to his home for her.

"Is Mommy through yelling at you, Daddy?" Katherine asked.

"Who's that?" Conner asked, more interested in C. J.

"Oh my God, these are your children!" C. J. exclaimed.

They got up from the movie and scuttled over to her. Conner looking her over minutely, as if gauging her worthiness, but Katherine ran up and hugged her leg.

Conner's expression was very serious, and his words were sharp and carefully annunciated. "Katherine likes you. Do you like my dad?"

"I love your dad," C. J. said, patting Kathy on the head.

"You're not going to break his heart, are you?" Kathy asked. "That's what Mommy did when she ran off with Toad. You won't do that, will you?"

"I'll try not to, honey." C. J. grimaced.

"Good, then I like you too," Conner told her seriously. "You look a lot more like a real mom than my mom does; at least you look at us." He threw himself on her other leg and hugged C. J. tightly.

"My God, they're adorable, and Kathy looks just like me!" C. J. laughed, almost looking at ease.

"Welcome to the family!" Flint smiled, leaning in close and whispering, "C. J., I hate to remind you of this, but you don't like kids, remember?"

She didn't hear him, apparently, because she was hugging them back and saying very un-C. J.-like things like, "Bless their little hearts!" and, "Well, then, show me your room!" and, "We're going to have to go shopping for girl things together, and Conner, you can show me what boys want!"

It was all very confusing for Flint, who found himself alone with his pipe. The kids dragged C. J. upstairs for a tour, and she appeared to go willingly. Flint sighed. It was time for a martini.

After he'd put the martini to bed, it was the kids' turn. C. J. helped, and she was surprisingly good at being firm after the necessary pillow fights, extra hugs, and bedtime stories. Eventually, the lights were out and Flint and C. J. headed downstairs.

"Look at this place, Flint; I could fit my whole house in your living room!" she said. "All you need is some decorating help—this place is Spartan. Have you ever heard of crown molding and real baseboards?"

"This is only eighteen hundred square feet, so I take it you're living in a well-appointed shack?"

"It's a cabin, but not much of one," she admitted, putting her hands on his shoulders and guiding him down the stairs to the kitchen.

Flint trembled at her touch.

"It's mostly for my animals," she continued. "It's in Idaho with a great barn, sixteen acres, a stream, and loads of peace and quiet."

"Are you living there all alone?" Flint asked, not really wanting to know. It was a dangerous question. He told himself he didn't care, he shouldn't care, because why on earth would he want to get involved with anyone—especially C. J.? Their romantic track record lived up to her nickname; it was cataclysmic at best. He'd rather deal with terrorists—seriously.

"I'm living with a guy named Roger, he's my rock," C. J. sighed. "I've got everything I ever wanted: a farm, my horses, no kids, no responsibility, no sex, and a guy with a good job that treats me great—at least when he's not drunk."

Flint grimaced. He'd heard varying shades of this before with C. J.—many times over. "What does he do when he gets drunk; does he beat you?"

"No, he doesn't beat me; he just yells a lot—I'm sure I deserve it."

"You ever think of settling down with someone who doesn't need to be saved, Mother Teresa?" He wondered if the same might not be true of him.

"Here we go again," she said, tousling his hair.

"Sorry, I'm sarcastic because I care. Remember, I've been listening to variations of this for almost twenty-five years now." At her request, Flint boiled some water for iced tea. Eventually, he asked the next question he didn't really want the answer to. "Idaho and Roger, is that where you see yourself in ten years?" He tried to make it sound like he was objective and didn't really care.

"Ten years? I don't know whether or not he'll toss me out in two days, two weeks, or two years," C. J. said, letting him go and opening the fridge. "You got room for horses out here?"

"There's always room for a few more critters!"

"I don't think you need six horses, three dogs, a dozen chickens, two geese, and eighteen cats—this place doesn't look that big."

"Eighteen cats?" Flint gasped; he hated cats.

"Eighteen cats, Wolfy; I'm a high-maintenance redneck woman—but I got a great rack and I like to run around naked."

"That sounds like a reasonable trade; I'll bet what's-his-name likes it."

"He does, but it never leads to anything—I sleep on the sofa most of the time." C. J. grimaced, rummaging around in the fridge. Then, as if to change the subject, she stood up straight, put her hands on her hips, and shook her head vigorously. "What's with you bachelors; don't you have any food?"

"Of course," he replied testily, opening the freezer. "There are chicken nuggets, meatballs, pizza, and veggies. What more do you want?"

"What about fresh food, Flint?" Her blue eyes flashed with disapproval. "You've got two young kids. They need fresh vegetables, fresh fruit, and something other than microwave meals!"

"Yes, Mother," he sighed. He pulled the bottle of gin out of the freezer and collected a bottle of wine. "Have they got running water in Idaho yet, or do you still have to drink out of streams and bogs?"

"Funny, Wolfy, I don't remember you with a sense of humor—at least not a good one. Just the tea, please. I'll show you how to make it right."

"Tomorrow, I'll cook you breakfast. You do eat breakfast, don't you?"

"I have coffee," Flint said jubilantly.

"Is that what you feed the kids?"

"I put a lot of milk in theirs."

"I may have to stay longer than I planned," she sighed.

"Stay as long as you like, C. J.," he smiled, patting her on the butt.

"Please make yourself at home, and if that means running around naked, I guess I'll just have to adapt."

"You'd like that, wouldn't you," she sniped, taking the kettle off the stove and throwing in a bunch of tea bags. "I always did like the way you leered at me. I may have to throw you a bone."

Flint went to make himself another martini and then thought better of it—he needed it too much. Then he thought better of it again and made the damn thing anyway. Still, he was determined not to enjoy it. He lounged against the counter not enjoying his martini, watching C. J. work her magic. He didn't mind. She was easy to look at; in fact, she had as good a body as she had in high school, maybe better. He ogled her.

She flashed her blue eyes and said, "Still looking at my boobs, aren't you? Some things never change. You're watching me with the same expression of tightly controlled gentlemanly lust you had on your face twenty-five years ago in art class."

"You look like you did twenty-five years ago, if not better."

"You're so good for my ego; you always were." She filled a couple of tumblers full of ice. "In this case, looks are not deceiving, Wolfy; they're just as perfect as they were back then." After the tea steeped, she poured it over ice. Then she got out some juice. "I've worked awfully hard on this forty-year-old package, and I've done a damn good job."

C. J. added the juice, a slice of lemon, and then more ice. She handed Flint a glass and said, "I'm a tea-aholic, but that's all to the good. Tea has less caffeine than coffee and lots of antioxidants."

"It tastes good, too; that can't be right."

C. J. smiled and patted his arm.

They were silent a minute, but C. J. kept looking at him.

"What?"

She shrugged, and said, "Nothing—well, that's not quite true." C. J. hesitated. Finally, she reached up and ran her finger along his cheek and jaw. It was a moment before Flint realized she was tracing his scar. "Alright, Flint, you asked me what you didn't want to know—am I living with someone. I told you. I'm not in love with him. I'm not going to marry him. When your sister told you you were divorced—"

"My sister told you that?" Flint interrupted her.

"I know she wasn't supposed to, but I begged." C. J. turned serious

97

for a minute. "I couldn't bear the thought of never seeing you again until we were old, wrinkly, and gray. I missed you. So she spilled the beans, and here I am."

"What does what's-his-name think?"

"He knows where I stand, but he doesn't know the friend I'm visiting is you." She stirred her tea. "Now, can you tell me what's behind that scar? I have a feeling it's not something nice."

"It's not. Do you really want to know, C. J.?"

"Really."

"Well, keep it under wraps, C. J., this isn't public information. There's a lot about 9/11 that didn't get into the papers."

"Those fucking bastards, we should just nuke the entire Middle East, that's what I say!" C. J. erupted. "I had an absolute panic attack when the terrorists flew those planes into the World Trade Center; I knew you were an airline pilot. I called your sister up, but it was a few days before she knew anything. Thank God your airplane wasn't hijacked!"

"Actually, C. J., it was," Flint told her, refilling their glasses with C. J.'s concoction.

C. J.'s jaw fell, and she stared at him with wide blue eyes. "Are you serious?"

Flint smiled and said, "Deadly serious. They gave me this little jihadist love mark; still, they're not around to gloat."

"Oooh, tell me more!" C. J. grinned. "You're getting me all hot and bothered!"

"Oh, C. J.," he sighed, not quite knowing what to make of her reaction. C. J. and he had never clicked physically—for her part, at least. What about now? No, Flint wasn't a cad, though as Orani had pointed out, maybe that was part of his problem. Then he laughed. What was he thinking? She couldn't see him as anything but a best friend; she didn't want sex from him.

It was pathetic. Funny thing, he thought bitterly, even after Vanessa cheated on him and left, he couldn't satisfy his needs while they were legally married—it was still cheating. Now, the old rules with C. J. just didn't go away. They were friends. She trusted him. She'd given him opportunities in the past, but he knew she only did so out of guilt.

He could never bring himself to disappoint her and fall to the level of every other guy she'd ever known.

Still, they were adults now not kids. C. J. wasn't married, and she was as enticing as ever.

She snuggled up next to him.

"Do you want to go out to the hot tub?"

"Only if you don't mind me going naked."

"That sure makes it a hard choice—fine," Flint said, trying to contain his eagerness. They took their drinks out to the back deck and Flint took off the cover. Then he took off his shirt and pants.

"Whoa baby!" C. J. cried. "Flint! You've got to be kidding. Vanessa left this body; what's the matter, didn't you want to have sex with her—I mean, not that I blame you!"

"No, she got it whenever she wanted it, but that was nearly never."

She took off her blouse and then her breasts bobbed out of her bra. Suddenly, she stopped and came closer to him. "What the hell, you're all bruised up, Flint. What happened?"

Flint just looked at her boobs.

"Flint!"

"Oh, sorry, you know how I've always been distracted by those things. You should have them registered." He eased himself into the hot tub. The warmth felt good on his aching body. "You know we should have a bronze cast made of them and send it to the Smithsonian."

"I know your game; even though you're right, you're avoiding the subject!" she snapped. She took off her pants and slipped into the tub. "Oh, that feels so good after a long drive!" Her eyes flashed at him. "There, you get to see me naked; now tell me what happened with the scars and the bruises. Do you wrestle tigers on the side?"

"Not tigers, cowards, but they have their dangers too," he said, and Flint told her his story.

After he finished, C. J. sidled up to him, pressing herself against him. She slipped her arm inside his and hugged him close, pressing her left breast against his arm. Flint fought for self-control, but he almost lost it when she cooed, "Flint, I've never been with a man who took charge like that."

Was she serious, or was she poking fun at him? "What do you

mean? Oh I know I was always polite and nice on the outside, but get me in a game and I was the meanest son of a bitch in the state, remember? That was the problem you had with me: Dr. Jekyll and Mr. Hyde."

She laughed. "You never played the part of a jock well, and you never took charge with me! Maybe you should have. Besides, I was an idiot; you were my best friend."

Flint took her in his arms and lifted her from the seat.

"What are you doing?"

"I've forgotten my manners," he smiled. He moved her to the lounge seat in the tub and set her down. Then he sidled his way down her legs, dragging his fingertips from thigh to toe, before settling his strong hands around her feet, C. J.'s weak spot. "You've driven a long way. I think you're in need of one of my massages."

"Oh, goody," she smiled, and she waved an imperious hand. "You may proceed with the massage, good sir knight, and make sure you're thorough!"

"Yes, my lady!"

He started at her feet, doing her toes and the balls of her feet. When she relaxed and lay back, Flint squeezed her heels in his hands and finished at her toes, wringing the stress from her entire foot. She moaned with pleasure. At length, Flint moved slowly up her leg, methodically rubbing her Achilles, calf, quads, and thighs. C. J. became limp, completely relaxed, and completely under his control. He moved further to her hips, moving his hands symmetrically, squeezing and then pulling down to her hams. She tilted her head back, eyes closed, lost in the joy of his touch. Her white breasts bobbed to the surface of the steaming water, nipples erect, standing out in the cool air. Flint reached up again to her hips, but this time he slid his hands under her, lifting her from the seat as he drew his hands across her buns. She floated up, revealing her neatly trimmed pubic fur and the hint of the Promised Land. He repeated this half a dozen times, drawing closer to her each time, wondering when she'd bark his name—the inevitable signal to stop. It had always come, and he'd always obeyed, but this time, C. J. simply lolled her head from side to side and made hardly to be heard exclamations of delight.

Flint kissed her left thigh, halfway up. She didn't protest. Then he kissed her right thigh a little farther up. Still, she didn't protest. One more kiss on the left. Was she okay with his advances? It had been a long, tough day for C. J., and she would never have meant for this to happen. He should back off. Flint sighed and began to pull away, but the presence of C. J. right there, inches from him, beckoned. *What are you thinking of; you're forty years old, for crying out loud! Flint, don't be a fool!* Before his newfound bravado faded to the haranguing logic of his virtuous self, Flint kissed her right where it counted.

All of a sudden, the gates opened, and Flint was allowed in. He'd always remembered C. J. talking about how she didn't like oral sex, either way, how she got bored and stopped it before it ever got very far. So he expected at any moment to hear her say, "Flint, what do you think you're doing?" Still, while he was waiting, Flint was determined to take advantage of the situation and satisfy his desire of twenty-five years to be exactly where he was now. If C. J. wasn't going to enjoy it, he'd enjoy it enough for both of them.

After a few minutes, however, C. J. showed no signs of being bored. In fact, if Flint had to hazard a guess, he would have theorized that the references to God, sweet Mother Mary, and Jesus Christ himself were a testament to her pleasure. He never knew that C. J. was that religious. Therefore, since C. J. didn't seem to want him to stop, he kept right on doing what he was doing. It got to the point where he was almost certain that her clipped exclamations, stranglehold on the side of the tub, and rope-taut muscles were a sign of unrestrained pleasure—but then it stopped. CG shouted something unintelligible, and then she clutched his hair and pushed him violently away.

"Don't touch me! Don't touch me!" she pleaded, and Flint was afraid he'd really overstepped his bounds this time. She drew away, wide-eyed and confused, saying over and over again, "What was that; what the hell was that?"

"C. J.," he started, but she was up and out of the tub, mumbling something about not being able to live there, she was an Idaho girl, and she'd finally found a great situation and now this! C. J. disappeared inside, leaving Flint wondering how he'd so thoroughly ruined everything yet again. Depressed, he put on a robe and went inside. C. J. wasn't downstairs. He checked her truck. It was still in the driveway, and she wasn't in it, so she hadn't left. He went upstairs and found the master bedroom door locked.

"C. J., are you okay?" He knocked ever so softly on the door, almost dreading a response.

A moment later, the door opened and C. J. poked her head out.

"C. J., I'm—"

She put a finger to his lips, stopping him. Then she kissed him tenderly on the lips. "You're a real bastard, Flint, but you were right. You were right about everything." She took a deep breath, closing her eyes, and then she grabbed the lapels of his robe. Forcefully, as if trying to convince herself, she told him, "Tonight was a dream, a really great dream, but it didn't happen. I belong in Idaho, do you understand?"

He nodded.

"Flint, it was a really, really great dream!" Then she handed out a pillow and a blanket and closed the door. He heard the lock close with a soft but definite snap!

CHAPTER 14: Halo of Flies

C. J. left the next morning after they dropped the kids off at school. As they stood in the driveway, saying good-bye, she said, "I think you should work for them. We're at war, Flint. God knows we need men like you to protect us against the fucking terrorists. If you don't step up and do it, who will? The media's on their side and so is the ACLU."

"I got the kids to think about," Flint said.

"Yeah, you better be thinking about Kathy growing up wearing a burkha!"

Flint shook his head, saying, "C. J., it's not as easy as that. I've done that sort of thing—it's easy to get lost in it."

"Tell me about it," C. J. said, hugging him close. "I've lived my life with all sorts of so-called men, but only one real man—you. After twenty-five years of avoiding you, I come to find out you can give me what no one else ever could. Holy shit! How am I supposed to live without that; how am I supposed to leave my horses for a big city and children—you bastard!"

Flint's brows drew together and he took a deep breath. He contained his disappointment by shaking his head and saying with a tight smile, "You've got everything you always wanted back there, and I have an insane ex-wife and kids—I can't expect you to make that trade."

"They're great kids, Flint, and you're, well, you're better than I deserve."

"Bullshit, now hit the road. I want you over the pass before it gets dark." Flint hugged her close.

She hugged him back, saying, "I better go, before we end up in the hot tub again—then I'll never be able to leave."

Flint watched her truck pull out of the driveway. She waved, and she was gone. The dust from her truck settled slowly on the ground, just like his unrequited dreams. He went back in and tried as best he could to forget about C. J. and whatever it was that happened the night before.

He was home for another two weeks before he went back to work. He flew a couple of trips to Hawaii and had another one scheduled for Maui. At the last minute, quite unexpectedly, the company changed his trip from Maui to a transcontinental flight to Chicago, Denver, and back to Chicago. The next day, he'd go back to Denver, then to JFK and New York City.

The trip was uneventful, but Flint stayed away from any conversation regarding 9/11. There were plenty of other subjects to talk about, however. There were rumblings that the company would enter bankruptcy—management was asking for 40 percent of his pay and his pension as part of a "shared sacrifice" plan.

The rumors were enough to keep him from worrying about New York, and Flint slept as soundly as he had in the past few weeks, which meant not at all.

The ringing phone was almost a relief.

"Wolfe."

A thrill of adrenaline shot through him. The clock read 4:00 AM. Where was he? Turning on the light revealed a notepad with the logo for the O'Hare Airport Hilton. He was in Chicago, and that made it 2:00 AM at home. What was wrong with the kids? The woman's voice on the other end of the line was familiar, but try as he might, he couldn't place it.

"I'm sorry, I missed whatever you just said," he replied with a thick layer of drowsy irritation in his voice. "Who is this again?"

"Orani, Mr. Wolfe, remember me?"

"Of course, sorry, I'm in kind of a haze right now. What's the matter?"

"As always, I'm looking out for your welfare," she said. "After all, you do have a fatwa on your head, don't you?"

The words struck Wolfe like an electric shock—he was instantly awake. He'd almost forgotten about that.

"What's going on?" he asked, feeling a knot growing in the pit of his gut.

"While you've been busy putting your domestic life back together, our friends haven't been idle, and they haven't forgotten about you. Listen carefully; this is important," Orani said without a trace of emotion. "You're flying to JFK today, and you'll be staying at the Marriot, room 712."

"You seem to know a lot about my schedule."

"As do other, less benevolent people."

"Shit!" Wolfe whispered to himself.

"Six blocks north of the hotel is a mosque. The directions are in the hotel guest book. That is the mosque of a prominent cleric, a Mr. Ahkmed al-Bashri, who is preaching jihad and is currently under investigation."

"Yes, I've heard of all of this before; will you please get to the point," Wolfe said, his patience wearing thin.

"The point is this: Mr. al-Bashri is not all talk. Moreover, he knows who you are and where you are staying. At 10:00 PM, two men will leave the mosque and enter a car parked across the street under the oak tree. Those two men will drive to the Marriot. The security guard, Ali, will let them in a back door. He comes on duty at 10:00 PM and he expects the two at 10:15. The two men already know your room number, but Ali will inform them of any changes. The rest you can guess."

Wolfe felt a surge of anger, but also a chill that settled into the pit of his stomach. "How do you know this?"

"It's our business to know these things and to protect our citizens," Orani said.

"Then what are you going to do about it?"

"We've already given you the information you need to act on the problem. Further help will be found in your nightstand drawer."

"You're not going to arrest these people?" Wolfe asked, his voice rising in disbelief.

"We have no power to do that," she said. "Intervention would require us to contact local authorities, which in turn would require us to provide proof of our suspicions. That would compromise some important surveillance activities."

"In other words, I'm on my own."

There was a pause, and then Orani's voice almost sounded as if it had feeling in it. "You're never on your own, Flint." There was another pause, and once again she was all business. "The Company is always here. Of course, the amount of help we can lend you depends on the services we get in return."

"You're trying to force my hand, Orani," Wolfe said flatly.

"Not at all, but wouldn't you like to see C. J. again? Congratulations on being a cad! I hope you enjoyed it. More importantly, it's up to you to see that your kids are not left without a father. It would be a tragedy if they were orphans because of your inaction. If you need anything else, I'm a phone call away. Good luck, Mr. Wolfe."

There was a click on the other end and the call went dead.

Flint didn't sleep the rest of the night.

He landed in New York at three-thirty the next day. Just as Orani predicted, he checked into room 712. Flint went straight to the nightstand. There was nothing there but a Bible. He shook his head, thinking the whole thing was too cloak and dagger to be real, but he picked up the Bible anyway. It was heavy. He opened it; the pages fell open to Exodus 21:24. On the left-hand page, the quote "an eye for an eye" was highlighted, but on the right, someone hollowed out the book. Inserted in the void were a Walther PPK, two clips, a silencer, and a picture. Wolfe took out the gun. The serial number was filed off. He put the gun aside and lifted the picture from underneath the clips. It was of a smiling Middle Eastern man of perhaps twenty-five. He wore a red security blazer with a nametag that identified him as Ali.

Flint sat down heavily on the bed and sighed. "So it's come to this. I don't have any choice." He picked up the gun and inserted a clip. The silencer screwed snugly into place with a sharp snick! He pulled the action back and loaded the first round. Then he flicked the safety off. His face grew stern with resolve, and he said, "I won't allow my kids to grow up without a father."

He tried to nap, but it was impossible. This was different. Before, the enemy thrust the moment upon him—he reacted to the crisis.

Now he had to anticipate it; he had to plan; and above all, he had to be patient.

Flint went to a local J. C. Penney and bought some clothes. He picked up two pairs of black sweats, black socks, two pairs of black shoes, and a small, black backpack. It drained his bank account.

"Going Goth?" asked the store clerk as she rung it up. She ran his card and frowned, saying, "Sorry, sir, your card's been refused."

"That's what divorce does to you," he growled.

"You shouldn't have cheated on your wife," she said.

He flushed red with anger and spat, "She's the one who cheated and ran out on me and two kids, missy. Now I have to deal with your crap!"

He turned to leave, but the cashier called him back. "Sorry, but it's usually the other way around. I'll tell you what; I'll assume the lines are busy and ring it up manually, okay?"

"Thanks," Flint replied, wondering whether he should, after all, be thankful.

At a drugstore, he got some rubbing alcohol and a lighter; then he returned to the hotel to try and get some sleep.

At 8:30, it was dark. Wolfe left the hotel wearing the black sweats and black shoes. In the front pocket of the sweats were the Walther, the silencer, and the extra clip. He left his ID in the room and taped the key card behind the "Do Not Disturb" sign hanging on the doorknob.

Ali wasn't on duty yet.

Wolfe slipped out the side door and walked to the mosque. He saw it from two blocks away. It was a nondescript building with an alley on each side separating it from the residences next door. A small, painted sign in Arabic was the only distinguishing mark. He stopped about a block away and waited under one of the oak trees that lined that side of the street. There was no car parked in front of the mosque.

It was now so dark that he was all but invisible. Several people passed by without seeing him under the tree. Then, at a few minutes past 9:00 PM, a car drove down the street from behind. It passed him and pulled in under the oak tree across from the mosque. Two men got out. He couldn't see their faces because the street lamp was behind the branches of the trees, but he could hear them talking excitedly in Arabic.

They crossed the street. In the middle of the street, the light fell on their faces: two young, pleasant-looking men with short-cropped beards. They looked like anything but terrorists. One of them rang the doorbell. In a moment, a large, bearded man answered and ushered them in. Wolfe noticed the hall light to the second story go on, but neither of the front windows showed any light.

Wolfe walked down the sidewalk to the tree immediately behind the car and hid in the shadows.

***

Hamdi and al-Bashri greeted the two assassins warmly. Hamdi showed them pictures of Wolfe and gave them the particulars of the night's plan. "One note of caution, brothers," he said seriously. "We know from our contact in the ACLU that he's an expert in hand-to-hand combat. His records at United Airlines show that he was a military officer for twelve years and fought in the first Desert Storm. Be careful! We don't want him to get away!"

"Don't worry," said one of the men. "Allah has guided us through dozens of operations. He'll not fail us now. The Crusader is as good as dead; that is, unless you want him alive. His execution would make for excellent propaganda."

"The High Mullah would consider that a great coup," the other man said.

"Can you do it?" al-Bashri asked.

"He's a Westerner," the first assassin replied with contempt.

Hamdi wasn't so certain and said, "It's more important to get him out of our way. We can't haul him around the country without raising suspicion. Remember, he worked for their government, and he's assuredly been in contact with them since the September operation. It's a steep risk."

"Let us worry about that," the second assassin told him. "We'll be back with him in the trunk, one way or another. Shall we say in an hour?"

Hamdi looked at his watch and said, "Unfortunately, I can't wait around. In case something goes wrong, I need to be out of here with the truck; otherwise, we're jeopardizing the operation in the West. Call me on my cell phone when the operation is successfully completed."

The two men nodded.

"Let us pray then, before you go," al-Bashri replied with a smile.

***

Across the street about half a block away, a black Chrysler 300 sat silently. Orani and another agent inside had a perfect view of the assassin's car and the front of the mosque. She raised a pair of infrared binoculars and said, "There he is, right behind the tree. He's waiting patiently; I'll give him that."

"Think they'll see him with an IR?" the agent asked.

"No, he's out of their line of sight. Maybe he thought of that," she said.

"I'll bet he shoots them from across the street and runs like a jack rabbit."

Orani shook her head and said, "I've seen him work; he's not scared of them."

"Fifty bucks says he doesn't even shoot them, he just warns them," the man said. "A hundred bucks says if he shoots them, it's from across the street."

"You think he's too squeamish to kill them after what he did on that airplane?" she asked skeptically.

"He'll warn them first."

"You're on," she answered, knowing the truth of the matter.

They waited patiently. At 10:00 PM precisely, they saw the door to the mosque open. The two young men stepped out. They each carried a large gym bag. Before leaving the landing, they turned around. An older man dressed in cleric's robes followed them and blessed them while another man stood in the doorway.

"Al-Bashri is highlighting himself. I wonder if our boy recognizes him."

"I imagine he does," Orani said. "Who's the other man? He looks familiar."

The agent paged through his files. "Right, here we are, Marwan Hamdi, bomb maker and engineer. He got his degree at Yale."

"The things we do for these people!"

The cleric turned around and went back inside, ending Orani's curiosity. The assassins went down the steps. Opening the gate, they made their way across the street. Nothing happened to waylay them. One of them took out a set of keys and opened the trunk. The other stood next to him. They faced the car, their backs to the tree where Wolfe was hiding.

"What's he doing; did he get cold feet?" the agent asked.

"I can't see him; wait, there he goes!"

The trunk of the car came up and both men leaned over to put their bags in. At that moment, the black shadow of Wolfe stepped from behind the tree. From about four feet away, they saw his arm raise, gun in hand, and then the two terrorists convulsed and collapsed over the edge of the trunk.

Orani's partner jumped in surprise.

Wolfe's action was so brutally efficient it caught even Orani completely off guard.

Wolfe stooped and picked something off the ground. Then he retrieved the gym bags and unceremoniously rolled the men into the trunk. They watched him point the gun into the trunk and two more silent shots were fired. Wolfe closed the trunk, tossed the bags in the passenger seat, got in, started the car, turned on the lights, and drove away. It all took less than a minute.

"Wow! That was slick as you please," Orani said, obviously amazed. "That's quite a leap from not wanting to be an assassin to this!"

"We're either dealing with a natural or a professional," the agent said. "What'd he do in the military besides flying? I mean, we have the Medal of Honor thing, but how did that lead to this?"

Orani shook her head. "There's no record of him working for us or anyone else. Maybe he's just smart."

"Yeah, right," the agent said. "He's been in the game before—we just didn't know it. We'd better follow him and see what he's up to now."

Orani started the car and took off after Wolfe.

***

Wolfe drove straight to the hotel, all the while making sure he didn't speed or run any stop signs. His heart raced, but he was only halfway through his job. If he was going to do this, damn it, he was going to be absolutely, viciously thorough.

He drove around the back of the hotel. There was a service door there. He stopped next to it, got out, and knocked. There was no answer. He checked his watch. It was 10:12. After waiting another minute, he knocked again. This time the door opened. It was Ali.

Ali said a few words in Arabic, and then he noticed it was Wolfe standing at the door with a gun. He shifted to English, putting his hands up and saying, "Please, sir, do not shoot! I have no money. We can get the money out of the hotel safe!"

"Shut up!" Wolfe grabbed the terrorist by the collar and threw him head-first down the stairs. The man hit the asphalt hard, rolling on his back and whimpering, "Please don't hurt me; please don't shoot me!"

"Get up, open the back door, and get in!" Wolfe ordered. Ali stumbled into the back and slid as far away from Wolfe as possible, his hands up, his lips quivering.

"Put your seat belt on. Good. Now sit on your hands!"

Wolfe shut the back door and got in the front seat. He turned around and pointed the Walther at Ali's head.

"You seemed pretty cock sure of yourself when it was me you were going to kill. What's the matter, haven't you heard of the risk part of risk-reward?"

"You're going to kill me, aren't you?" Ali stammered.

"I wouldn't have you buckle up for safety if I was going to shoot you, Ali," Wolfe told him in a soothing voice. "Don't worry, you're just small fry. All I want to do is to talk to al-Bashri so we can clear this up. Then I can get on with my life, and you can get on with yours. Understand?"

Ali nodded.

"Now I'm going to have you take me to his office. To make sure you don't pull a fast one, I want you to tell me how we get there from the back door."

Ali swallowed hard and said, "I go up the back stairs. His office is on the left as you exit the stairway."

"How many guards does he have?"

"Just Abdullereda. He's the only one who spends the night with the imam," Ali said shakily. Then, lips quivering, he said, "You are going to kill me anyway, aren't you? You're going to kill me even though I told you everything!"

111

"Ali, I'm going to show you the same consideration your friends were going to show me in my room." Ali turned white and began to whine incoherently. Wolfe squeezed the trigger twice. The gun pinged, and two red holes appeared in Ali's chest. He slumped against the back door, eyes wide and vacant. A red stain spread across the white shirt.

Wolfe nodded, "In other words, yes, I'm going to kill you, Ali. You chose to be a terrorist; you pay the price—the only price possible with you people."

The deed done, he searched the assassins' gym bags. He had time. al-Bashri wouldn't expect the assassins back at the mosque for a while yet. In each bag, he found a passport, money, plane tickets from New York to Frankfurt, Germany, clothes, and a 9mm with a silencer and an extra clip each. He took the money, several thousand dollars at least, and the guns. He wiped down the Walther and placed it on Ali's lap, slipping his picture under the gun.

After chambering a round in each 9mm, he drove off.

CHAPTER 15: The Double-Edged Sword

Across the street from the hotel, the black Chrysler waited. Orani and the man watched Wolfe pull around back and then disappear behind the hotel. He came out the side alley a few minutes later.

"He's got someone in the back seat," the man said.

"Is it Ali?"

"I can't tell, but who else would it be?"

"Now where's he going?" Orani asked, pulling the car out to follow Wolfe again.

"I assume he's going to dump the bodies."

"You want to bet?"

"Why, where else would he be going?"

"It looks like he's headed back to the mosque!"

"Goddamn it, he's not going to make al-Bashri a martyr, is he?"

"Wolfe is sending a message to all involved, that's for sure!" Orani said, stepping on the gas. They caught up to Wolfe just in time to see him drive into the mosque. He took the alley to the right and went out of sight behind the building.

"Should we go in after him?" the agent asked.

"Isn't this what we wanted to hire him to do in the first place?" Orani replied. "Let him do his job, and hope to hell he's competent enough not to blow it. If we interfere, then we involve the Company in this, the administration, and God knows who else. Take it easy. If he gets caught, he takes the fall, and either way, we'll be rid of al-Bashri."

The agent sighed and said, "So, we let the good guy fry after egging him on?"

"If he still doesn't want to play ball after this, then in order to avoid an international incident—yes," Orani said with finality, although privately, and she chastised herself severely for this, she prayed for Wolfe. She wanted him to succeed, of course, but she wanted him to get through this as well.

"Jesus, sometimes I hate this job."

***

He turned onto the street and saw the mosque, but Wolfe had to wait as a yellow Ryder rental truck pulled out of the driveway. He didn't have time to wonder what it was doing there; he had a job to do. He pulled into the driveway and drove to the back. There was a large asphalt parking area between the house and the carriage house—enough for four cars at least. He parked just outside the light.

Wolfe opened the door and got out of the car, a gun in each hand. He kept to the shadows along the high overgrown hedge—apparently, the jihadists didn't hire gardeners. When Wolfe was halfway way to the back door, it opened. The security guard was obviously expecting the assassins because he opened the door wide and addressed Wolfe in Arabic. Wolfe raised both guns and shot. The guard spun around with a cry and fell sideways over the wrought iron rail. He slid down the rail leaving a bloody smear on the chipped paint. Halfway down he came off and lay sprawled head downwards on the stairs like a disjointed doll. Wolfe put another bullet in his eye and stepped over his still quivering form.

Rushing inside, Wolfe turned off the hall light and the outside light just in case the neighbors heard anything. Then he headed to the back stair. Climbing the stair, Wolfe turned left at the top, as Ali instructed. There was a paneled door. A light shined beneath it. Wolfe listened for a moment, turned the handle, and stepped into the room. al-Bashri was just crossing the office to the door.

He was clad in dun-colored robes with a white Kufi. He was carrying a manila folder and apparently reading the contents. The cleric's watery brown eyes looked up at Wolfe over a pair of small, rectangular spectacles. His face was smiling as if expecting good news, but his expression changed dramatically when he focused on Wolfe. At first, he was confused, asking in thick, guttural English, "What are you doing? You are not allowed in here. It is only for Muslims!"

Then, in obvious shock, he recognized Wolfe.

Wolfe raised his guns and shot the terrorist four times in the belly from about five feet away. al-Bashri staggered back with a cry, dropped the folder, and collapsed against his desk. He slid down to the floor and came to rest sitting up, his back against the bloodstained desk, staring wide-eyed at Wolfe. A pool of dark blood sluggishly spread down his robes to the carpet.

Wolfe glanced down at the folder. A picture slid halfway out; it was a picture of him in his airline uniform.

"What have we here?" he asked, shoving one gun into his waistband and stooping to pick up the folder. Upon opening it, he saw the picture was an enlarged black and white Xerox of his airline ID badge. Beneath the picture were pages of information, much of it written in Arabic, but quite a bit in English. To his consternation, he noticed his address and telephone number. The file also listed his company computer user name and password. "They've got to have someone inside the company to get this!"

Behind his personal data was a bundle of papers stapled together. They held a very detailed account of his actions on 9/11. How they got the narrative was a mystery, until Wolfe noticed a name and phone number scrawled in the margin of the notes: "D. C. Dallas, ACLU, (555) 733-2666"

"You've done your homework, it seems, and gained some friends in unfriendly places," Wolfe said grimly, glancing at al-Bashri with cold fury. "However, you didn't delve far enough into Western character. Did you think I'd wait for your goons to come and get me, al-Bashri? Is that what you remember of the West?" Wolfe squatted in front of the cleric and looked him straight in the eye. "Well, let this be the last thing you hear on this earth. We won't wait for you. Do you understand me? Like Leonidas and Richard the Lionheart before me, I will come to you, and I'll make you bleed!"

The wounded man tried to speak, but Wolfe simply stood up and pointed his gun at the cleric's forehead. "You have nothing to say in this world or the next. You people have to learn: you either enter the twenty-first century with us, or you don't enter it at all."

Al-Bashri stared in horror at the barrel of the gun; as if suddenly afraid to face the doom he so easily dealt on someone else.

"What's the matter? You have no trouble having a teenage girl stoned to death, or ordering children beheaded. What's the matter now, you fucking coward!"

Al-Bashri trembled uncontrollably, sputtering and gibbering. Drops of blood sprayed his gray beard.

"I didn't want this, you bastard. I don't need your blood on my hands, but you gave me no choice. You should've stuck to religion and stayed out of terrorism—they don't mix." He gave the cleric a wry smile. "Besides, a fatwa works both ways."

Wolfe fired twice. There were two soft pings and a pair of dark holes appeared on the terrorist's forehead. He shuddered and grew still.

Wolfe said, "This shouldn't happen in the house of God, but you would have been happy to bring me and my kids here and cut our throats while praising the name of Allah. So be it—this is your game, not mine. You made the rules; you have to die by them."

Wolfe was about to leave when he noticed a safe behind the desk—its door ajar. Curious, he hurried over and opened it. Inside were some scrolls, old books, several folders, and bundled stacks of cash. The cash was in hundreds and fifties. He took the cash and put it in his backpack with the lawyers in mind, and then he took out the folders.

"Why keep them in here instead of in the file cabinet?" he muttered aloud. Interestingly enough, the labels on the folders were in English. They read "Jihad America" and "Jihad New York."

He opened "America." Inside were lists of names, phone numbers, and addresses. There were dozens of pictures of various sites in the country, including the Gateway Arch in St. Louis, the Space Needle in Seattle, and the Lincoln Memorial in Washington, DC. Equally as interesting were bundled photos of very specific sites stapled to the recognizable pictures. For instance, behind the Space Needle was a picture of a run-down yellow house, a ferry boat, a restaurant front, and an underground parking space.

"My friends should be interested in these," Wolfe said grimly.

The "Jihad New York" folder made him break out into a furious cold sweat.

The folder had landmarks, but it also showed public facilities like the water works, natural gas facilities, and malls. By far the most chilling were the pictures and locations of half a dozen schools.

"You fucking bastards! You're planning to kill kids; what kind of sick monsters are you?" Wolfe stuffed the files in his backpack and added al-Bashri's laptop. As he slung on the backpack, Wolfe noticed the trash can next to the desk. Strangely enough, someone had burned the papers in the can.

Wolfe poked through the ashes. There was nothing discernable except the top corner of a multi-page yellow receipt. Carefully taking it out, Wolfe could read the top left corner of the stapled first and second page. It read:

Ryder Rentals
Rental Period: *04-23-02 to 05-*
Invoice Number: *72890-997-0*
Vehicle License: *NY 273A*
Renter: *Marwan Ham*
New York, NY to Se

The yellow truck that left as he arrived came to mind. With a sense of urgency, he searched the rest of the house.

Wolfe didn't find anything else incriminating in the house. For good measure, he searched the carriage house and garage out back. There, he found another surprise. The carriage house was a dormitory, but it was empty now. The garage had several vans and a car but nothing of any great interest. The basement was another story. Next to the old furnace were ten fifty-five gallon drums. The packing labels identified the contents as ammonium nitrate. Next to the drums were a dozen metal cans of fuel oil.

"Well, well, what have we here, religious material? That's enough to take out the block!" To make matters more disturbing, the drums sat on pallets and were at one point wrapped with cellophane. Someone had cut the cellophane and taken at least ten drums. Wolfe examined the drums and found labels on each drum reading, "Harvest Agricultural Supply, Ithaca, New York."

"You'd think we'd learn from this stuff!" he said, with slow-burning anger. Wolfe tore off one of the labels and stuffed it in his backpack. He didn't need to see anymore.

Working quickly, he carried the cleric outside and put him in the car next to his bodyguard. He loaded the trunk with the fuel oil and unscrewed one of the cans, splashing the liquid all over the carpet in the trunk and over the bodies.

He changed into his spare sweats and shoes, washed the gunshot residue from his hands and face with the rubbing alcohol, and left the old clothes in the trunk with the fuel oil. The two shooters he left draped over the open trunk, putting half-smoked cigarettes in their mouths.

"They shoot al-Bashri and his bodyguard and drag them out to the limo to dispose of them. They open the trunk, releasing the fuel oil vapor and exposing it to an ignition source and oxygen—stupid terrorists. I doubt there'll be anything for even Grissom to find when that much fuel oil goes up!"

He took another cigarette and lit it from a safe distance; he flicked it into the trunk. Wolfe ran.

The whoosh of flame was audible, but he didn't turn to look. The fuel oil cans ignited when he was about thirty yards away; he felt the heat on the nape of his neck. As he reached the sidewalk, the gas tank blew up.

Wolfe slowed to a jog on the sidewalk, like any other man running at night. He jogged up to the black 300 and tapped on the driver's window. It slid down to reveal Orani and a dark-haired man with hard eyes.

"You wouldn't mind giving me a ride back to my hotel, would you? It's a long walk, and it looks like this place is going to be hopping when New York's finest arrive."

"Get in," Orani said gruffly.

Wolfe opened the back door and slid onto the leather seat. "Nice to see you, Orani; you're looking the elegant espionage part as usual. Who's your friend?"

"You don't need to know, Mr. Wolfe," the agent said.

"They pair you with some awfully chatty fellows, Orani. Is it you or simply company policy?"

"What'd you do with the gun?"

"It can't be traced, can it?"

"No," she said, turning onto the main drag. The hotel was a block away.

"Then it's still doing its job," Wolfe told her. "Listen, do us all a favor and get the fire department over here. There are ten fifty-five gallon drums of ammonium nitrate stored in the basement of the carriage house. I'd really hate to see them go up when we're this close, and I don't want to see any of the good guys get hurt."

"Shit!" the agent cursed. He got on the phone and tipped off the fire department.

"And what about Ali?" Orani asked. "Wasn't that him in the back seat?"

"Whoever rented that car had him killed," Wolfe said. "Maybe he was stealing from the mosque. That's a bad idea, considering these people." Wolfe unzipped his backpack and handed the files and the laptop to her partner. "Here's some reading material, and al-Bashri's laptop. You were right, Orani; they've got operations planned, from schools to national icons. Al-Bashri even has a file on me—thanks to Dixie Dallas."

"That's interesting. I'm glad we got it before the cops did; otherwise, we might never see it," Orani mused. "Good work, Wolfe."

The other agent gave the files a cursory study, but even he sounded impressed. "This is excellent stuff—a gold mine in names and contacts. No way would they want us to know about this. If we work fast enough, we can track these people and get wiretaps and tails in place."

"Why not arrest them for conspiracy and pump them for every bit of information they've got—isn't that what you do?" Wolfe asked testily.

"No, Mr. Wolfe, it's unfortunately not that easy," Orani said. "That's why we want you. You see, we either wait until the bad guys do something wrong or we have enough evidence for a trial—then we get to move in and get them. That's how the game works."

"That's going to get a lot of people killed," Wolfe replied unhappily.

They pulled into the hotel parking lot. "In case you didn't hear, they're targeting schools."

"Bingo! Let there be light!" the other agent said, throwing him a sarcastic glance that was more venomous than amused. "Why the hell do you think you're here? Good God, man, open your eyes!"

"My partner is right, Mr. Wolfe," Orani added. "That's exactly why we've been trying to recruit you. We need to nip these things in the bud." She pulled the 300 into a spot, put it in park, and turned around, looking at him with those deep brown eyes. "There are going to be times when we have enough evidence to know what they're up to, but not enough to bring it to court. That's where you come in."

"You want me to take the gray area out of the equation."

Orani's man laughed. "That's it in a nutshell. We'll walk back to your room with you and then explain your options, Mr. Wolfe."

"That sounds final," he said with narrowed eyes.

"It is," Orani said.

CHAPTER 16: A New Vocation

"We think it's time you took some time off, and disappear," Orani told Wolfe back at the hotel.

"I have an idea; how about a vacation?" Flint smiled. He was in a good mood for a change. That wasn't to be wondered at, considering he was alive and the deadly work of the night was over. He didn't want to admit that part of his good feeling was from seeing Orani again, but enough of him was cognizant of it to suggest a cruise. "We could go to the Bahamas and act like an old married couple. We'll lie around the beach all day drinking pina coladas. I'll burn, and you'll just get more beautiful. Then, like most married couples, we'll go to bed together and find an excuse not to have sex."

Orani laughed, rummaging through the liquor cabinet. She poured the agent a scotch and herself an amaretto on the rocks and made a martini for Flint. "Sorry to burst your bubble, but I'm talking about a working vacation," she said, handing Wolfe the drink. "You're going to Virginia."

"Virginia—no one goes on vacation to Virginia!"

"You are."

Flint raised the glass to his lips, but then he unconsciously stopped.

"What's the matter? Surely you don't think I slipped a mickey into your drink?"

"No, but I almost forgot; I've got to fly in ten-and-a-half hours. Twelve hours bottle-to-throttle, those are the rules."

"Drink it; you're not flying tomorrow," she said. "We're taking you down to DC for a quick indoctrination. It'll take a week—don't worry, I've already had United call your parents. They think you're quarantined for an anthrax scare on your plane. You can call them tonight. After that, we'll fly you back home. You've got two weeks to rest, recuperate, and pack. Then we're bringing you back here for a couple of months. You should be back flying by spring."

"What's this all about?" Flint asked, sipping the drink. Damn, Orani made good martinis. Did they teach her that in spy school? He didn't doubt it.

"We're sending you to training," she said. "You'll learn the intricacies of what you did tonight, along with a variety of techniques. I know you're a family man, so you can take your kids with you. We have a school and a day care facility."

"Assassin day care—you really keep up with the times," Flint said, sipping at the martini. "And if I don't want to go?"

"We can protect you and your kids far better if you're on the inside than on the outside, Wolfe—how many times do I have to say it? You know how the government works. Besides, do you really want the IRS prying into that backpack?"

Flint gave her a wry look and asked, "Will the Company pick up the tab for my legal challenges from the ACLU?"

Orani leaned over the table and said, "We'll make them disappear."

"Are you my contact at the Company?"

"Do you want me to be?" Her eyebrows rose as if truly curious.

Flint glanced at the other agent. "No offense, but if I'm going to take orders that lead me to my death, I'd rather get them from you than him—at least I'll enjoy the view."

She nodded and raised her glass. "Is that the only reason, Mr. Wolfe?"

He touched her glass with his and turned serious. "I saved your life once. It may not count for much, but someday I'm hoping you might return the favor."

"It counts for something, Flint," she said with a slight laugh. It sounded as though she was treating his statement lightly, but Flint noted, for the second time, that she used his Christian name. That was enough.

"I guess that's it, then. You got me."

Orani's partner got up and went into the bedroom. He returned a moment later and handed a small leather billfold to Wolfe. "Welcome to the Company, Mr. Wolfe. It'll be an honor working with someone of your stature."

Flint opened it up. It was an ID with his picture. There was a holographic icon in the center that read "CIA." He swallowed hard and sighed, but for some reason, he didn't feel angry, cornered, or threatened. He felt as if he were doing the right thing—even for, and maybe especially for, his kids. "Well, I guess that makes it official."

The formerly stoic agent smiled and held out his hand. "By the way, I'm Walter, Jason Walter."

Wolfe shook his hand.

Before he'd finished half his drink, he'd become a paid assassin.

Orani went into her room and came out with two garment bags and a black gym bag. She dropped the bag at Wolfe's feet. "Here's your new wardrobe, including a suit and a new uniform."

"What's that for?" Wolfe asked, taking a garment bag and unzipping it. Inside were a blue pilot's uniform and two white shirts. "I already have a uniform."

"This isn't simply a uniform," she informed him. "The fibers in the cloth are aramid fibers. They are synthetic fibers from the same family as your air force issue Nomex flight suit, but they're five times stronger than steel. There are not plates, so it's not true body armor. It doesn't distribute the force of the blow, but the weave has close to a no-yield point. We've sacrificed some protection to improve suppleness, but this cloth will still stop a bullet or a knife, and it's a lot more comfortable than wearing a Kevlar vest all the time."

Orani and Walter spent the rest of the evening going over the folders Wolfe liberated from the cleric's office. Out of professional courtesy, that was Flint's opinion, they had him look things over as well. He paid close attention to the pictures of Seattle, as it was his hometown. Nothing jumped out at him except the photo of the underground parking spot. For some reason, it struck him as familiar, but he had no idea why. He'd been to the Space Needle, but he'd never been to the parking garage. It wasn't valet parking, which was for certain. The spaces were set against a concrete wall with a loading dock to the right.

Even more mystifying was the folder "Jihad New York." It had self-explanatory photos of New York landmarks—including the Twin Towers of the World Trade Center, which were irritatingly crossed out in black ink. Yet there was nothing at all indicating how the jihadists would attack such a wide array of targets. The jihadists would need hundreds of fighters working in close concert.

"They simply couldn't keep something that big quiet," Orani noted. "I think this has to be a wish list yet to be prioritized."

"Then they're dreaming big," Flint said, pointing to the last page in the folder. On it was a list of every major city on the East Coast, from Boston to Miami. At the bottom was a scrawled note in Arabic.

"It says, 'blessed be the Wave of Allah that will strike his enemies down with a single stroke!'" Orani translated.

"Good God, they can't be thinking of striking all these cities at once, can they? They'd need thousands of people. We'd hear of something long before it happened."

"Not if they use the mosques," Flint ventured. "Our own laws will protect them; that is, unless you have the mosques bugged."

"Wishful thinking," Orani muttered. "Don't worry, they're fanatics; their eyes are bigger than their stomachs."

Flint wasn't so sure, especially after 9/11.

***

It was a long week full of paperwork, briefings, meetings, and a million other things. Fortunately, the flight back to Seattle was uneventful. Flint exited the plane, took the train to the main terminal, crossed to the parking garage, and took the elevator down to the first level. As he crossed the terminal, he retrieved a text message sent by Orani. It read, "Ryder truck arrived in Denver day before yesterday with Marwan Hamdi and Gamel Khallida. Hamdi is a native New Yorker and a Yale-educated engineer on our watch list. Khallida graduated from the University of Washington with a degree in nuclear engineering. They are staying with Dr. Yusuf Kadir, the director for geophysics at the U of Colorado. Pictures below—be ready for a tasking."

Flint traversed the underground rental car lot, perusing the pictures of the two bomb makers and the physics professor.

What does a geophysicist have to do with two highly educated terrorists? he wondered as he reached the bus stop next to the main road. *Oh, well, that's Denver's problem right now.*

Flint checked his watch; it was five o'clock. The next bus wouldn't be there for ten minutes. He sighed and resigned himself to wait, pacing as he always did along the sidewalk. The tunnel's high ceiling was slick with condensation. Pipes ran thirty feet above him, dripping with water. No matter the season, the tunnel was cold and wet. Flint let his eyes wander, bored, looking at the strangely thin rectangular columns. He wondered, as always, just how they'd stand up to an earthquake if it shook a certain way. The thought made him stop. A shiver ran down his spine, and his breath caught in his lungs.

Flint dug in his bag until he found the file folder Orani left with him. She'd given him his own file to study, but also the Seattle file. Digging through, he took out the large photo of the Space Needle with its accompanying detailed photos. In short order, he found what he was looking for: the picture of the parking space.

There, behind space B-2, was a chest-high cement wall with steel railings, and on the right-hand side of the picture just to the side of the loading dock, there was the base of one of those strangely out-of-proportion columns unique to SEATAC airport.

"So it wasn't the Space Needle after all!" he exclaimed, leaving his bag behind and running along the road. There were parking spaces at intervals along the way. Parking space B-2 was about a hundred and fifty yards from the bus stop. There was nothing there. Flint ran up the stairs to the third level of the garage, the baggage-claim level. Sprinting outside, he found himself right in the middle of the terminal. If a bomb went off from that parking space, it would collapse the airport road and the baggage claim area in the very center of the terminal. Above that were ticketing and the brand-new rotunda crammed with shops and restaurants.

"Ten drums of ammonium nitrate will take out the terminal and touch off the gas lines beneath it," he muttered. Digging through the folder, he found the burned rental receipt. He keyed in the toll-free number.

"Good afternoon, Ryder Truck rentals. I'm Melissa; can I help you?"

"Yes, this is Mr. Hamdi, I'm sorry to bother you," he said in as calm a voice as he could manage. "I've rented one of your trucks for my trip to Seattle, but I'm afraid I've lost my paperwork. I'm running a bit behind, and I can't remember when it was I was supposed to bring the truck in or where—I don't want to turn it in late."

"Do you have any information that could help me track the truck, Mr. Hamdi?"

"I have the license plate number; will that help?"

"Give it to me."

"NY 273A."

"It looks as though the truck is due in today at 8:00 PM at our Bellevue location. Do you need directions?"

"No, thank you very much for your help," Flint said, hanging up. "They're going to detonate it at the evening rush!" The hour between six and seven PM were abnormally busy. Businesspeople were either leaving on trips for early-morning meetings or returning in time for a late dinner. From what he could see at the baggage claim level, today was no exception.

"There're at least ten thousand people here," he gasped and ran back toward the parking space. It was empty. He opened his phone to call Orani, when he heard the sound of a truck.

It was the Ryder truck, and just as he anticipated, it turned into parking spot B-2. Wolfe drew his gun and screwed on the silencer. Then he froze.

The driver was a blond man who looked like a California surfer bum. The passenger was a young, curly-haired brunette of pale complexion—she couldn't have been eighteen.

Where were the two Arabs?

CHAPTER 17: Misconceptions

Wolfe was stunned. He didn't know what to think. He double-checked the license plate number—it was the same. The parking spot was the same as the information from al-Bashri. There could be no mistake. What were these kids doing in the truck; were they duped into carrying out a deadly plot?

He holstered his gun and stepped out from behind his vantage point. Flint had to warn them before they got hurt.

The young man turned away, digging something out from behind the seats. He dragged a heavy canvass vest over the seat back; it was a suicide vest—no mistake about it.

Wolfe stopped.

The girl turned from the young man and looked straight at him. Her blue eyes grew round as saucers. She obviously said something to the boy, as he turned quickly around and pushed the vest below the console.

Wolfe's mind worked furiously, but outwardly he smiled and waved, heading for the passenger side of the truck as if that's what he meant to do all along. His calm demeanor hid his confusion. Could these be the terrorists? How? They couldn't have any connection to Al-Qaeda, could they? Immediately, he cursed himself, and the shock melted away to pure, chilling fury. Fool that he was; he'd let his emotions jeopardize thousands of people. Just like the traitor John Walker Lind, these kids were brainwashed. There was no saving them. If they detonated their vests or the truck before he got to them, thousands would die.

Wolfe walked casually up to the girl's window. She looked angry but rolled it down anyway. The young man fiddled with something Wolfe couldn't see—he'd have to be careful and quick.

"What do you want?" the girl asked.

"Sorry, I just wanted to let you know your pass isn't showing," Wolfe told her. He looked her right in the eyes. There was nothing human in them. Whatever was in there was no longer anyone's daughter. She was lost. "You can't be too careful these days; you never know when or where those terrorists will strike."

She smiled an amused, thankless smile that was more revealing than any words and replied, "No, you never can tell."

Wolfe pounded his left hand against the yellow door of the truck, right beneath the handle, and slipped his right hand into his jacket. "The godless bastards have no conscience, no morals, and no future! But we'll crush them in the end. Every one of them will end up sleeping in hell—so much for their seventy-something virgins. What a bunch of sick bastards!"

Her eyes flared in anger. "You're obviously ignorant of their aspirations—hey, back off!"

Wolfe whipped his gun out and grabbed the door handle, swinging himself onto the running board. The girl tried to push him away with her hands, but he hit her in the temple with the butt of his gun. She reeled, momentarily stunned. The young man glared at him with teeth bared, like an animal, frozen by Wolfe's sudden action.

Wolfe shot blindly, firing twice as the girl scratched and clawed at his arm and face. The boy reached for a glowing red switch, but the impact of the bullets jerked him around. A red blotch appeared on his left shoulder and a splash of blood spattered the driver's window. He cried out as a second round, red hole appeared on his left breast, and he slumped into the corner of the seat.

"Crusader dog!" the girl exclaimed, scrambling for the red switch.

Wolfe grabbed her by her hair and jammed the barrel of the silencer under her chin. "Stay still, missy, if you want to live!" he told her harshly.

"You'll all perish in the flames of Allah's new world!"

The girl kicked and flailed for the red switch. To Wolfe's horror, her foot missed it by less than an inch. With a cold, sick rage, he pulled the trigger twice. The girl's head rocked in his hand as if she were nodding, and then her blue eyes—so much like his daughter's might look in ten years' time—stared up at him in that dull, dead, vacuous gaze.

He let her head go and, in fury, put another round in the young man's skull.

"You fucking traitorous bastards!" The fury faded. Wolfe's job wasn't finished.

He opened the door, careful not to let the girl's body fall out of the truck or accidentally onto the switch.

"You've got to have a timer on the bomb back there as well, otherwise why take the trouble of having suicide vests? You bastards probably planned to watch the detonation and then blow yourselves up amongst the first responders."

Squeezing into the cab, Wolfe checked the device with the red switch. It was a simple black box with a pair of wires running back beneath the seat. On the box was a toggle switch that read "Arm" on top and "Disarm" on the bottom. It was in the armed position. Next to the toggle switch was the red rocker switch.

He threw the toggle switch to "Disarm" and the red rocker switch went dark. Wolfe cut the wires with his Leatherman pliers. Then he rooted through their keys and unlocked the back. It smelled heavily of fuel oil. There wasn't much room in the cargo compartment. It was filled with the missing drums of fertilizer. Wolfe squeezed in between the drums and closed the cargo door. A dim blue glow showed from the front of the compartment. Wolfe figured that was the control panel. He worked his way forward. Sitting on top of the drums of ammonium nitrate was a PDA wired to a car battery. The screen on the PDA was counting down from 00:14:20.

"That's not much time," he muttered to himself. "But how do I know there's not a dead man's switch? Damn!" Wolfe checked his watch. It read 1815.

"Alright, I'll give myself to 1825—no later."

Wolfe hustled out of the cargo compartment. He got in the driver's side door, shoving the beach boy headfirst into the passenger foot well.

Grabbing the dead girl's hair, he pulled her down and out of sight. Her head plunked onto his lap. He pushed her roughly away.

"Sorry, there's no time for that, honey."

Wolfe started the truck and backed out, heading out of the tunnel. He came to the bus stop, and there were a couple of crewmembers looking over his bag. He screeched to a halt, jumped out, and grabbed his bag.

"Sorry, I forgot this!"

"We thought it was a bomb!" a pilot joked.

Wolfe threw him a wry glance and tossed the heavy bag through the window and on top of the girl. He gunned the engine and sped off. It was 1818.

It was less than a minute to the guard shack. Wolfe stopped opposite it and rolled down the bloody window.

The guard stared at him, his dark, puffy face going red and a dumbfounded expression in his eyes.

"Weren't you supposed to stop the terrorists from getting into the airport?"

The guard ignored the 9mm in his holster and reached behind the door of the shack. He came out with an AK-47.

Wolfe shot him twice in the head. The baseball hat with the yellow security badge tumbled off the guard's head; he flew back into his chair and rolled to the floor. A pool of blood slowly spread across the dirty concrete.

1820.

He hit the gas and drove the truck down the airport access road toward the north parking lot. There was a large, open space next to a water tower there. Wolfe looked at his watch every few seconds or so, and almost as an afterthought, he called Orani.

"Wolfe! What is it?"

"You have any idea how I can disarm a bomb without blowing myself up?" he asked as he careened around a tight corner, ran a red light, and flew across the bridge over the highway. The parking lot was three hundred yards ahead. He could see the trees surrounding the water tower.

"You're serious?"

"Absolutely! I'm in that rental truck from New York; the one with the ammonium nitrate and fuel oil that's not supposed to be here. Now there's a PDA attached to a car battery and then the ammonium nitrate and fuel oil. Can I cut the wires, or is it going to blow up if I disconnect the power source?"

"Hold on a second; how much time do you have?"

"Roughly five minutes; the bomb is in the back of the truck—I'm driving it away from the airport as we speak."

"Hold on."

He passed the first gate; then after two hundred yards, he turned hard onto the parking lot access road. To his right was the Boeing plant, and to his left, the water tower. The truck protested as he turned onto the dirt access road. He gunned it to the water tower and skidded to a halt at the steel gate. Wolfe jumped out of the truck and checked his watch.

1825.

"Orani, I've got four minutes!" he yelled over his earpiece, scrambling into the back of the truck. When he reached the PDA, he corrected himself. "I've got two minutes and thirty-seven seconds!"

"Mr. Wolfe, are you there?" asked a male voice.

"I'm here."

"Good. Now, there should be two wires going from the power supply, to the PDA and then to the device itself; do you see them?"

"I see four wires going from the battery to the PDA and four going from the PDA to the bomb," Wolfe replied, now beginning to sweat.

"Are there two black wires and two white wires?"

"No," Wolfe said, squinting in the dim light, "it looks like each wire is a different color."

"I was afraid of that," sighed the man. "That's Hamdi's signature: a dead man's switch and the real switch. If you disarm the wrong one, you go boom! Is the bomb in an unpopulated area?"

Wolfe looked at the PDA.

00:01:42.

"Sort of," he admitted. It was the best place he could find in such short notice—he certainly couldn't get on the highway.

"Is the area clear for at least three hundred yards?"

"No." He wiped the sweat from his forehead. "Do you have any idea which wires I need to cut?"

"One dark one and one light one," the voice said. "They should be on the same side of the PDA. Pick a side. Hamdi's left-handed, but of course, he won't admit it. I'd choose left. Still, if I were you, I'd run."

00:01:20.

"Alright, I'm cutting the wires between the PDA and the battery on the left side," Wolfe said, trying to sound calm.

"No! Between the PDA and the bomb, Wolfe! Cut the wires between the PDA and the bomb! The PDA's the switch, but it may have enough juice to set off the bomb!"

"Alright! Alright!" Wolfe shouted.

He took a deep breath and cut the wires.

The PDA beeped harshly. The screen flashed red with white numbers blinking off and on, "10 ... 9 ... 8 ..."

"Wolfe, what was that beep?"

"Orani, tell my kids I love them and I died for my country, or some shit like that," Wolfe said with finality.

"Wolfe!"

"3 ... 2 ... 1 ..."

CHAPTER 18: Ghosts in the Machine

Wolfe refused to close his eyes. If he was going to meet death, it would be with his eyes open. He just didn't figure it'd be because of a bunch of fertilizer.

The PDA hit 0 and the alarm rung. The screen turned white. Involuntarily, he closed his eyes. An enormous rush of sound assailed his ears, and a wave of heat swept over his flesh.

That's it? he thought. *That's all there is to it? I suppose that is really and truly it, then.*

"Wolfe?"

"Saint Peter?" he asked aloud, not very happily. All the things he'd yet to do suddenly flooded back into his mind—especially the unfinished business with his kids. A growl escaped his tightly clenched lips. "Damn it, what right do you have to take me now?"

"I don't understand," said the voice in apparent sincere confusion.

"Don't you dare judge me! Hell, you knew him and denied him three times—so don't you dare damn me. I've been faithful with all my faults!"

"Wolfe! Why aren't you dead?"

It was Orani's voice.

Flint opened his eyes. The PDA was still flashing "0," but otherwise, the barrels of ammonium nitrate were still sitting there, intact. He sighed in very pleasurable but embarrassed relief. Somehow, someway, he must still be alive.

133

"I really don't know; it counted down to zero."

He walked to the back of the truck and peered out toward the runway only a hundred yards away. A 747 just landed. That explained the noise and the jet exhaust explained the heat.

"You're alive!"

"It seems so," he admitted.

"Then I must sound an awful lot like Saint Peter."

"Sorry, I've been preparing that speech for quite a while."

"Save it for later, please."

"Mr. Wolfe, I still don't understand why you're alive," said the man. "What exactly did you do?"

"Exactly what you told me to do, except—" Wolfe hesitated and went back to the intact wires. He traced one set from the PDA to the battery, but the other two went down toward the bomb, then turned and ran to the front of the van. They ran through a small hole bored into the front of the compartment, came back out the hole, and went to the bomb. Wolfe understood.

"Except what, Mr. Wolfe?"

"I didn't have time to trace the other set of wires," he explained. "The terrorists had an arm/disarm switch in the cab. I disarmed it and cut the wires. That must've interrupted the entire circuit."

"Of course, Hamdi would've wanted his people to detonate the bomb if they were stopped—to get something out of it."

"Alright, I think I've had about enough for one day." Wolfe sighed.

Sirens broke into the air.

"Oh, bloody hell, they've found the security guard," he sighed. Then he got out of the truck, closed the back door, and locked it. "Say, you got anyone in this town who can pick up the truck? The cops are going to be thick as thieves here, and I don't want any part of it."

"Hold tight," Orani said, "we're looking up the people now."

Wolfe returned to the front of the cab and climbed back into the front seat. The smell of blood was heavy in the cab. He picked up the girl's head by her hair and said, "Now that I've got a moment, here's another mystery for you, Orani; these aren't the two terrorists you tracked from New York. These are two white kids; it's a young guy and a gal in their late teens-early twenties. How they got into this, I don't know."

"Insanity isn't limited to people from the Middle East, Wolfe."

"I know that; I have an ex-wife, remember?" he retorted, digging through their clothes. He found the man's wallet and the woman's purse. He found their driver's licenses and another form of ID he didn't expect. "Orani, we have here Cat Lloyd and Anita Sunstein; they're both students from the University of Colorado. Hey, isn't that the home of the traitor, the 'Little Eichmann' guy?"

"I wouldn't be surprised if they were in his classes, but we've got another professor there who is a person of interest. That area seems to be a hotbed of dissention; it's strange considering how wealthy they are," Orani said. "We'll check up on them."

He heard a siren and looked in the rear view mirror. A cop was pulling into the access road. "Any word on those people, Orani? I've got company."

"Who?"

"It's your friendly neighborhood police. Can I flash them my ID?"

"We'd rather you didn't."

"Orani, I've got two dead kids in the cab, the gun that killed the security cop who was in on it, and one big-ass bomb in the back of my truck. What am I supposed to tell him?"

"Do what you need to do, Wolfe, and good luck," Orani said.

"Orani, I'm not going to kill a cop ... Orani!"

The line was dead.

Wolfe swore as the cop car pulled alongside. He opened his door and stepped down, saying, "Good afternoon, officer, can I help you?"

The cop kept his right hand at the top of his holster, walked around the front of his car, and asked, "This is kind of a strange place to park a rental truck. You commute in this thing?"

"No, I couldn't afford the gas bill with all my pay cuts," Wolfe smiled. "I just moved up here, but I don't have a pass for the employee lot yet. I drove the truck out from New York, where the company based me before, and I left it here while I flew a trip. I know it's not quite kosher, but I couldn't afford the four-day parking fee, so I parked it here out of the way."

"Do you have any ID on you besides your airline badge?"

"Yes, sir," Wolfe said, opening up his jacket so the cop could see his breast pocket before he reached in it. He pulled out his federal flight deck officer ID, the one that identified him as a deputized air marshal. He handed it to the cop.

"Thank you for that," replied the officer, meaning Wolfe's mannerisms—every cop appreciated non-threatening behavior. "So you're one of the guys who can carry when they fly; what do you use, the Glock?"

"Yes, sir, they had a surplus on them, so that's what they gave us. It's a good weapon—not what I'd choose, but a good weapon. It's in its lockbox inside my bag."

"Mr. Wolfe, I'm glad to see you're one of us," the officer said, handing Flint back his ID. "Excuse me, but I have to ask you a few questions. You see, we've had some trouble down at the guard station, and about the same time, witnesses saw a Ryder truck drive out of the tunnel."

"It must've been someone else," Wolfe said evenly. "What kind of trouble did you have?"

"A cop is dead," the cop told him.

"A cop, here at SEATAC, shit!"

"Do you mind if I have a look in your truck?"

"Not at all," Wolfe said, wondering what he was going to do without spilling his identity. "Do you want to see the front or the back first?"

"Show me the back, if you don't mind," the cop said.

Wolfe led him to the back of the truck, wondering just how he was going to explain the lack of furniture and the presence of a very powerful bomb. He had no choice; whether Orani wanted him to or not, he had to reveal himself. He took off the lock on the rear door and turned to the cop.

"I ought to tell you, officer," he began, but the cop's radio crackled and the officer held up his hand.

"Two-victor-eleven, go ahead," the officer answered.

"Two-victor-eleven, we've got clarification on the rental truck. It was a *U-Haul,* not a *Ryder,* repeat, a *U-Haul* truck. How copy?"

"Two-victor-eleven copies, cancel the code. I'm back on the road," he said, and he looked wryly at Flint. "Sorry about that, Mr. Wolfe, mistaken identity. Now, you were saying?"

"I was just going to ask you to stand back, officer." Flint smiled, stuffing his wallet back into his jacket. "I'm a pilot, not a mover, and all this stuff's liable to fall on you—I've got it packed to the gills."

"Don't worry about it; this isn't the truck they're looking for," the officer said, turning away and heading back to his car. "Sorry for the hassle. Have a better one, and next time, park the truck where it belongs."

"Will do, officer," Wolfe smiled.

The cop turned away, but then stopped and asked, "How big a pay cut did you guys take?"

"Forty-one percent officially, but with the loss of seniority, it was about 65 percent take-home for me, not including the loss of pensions—but management got its bonuses, so it all evened out. I live vicariously through our benevolent CEO."

"It's a crappy world for the little guy," the cop said, shaking his head. "Fly safe!"

Two men showed up an hour later to take the truck. One of them wore Ryder coveralls. They both showed him their IDs. They worked for the Company.

"We'll go over this with a fine-tooth comb and let you know what we find out, Mr. Wolfe," the man in the suit told him.

"You should probably tell Ms. Orani instead," Flint replied.

The man shook his head and opened the cargo door, looking a bit confused. "No, sir, we were told you were the agent in charge, so unless I get a change of orders, you'll get my results in your company e-mail."

His partner opened the cab and started hauling the bodies to the back. "Nice bit a tail, this one," he said with a distinct New York accent. "A shame she went wrong."

Flint stared after him for a second and then looked back at the other man. "I don't have company e-mail," Flint said, his voice trailing off in wonder, "do I?"

"Of course you do, Mr. Wolfe." The man smiled and climbed into the back. He checked the PDA, clipped the rest of the wires, and took a few pictures with his cell-phone camera. "By the way, it's an honor to meet you."

"Likewise," Flint said, mystified.

"We'll process this tonight and have a report for you first thing in the morning. That'll give you time to get your report out to HQ before close of business DC time."

"I appreciate that." Flint sighed, not knowing which was worse: the blood on his hands or the paperwork it entailed.

When he got home, the kids were still in school. He showered, shaved, checked his mail, and finally removed his laptop and turned it on.

As soon as he'd logged in, a voice said, "Good afternoon, Mr. Wolfe, you have mail."

"What the hell?"

A gray box sat in the middle of the screen. Inside it said, "Software update available … Select *OK* to accept … Always trust software from the Company."

"Someone has a sense of humor over there," he said, and clicked the button. It took a minute to upload, and then a voice came over the speaker.

"Mr. Wolfe, your computer is now secure. You can access your e-mail under the heading *Astrophysical Journal.* Communications will be through this area until we issue you a secure cell phone. You have a new assignment. Please check the status at once and acknowledge receipt."

"Hey, I haven't even been trained yet—or whatever they call it!" Flint complained, but he obediently sat down and opened the flashing mailbox anyway.

The pictures of three Middle Eastern men appeared at the top. Their names and occupations were in captions underneath. The first man was an older, pleasant-looking man with an innocent face and a close-cropped white beard. His name was Dr. Yusuf Kadir, and he was the department chair for geology at the University of Colorado. The other two men were younger and had captions that were more sinister. They were the well-educated terrorists.

Beneath the images was an itinerary.

"Dec. 1, 1400 Flight 722 SEADIA as Dr. Edward Strait, PhD, MIT, Astrophysics Dept., with wife and kids."

"My wife? They've got me married off already."

"Pick up at DIA door 612, center island, by Agent Conrad. C-M-73-245. C&R: *Hard Winter/Late Spring.*"

He had to think about that. Agent Conrad would be a white male, seventy-three inches tall—that would be six-one—weighing two-forty-five. He was a big boy. The challenge and response would be something with hard winter and late spring.

"Boulder Sheraton. Thursday, Dec. 2, 1515: You are to give a lecture at the University of Colorado on 'The Impact of the Moon on Terrestrial Geology.' Details in attachment. After your lecture, Dr. Kadir will lecture on 'The Geologic Instability of Ancient Volcanic Formations.' Observe the lecture and try to ascertain the relationship between Dr. Kadir and Hamdi and Khallida; i.e., is Dr. Kadir passively involved or actively involved, and what is the purpose of Hamdi and Khallida coming to the university?"

The lecture was in two days.

"I'm going to look like an absolute idiot," he mumbled to himself. "What's the point?"

"After the lecture and before your departure, you will have an opportunity to investigate further. You are not to eliminate Hamdi or Khallida yet. We want to know what they're up to. Their files are attached. Company day care will be provided for the kids."

"Good God, I'm supposed to take the kids along?"

"Dec. 3, Flight 176 DEN IAD, 1237 dep. You will be picked up at the airport by Agent Kowalski. AA-M-75-195. C&R: *Congress/Idiots*."

"Well, at least that makes sense."

That was all.

Flint leaned back in his chair and asked aloud, "Good God, what can happen now?"

Apparently, it was the wrong thing to say or to think. He heard the doorbell ring. A wave of weariness passed over Flint, and he couldn't get himself to get up. Then he heard the door open. The Danes were barking. He heard the kids' voices and a woman's voice. Flint leapt up and ran to the front door.

A woman in pink leaned over the kids. She had bobbed blonde hair and a Cheshire cat smile. Behind her, there was a cameraman.

"Conner and Katherine, what beautiful names," she was saying. "Did you know your daddy is a murderer?"

"What are you doing here?" Flint asked, rushing to the kids and pulling them from the clutches of Dixie C. Dallas.

She smiled and said, "They're just adorable, but do they know their father's a monster?"

"He's not a monster, lady, you are!" Conner said, immediately coming to his dad's aid.

"How sweet, just like his dad!" she said.

Flint's blood boiled, but he sent the kids off. "Get to your room, guys, I'll be right up as soon as I take care of this stranger."

"Are you going to beat her up like you did Toad and his gang?" Conner asked excitedly.

"I want to watch," Katherine added, trying to wriggle out of his grasp.

"No!" Flint said. "Now, please, guys, I mean it. Go to your rooms!"

Reluctantly, the kids did as they were told.

Flint turned around to find Dixie and the cameraman let themselves in. "Get out!" he said sternly.

"Not before I give you this," she said, handing him an envelope. "It's a civil suit I filed on behalf of the families of the five men you murdered on that flight that never was—do you remember?"

"You filed suit on behalf of terrorists?" Flint asked, completely stunned. "Do you know what happened on 9/11, Dixie? Do you have any clue? Those men who hijacked the airliners killed thousands. Why on earth would you defend them?"

"Hey, they've got the same right to express themselves under the Constitution that you and I do—it applies to everybody," she said, and she put her hands together as if saying grace. "By the way, thanks for admitting the flight that never was actually happened; I've been stonewalled by the government since September 2001."

Flint sighed. He was angry, really angry, but Dixie's psychosis was so unbelievable that it disarmed him. She'd gone absolutely stupid. Exasperated, he approached the cameraman, who was still filming. "You're in my house, and I didn't invite you in." He ripped the camera out of the man's hands.

"Hey, that's private property!" the cameraman said.

"It's on my property," Flint replied. "So are you, by the way. Check the Constitution—you can't just barge into a citizen's home and violate his privacy. Citizens are protected under the Constitution, not criminals, or those enemies of the state—foreign or domestic. Now get out, or I will throw you out—you've been warned."

The cameraman moved toward the door, but Dixie stayed put.

"If you touch me, it's assault."

"Very well, if that's how you want to play it," Flint said, and he picked her up and threw her over his shoulder like a rug. Dixie yelled and screamed, but it was to no avail. Flint carried her out, ushering the cameraman ahead. When he reached the edge of his property, he put her down and said, very calmly, "Can you stop yelling for one second; is it possible for you to be rational?"

She stopped, perhaps wondering what he might have to say.

He leaned close and whispered, "Your pursuit of this endangers my life, Dixie. I've already got a fatwa on my head; believe me, they don't need your help."

"You should have thought of that before you murdered those men!"

"Well, if I hadn't done what I did, we wouldn't be having this little conversation, would we? We'd be dead. That would put a crimp in your little ACLU crusade, now wouldn't it? Who would defend the pedophiles?"

"You're working for the government, aren't you; that's why you're so gung-ho about killing anyone who might disagree with them!"

"You live in your own little world, don't you?" Flint said, shaking his head. His voice lowered to that dangerous octave again. "Be careful; you're trespassing on my world, Dixie. I can forgive you endangering me, but if this puts my kids at risk, then there's not a single place you can hide from me—remember that."

"Is that a threat?"

"It most definitely is," he said, and he turned on his heel and left them.

CHAPTER 19: Academia

Flint's wife showed up that evening. It was Orani. When the kids found out she was Dad's friend, they adopted her into the family, demanding that she sit down and watch a movie with them. She did, and Flint was relegated to making popcorn, almost like a real family. After the kids went to bed, she kept him up, briefing him on his cover and on the assignment. "This is our target of interest, Marwan Hamdi, the Kuwaiti responsible for the truck bomb in Seattle. Again, he seems to be at the center of things. He had contact with the New York mosque, but we don't believe either he or Khallida had anything to do with the assassination attempt. We doubt he knows anything about you.

"However, he's very intelligent and very, very committed," Orani told him, showing Wolfe several photos of Hamdi from Yale, Paris, and Afghanistan. "He's their chief engineer and bomb maker. Whatever it is they're up to, he'll be behind it. He was married to a very independent Iranian girl from a wealthy family. She had a daughter, but they were estranged because she wanted an education and he of course didn't believe in that."

"What happened to her?"

"She died three years ago under suspicious circumstances. I would hazard to say that Hamdi killed her under the guise of an honor killing, but the police called it an accident."

"He never owned up to it?"

"The girl's family is very powerful; he didn't dare. I think it's safe to say that's a soft spot with Mr. Hamdi. She was, by all our information, his equal intellectually and certainly his superior otherwise. It was a poor match."

Wolfe stood and stretched. "Speaking of matches, shouldn't we turn in? We have to get to the airport early tomorrow."

Orani smiled and said, "I suppose we better start the married couple charade tonight." She got up and surprisingly, she took his hand, leading him up the stairs. Wolfe followed obediently, his heart beating like a drum in his breast. She stopped by the kids' bedroom and peered in through the door. They were sleeping soundly. Then she led him into the bedroom and directly to the bed.

Wolfe swallowed hard, telling himself, *come on, it's not like this is your first time!* He looked Orani over, admiring her—no, after the abortive rendezvous with C. J., Wolfe practically devoured her with his eyes. She stopped at the bed, bent over for a moment, and then turned around. Wolfe began to reach for her, but there was a pillow and the comforter in the way. He stopped, not quite comprehending what was going on until she smiled. He got it.

"Damn it!"

"Sorry, but you sleep on the sofa."

"Just like my married life!" Wolfe grabbed the bedding and headed back to the door. Before he left though, he glanced back at her. "What is it with you, Orani? Is there a man waiting for you back in DC, a Mr. Orani, kids?"

Her smile became a bit more strained, but she shook her head. "No, there's just me."

"Why?" When she raised those perfectly arched eyebrows, he added, "Why not, you're beautiful, driven, intelligent—even likeable. You'd have men standing in line; what's the matter, don't you like men?"

"No, I like men." She seemed surprised at the question.

Wolfe shook his head. "You don't want to let anyone in; I can understand that. I don't know why you don't want anyone in there, but I can understand it." He walked back into the room, but he didn't drop the bedding. Something about Orani's manner told him she was vulnerable at this moment, so it was no time to press the issue. Still, he couldn't help but care at least a little bit. Maybe it was empathy, maybe he just hated to see such beautiful eyes questioning things. "Hey, forget about the James Bond bravado. I'm a guy, but I'm a person too. If you need an arm around you while you sleep, let me know, it won't go beyond that."

"Do you really think you could stop there, at just snuggling?" She cocked her head to the side in that singular way of hers, obviously questioning his sincerity.

"Ask C. J.," he told her. "Now, don't spread this around, but I actually care about what you think of me. I'm one of those pathetic dinosaurs that believe in chivalry. Sorry to destroy your Neanderthal image of me." He stepped next to her and kissed her on the cheek. "Good night, Orani, and don't worry. No one's going to bother you here. Sleep tight!"

***

Yasmina tucked herself in and turned out the light. Two minutes later, she turned it back on. After staring at her cell phone for five minutes, she finally picked it up and dialed.

"Hello?" It was a woman's voice.

"C. J.?"

"Yes, who is this?"

"It's Orani," she said, so used to just giving her last name she almost forgot how to use her first name. "It's Yasmina Orani, Flint's friend at the Company."

"Is everything alright; is Flint alright?" Her question was sudden and hinted at instant hysteria.

"He's fine, C. J., he's fine," she said quickly. Then she hesitated. She was about to hang up when she forced herself to speak. "Listen, this call is for me, not for Flint. He said something tonight, something so strange and unexpected that I had to follow up. It's my job to get to know him. I thought maybe you could enlighten me."

"What did he do?"

"It's more about what he said he wouldn't do," Yasmina admitted. "In this job, we're forced into some close quarters, and I admit, I've kind of led him on with some innuendo—I don't know why."

"It's because you can trust him," C. J. said evenly. "Yasmina, listen, that's the one thing that's rock-solid about Flint. Oh, he has a temper, and he's kind of strange in a Sir Lancelot type of way, but when it comes down to it, you can trust him. We used to go camping all the time, and me, I like to sleep naked and run around naked in the woods. I told Flint straightaway that I wouldn't hold it against him if he jumped my bones—he didn't, and you know what he said?"

"What?"

"He said that he thought about it, but if he'd done it, then he'd be just like every other guy I'd ever met. He knew I didn't really want to, and he knew I trusted him. That was important to him. So I slept naked and he slipped out of the tent to sit in a mountain stream every time it got too hot for him."

"Why didn't you marry him?"

"I don't deserve him," C. J. said emphatically.

"Oh, come on, C. J.!"

"No, really, I'm serious; in fact, I think that's why Vanessa divorced him. I think she felt so guilty being married to such a great guy, she couldn't take it anymore. She went and found Toad, someone who would treat her as badly as she thought she should be treated."

"You're serious about all this," Yasmina said.

"I am."

"Thanks, C. J. that helps."

"Are you thinking about sleeping with him?"

"We all think about sleeping with the men in our lives, but it would be problematic, maybe even dangerous in our circumstances. That's something I intend to avoid. Don't worry, C. J., he's all yours. I won't interfere."

"Listen; just between you and me, I've put Flint through the ringer. I've known more guys than I ever want to admit to. If Flint gets a little more mileage on him, well, I've got no right to complain. If we ever get together, then maybe we'll be on more even terms. I can live with that."

"Thanks for the insight, C. J. Good night."

"Bring him back safe. Good night."

Yasmina got out of bed and went downstairs. She stepped around the huge Danes and stood next to the sofa, looking down at the sleeping form of Flint. He looked enticing, and she actually lifted the corner of the comforter. One of the dogs woke up and gave a low woof! Flint stirred, and he almost woke up. Yasmina dropped the comforter and scampered up the stairs like a little girl caught sneaking into the boys' room at a slumber party.

***

The next morning, Orani was all business. She gave him his disguise. It was surprisingly simple, and she explained, "We know they have your photo ID, but I don't know if Hamdi or Khallida have seen it. Besides, the photo's six years old, so it doesn't have your scars or the wear and tear of your divorce."

"Thanks so much for noticing," he replied. "Do we know where they got my file?"

"Yes, we do. They got it through Dixie C. Dallas. There's no terrorist conspiracy there, just a girl working in Chicago as a clerk who has a brother on the ACLU payroll. We're leaving the link intact and doctoring everything involved with you and the airline."

She handed him a bottle of hair gel, contacts, and a pair of glasses. "Put on the hair gel and comb your hair straight back. The contacts will make your eyes blue. The glasses have transition lenses, which will make it harder to gauge your eyes." Flint did as he was told, although he had a bit of trouble with the contacts. Still, when he was done, he looked at himself in the mirror, astounded at the transformation. The hair gel made him a blond, and slicking his hair back made his already strong features stand out. With the blue eyes, he looked positively German. The long, ragged scar added a sinister aspect to his demeanor. "All that's missing is the monocle and the Gestapo uniform."

The kids were quite excited about the new look, but Orani shook her head. "It does what it's supposed to do, but it doesn't do you any favors. I like you the way you were before."

Flint smiled and wrapped his arm around her slim waist, pulling her to him. "It's so nice to know that my wife still cares about the little things!"

She gave him an exasperated pat on the cheek and said, "Down, boy, it's time to go."

They boarded a flight to Denver. After landing, Agent Conrad picked them up and drove them to the hotel in a black Lincoln. The rest of the evening, Flint boned up for his presentation. It wasn't as difficult as he feared. Someone, he didn't know who, took an old paper of his on the gravitational tides of the Jovian moon Io and applied it to Earth. It wasn't completely applicable, but it served the purpose.

Orani got him dressed for the lecture, briefing him on the latest information. As she combed his hair, she told him, "Expect the two men in the file, Hamdi and Khallida, to be hanging around Dr. Kadir. We need to know what they're there for and how close they are to Dr. Kadir. I doubt they'll even notice you're there, but if you do meet them, don't be belligerent."

"What if they suspect something and start prying?"

"Use me as a foil," she told him. "Fundamentalist men are psychotic when it comes to Muslim women. If you mention that we're married and happy, it'll drive them insane. The mere fact that I'm running around without a headscarf instead of half-naked in a harem is infuriating to them."

"I kind of like the image of you in a harem costume."

She finished his hair and brushed the shoulders of his aramid-tweed suit. She flashed him a smile and said, "Wolfe, you have no idea how good I look in a harem costume, and you never will, but keep that image in your head and remember that we have a great sex life. If you even so much as hint at that, they won't be able to remember anything else."

"Either will I," Wolfe mumbled.

"Go give a good lecture; I'll be listening on the wire."

Flint gave his lecture and even muddled through the question-and-answer session without embarrassing himself, or worse, blowing his cover.

During the lecture, he watched Dr. Kadir. He seemed bored, but the two Middle Eastern men next to him, Hamdi and Khallida, eyed Flint with dark expressions. When he sat down, they whispered among themselves. Flint busied himself with his notes as Dr. Kadir went to the podium.

To his surprise, Hamdi and Khallida got up and sat next to him, one on either side. Their cologne rolled over Flint like a noxious cloud.

He looked up and glanced over the cheater glasses he wore for the occasion. The man on his left offered his left hand. Flint simply raised a brow, but didn't accept the insult.

The man withdrew his hand and said, "That was a very interesting lecture, Dr. Strait, is it?"

"Yes, Edward Strait, nice to meet you," Flint said.

"I would never have believed that the Moon could affect our planet's geology—it's all rather far-fetched, isn't it?"

"The data doesn't lie. Io has the highest level of volcanism in the solar system because of the gravitational tides of Jupiter and Europa, and the Earth and the Moon have a much more dramatic mass ratio," Flint said, leaning away from Hamdi, because the terrorist was so close that their shoulder's touched. He bumped into Khallida.

"You weren't listed on the schedule; when was it you were called?"

"I'm sorry, is this some sort of interrogation?" Flint asked. "Now, if you please, I'm quite interested to hear what Dr. Kadir has to say; he's got a very good reputation in our field."

"Yes, it is much more extensive than yours, Dr. Strait," Hamdi said.

Khallida added, "We are interested in it as well; we'll sit and listen to it together, if you've no objection."

"None," Flint said.

It was an uncomfortable lecture to say the least, but as Dr. Kadir's subject became clear, the two terrorists' intentions became transparent and positively gruesome.

At the mid-point of the lecture, Dr. Kadir brought a slide up showing the cliffs of an ancient volcano in the Canary Islands. They plummeted several thousand feet into the sea. He ran his pointer along a jagged rift of rock slightly inland from the tops of the cliffs and said, "Here we see the fault on the island of La Palma left by the 1949 eruption. The western face has already fallen several meters toward the Atlantic. A major earthquake in this region could trigger an enormous landslide, releasing approximately 500 thousand million tons of material into the Atlantic Ocean. This would trigger a mega-tsunami—such as the one documented in the Aleutian Islands and the island of Reunion discussed previously. This landslide would send a wall of water up to fifty meters high across the United States East Coast and the Caribbean. The wave will reach up to twenty kilometers inland with catastrophic results." Dr. Kadir paused and looked out at the audience, adding, "The saving grace for this scenario is that it would take a major quake, one of at least eight on the Richter scale, to trigger the slide. Also, chances are that the fault will not give way evenly or in its entirety. What will probably happen is that parts of the fault will give way and the mainland will be subject to a series of serious, but not catastrophic tsunamis—unless, of course, the Moon is in the correct alignment and Dr. Strait's gravitational tides conspire to bring it all down at once!"

There was scattered laughter, and Hamdi gave Flint a gentle prod, saying, "It appears our Dr. Kadir doesn't think much of your lecture either!"

Flint raised his hand, and when Dr. Kadir nodded his head, he asked, "I assume you're monitoring the fracture zone for subsidence as well as earthquake activity?"

"The university has an ongoing project at the site," Dr. Kadir said flatly. "We've bored over a hundred test shafts into the fracture. Each is a thousand feet deep and has a package of monitoring equipment at the bottom. We're monitoring the site with the same rigors as Mount Saint Helens—but, of course, the mountain caught us by surprise anyway."

Wolfe listened intently to the rest of the lecture, but he really wanted to leave and get on the phone with Orani. This made the notes he found in the New York mosque terrifyingly clear. *The Wave of Allah! So this is what they're up to. It's perfect; not only do they cause mass destruction, but they can blame it on an act of God. Millions will flock to the jihad! The only question is how do they intend on triggering it?"*

Dr. Kadir left that question unanswered, but when the lecture finished, Hamdi turned to him.

"Perhaps we could meet for a drink later on. You are staying at the Sheraton, I assume?"

"Yes."

He smiled and added, "Yes, I thought I saw you checking in with your children and your lovely wife. She is from the Middle East?"

"Iran, actually," he replied, shoving his notes in a leather briefcase, trying to act bored and academic. "Her parents were academics there before the Revolution. We met at a symposium. They didn't make it out of the country, unfortunately."

"There are still in Iran, then?"

Flint straightened his glasses, showing some irritation, and shook his head. "No, they were murdered by fundamentalists. I suppose they were too intelligent to be allowed to live in Khomeini's medieval state."

"That medieval state, as you call it, has brought many people closer to Allah." Khallida smiled good-naturedly, but his eyes were dead serious. "That is what matters in the grand scheme of things, even if there are a few regrettable incidents along the way."

"Right, now did you have something relevant you wanted to talk to me about, because it's obvious that politics isn't going to work."

Hamdi laughed and clapped Wolfe on the shoulder. "You are a funny man, Dr. Strait, and strong too!" He looked at his hand, which had slapped against very solid muscle underneath the tweed jacket. "For goodness sakes, you are like an American football player beneath." Hamdi eyed him with narrowed eyes, but he smiled nonetheless. It was like looking at a man with two completely different faces. "Forgive me for noticing, but that is a terrifying—did I use the right word?—scar on your face. It looks recent. You must be an active man." He looked around and shrugged. "I don't see many American professors that look like you. Do you have dangerous hobbies such as skiing or perhaps flying?"

"Hockey," he replied evenly, realizing Hamdi was suspicious. He pointed to the scar. "It's a couple years old, and it came from a skate. Hockey's big in the Northeast; half the MIT faculty is in the league. It's kind of rough for someone my age, but it keeps me in shape, and when you have a wife as beautiful as mine, it pays to keep in shape." He grinned wickedly.

"Yes, you have a very beautiful wife," Hamdi said, but his voice lost its edge, and his expression turned dour.

Khallida jumped in, saying, "I hope she remembers her roots, as you say. Iran is a proud country with a great heritage. She's still a practicing Muslim, I hope; you haven't converted her?"

"She is still a Muslim," Flint said, moving past the terrorist.

"Really, because she doesn't even wear a headscarf," he said disapprovingly.

"She dresses modestly," Flint informed them. "That is all her prophet asks—if I remember the scripture correctly."

"That is subject to interpretation."

"Isn't everything?" Wolfe headed toward the exit, but he hesitated, turning toward the two men. "Gentlemen, I have to get back to my family. My wife doesn't like to be kept waiting and I don't like to keep her waiting. So if you will excuse me, this was a stimulating meeting. Good evening."

"Forgive me, but it's not often that I get to converse with someone who has such an interesting resume. Perhaps we could get together later on—at ten o'clock in the bar?"

Wolfe scratched his chin and grimaced. "That's usually the time my wife and I have our private time," he explained. "The kids have gone to bed, so it's our time to relax. It's been a long day flying from Boston on such short notice."

"I'm surprised you brought your family along," Hamdi said, and that conspiratorial glint returned to his eye.

Wolfe shrugged. "The symposium called at the last minute because of a vacancy. I agreed to do it if they bought tickets to Hawaii for me and my family. I was joking, but they agreed. We're going on to Maui tomorrow. I couldn't pass it up. How often can you get to Hawaii on a professor's salary?"

"You are a dedicated family man," Hamdi said, and his voice softened again.

"How could I be otherwise with a woman like that waiting for me?" He took out the card that came with his persona and handed it to Hamdi. "I'll check with Yasmina and see if it's alright to meet you for a drink—she's the boss. Give me a call if you're still interested." Wolfe waved and left.

Flint ducked out of the lecture hall with the rest of the crowd and ducked into a dark classroom. He called Orani.

"Yes, I was listening to the lecture via your wire. Hamdi suspects something, but you got them all wrapped up in me—good work. They get very emotional when their women are unchained and not following what they consider the true path. Hamdi is especially vulnerable, considering his late wife. Use that again if you need to. We have to be careful at this meeting. It's a setup of some kind."

"Fine, they've left with Dr. Kadir. I'm going to go see what they're up to."

"Good. Don't worry about us. We're snug in the backup room; no one's the wiser. If something goes down, I'll text you."

"If I learn enough, should I make a move?"

"In public, no! We don't want to blow this open yet."

Flint hung up.

He exited the room. The lecture hall was empty. Dr. Kadir, Hamdi, and Khallida were gone.

Flint made his way quickly to the geology wing. The hall was dark, but he could see light coming from a door at the far end. The wing entry doors were locked, but Orani supplied him with a passkey. He swiped it and the lock opened with a light click.

Flint ducked in, shutting the door silently behind. Treading softly, he approached the lighted door. The door was typical of universities, solid wood with a large pane of safety glass. It read, "Geophysics Lab."

He could hear voices inside, though only barely.

Flint tried the door. It too was locked. He couldn't see anyone in the lab, so he swiped the lock. The lock opened, making what felt like an inordinate amount of racket. There was a sudden silence in the voices.

Wolfe had to decide what to do in an instant; almost without thinking, he slipped inside, silently closed the door, and slid across the narrow gap to one of the lab tables.

The lab tables were made up of double rows of cabinets with a thick laminate tabletop for experiments. Wolfe hid behind the cabinets, but he heard two distinct voices say something in what sounded like Arabic, and footsteps coming toward the door.

Bending double, he ran to the end of the table and slid around the corner. Peering from behind the cabinets, he could see a man at the door. He checked the door and then opened it, looking both ways down the hall. Seeing nothing, he returned to the other end of the lab and continued his conversation in Arabic.

Wolfe took out his Bluetooth and plugged it in his ear. He dialed Orani.

"Hello!"

"Translate!" he whispered, and he moved carefully toward Dr. Kadir and the terrorists.

"You're too far away," Orani said.

He glanced over the tabletop. They were five rows beyond him standing next to a large Plexiglas structure. Moving with extreme care, Wolfe crept from row to row, until all that separated him from the terrorists was a single lab table.

"There we go, I can hear them now," she said, continuing, "devices need to be set incrementally, about two hundred and fifty meters apart, all along the fault line. The shafts are designed for the purpose. Even though they now carry scientific equipment, Allah wills that they should serve his purpose. My friends, it will require at least seventy-five nuclear devices to ensure the fracture is large enough to cause the desired tsunami—and mind you, the detonations must be near-simultaneous to avoid setting up a destructive interference pattern or vaporizing the conduits; therefore, the distances must be precise, and the firing sequence must take the distance into account. Each device must be a minimum of ten kilotons—how you're going to get that many devices, I do not know. So there it is. I've done what you ask. Here is the detonation sequence." He paused. "The project is feasible, but I'm sorry to say, improbable. To find so many devices and get them there with no one the wiser seems an impossible task."

"Thank you, Dr. Kadir; we will leave that to Allah."

"God be with you."

"And with you."

Dr. Kadir led Hamdi and Khallida past Wolfe and to the door. He turned off the light and left with them.

"I'm alone in the lab now," he said, moving over to the table where Dr. Kadir had a plaster model of the island with red dots marking the shaft locations. "I'm going to get some pictures of this; that is, unless you're going to raid this place and take it yourself."

"We can't do that," Orani said.

"If I hear that one more time," Wolfe growled, turning on the overhead lights.

"I didn't write the rules, Wolfe."

"Alright, I'll be a few minutes; I've got to hang up to take the pictures."

He hung up and switched the phone to camera mode.

Fools! he thought, moving around the model and snapping pictures. *We have them dead to rights! They're right here planning to kill mil-*

lions and we're not going to do anything about it? It's madness! Wolfe took a dozen photos and then rummaged around the table. He found several sets of papers that were noteworthy; among them were diagrams for the shafts, a list of the shaft positions in latitude and longitude, and other diagrams whose purposes weren't immediately apparent. He took pictures of them all, turning off the larger overhead lights and using only a desk lamp for illumination.

"This is like something out of *Hogan's Heroes!*" he muttered to himself.

The lock turned in the door.

CHAPTER 20: Divine Intervention

Flint looked around. The only other door was the one to Dr. Kadir's office.

He reached for the light, but the door started to open—they'd notice it if he turned it off. Wolfe ducked under the counter and ran to the office door. Swiftly, he opened it and stepped inside. Wolfe stood in the dark, peering through the glass pane with Dr. Kadir's name stenciled on it. The geophysicist entered with Hamdi and Khallida in tow.

"Didn't I turn off that desk lamp?"

Hamdi said something in Arabic. He and Khallida took opposite sides of the room and began to search it. Kadir headed toward the office—and Wolfe.

Wolfe took out his gun and fitted the silencer in one smooth, slick motion. He knew with every fiber of his being that he should end this here and now. He'd seen enough, but Orani's direction tolled in his head. She was quite specific—not yet. Wolfe almost gave in to temptation, but his military training interceded. Still, if they discovered him, he'd have no choice.

With that in mind, he hid in the darkness behind the glass door. It was the most obvious place to hide, and the most certain of discovery. *Come on,* he thought, as Dr. Kadir came directly to the door; *give me a reason to end this now!* Kadir opened the door and turned the light on. He passed right by Wolfe, who could see him quite clearly through the glass, turned away, and went to his rather unkempt desk.

"Everything is as it should be," he called out in English. "Nothing is disturbed; I must have left the light on."

Wolfe waited for the doctor to turn around and see him when he noticed Hamdi at the door. The bomb maker wasn't two feet from him, but in his hand was a 9mm with a silencer.

"You are certain nothing is missing?"

Dr. Kadir turned around, but whether there was a reflection hiding Wolfe or Kadir was focusing on Hamdi, he couldn't tell, but somehow, he still didn't see Wolfe.

"Nothing is missing."

"We have everything, then?" Hamdi asked.

"You have everything; go with Allah's good will."

Wolfe prepared to step out from behind the door.

"Allah be praised," Hamdi said, and he raised his gun. The silencer pinged twice and two shell casings clattered onto the floor.

Dr. Kadir clutched the red blotches on his chest and fell back into his chair. The chair spun around and dumped him onto the linoleum floor. A pool of dark-red blood spread over the cracked brown tiles. Kadir didn't die immediately, but stared in horror at Hamdi. He tried to say something, but nothing came out of his mouth except blood.

"You've done your part, doctor, but alas, the infidels may trace me back here. They would undoubtedly get everything they wanted to know from you." He shook his head. "You were dead when you volunteered your services, but then, so are we all. Go then to paradise!" He raised the gun again and shot Dr. Kadir between the eyes.

Hamdi flicked off the lights. Then, without ever seeing Wolfe, he closed the door. Wolfe followed him with his eyes. Hamdi and Khallida took the files from the table and stuffed them into a red-and-yellow backpack.

The jihadists then went from table to table and turned on the gas for the Bunsen burners.

A thrill of panic coursed through Wolfe's spine. There was a single small window high in Dr. Kadir's office. He stumbled toward it, slipped on the blood-slick floor, and then stepped on Kadir's corpse. Wolfe threw open the latch and pulled himself up, but he was too eager and he cracked his head against the upper frame of the window.

His head swam, but he didn't let go. He threw an arm outside the window and grabbed the exterior ledge, hauling himself through. Wolfe fell headfirst out of the building. Whoosh! A wave of heat scorched his legs and the window blew out. He dove ten feet into some shrubs, rolling to the freshly cut grass outside the geology department.

It was only when he sat up that he realized his trousers were on fire.

With a cold sense of panic, he beat out the flames; there were already sirens wailing.

He sped across the grounds toward the campus fence.

Ten minutes later, he was at the hotel, but to his surprise, there were Hamdi and Khallida, ahead of him, smoking cigarettes outside the front door. He ran around the back, but there were two men there as well. He called Orani.

"Where are you?" she asked.

"I'm outside the hotel. I can't get in," he told her, making his way back to the front of the hotel where he could see their room. He looked up and counted floors. There it was on the seventh floor. Orani was out on the balcony looking over the mess at the university. "Hamdi has both exits covered; if they see me coming in, they'll know I was at the lab."

"What happened? It looks like all hell broke loose on campus; what did you do?"

"It wasn't me, Orani, it was Hamdi and Khallida. They shot Kadir and set fire to his lab—now they're expecting me for drinks in about half an hour. If I don't show, my cover's blown."

"That's a problem," she answered.

"No, it's not," he told her forcefully, picking a spot behind a planting of trees. "I can pop them both off from here and then do the two at the back; no one will be the wiser. Then this whole crazy thing about flooding the East Coast goes away."

"You're turning bloodthirsty, Wolfe."

"Isn't that what this is about?" he said testily. "What the hell are we waiting for?"

"Wolfe, these aren't the only people in the know," she said. "If they're really serious about this, they have to have a source for the nukes; we cannot, I repeat, we cannot do this before we find out where those nukes are supposed to come from. Strap it back in, Flint, and get up here. You've got to make that meeting."

"How am I supposed to get up there?"

"I suggest you climb, but be careful. I can see Hamdi from here, and he's been checking our balcony out. The sooner he sees you up here with your wife, the better off we'll be."

"You've got to be kidding," Flint said, and he meant it.

"No, get up here."

"Orani," Flint moved over to the patio of the room directly beneath theirs—seven stories beneath theirs. There was a railing around each balcony. If he stood on the railing, he could reach the lower rail of the floor above. It was possible.

"What are you waiting for, Wolfe?"

"I hate to tell you this, Orani, but I've got this fear of heights thing," he said through clenched teeth.

"You can't be serious; you're a pilot."

"It's actually quite common in pilots," he explained. "Type A personalities often choose professions that confront their fears. Believe me, it doesn't always work."

"We don't have time for this, Wolfe," she told him forcefully. "I'm standing here watching the fire, and they're wondering where you are. Get up here."

"Can I at least say good-bye to my kids before I fall to my death?" he asked, gauging the jump to the second floor rail.

"They're in bed," she replied. "Now hurry up. If you get up here, I'll let you make out with me on the balcony. We can appear to be the happy couple for their eyes, and it'll push all of Hamdi's fundamentalist buttons—that should settle their doubts."

"Great," Flint said, and hung up.

He tucked his cell phone in his pocket, slung his leather satchel over his shoulder, and gathered himself. He jumped. Wolfe had always had a great vertical leap—at least he *had*. Although he still possessed powerful legs, the old scars left their mark. What looked to be an easy jump was anything but that. He grabbed the lower crossbar of the second-story rail, but just barely. He swung there for a second and then pulled himself up. Hooking his right foot on the balcony gave him enough leverage to clamber up.

"One down, five to go," he whispered. Without looking down, Wolfe worked his way on top of the rail, using the building to stabilize his climb. There wasn't much to hold on to, and it was precarious at best. He didn't think about the gulf behind him. Standing, he grabbed the lower rail of the third floor. Wolfe repeated this twice more and was in the middle of clambering up to the fourth-floor balcony when its exterior light went on. He froze with his right foot hooked on the floor and his arms wrapped around the iron railing.

The sliding glass door opened and a man stepped out.

"Honey, look at this; the university is on fire!"

Wolfe was about to ease himself back down to the third-floor balcony when that light when on as well. Most of his body hung in the void between the third and fourth floors—readily apparent to even a blind man. Clenching his teeth to stifle the effort, Wolfe lifted his torso and left leg, hanging like a rolled-up window shade from the side of the fourth-floor balcony. All of his weight rested on his arms and right foot; he couldn't keep it up for long.

"Okay, do I go up or down," he mused. "Either way, I'm screwed. As soon as they make a commotion, Hamdi and Khallida will see me—then I'll have to kill them!" To make matters even worse, his cell phone rang.

"Is that my phone?" he heard from both balconies.

The man on the fourth-floor balcony turned and went inside.

Wolfe didn't wait. He was up and onto the fifth floor before the man could turn around. Swiftly, he silenced the phone, tucked it back in his pocket, and then he was up again. He took the next two floors quickly, not wanting to stop and think about what he was doing. He just did it. Then he was up and over the rail to his balcony.

Orani was waiting for him with a drink.

Flint couldn't speak. He was sweating profusely, and now he started to shake. He gulped down the drink she gave him. It was Bombay Sapphire on the rocks.

Orani stripped off his satchel, threw it inside, and dragged him over to the other side of the balcony. They watched the fire while Wolfe caught his breath.

"They're watching," she told him, glancing down as she turned to wrap her arms around his neck. "We need to put some pressure on him. We're only half done, Wolfe, now wrap your arms around me and kiss me!"

"Orani!" he stammered.

"I'm serious; we have to give them a show," she said, throwing her arms around his neck and kissing him. "Come on, Wolfe, this is for God and country. Now grab something and kiss me!"

Wolfe relented, but to his dismay, it wasn't as difficult as he wished. Orani had a fine figure. The first thing he noticed was the suppleness of her lips and the warm fragrance of her breath. The luscious firmness of her large breasts pressed against him. She wasn't wearing a bra, and one of her nipples poked him as it slid within the lapel of his jacket. She grabbed one of his hands, he couldn't readily say which one for some reason, and put it on her ass.

"Squeeze," she instructed. "Pretend like you're enjoying it."

Flint pretended as hard as he could. It was working.

"That's my boy," she said, almost giggling. She slipped her tongue into his mouth.

Flint was taken aback; he thought of C. J., and a wave of guilt swept over him. Then he remembered that she left him—again. He ardently returned the kiss and slipped a hand up her skirt and beneath her panties to squeeze her naked cheek.

Orani took a shuddering breath and asked, "Are they watching?"

"What?"

"Are they watching?"

He moved to nuzzle her neck and glanced down below. Hamdi and Khallida were indeed watching; he could feel their ill will from there.

"Yes, back to work," he said, and his kisses moved down her neck, to her shoulder, and to her breast. He mouthed her nipple and sucked it through her silk blouse. His hand, the one not engaged with her ass, fumbled with the buttons on her blouse.

"You're learning fast," she said earnestly, "but let's not overdo it; we can't end up humping out here in front of everybody."

Wolfe swept her up in his arms and carried her inside. He headed for the bedroom.

"The kids are asleep in there!" she protested.

He took her to the sofa and laid her down. He got on top of her, but it wasn't all that large a sofa.

"There's not enough room!"

He picked her up and kicked aside the coffee table.

"They can't see us anymore," she told him between kisses.

He knelt down and laid her on the carpet, saying, "They could have the place wired; are we undercover or not?" He lay down next to her, a hand sneaking within her blouse to fondle her breast. Then he had her blouse open and an olive-hued breast popped out, large and round and firm, with a dark, erect nipple. Flint's mouth surrounded it.

His mind raced. Yes, C. J. left him again. She was in her world and he was in his—but he didn't want to be in this world. Still, he was here, and Orani was here, and that wasn't a bad deal; he might as well indulge himself. It didn't hurt that she was a beautiful woman, but he didn't really have any choice, did he? After all, they expected him to perform for his wife. That was part of the deal.

Flint slipped his hand up her skirt and kneaded her through her panties.

"I think we got our message across to them," Orani said. "We can—oh my!"

He slipped the hand into her panties.

Orani arched beneath him, her head tilted to the side, but she said, as she gasped for breath, "Really, Wolfe, we don't have to carry this too far."

He moved down onto her, his kisses falling on her tummy, her hips, then onto her thighs. Wolfe stripped her of her panties and tossed them out the balcony window and over the rail.

Orani stopped protesting.

The hotel phone rang.

Wolfe's head popped up, but Orani grabbed his hair and shoved it back down.

"I'll get it!" she told him, fumbling for the receiver. She dropped it, picked it up, and finally, in a forced voice, asked who it was. A man's voice answered, but Wolfe couldn't catch what he said. Orani said, in rather an irritated manner, "Do you mind? He's had a long day and he's unwinding with his wife; believe me, he doesn't want to be disturbed!"

The voice said something else, and Orani pushed Flint's head away.

"Oh, why, yes, I'm so sorry, he did mention he had a meeting with you. Hold on, here he is."

She handed him the phone and tried to extricate herself from the compromising position. With a grin, Flint just stayed where he was, effectively pinning her to the floor. She finally gave up and blew a long, black strand of hair from her face.

"Dr. Strait here, can I help you?"

"Dr. Strait, this is Marwan Hamdi. I'm down at the bar. Did you forget that you promised to have a drink with us?"

Flint looked at Orani, disheveled and half-naked, and said, "Can I take a rain check? I'm really rather beat. It's been a long day."

Orani shook her head, whispering, "You need to meet them!"

Hamdi echoed her, saying, "We're leaving tomorrow and I would hate to miss this opportunity to meet you and discuss your theories; after all, that's what these conferences are for, isn't it—exchanging ideas?"

Flint sighed. "Give me a few minutes and I'll be down."

He hung up the phone and smirked. "We have a few minutes!"

She wriggled free and covered herself. "Good, then you have time to change and take a cold shower!"

Wolfe relented, changing out of his bloodied and burned clothes. He put on another set of clothes, except for his original tweed jacket and brown roper boots—after brushing them clean. Orani was sensitive to not changing his wardrobe too much—the jeans and golf shirt he threw on were more casual than the shirt and slacks he wore to the lecture—that was expected.

"Now remember, you're an academic, Flint, don't forget your cover," she said, brushing the shoulders of his jacket once more as if to make sure there was no dirt, grass, or glass from his adventure.

Flint shook his head and griped, "That begs the question: why do they want to see me in the first place? After all, it's not like I was a signature speaker at the lecture. There's got to be a reason they want to see me."

She sighed, and her brows contracted, as if he raised a good point. "There's no way to know if you don't go down. The rule of thumb is to take advantage of all opportunities."

"Orani, I don't know how to handle this!" he told her pointedly.

"I don't have any problem with the cover, but what am I looking for? What am I supposed to find out?"

"I've no idea," she said, patting him on the chest. "You've done great so far. Don't worry, I trust you."

"Great," he snarled, stomping into the bedroom where the kids were asleep.

"Where are you going?"

Flint kissed the kids goodnight and retrieved his knife and the Walther.

"You're just going to the bar; I don't think you'll need to go armed."

"Well, you're not the one who's meeting two international terrorists;" he said with an angry edge to his voice. He tucked the gun in the back of his pants. The silencer went in his coat pocket. The knife went in his right breast pocket. "They've already killed one man tonight; the one thing I'm certain of is this: they wouldn't mind seeing me go away either."

"Well, don't kill them, Wolfe."

"We'll see," he said, forcing a smile and opening the door. He turned and asked, "Do I get a good-bye kiss, honey?"

She leaned over and kissed him on the cheek; he took the opportunity to reach around and squeeze her on the cheek.

"Just staying in character," he said.

"Remind me not to be your wife on the next assignment," she sighed, and shut the door.

Wolfe rode the elevator to the lobby and stepped out. The bar was to the right. He walked through the glass doors into a dimly lit, comfortable room with tables, booths, and a long, ornate wood bar. He saw Hamdi and Khallida at a table. They waved. There was a drink waiting for him.

Wolfe stepped up to the table.

The two jihadists rose. Hamdi once again offered his left hand.

"Is there something wrong with your other hand?" Wolfe asked, sternly, avoiding it. "Do you actually think that I could be married to an Iranian and not know your customs?" He took a seat and glanced at the two men. They sat down; their faces wore false smiles—like a hangman in clown paint. "Now, gentlemen, what did you want to see me for?"

"Come now, Dr. Strait, there's no need to be so unpleasant. We're all colleagues here," smiled Hamdi.

"Really and where are your degrees from?" he asked. "You took great interest in my credentials; it seems to me, it's only fair if I reciprocate."

"Dr. Strait, please, I'm sorry we got off on the wrong foot," Khallida said soothingly. "We didn't mean to come across that way—put it down to cultural differences. We mentioned our encounter to Dr. Kadir, who took great interest in your lecture, by the way, and he urged us to make amends. We've taken the liberty of purchasing you a drink, on us, isn't that the tradition in the West? It's a martini with Bombay Sapphire and a twist of ginger—is that acceptable?"

Wolfe lifted the glass and sniffed the drink. It smelled perfectly normal. There was the Sapphire, the ginger, and apparently nothing else. Who was he kidding? How the hell would he know if they slipped something in it or not? They looked at him expectantly. He raised the glass to his lips, feeling as if he must drink from it for appearance sake.

CHAPTER 21: Taking Charge

Bullshit! he thought to himself. *I'm not going to be an idiot about this!* He put the glass down.

"I'm sorry, as much as I appreciate it, I can't," he said. "I promised my wife I'd have a drink with her this evening. I'll just order something non-alcoholic, if you don't mind," he said evenly, raising his hand for the waiter.

The jihadists seemed taken aback. "Surely, a single drink won't make any difference?"

"I have some work to do tonight—I have a deadline for the *Astrophysical Journal* on Monday," he shrugged. "If I have more than one drink, it muddies the mind and makes me useless. I can't afford that— you as academics can appreciate that. Still, I'd hate to see it go to waste. You're welcome to it." He picked up the glass and placed it in front of Hamdi, who had a martini glass.

Hamdi turned pale.

"I'm not fond of ginger," he said, swallowing hard.

"My mistake," Wolfe said, reaching for the glass. He offered it to Khallida, who refused. Then he set it back down in the center of the table, but the bottom caught a saucer and the martini spilled onto the table.

"Bloody hell!" Wolfe swore, and he mopped as much up as he could with his napkin.

The waitress hurried over.

"I'm sorry about this," he said apologetically. "It's been a long day; I can't even be trusted to handle a glass! Could you just bring me a ginger ale please, and put it on these gentlemen's tab."

The waitress swept up the mess with a towel and took away the drink. Wolfe tore off a sodden corner of his napkin and threw the rest on her tray.

Hamdi smiled and said, "You are very disciplined, Dr. Strait."

"Thank you, now what can I do for you—my time, as you can see, is limited."

The men looked uncomfortable, as if they were unprepared for an extended discussion, but after exchanging glances, they settled back and smiled. One of them, Hamdi, reached into his pocket and took out his cell phone.

"I have a text," he said, mocking rude Western fashion. Wolfe watched him busily punch his keys without taking the time to read any message.

Who was he texting and why?

Khallida must have seen Wolfe's attention on his partner and belatedly tried to distract him. "Dr. Strait, would you mind expanding on your thoughts—about gravitational tides, that is. Frankly, the idea is otherworldly."

Wolfe glanced at Khallida, grimacing. These two might be high-level jihadists, but in the art of undercover work, they were as green as he was. "Read the papers published by the symposium, or look up the Jovian moon Io on the Internet—I don't have the time or the inclination to give you a lesson in basic physics."

"Why so hostile, Dr. Strait, I don't understand?"

"Oh, I don't know, you bash my theories without knowing the basic physics behind them; interrupt time with my family; repeatedly insult me with crude and juvenile cultural tricks; and then text people while you're with me," Wolfe retorted. "I don't know where you're from, but I've been a lot of places, and that's inconsiderate behavior no matter where you're at."

"I'm so sorry, Dr. Strait, but it was unavoidable." Hamdi smiled, putting his cell phone back in his pocket. "I've been watching too many of your youths; I think I've picked up some of their bad habits." He chuckled at his own joke, and then leaned back in his chair. "Let's lay aside science for a moment, if that's an irritant for you."

"Very well, what do you want to talk about, family?"

Hamdi laughed. "That reminds me, America is so strange. We were out watching the fire at the university; did you see it? Well, the next thing we know, it's raining panties!" He pulled out the pair of panties Wolfe tossed over the balcony railing. "American women seem to be trying to perfect the art of debauchery, don't you agree?"

Wolfe snatched the panties from Hamdi's grasp, correcting him. "If that's what you think about American women, or any woman, for that matter, then you're more ignorant than I could ever have imagined." He took the panties and folded them very neatly on the table before tucking them into his pocket. "In fact, I've never seen anything more tragic or infantile than the way they treat women in other parts of the world. Take the Taliban, for example, considering women nothing more than walking wombs. What fools! What a waste to subject half your population to conditions as bad as slavery."

"So you would have a woman take your job at MIT?" Hamdi asked.

"If she were more qualified and smarter, absolutely," Wolfe said firmly.

"What about your wife, Mrs. Strait? Does she share in your lofty opinion of women?"

"She's one of the reasons I have such a lofty opinion of women," Wolfe said seriously. "If you met her, you would at first notice how incredibly beautiful she is, far too beautiful for the likes of me! If you got to know her, however, you'd learn that she's the consummate professional, smart, tough as nails, sure of herself, and yet easy to be around. She's one of the most incredible people I've ever known."

"I'm sorry to say it, but that confirms the impression of Western men as soft, don't you think?"

"Really, and what makes a man hard?" Wolfe stared at Hamdi. "Do you think by beating your wife, or killing her, if necessary, that you prove yourself to be a man?" Wolfe saw Hamdi shudder, and he smiled. "Such men are cowards. In the West, we hold such men in absolute contempt!"

"I think that is weakness; it tells me you can't control your women."

"Why should I want control?" Wolfe asked, and he was sincere.

"Why do I want a woman to submit to me through force or threat of force? That's a shallow victory. I'd much rather win her favor willingly."

"Is that how it is with Mrs. Strait?"

"I respect her far too much to ever consider taking advantage of her, even though she is my wife." He took a drink of his ginger ale, and then he smiled. "Your problem is that you view strength only through subjugation, through force. A strong man, a strong nation, a strong people has patience, understanding, and wisdom."

"Yes, I see," Hamdi began to get agitated, waving his arms around and raising his voice. The other patrons of the bar began to glance over to their table. "You are a nation that likes to talk, and if you do not like what you hear, you bomb people from afar. That is how you settle things. That is how you settled things in the Crusades!"

Wolfe nodded, "The Crusades were a noble undertaking that was horribly botched."

"A noble undertaking, you say," Hamdi laughed. "You call invading our lands noble, how typical!"

"They weren't your lands. The Roman Empire was invited to administer and protect the Holy Lands over seven hundred years before Mohammed was born. They'd been Christian for almost four hundred years. Yet even after the *Muslim* invasion, the West reacted with restraint. It wasn't until the Muslim governors began destroying the most holy sites in Christendom and slaughtering pilgrims that the West called for a Crusade to stop it. Really, how would you react if we took over Mecca and started murdering worshipers at the Rock? Would you have acted any different?"

"That's what the Crusaders use as an excuse for murdering thousands of Muslims!"

"True, many Muslims were killed," Wolfe admitted. "However, more Muslims died by Saladin's hand when he consolidated power than were ever killed by Crusaders."

"What about Acre, when your Richard the Lionheart executed 2,500 helpless prisoners? That is a black crime that we still tell our children about!"

"And yet you don't tell them about the aftermath of the Horns of Hattin, when Saladin ordered the execution of the Crusaders?" Wolfe shrugged and said, "Richard was perhaps swayed by vengeance for Saladin's crime, but he did at least offer to ransom the prisoners. Saladin refused, leaving Richard with few options." Wolfe shook his head and sighed. "Mr. Hamdi, we'll never agree on everything, but here in the West, we at least talk and attempt to start a dialogue. If we really were as bad as you claim, we wouldn't be having this conversation."

Hamdi seemed taken aback. "What do you mean?"

Wolfe leaned forward and spread his hands out as if to say, "It's obvious!"

Hamdi still didn't know what he meant.

"Mr. Hamdi, we have had the bomb for over fifty years," Wolfe explained. "We have twenty-five hundred warheads. If we were as evil as you claim, as single-minded in our desire to wipe out other religions, cultures, and beliefs as you claim, then there wouldn't be a problem in the Middle East. The Arabian Peninsula would be a parking lot. It's really no problem to drill through glass to get at the oil."

Hamdi looked stunned. Wolfe paused and added, "The ironic thing is we don't fear the bomb. We've used it before. The fundamentalists like Bin Laden would use the bomb in a heartbeat, and they'd crow about how many men, women, and children they slaughtered. At the same time, these fundamentalists aren't afraid of us using the bomb on them, and you know why? I'll tell you; it's because they realize we're strong enough, moral enough, and good enough to not use it. They don't have the same moral fiber or the same strength. They're cowards, and they know it. That's the difference between us. Good night, Mr. Hamdi."

He headed out of the bar. He wasn't entirely pleased with himself; he'd let his temper get the better of him. *Maybe I'm not cut out for this,* he thought. *James Bond wouldn't let himself get flustered; that's probably just what they wanted.*

Flint headed to the elevators. As he pressed the "up" button, two men entered the hallway. One was a black man wearing sunglasses, and the other was a clean-shaven man of Mediterranean or Middle Eastern heritage. He remembered the two men posted in the darkness of the back entrance to the hotel. Could these be the men Hamdi texted?

The elevator door opened.

Flint hesitated—go in or not? He shouldn't, he knew, but that

Christopher L. Anderson

thought of caution caused an immediate angry reaction. *I'm tired of these bastards dictating my actions!* he thought viciously. He stepped in and pressed the button for the ninth floor and the room he checked into originally.

"What floor?" he asked naturally, just as he always would. He didn't want to tip his hand and pull out his gun; he could be wrong after all.

"Same floor, thanks," the black man said, and he stepped to the back of the elevator. Strangely, his companion didn't move next to him; rather, he stayed in front of the door right next to Wolfe.

Wolfe stepped to the back right corner of the elevator where he could see both men.

The door closed and the elevator started to move.

As it passed the third floor, the man in front reached over and pushed the emergency stop button. His partner whipped out a knife and stabbed at Flint's stomach. Almost at the last second, Wolfe blocked the knife thrust aside with his left forearm. He felt a sharp burn in his side as the blade creased his flesh slightly above his belt. The attacker's momentum carried him off balance, right into Wolfe, but he did the correct thing and continued his charge trying to pin Wolfe into the corner of the elevator. It worked.

The larger man crashed into him and drove him into the corner. Almost immediately, the terrorist brought the knife back to stab again, seeking the soft vitals of Wolfe's left side. Instinctively, Wolfe blocked the knife hand into the back wall of the elevator; it was a precarious hold, but he had no other recourse. He smashed upward with his right knee, bringing it up again and again into the man's groin. The attacker grunted, but he didn't let go and succeeded in sliding the knife hand out of Wolfe's block.

His attacker stabbed like a machine, but he had a bad angle, and each time Wolfe parried the blade into the wall. The edge scraped across the stainless steel and after a few strikes it got caught between the elevator hand rail and the wall. Wolfe struck him hard in the jaw then ducked and wriggled out of the terrorist's grasp. Pushing off with his right hand against the black man's torso and twisting his hips spun out of the corner and into the open.

The second terrorist came at him, but his overhand stab was wild and unlike his partner, he allowed it to carry him off balance. Wolfe

170

backed out of the way to the terrorist's left, his back to the elevator buttons. He slammed the emergency stop button off, and the elevator started to move again. He was behind the second terrorist now, and he lowered his shoulder and drove it into the terrorist's back. His powerful legs shoved the terrorist into his partner, pinning the better fighter of the two into the corner. There was a lot of grunting and shouting coming from the two, and the black man was trying to twist around to bring his knife into play again. The second terrorist wasn't strong enough to do anything but blindly flail about with his knife—that left his arm exposed. Wolfe snatched it up with his left hand and cranked it around in an arm bar. He wrenched it until it snapped.

The terrorist screamed and dropped his knife, rising up to his toes in a vain attempt to relieve the pressure on his joint. Wolfe yanked the wrist up and around, turning it like a flesh-and-bone crank to some terrible pain machine. The terrorist's screams turned into a high-pitched howl, and he slumped to the floor, sobbing and shrieking.

In one quick motion Wolfe swept up the knife and plunged the blade into the terrorist's back, sliding it between the ribs and into his lung—after a swift, cruel twist, he yanked the blade free. The terrorist shuddered and collapsed in a fetal position, quivering and gurgling.

Wolfe drew his other knife, holding both out, ready for the other terrorist who eyed him with cold fury.

"Allahu Akbar!" he yelled, holding his knife to stab overhand, but instead, he slashed in a wide arc, back and forth, making a wide figure eight with the edge of the blade.

Wolfe was no knife fighter. He instinctively ducked the first slash, but that left his neck exposed for the second. His head craned to his right, his body leaning that way as well, and he was off balance and exposed. The terrorist's knife slashed down from his left, but again, instinct saved him. Wolfe whirled in his crouched position, a compact turn that brought his knife arm against the terrorist's arm and knocked it away at the last moment. He stabbed with his other knife, but the terrorist clamped down on his wrist with his free hand. The terrorist's impetus carried him into Wolfe and they crashed into the corner of the elevator.

"I'm going to cut you up, white boy, and feed your carcass to the dogs!" the terrorist growled in an unmistakable Midwest accent. "Allah be praised, I'll be raised on high as a hero for sending you to hell!" The larger man leaned on Wolfe, trying to overwhelm him with his size and strength.

"You're nothing but a damned traitor!" Wolfe breathed, but despite his fury, the man was larger, stronger, and younger. Relentlessly, he pushed Wolfe deeper into the corner, and his knife came closer and closer to Wolfe. He thrust hard with his legs, and the knife blade nicked Wolfe's cheek. With a surge of desperation, Wolfe pushed the knife back, but the terrorist redoubled his efforts and the blade started to close in on him again.

With a sickening sensation, Wolfe realized he was about to lose. He was about to die.

He grunted with effort, pouring everything into trying to hold back death. The terrorist's eyes became enormous and white. Sweat shook from his ebony skin. "I'm a holy warrior; die, Crusader, die! Allahu Akbar!"

Ping! Ping!

The terrorist's eyes went glassy, and he crumpled to Wolfe's feet. Orani stood behind him, her gun smoking.

Wolfe stared at dead terrorist, his breath coming in ragged gasps. Getting a hold of himself—for the moment at least—he swallowed hard and straightened his jacket.

Orani simply stared at him. Then she stared at the bodies.

Wolfe understood. It was her first kill. He stepped over the huddled forms of the would-be assassins and took her by the shoulders. "Go back to the room and wait for me there," he told her gently but firmly. "I'll be right back. Go!"

Orani shook her head, but then she did as he told her.

Wolfe punched the button for the parking garage. The doors closed. The elevator ride to the garage was only eleven floors, but it seemed like forever. His mind was racing with conflicting thoughts. *Please don't stop for someone; what do I do with the bodies; is Orani alright; where are Hamdi and Khallida?* Somewhere in the back of his mind, pushing insistently on his consciousness was a strident voice, half angry, half panic-stricken, yelling, *What are you doing? You idiot you just about got yourself killed!*

The bell rang and the door opened. He was in the garage. Like a robot, Wolfe dragged the bodies to the hotel dumpster. Before he got rid of them, he ran through their pockets, looting them of their cell phones and wallets. Then he lifted the bodies into the dumpster. There was a fire extinguisher in the garage. He broke the glass and took it out, using it to douse the interior of the blood-spattered elevator. That was all he could do.

He ran the stairs to the seventh floor and let himself into the room. Orani was on the sofa, cradling a drink in her hand. He stepped up to her and knelt by her.

"Are you alright?"

She nodded, still shaken, still pumped up from the action. "I was listening on the wire," she started to explain, but he put a finger to her lips.

"You did what you had to do, Yasmina. They were coming after you next." He wanted to stay with her, but he couldn't. Wolfe felt a rising wave of something deep within his gut. He couldn't tell what it was, but he needed to get out of the room. He walked stiffly to the bathroom and closed the door.

The first thing that struck him was his image in the mirror, bathed in sweat, pale, and frightful. He tore off his coat, feeling suddenly hot, then his shirt. He started the water, washing his face with a messy torrent of cold water, or rather he tried to. His hands began shaking so badly that he couldn't cup water in them. Then his knees began to go. Wolfe threw himself on the commode just before his legs gave wave.

Violent shaking overtook his body. He clutched himself to stop it. It did no good; instead, it got worse, and now he was clenching his teeth to stop the choking sobs rising from his throat. Tears welled up in his eyes. For what, what was he freaking out about? He didn't give a damn about those two men! Then he realized it wasn't that.

"I should be dead! My arrogant ass should be dead in that elevator! Good God, what an idiot I am!" The door opened and Orani poked her head in.

"Wolfe, are you alright?"

"No," he admitted, struggling mightily for self-control. "I'm just coming to grips with my own stupidity!" His voice was harsh with self-loathing. Wolfe took his head in his hands, muttering, "What am I doing with my life? My kids are in there sleeping and I'm trying to play a game that's going to get me killed! What the hell am I doing?"

Orani stepped in, her own trauma pushed aside for Wolfe's meltdown. "You're not playing a game, Wolfe. You're a soldier in this war."

"Yes, a soldier who kills, kills some more, and then kills some more! I'm nothing but a goddamned killing machine! What good is that to anybody, anybody that I love? I'm nothing more than those two bastards in the elevator—nothing more!"

"You're more to me, and you're more to those two kids in there; you have to be, Wolfe, you can't give that up."

"I can't—" he started, but then a cell phone rang. It wasn't his, but the ringer came from his pocket. It confused him for a moment, and he stared dumbly at the bulge in his pants. Of course, the assassin's phone! He took it out and flipped it open.

"Hello! Kamil is the operation complete?" said a familiar voice. It was Hamdi.

A cold wave of anger pushed Wolfe back into sanity, herding his disquiet into a deep, dark corner of his mind. He put the phone to his mouth, and his voice was once again controlled, laced with hidden menace. "Hello, Hamdi, I see you took our little talk rather too personally."

"Mr. Strait, or should I say, Mr. Wolfe!" the terrorist said, but it was obvious he was shaken.

"Look over your shoulder, Hamdi, I'm coming for you!"

Click! The line went dead. He put the phone on the counter.

"Are you alright?" Orani asked.

"No, but I'll get through it. How about you? How are you doing?"

"I'll get through it."

Orani stitched Wolfe up and they turned in, exhausted. Wolfe led her to the bedroom, meaning to sleep on the sofa, but she didn't let go of his hand. She lay down on the bed, curled up on her side, and Wolfe lay down protectively next to her. The kids breathed softly, ignorant of the violence that went on around them. Soon, Orani's breathing became smooth and regular. Wolfe drifted off, snuggled up against Orani. Her head was on his left arm, and his right arm was wrapped around her. His hand was on his gun.

CHAPTER 22: The Professional

There was something ghoulish about the next six weeks. Flint trained for ten hours a day, and then he went home to a bungalow and spent a quiet evening with the kids.

It was the fourth week of training, on a Thursday, and Wolfe was just sitting down to a light lunch. It was a nice day. A fresh winter snow gave Virginia a heavy, fresh smell. He took a seat at a small table on the back porch of a brick building with colonial trim. His view was of an inner court. It could have been an Ivy League college campus, but it was a government complex, and the people there were wore gray overcoats and carried briefcases.

He surveyed the sandwich he'd made and was about to take a bite when Orani stopped at the table and smiled.

"Do you mind if I join you?" she asked.

"Please do, all I've seen all day are grizzled, macho guys," Flint told her.

"So, how's it going so far?"

"I'm sure you know all about that, why ask?" Flint replied, taking a bite out of his sandwich.

"Come on now, Wolfe, are you still mad at me for cajoling you into the Company, or is it something else?" Her dark eyes flashed at him in a quizzical way.

"Nothing at all," Flint said, not wanting to admit to Orani, or himself for that matter, that he wouldn't mind exploring their relationship further—physically at least. He was, after all, a bloke. Unfortunately or fortunately, he wasn't sure which; Orani was now a complete and cold professional. It was frustrating. He sighed and shrugged. "I don't really want to be here, that's all. I didn't aspire to this line of work, and present company excepted, there's not really much in the way of companionship. Are you sure you shouldn't be masquerading as my wife—just to give me someone to talk to after the kids go to bed?" He shook his head, gauging her eyes for a reaction. "Even a guy can watch only so much ESPN."

Orani chuckled, but her eyes didn't betray and emotion whatsoever. "Sorry, Wolfe, I've got a home and a life here. That was part of the assignment."

"You married, then?" Flint asked, trying to sound uninterested.

She gave him a half-smile. "That's none of your business."

"You know all about me," Wolfe told her pointedly, "but all I really know about you are the curves under that nice suit you're wearing."

"Now, now, Mr. Wolfe, I know the transition to this life is jarring," she said in a soothing tone, making him wonder whether she was trying to sound sincere or really was sincere. "The emotional aspect to certain parts of this job takes some getting used to. You have to learn to detach yourself in order to accomplish the task at hand. If I led you to think something was there when it isn't, I'm sorry. I tried to play my role—that's all."

Flint felt a blush of embarrassment creep into his face. It irritated him. In a tone more combative than he wanted, he said, "No need to apologize, Orani, I'm just lonely for some adult company."

"Why don't you give C. J. a call? I'm sure we can afford to fly her up here."

Flint laughed in his bitter, half-strangled way. "She's staying on the farm in Idaho with what's-his-name. She can't leave her horses."

"Even for a weekend?"

"She's decided to stay, so I don't want to complicate things further, even if they aren't married. I'm not into affairs, Orani. As strange as it may sound from a man, sex for the sake of sex is too complicated to be that enjoyable."

"Really, well, that is a strange point of view for a man; I wouldn't have guessed it from our trip through Colorado."

"It had been two years, Orani, and I hate to tell you this, but you're absolutely gorgeous." Wolfe shrugged and took a large bite out of his sandwich. "You make it much too easy to get carried away. Next time I need a wife, let's find someone other than you!" He turned back to his lunch; he wasn't in the mood to talk anymore.

"It's a trust issue with you, isn't it?" Orani laid her slender chin in her hands and looked at him with those large, almond eyes. "You like to be trusted, especially by women."

Wolfe sat back in his chair and finished chewing before responding. "What's this all about, Orani? Are you building a character profile on me? If so, then just ask me what you will. The cold shower routine is irritating."

"You read people from your experience as a civilian, Wolfe, not as an operative. I was your wife in Colorado, and even though we both know otherwise, I don't expect you to be able to turn your emotional switches on and off as I do. You'll learn. It's one of the toughest things about this business, but it's usually women who associate sex with emotion. Most guys just view it as a bonus."

Wolfe felt himself blush again and warned her, "Don't try and get in touch with my feminine side, Orani."

She laughed again and thanked the waiter who brought her tea. Stirring the tea, she observed, "You use sarcasm and humor to cover yourself when something makes you uncomfortable."

"I'm that transparent?"

"You're that consistent."

He rocked the chair back and crossed his arms, tilting his head to the side. "I don't know, maybe you're mistaking discomfort for frustration. I enjoyed rolling around with you. Maybe I just want some more."

"Now you're angry; you tend to be blunt, even crass, when you're angry."

Wolfe dropped his chair on all four legs with a thump and pushed noisily away from the table. He sprang up and said, "That's enough of that; I've got a sniper course this afternoon. That's good. Right now, I feel the need to shoot something."

"You're mad at me," she sighed. "Is this a divorce?"

"I've been through one of those already, thank you very much." He turned to leave.

"Wolfe!" she called after he'd taken a few steps. He turned with a scowl.

She got up and approached him. Crossing her arms over her chest, she looked at him with a clinical expression and shook her head. "You're really not that easy to figure out. When you're in the company of other men, you're ultra-competitive, suspicious, and ruthless when you need to be. When you're with women, you're respectful and doting, and you seem to enjoy pleasing them over being pleased."

"Meaning?"

"Meaning, you'd just as soon shoot a guy as look at him, but when you go to bed with a woman, you're not there just to get your rocks off."

"Your point being?" Wolfe was getting tired of being analyzed, and he tried to show it by crossing his arms and scowling.

"You don't often find the one with the other—that makes you vulnerable." She took her red-nailed index finger and jabbed it into his chest.

"Meaning Mata Hari is going to shoot me in my sleep? Does that worry you?"

"It should," Orani told him, and her stern look melted into a slight conspiratorial smile. "But having been your wife, I can't imagine any woman who could do it; we'd all like at least one more crack at you."

Wolfe stared at her, not knowing quite how to respond.

She laughed and patted him on the chest. "There's nothing we can teach you there, Flint. You don't have the Casanova's ego, but you ought to. Now go shoot some things and make me proud."

She turned and left with a wave, sashaying her hips and tossing her hair. Flint glowered at her, having no idea what to make of her. He gladly went to the range and shot things up.

Wolfe didn't mind the shooting, the martial arts, or the academic training. Even the endurance training wasn't so bad. It was the little things he hated. His sixth week provided the perfect case in point.

He was sitting at a computer desk going through a presentation on escape techniques. It was a basic review with a test; he'd already gone through the hands-on training with handcuffs, plastic cuffs, etc. He finished the test thinking it was a waste of time, and he heard a hiss followed by the sensation of a slight puff of air in his face.

Everything went black.

Wolfe woke up to darkness.

His first instinct was to try and sit up, but he bumped his head on something solid only a few inches away.

"Ouch!"

Wolfe's hands were cuffed behind his back, and tape bound his arms and legs. By feeling around with his feet and wriggling, he ascertained that he was in a coffin-like box. The air was hot, stuffy, and smelled of wet earth. They were trying to simulate the feeling of being buried alive, trying to instill panic. They were doing a really good job.

Rule number one, don't panic! Yeah, right, so he jumped to rule number two: concentrate on one objective at a time. That was obvious. He positioned his hands behind his back, trying to concentrate on the techniques they taught him, not the walls of the box that got closer by the minute. Digging at the seam of his back pocket, he could feel the length of wire conveniently sewn into the pants. The definition of convenience was different for the Company than it was for Wolfe, and it took several minutes to extricate it—then he dropped it anyway. Fortunately, it couldn't go far and he eventually found it. Wire in hand, he began the laborious task of picking the lock of the handcuffs with his hands behind his back, lying on his stomach, duct taped at the arms and legs, and buried in a coffin.

Best not to think of it that way, he reminded himself. In that respect, the Company was right—one miracle at a time. He set to his task. The work actually helped. It gave him something else to think about besides claustrophobia.

"So what do you want to talk about, Wolfe?" It was Orani. Her voice came out of a speaker somewhere in the darkness near his head.

"I'm busy!" he told her.

"You need to compartmentalize; I thought pilots were good at that."

He didn't answer. He bent the tip of the wire and felt for the notch in the lock, but it wasn't easy. His hands were already half numb. "How the hell did I get myself into this?" His wrists chafed and his fingers were already cramping. This was much easier in a classroom.

Wolfe was getting angry.

"Is there a problem, Wolfe?" she asked in a sickeningly sweet voice.

He bumped his head on the coffin in his efforts, causing a loud thump, and the wire slipped from his fingers again. "Damn it, you people are worse than the terrorists! You better be on your way out when I finally get out of here—if I get out of here."

"Calm yourself, Mr. Wolfe; it'll go much easier if you're calm."

Biting back a reply, he searched for the wire. It didn't take long to find. Concentrating hard, he slipped the crook into the notch of the lock and felt for the tumbler, hardly daring to breath. He found it, so he thought, and twisted. There was a click, and the left cuff loosened.

"How are we doing?"

"Are we a team now? I'm the one buried in the hole!" He worked his hands to his sides and then to his stomach, which wasn't easy. Duct tape pinned his arms to his sides. He had to grab an edge and tear it, so they told him, but once again, what was simple in a classroom was markedly more difficult in a stifling box while holding a conversation and trying not to scream.

"There's a practical side to this beyond the pleasure of hearing my melodic voice," she continued, obviously from a very comfortable chair in a large, air-conditioned room. "Say you're tied up and being questioned. We want you to be working on your escape during the interrogation, as there might not be a chance afterward."

"Alright, you win," he growled, "anything to keep you from reminding me what a good idea this was!" Still, he didn't want to make it easy on her. "Let's talk about something I really don't understand? You know what gets me: I can't understand the Muslims in America. After all, I haven't heard squat from your community condemning 9/11. At most, I hear we asked for this, or that we need to understand where the terrorists are coming from. As far as I'm concerned, no offense intended, the CAIR organization is simply a front for al-Qaeda."

"Of course it is; whatever made you think otherwise?" Orani's voice was irritatingly calm, and it betrayed no anger whatsoever. He was really beginning to dislike that about her. "Like Christianity and Judaism, there are reasonable people and unreasonable people. This is a war on unreasonable people and not on Islam."

"I really hate it when you're like this," Flint replied coldly, managing to use the end of the open cuffs to pierce the tape and produce a ragged edge to be torn. The effort caused a stinging pain in his shoulder. He stopped and tried the left hand. It was awkward, but there wasn't any pain. *Good God, my body's a wreck!* he thought, but he said, "I'm not the one who started this little war. This wasn't my idea. My point is American Muslims are in just as much, maybe more, peril than Christians, Jews, and whatnot. If you're not part of the jihad, you're a collaborator. They're busy cutting off the heads of your children if you talk to Americans over there—what happens if you are an American?"

"You have a poignant and maddening point. Unfortunately, in my opinion, our biggest problem is not the active terrorists, but the silent majority of Western Muslims who don't realize that they are active terrorists just by doing or saying nothing. If they hear of a plot, they don't feel it's their duty to expose it for the evil that it is; that makes them just as much a terrorist as the bomber."

"You're smart and gorgeous, who'd have thought it? Will you marry me?"

"We've already been married, Wolfe."

"So this is how you divorce me: bury me alive frustrated and unrequited!"

Wolfe ripped the tape all the way through and wriggled his arms completely free. He couldn't undo his legs; the space was so cramped he could only start ripping the tape at his thighs, but he didn't have enough leverage, or strength, to get much farther.

"If you get out of there, maybe we can work on that?"

"Work on what?" Wolfe forgot his train of thought.

"Focus, Mr. Wolfe; the balcony in Boulder, remember."

"Oh!" He chuckled at the thought—it was a good one. "That is motivating!"

"Thank you for the compliment."

He knocked on the lid to his coffin. It sounded hard and firm. He pushed. It didn't budge, and he had no leverage. "Great—now what?"

What to do?

Think, stay calm, and don't give in to panic— easy for them to say while clicking their way through a slideshow. Here, even in this exercise—was this an exercise? No, he couldn't think that way. This was an exercise, that was all, but it wasn't a classroom, it was terrifyingly different.

The answer was, as always, simple. Step one: he had to get out of the bindings. Step two: he had to get out of the box. Step three: he had to get to the surface. Step four: he was going to kill someone up there.

There was always a weakness somewhere.

It had to be the end of the box; he tried not to think of it as a coffin. If he kicked out a side, the top would collapse on him. It had to be one of the ends. He kicked at the bottom. It sounded solid. Squeezing his hands by his chest, he reached for the top. The cramped space made it tough to get his arms over his head, reminding him how close, dark, and terrifying it was to be buried alive.

Wolfe fought the rising urge to panic.

He really was going to kill someone.

"If you're trying to get me all worked up, you're doing a good job, Orani," he growled, trying to re-focus his mind on something other than claustrophobia, darkness, and who knows how much dirt over his head. "Quite frankly, Orani, I've got more important things to do than go around popping off fanatical Muslims, but seeing as they've already tried to off me, I don't suppose I have much choice."

"You're defending your country, Wolfe; what's more important than that?"

"Being a father," Flint said, knocking against the end. "Going to a Vikings game, taking you out to dinner, watching a good movie—the list goes on and on." The end was satisfactorily hollow. He hit the corner with the heel of his palm. After a few strikes, he heard the nails creaking and felt the wood move. "I didn't ask for any of this—especially the crap you're putting me through now. I'd advise you to be far, far away when I get out of this."

"I thought you wanted to take me out to dinner?" Orani laughed, ignoring his threats. "Let me ask you, if you don't defend your country, who will? Let's just say they win. Your kids, providing they live, would end up growing up under sharia law. Your daughter wouldn't be going to school, and your son would be educated just enough to strap a bomb on his belly. Even if that never happens, they could destabilize the West enough to collapse our economies and put civilization itself in jeopardy. Do you want that for your kids, all because you don't want to get involved or go through a few uncomfortable exercises?"

"You call this uncomfortable?" One end of the back panel came free, and after a few more strikes to the other side, it came off. "You and I know firsthand what they're capable of—and I have the scars to prove it."

"As do I," Orani said.

"Divided loyalties?" Wolfe asked, figuratively twisting the knife in his own turn. He pushed the panel aside and felt beyond the box. It was dirt, but it wasn't hard-packed. There was a void in the dirt about twice the size of his head. He couldn't be too deep or the weight of the dirt above would've collapsed the small pocket. Of course, they bound him, so why take the extra time and effort to bury him deep?

"Not at all," she replied, "but I not only face an assault on my life, liberty, and the pursuit of happiness, but an assault on my religion. Think of it this way, Wolfe: it's like the KKK hijacking Christianity for their pro-white aims. I doubt whether Jesus of Nazareth would approve."

"I told you how smart you were—remember?" Wolfe used the end piece to scrape at the soil on the roof of the pocket. It came down easily. He took the loose soil and laboriously shoved it into the box toward his feet—there was nowhere else to put it. It was dirty work, but the lid of the box kept the dirt from falling on his face. Eventually, however, he'd scraped as high as he could reach. He had to crawl out of the coffin and into the hole he was digging. If his tunnel collapsed, there was nowhere to go. It didn't make him feel any better that they'd dig him out.

Wolfe swallowed hard and pulled himself in the void he dug. He took a moment to rip the tape off his legs, now that he could reach them.

Orani's voice came out of the box deadened by the dirt. "So what is it, Mr. Wolfe? Is the honeymoon over? If there's something you want to get off your chest, now's the time. You're going to have a handler whether you like it or not, so if you've got a problem with me as a Muslim or as a woman, now's the time to bring it up."

Flint laughed. "I have no problem with you, Orani. God knows there's no way I'd possibly act out the whole *partner* thing if you were a man!" He grimaced and scraped at the roof of his cave. Dirt fell onto his face and into his eyes and mouth. He stopped, spitting it out and wiping the grime from his eyes. Having his eyes open in this darkness was almost as stupid as having his mouth open. With a different plan of attack, he returned to work.

"It's not you, Orani, it's me. You see, I thought I left my past behind. All the death, destruction, and juvenile glory-seeking was over and done with. I survived it once. That's a nice position to be in. I'm not quite ready to trust my luck again—I don't know how much luck I have left."

"Sorry, Flint, duty doesn't always call when it's convenient."

"I don't just have myself to think about now." Wolfe dug upward, slowly inching further up the tunnel, pushing the loose dirt into the coffin. The sharp edge of the panel caught on something. He shuddered to a halt.

Reaching up in the darkness, Wolfe felt the roof of the hole. His fingers dislodged pebbles. They clattered onto him. There was something else though, something that felt like moist, wiry hair.

"Have I run into a corpse?"

There was no head, though, and the tendrils of hair grew larger, with branches that joined into larger strands. He sniffed the darkness. He smelled wet earth and greenery.

He realized they were grass roots—the surface! Taking the edge of the panel, he stabbed upward. Hacking away, Wolfe brought down enough dirt to see a sliver of light. Without waiting, he stuck both hands in the crease and drove upward. The ground split and Wolfe emerged into the light of a large area of sod. He was chest-deep in a section of grass cleared of snow.

Orani sat in a lawn chair wearing sunglasses and a long, black leather coat with a fur collar and sporting a bright red scarf. She applauded.

"Bravo, Mr. Wolfe!"

Wolfe climbed out of the hole, feeling angry and vastly relieved. Grabbing the arms of her chair, he loomed over her. "You have no idea how torqued I am right now!"

"Oh, come on, Wolfe, it's better you confront your fears here in a controlled environment than out in the field," she scolded him, pushing him away. "Stop it; you're getting dirt all over me!" She brushed the dirt and sand from her coat. "Look what you did; I see chivalry is dead."

Wolfe stepped back and shook the dirt out of his hair. "I'm heading for the showers. That's it for me today. Go home to your doting husband; I'm sure he has a glass of merlot and a back rub waiting for you. I've got to clean up and make dinner for my kids—after I stop shaking, that is."

"I doubt I rate that kind of treatment," she said, scribbling down some notes.

"You need to look in the mirror and then listen to yourself, Yasmina. If I had a wife who looked like you, with your brains, I'd show you what chivalry means."

"My dear Mr. Wolfe, are you trying to seduce me?"

"You just planted me in the ground," he said, blushing, shaking the dirt out of his sleeves.

"And you're trying to decide whether to bed me or strangle me, is that it?"

"Sorry, I'm not in the mood—even with you," he told her testily, evading the subject he opened—why? He stomped off to the showers without another word, leaving a trail of dirt behind.

Wolfe had dinner with the kids and put them to bed. It was early, only nine o'clock or so, and he was restless. He stopped at the computer, checking on his accounts, e-mails, and sundry. As always, he verified his schedule. Tomorrow was a Saturday, but they always had something for him. Strange enough, there was nothing listed.

There was a soft knock on the door.

None too careful, Wolfe retrieved his Walther and answered it. It was Orani, still in the long, black leather coat and red scarf. She held a bottle of wine in one hand and a plastic shopping bag in the other. Giving him a peck on the cheek, she said, "Hi, honey, I'm home."

She walked by him and straight into the kitchen, where she retrieved a couple of wine glasses. Expertly, she uncorked the wine and poured it out. "You've graduated, Wolfe. Congratulations, you are now a fully fledged field agent of the CIA, though of course you can't tell anyone about it." She swirled the wine in each glass and handed him one. "What's the matter? Why the serious expression? I know you like wine."

Wolfe took it, glancing suspiciously at her. "Sorry; it's not that I'm unhappy to see you, only surprised." He didn't want to admit that he was indeed happy to see her, but that he wasn't looking forward to an evening of innuendo and frustration. He'd rather she went home to her mysterious life and left him alone with a porno.

"Surprised? I thought you offered me a merlot and a back rub?" She raised her eyebrows. "Oh, I know you've got these ideas of me being a Muslim woman. I assure you, I'm a thoroughly modern woman. I'm just as determined to fight for the right to bring the wine—but if you have other plans—" She put her wine glass on the counter.

"Of course I don't have other plans," he told her, picking the glass up and handing it back to her. "Can I take your coat? Stay awhile." He was about to add a cryptic remark, but he was tired of the games, so he just said, "Please."

She sipped her wine and smiled. Putting the glass down, she unbuttoned the coat. He stepped behind her and slipped it off. She was wearing only the red scarf and black boots. He felt a sudden rush of adrenaline; he was a teenager again, flashed for the first time. Picking up her glass of wine again, she turned to him and sipped it. With a flash of her lovely brown eyes, she picked up the bag and said, "Give me two minutes, and join me in the bedroom." When he didn't say anything, she patted his cheek. "Didn't I tell you that I'd like to have another crack at you? I wasn't teasing, Flint, not this time. Now come on and show a woman that chivalry isn't dead!"

Orani walked luxuriously into the bedroom. Wolfe waited, glaring at the glacial movement of the second hand on his watch, not knowing whether he was being set up yet again or whether it was for real. At two minutes exactly, he opened the door. The lights were off, but Orani had six candles lit. The scent of jasmine wafted appropriately into the air. She lay on the bed in only the scarf and boots.

"Close the door; we don't want to scar the kids for life!"

He obeyed, and she held out a long, toned leg. "Do you mind taking off my boots?"

Flint took off one boot, and then the other. Sliding between her legs, he crawled forward to kiss her. He let the kiss linger, soft and luxurious, enjoying the playful warmth of her tongue and the firmness of her lips. Flint moved to nibble on her ear, down her neck and shoulder, and on to her firm breasts. He lingered on her nipples, drawing a slight chirp of pleasure. Down across her flat belly, and then he paused at the well-trimmed patch of pubic hair. C. J. came to mind, and with that thought, a pang of guilt. Was he cheating? Even if he wasn't cheating in true sense, wasn't he in his heart?

Reality struck. C. J. was in Idaho in bed with another man. He was with a beautiful, desirable, and willing woman—it had been years. It was time. Flint kissed her and nuzzled his way further down.

Orani grasped his hair, forcing him further down, but then pushed his head away. Flint looked up. She was smiling, a feral cat-like grin, and she pushed him back and away, forcing him to stand. She scooted to the edge of the bed, sitting there, and she reached for his belt buckle.

"It's been years for you, Flint, and it's been five years for me," she said, and her breath came in gasps. "Five years since—since I've had a man." She yanked down his trousers, and then he was inside her.

Flint didn't know if it was right or wrong. He cared whether it was, but he cared for Orani, and truth to tell, he cared for himself too. He needed this. The time for reflection was over. He stopped arguing with himself and gave in to being simply human.

Sometime later, much later, Yasmina pushed him away and gasped, "That's enough; you've made me a believer in chivalry! Good God, Flint, I need to use my legs again sometime in the near future, oh, sweet mystery of life!"

CHAPTER 23: Shadows of Youthful Indiscretion

After dropping Wolfe off at the airport, Orani drove into the city. She turned into Georgetown, making her way through the congested streets to a small townhouse. She parked across the street, but before getting out of the car, she put on a headscarf and a long, black shawl that reached almost to her feet. Taking out her phone, she dialed a number. A man's voice answered. "Come on in!" Orani crossed the street, looked both ways along the row of houses, and then walked down the steps to the door. Her key fit the lock perfectly. She opened it and stepped inside.

"Papa, Lufti, I'm home!"

Lufti came running. "Mama!" She hugged Orani close.

"Hello, my dear!"

"Grandpa is almost done with dinner, and I helped!"

"She did indeed." Hamdi's father smiled. "You're just like your mother: responsible, respectful, and resourceful. You're growing up to be a fine young woman, Lufti." He patted her dark hair. "Now go and set the table, please."

When she was in the other room, the old man asked, "How was work today?"

"The immigration regulations have been tightened," she said, laying her purse aside on the front hall table and hanging the shawl next to it. "Every application takes three times as long, and that many more are refused."

"I don't understand why they don't close the borders," the old man said.

Orani looked at him in surprise. "Why do you say that, Papa? This nation was built on immigration. We can't simply choke off opportunity for less fortunate; that goes against our ideals."

"If this country let in fewer hotheads, like my son, we'd all be better off."

"What is the matter?"

He shook head, rubbing his temples as if they were painful. "I can't say for certain, but you know better than anyone what kind of fury lies in Marwan's soul." He looked at her tenderly. "A man couldn't have asked for a better wife, Yasmina; how could he have done that to you—I am shamed for it!"

She touched his cheek and said softly, "Papa, you saved my life. If you hadn't gotten me to the hospital after he—" she stopped herself and smiled. "Well, I would have died, and Lufti would have grown up without a mother—even one who isn't supposed to exist anymore."

"We need to be careful now that he's back in the country," he said, checking to make sure Lufti, who didn't know about her father's crimes, was still busy in the kitchen. She was putting the silverware next to the plates, forks on the left, knives and spoons on the right, Western style. "I never know when he may pop up!"

"The Department of Immigration is keeping track of his location," Orani told him.

"Yes, but there are those new friends of his from the mosque," he said nervously. "They are full of unsavory ideas, and I think, I fear, that Marwan believes in them also."

Orani acted innocently. "What ideas do you mean?"

"Jihad, he bought into this crazy talk of jihad!" He was insistent, but he smiled and apologized. "I worry, as a father, but more so for Lufti, and for you. After what Marwan has done, after all I've done for him; after all I've tried to teach him, it's hard, that's all. It's hard to have a son turn out as he has only to face the possibility that he's going to fall even further into," he stopped, but then finished, breathless, "evil."

"Have faith that things will work out as God intends, Papa," she said, taking his hand. "We cannot control the fate of others; we can only try to guide them, and pray."

He squeezed her hand.

There was knock on the door.

The elder Hamdi looked at it in consternation. "The one thing I dislike about the West is the rudeness. It is dinner time. Who could that be?"

He went to the door and opened it, already bristling and muttering, ready to chastise whoever it was and send them on their way. The old man opened the door with a jerk and then stopped short with a gasp. "What do you want?"

Three young, bearded men stood there smiling. "Good evening, Mr. Hamdi, your son asked us to check up on you and to join you for evening prayers on occasion. We have chosen this evening to fulfill his desires. I am Ahmad."

Ahmad named the other two men, but the elder Hamdi wasn't impressed. "This is not my son's house, and though he means well, I did not invite you. Thank you for stopping by, but good evening to you!" He moved to shut the door, but Ahmad forced his way in, followed by the other two men.

"We insist!"

Orani stepped forward, saying curtly, "Did you hear what Mr. Hamdi said? He did not invite you into his home, please leave!"

Ahmad turned to the elder Hamdi disapprovingly. "Do you always allow women of your household to speak to men outside their family and in so disrespectful a fashion?"

"We do not live under the Taliban! I thank my niece for helping to provide for me in my retirement, which is more than I get from my idealistic son."

Ahmad sneered, "My family is from Kabul, and there we do things the old way. A woman such as yourself would be caned for such immodesty in her own house, worse if she were audacious enough to act this way in public. Our women and our elders know their place back home."

"Leave my house!"

Ahmad made no move to leave, but wandered around the room.

Orani lifted her cell phone and said, "Leave or I'll call the police!"

A man snatched the phone from her and lifted his hand, growling, "You dare threaten a man? I should beat you for such arrogance!" He lowered his hand at a word from Ahmad.

"Forgive Jamaal, he oversteps his bounds." He picked up a black-and-white photo of the elder Hamdi, Marwan, and a woman holding a baby. "Were Jamaal in his own home, he would have every right to beat you as thoroughly as you deserve, but we are in Marwan's house. Discipline is his responsibility." He looked at the woman, and then at Orani. "This is Lufti's mother. She was your cousin?"

"Yes," Orani said. "Marwan beat her to death. I'm sorry, he disciplined her to death."

"I see the family resemblance, as well as the resemblance in temperament." He smiled, handing her the picture. "Be careful that you do not make the same mistakes that Lufti's irresponsible mother made." He turned back to Mr. Hamdi. "I think I would like some tea; isn't that the customary way to welcome guests?"

"You are not guests! Leave my house! If you do not, then I will call the police myself and tell them you forced your way in here spouting your Taliban propaganda. I'm sure the police or some other agency of the American government will be very interested to question you about your beliefs—especially after the blasphemy of 9/11."

Ahmad stopped, glaring at the old man. His two companions urged him to take action, seething at the insult, but he held up his hand. "We do not want to attract attention," he told them. Then he turned back to the elder Hamdi and Orani. "Both of you have been poisoned by the West. Don't think that I'll forget this. Good night!"

***

Ahmad left the house and dialed Hamdi on his phone. He related the events of the evening. "I did not want to draw attention to the mosque, Marwan, so I took no action. Do you want me to inform the imam? Perhaps he can speak to your father. He may have some of the elder women speak to your cousin as well. The West has obviously corrupted her; she's a perfect she-devil!"

There was a long pause on the other end of the line. Finally, Hamdi said, "I have no female cousin."

CHAPTER 24: A Vixen in the Ointment

Life was getting back to normal. He'd no tasking from the Company. He finished school for re-qualifying on the Boeing 777, and he flew a few trips to Asia and Europe. It was almost as if the world forgot about him and left him to his own devices. It was nice.

He got back home from the store with the kids, and there was a white Silverado in the driveway. Flint felt a wave of guilt hit him. It shouldn't have, he knew that, but it did anyway. After all, he'd been celibate since the divorce, and he always thought he should give C. J. the first crack at him. It didn't work out, but still, for some reason he felt guilty about Orani. Now here was C.J., apron strapped around her waist, cooking dinner.

"C. J., what in the world are you doing here?" Flint asked in abject shock.

Before she could answer, the kids tackled her and she was caught up in a whirlwind of hello's, do you know what's, and guess where I've been. It wasn't until Flint got them off to bed that the house quieted down and they were alone.

Flint mixed a couple drinks and led C. J. out to the hot tub—he felt he needed both.

"Are those new scars?" C. J. asked in alarm when he dropped his robe.

"Which ones?" Flint asked honestly, climbing into the tub. The hot water felt especially good after the long flight. He sipped his martini and added, "Nothing serious."

"I'm rethinking the advice I gave you last time I was here," she replied, letting her robe drop and displaying her voluptuous figure in the hot tub lights.

Flint leered at her, squeezing her ass as she sat down next to him.

"Last time you were here, you were leaving for Idaho, and I had a great dream, a really great dream," he reminded her. "What made you come back?"

"Orgasms," she said flatly.

"I doubt that's the explanation you gave what's-his-name."

"Roger."

"Sorry, Roger," Flint said sourly. "What explanation did you give him?"

"Same as last time, the truth, I'm coming out to help a friend. Do you have a problem with that?" She was getting defensive; it brought out the bitch in her.

"I don't have a problem with seeing you, C. J., after all, you're not married, but I think you have a problem with it. That concerns me; I don't want to be the source of your misery."

"You shouldn't have given me those orgasms then," she complained.

"It was only the one time," he smiled, draining his glass and refilling it with straight Bombay Sapphire.

"Well, how was I to know you were so good?"

"I told you!"

"That's what every guy says," she reminded him, and it was the truth. No guy ever said he was bad. "Besides, you weren't so great that New Year's eve in '84!"

"Now, don't bring that up again," he warned her. "The male libido is a delicate thing. You snuck off for the midnight kiss with someone else, remember?"

"Oh, yeah, that must've been Jack, you know, the guy I married."

"That worked out well, didn't it? It's just as well I didn't know. If I knew you snuck off to kiss a guy who turned out to be gay, I'd have probably joined a monastery."

"Jack's not gay."

"How often did you have sex in your two years of marriage?"

C. J. grimaced and said, "Four or five times, but only if I got him drunk enough."

"Stand up; go ahead, stand up!" Flint ordered.

C. J. did so. The upward shining lights of the hot tub gleamed off her shining body, showing it off marvelously. She was wantonly voluptuous, with a striking hourglass figure that made him shudder with anticipation.

"Now what red-blooded man could keep his hands off that body?"

"You have a point there," she sighed, sinking back into the tub. "How about giving me some of that gin?"

"Take a sip of mine before we waste it."

She did. Her face screwed up so tightly, Flint thought she'd never get it straight again. He got out of the hot tub, grabbed her empty glass, and sloshed his way to the kitchen. As he refilled her drink, pouring out fruit juice and amaretto, the phone rang.

He looked at the number but didn't recognize it. The area code was from Idaho.

C. J.'s father or his sister, he thought, and picked up the phone.

"Hello?"

"Is this Flint Wolfe?"

"Last time I checked," he said, glancing at the clock. It was 10:17. "It's a little late, don't you think?"

"Is Jane there?" The man's voice sounded strained, testy. He understood.

"She's asleep in her room; can I take a message?"

"She doesn't go to bed this early. You're lying."

"Don't take that tone with me, buddy, or this call is over—now, just for the record, who are you?"

"You know who I am!"

"Let's say I do, what do you want?"

"Stop having an affair with Jane!"

"As far as I know, I'm not having an affair with her," Flint growled, "but even if was seeing her, why should you care—you're not married."

"We have an understanding."

"You've had an understanding with her for five years, Roger," Flint told him tersely, already weary of the situation. "Listen; take my advice, the advice of her best friend. Propose to her. Marry her. Make a commitment. That's what women want. Quit leaning on an 'understanding.' All that means is you want an out if things get too rough—marry her."

"She doesn't want to get married."

"Then that should tell you something right there."

"Stay away from her, you dishonorable bastard!"

"Roger, I'm going to say this once, so you'd better listen." Flint's voice sank into that low, menacing baritone. "It's simple. I've been C.J.'s friend for twenty-five years, and in my book that trumps five years and an 'understanding.' Solution: you make C. J. happy and I'm your biggest fan. If you don't, then don't waste my time with idle threats."

"I can't fight you!"

"Don't worry about me; you have the trump card."

"What do you mean?"

"I have kids and you have a farm for her horses—done deal. Goodnight!" He hung up the phone and disconnected the cord. Snatching up C. J.'s drink, he grumbled, "How the hell does James Bond do it?"

He went back outside. C. J. wasn't in the hot tub.

"C. J.?"

"Shhh!" she whispered, her head popping up from beneath the lip of the tub. "There's someone out there! In the woods, I heard them and saw the kitchen light glint off something!"

"Relax and have your drink," he whispered. "I'll check it out."

He went back in the house and slipped his slacks and shoes on. He had a black sweater in his office and a black knit cap in the closet. Suitably dressed, he strapped on the Walther and retrieved the night scope from his rifle. From the office window, he could see C. J. Turning the night scope out the window, he scanned the woods and found his target. There was a man lying prone about twenty yards from the back deck.

Wolfe slipped out the front door. He entered the woods on the street side of the house, the man's most probable escape route. Checking the target's position with his night scope at four-step intervals,

Wolfe crept up on him swiftly and silently. He didn't have any apparent weapon, not a rifle at least, but he had something in his hands. Wolfe stopped three paces behind the target and drew his Walther. He stayed there, quiet and still, until his eyes accustomed themselves to the darkness; then he pounced.

In two long strides, he was on the target, his knee in the small of the man's back and the muzzle of the Walther pressed against the back of his head.

"Don't move!"

The man froze and said, "Easy, easy!"

"I'll be the judge of that," Wolfe said, taking the man's left wrist and cranking it up behind his back.

"I'm not a terrorist!" the man said, wincing. He spoke English with no discernable accent, but in Wolfe's experience, that didn't mean anything. "Jesus, she said you might be jumpy, but ouch!"

"Who said?" Wolfe asked, after cranking the man's arm sharply.

"Dixie C. Dallas!" he said. "Damn! I'm a SEAL; how the hell did you sneak up on me like that?"

"I saved a SEAL once, but I'm not so pleasantly inclined right now."

"Alright, listen, I have this camera, that's all. I'm just supposed to get pictures—nothing else."

"Leave your camera on the ground." The man threw it ahead of him. "Now, nice and careful, I want you to get to your feet. Just in case you're thinking about trying something, I should let you know something; you wouldn't be the first guy I took out at close range. I've got a shooting license."

"I understand," the man said, and did as Wolfe asked. Wolfe marched him out of the woods and to the side yard, then along the driveway to the front where the light was on. He pushed the man into the light and told him to turn around. Wolfe stayed in the darkness of the shadows.

The man turned around, squinting in the bright light of the front porch. He couldn't see Wolfe. "What now?"

"Empty your pockets and then strip!"

The man shook his head but said, "You're calling the shots, boss."

He took a wallet and a cell phone out of his pockets and stripped.

The man was younger than Wolfe, somewhere in his twenties. He was white, toned, and had a SEAL tattoo on his left shoulder. When he was down to his socks, Wolfe could see he was unarmed.

"Turn around," Wolfe ordered. When the man was facing away, he picked up the wallet and the cell phone. After scanning the wallet, he said, "Well, Jason Hubbard, what am I going to do with you? I suppose I should shoot you, just to be safe."

"Sir, I've got a wife and two kids at home, just check the pictures!" he said in earnest. "That's why I took this gig; this Dallas chick offered me five hundred bucks a night for pictures. Navy pay hardly covers the bills, so I took the job."

He checked the wallet. There was a picture of a pleasant-looking woman and two kids as well as one with the SEAL and his buddies. "Alright, Mr. Hubbard, what are you doing away from your home station?"

"We're doing cold-water harbor training at Bremerton Navy Base, sir."

"Who's your CO?"

"Lieutenant Garner, sir."

"Bob Garner, really?" Wolfe smiled, and he could see the SEAL turn white under the porch light. He came out of the shadows and walked past the naked SEAL. "Get dressed. I'll be right back, and you better still be here."

"Yes, sir."

Wolfe retrieved his cell phone and rejoined Hubbard. After scrolling down to Garner's number, he sent the call.

"Lieutenant Garner."

"Bob, it's Flint."

"Flint! How the hell are you, Zoomie? Hey, I'm in your neck of the woods. Are you still out in Idaho? Maybe I can get out there this weekend."

Flint couldn't help but smile at Hubbard's crestfallen expression.

"Actually, I'm just a few miles down the road on Vashon. Say, Bob, I need your help with a slight problem: I got one of your boys …"

Hubbard covered his face with his hands.

"Or, should I say, I have his wallet. He left it at the titty bar down here—don't ask me why I was there; I'm divorced now. Anyway, I saw the SEAL ID and thought of you."

Hubbard's expression told him, "I'm your slave for all time."

He obviously knew Garner, and what a navy brig was like.

"He's one of my boys—he's not in any kind of trouble, is he?"

"Nothing like the kind of trouble you were in back in the desert," Wolfe laughed.

"I owe you—you know that."

"Why don't we have a drink tomorrow after duty, and I'll return your wayward boy's wallet."

"I'll tell the main gate to expect you. How about the officer's mess at noon?"

"See you there, Bob."

"It's great to hear from you, Flint."

He clicked off the phone and told Hubbard, "You're in luck; I saved his life in Desert Storm—he owes me." There was an audible groan from young Mr. Hubbard. "I don't think I need to tell you what Garner will do to you if I tell him about your little adventure tonight."

"Please, sir, I'll do anything."

"I'm sure you would, but I can't trust you," Wolfe told him. "If Lieutenant Garner doesn't hear from the MPs at the main gate in about an hour, he'll start asking questions."

Hubbard dressed hurriedly and asked, "You won't say anything about this?"

"Not if you're where you're supposed to be."

"I'll be there, sir, and thank you."

"One more thing."

"Sir?"

"If you show up in my yard in the middle of the night, tonight included, I will kill you. Do we understand one another?"

"Yes, sir!" Hubbard gulped, and he ran off into the darkness.

Wolfe knew better than to think the SEAL was afraid of his threat. The only thing a SEAL feared was his commanding officer.

Shaking his head, Flint went back to the woods, retrieved the camera, and rejoined C. J. in the hot tub.

"So, what was that all about?"

"Neighborhood boys," he smiled, scrolling through the pictures on the camera. "They seemed to be focusing on your boobs; I can't say that I blame them."

"Let me see!" C. J. exclaimed, taking the camera. Her eyes sparkled as she appraised herself. "You can't blame them. Look at those. Not bad for forty, I mean, twenty-something tits, are they?"

"You look like an eighteen-year-old, dear." He kissed her and climbed into the tub, trying to relax. *Is this what I'm in for the next forty years?* he asked himself. *Every evening of every day, I'll be looking in the shadows for someone who's trying to kill me. All of this is because I defended myself—how fucking presumptuous of me!*

He couldn't think that way. He had to think of the now, the present, and that meant C. J. He looked at her, and he sighed. "Don't think I'm not happy to have you here, C. J., but you know I was always more concerned with your happiness than my own. Are you sure you should be putting your situation in Idaho at risk?"

She looked at him over the rim of her drink. "What are you trying to do, break up with me?" She sidled over to him with a feline grin. "If this is because you haven't fucked me yet, that's a problem I can handle."

C. J. slipped her hand around him, which normally would've sent Flint corkscrewing into the sky like a mad rocket. This time was different. He kissed her on the forehead. "I'm concerned with what you want from me, and what I need from you. After all, I've got two kids up there. They are and always will be the center of my life, but if I remember correctly, you have always needed to be the center of any man's attention. Between my kids and my profession, how are you going to deal with that? Where do you see this going?"

"So you are trying to break up with me," she frowned, letting go and moving to the other side of the tub.

"I'm not rejecting you; I'm trying not to make you miserable."

"Too late, I'm miserable," she sighed.

"You need to be happy, C. J. Am I the guy who is going to do that, or is Roger that guy?"

"Roger's not the guy. He was a project. He was a mess when I found him, and now every girl I know is after him, but he only wants me. He's great to me, kind, considerate, and he doesn't throw vacuum cleaners at me!" She chuckled but then grew serious. "When I look at him, though, I don't see my being with him the rest of my life. I'm not going to marry him."

"Then don't torment him."

"Meaning I should torment you instead?"

"C. J., there's something you should know," Flint started, knowing it was time to say something about Orani.

"Are you two a thing?" she asked, catching him off guard. How did she know? "She's beautiful, a professional, and she's got a great rack. I know how you like boobs, Flint. I'd do her, if I were you. Are you serious, I mean in a relationship?"

"No!" He was as emphatic as was Orani. "No, there's nothing like that, C. J.," he told her. "It was more professional than anything else, but I think you need to know that something happened."

"Did she enjoy it?"

Flint didn't know how to react to that. He wasn't in the habit of bragging about other women to other women—especially this woman.

"She must have," C. J. said, floating over next to him. "Otherwise, she wouldn't have sent you back and gotten as far away from you as possible. You were a threat. Now you're a threat to me and my life." She latched onto him again. "Thing is, I've been searching for this my entire life. Now that I've got the brotherly image of you out of my mind, it's time we explore the other facets of our relationship, Flint."

"You mean—" he hesitated.

"Yes, that's exactly what I mean!"

Straddling him, she took his hands and placed them on her round hips. Then she leaned over and kissed him lightly, allowing her lips to linger on his before moving to his cheek, his neck, and then his brow. With a smile, she began to massage his shoulders and neck. Flint had never been into massages, but C. J. had a special touch. Maybe it was because he'd wanted her hands on him for so long that the circumstances didn't matter, or maybe it was the electricity in her caress—he didn't know. Against his will, Flint began to relax.

Her voice cooed in his ear, deep and mysterious. "You can't resist me, Flint, give yourself to me; give yourself to the dark side."

Flint chuckled, and C. J. giggled back. She massaged his shoulders, moving down his arms, repositioning his hands on her round buns.

Then she dragged her fingertips up his arms, over his shoulders, up his neck, and to his temples. Slowly, she rubbed the tension from his temples and tousled his hair. Flint actually moaned with pleasure.

"That's my man," she whispered.

It was a moment before he realized what she meant. C. J. was slowly grinding herself on his crotch, and the monster beneath seemed to have forgotten his trials of the day. He caught her eyes. They were hooded by her long lashes, locked on him like a starving tigress.

"It's time, Flint," she told him. She grabbed a handful of his hair and drew his lips to hers. She kissed him hard and hot, fencing his tongue with her own. Her other hand left his face and raked his chest with her nails. She grasped him, and she raised herself slightly. Down she plunged, engulfing him within her, a slight gasp escaping her lips. She threw her head back, eyes closed, and rode him, forcing his mouth upon her swollen nipples.

Flint never thought to protest. He didn't think of Orani, he didn't think of the day or of anything else. He simply allowed himself to be lost within C. J.

CHAPTER 25: Insider Trading

Flint tipped the bottle of beer and took a swig. He didn't drink beer that much anymore, but in the officer's mess, anything else carried a stigma with it. He'd caught up with Bob, who he'd carried out of Iraq slung over his shoulder like a sack, but he didn't intend on discussing professional matters. Bob brought it up.

"I know about 9/11, Flint."

"A lot of people know about 9/11, Bob," Flint told him, evading the question.

"Not many know about flight 23, though."

Flint sighed. He just wanted to have a beer with a friend today. "How did you find out?"

"Special Forces received full briefings on all the flights, especially yours," Bob told him, finishing his beer and ordering another. "There was some surprisingly good footage from that ACLU chick's cell phone—confiscated, of course—good technique, Flint. I'm glad to see civilian life didn't smooth all your rough edges."

"It doesn't take much for that veneer of civilization to come off, does it?"

"I would've called, but we were and are under orders to minimize any contact. We know about the fatwa, and the higher-ups didn't want to expose you unnecessarily."

"It's nice to know they care," Flint said sarcastically. "Am I going to get you in hot water by meeting with you?"

"You initiated contact, and I'm facilitating the transfer of information."

Flint noticed the look in Bob's eyes. "Is there something I should know?"

"Are you packing?"

"Government-issue Walther and a silencer."

"Good, you should be," Bob told him, and his voice was emphatic.

"For crying out loud, Bob, I'm in the center of a navy base!"

"All the more reason," Bob said. "It's bad out there; I actually had to shoot one of my guys after 9/11, a closet Muslim. It was an operation in Afghanistan. The details are unimportant, but I had to, no shit, shoot one of my own guys. If I hadn't, he'd have taken out my entire team."

"But why does that pertain to me?"

"Flint, give me a break. These guys are willing to give themselves up to blow away their friends; they'll walk in here and pop you off, no questions asked. Prison or even the hangman is nothing compared to the glory they'll get from fulfilling the fatwa on you."

"You think there are still sympathizers in the navy?"

Bob nodded and accepted his second beer. "The military is the toughest nut to crack, but it also has the greatest rewards. They're being very aggressive trying to recruit Muslims, malcontents, and guys in credit crunches. You'd be surprised what a guy would do if he's about to lose his house, his car, his wife, and his kids. Suddenly the American Dream doesn't look so American. It's sad and stupid; like they'd have it any better if the jihadists were in charge!" He looked over his shoulder as the mess door opened. A couple of officers entered the mess. They headed for Flint and Bob, but the bartender ushered them to the opposite end of the bar. "One of my guys—" Bob told him. "Listen, Flint, we're not up here for cold-water training. You know as well as I that all our stuff is in the Med and the Red Sea right now, but there's something going on up here—we're pre-positioned."

"Why are you telling me this, Bob? I'm a civilian."

Bob thought for a second and then asked, "You still know how to shoot a rifle?"

Flint shrugged and said, "It's been awhile, but I could probably pick off a pumpkin at fifty yards."

Bob laughed and laid a ten-dollar bill on the bar. "What do you say we go find out?"

"Sure, I don't have to pick up the kids for another four hours."

They walked outside, and Bob told him, "Let's take your car, but hold on a second." He went to his car, a nondescript blue Chrysler, and took a canvas gun case from the trunk.

When they were in Flint's van, Bob couldn't help but say, "You didn't pick this out, did you?" meaning the van.

"No, it was a parting shot from the ex. A few months before she dropped the bomb, she insisted she needed a van if she was going to be a soccer mom. She picked it out, and then she left me with the van, the payments, and the kids."

"It's not exactly a babe magnet, you know."

"I'll worry about that when the time comes," Flint replied, following Bob's directions to the firing range. "So what's the field trip all about?"

"You know I have a boot on each side of the fence—hell, half the work we do has the Company stamp of approval, and more importantly, Company funding. A spook by the name of Orani briefed me on you. Say, does she like minivans and kids?"

"Don't go there, Bob," Flint told him.

"I don't know, man, she sounds hot."

"You were going to tell me what's up in Seattle?"

Bob sighed. "You foiled the Ramadan thing at the airport before it blew—kudos to you, buddy. Apparently, however, that was one part of a multifaceted plan. They've got more things planned. The Space Needle's the obvious second target, but my gut has me worried about other things. There's the range. Park anywhere you want." He got out of the van and scooped up the rifle, looking around as he did so.

The firing range was basically an alley cleared of trees almost two thousand yards long. A small building housed the armory, and that was it. They signed in and walked out to the range. Bob took his rifle out of the case.

Flint took it and loaded a round, setting up for a standing shot at the one-hundred yard target. Bob picked up a pair of binoculars. "You're clear to shoot whenever you're ready, Flint."

Flint sighted the center of the target, exhaled, and squeezed the trigger as if it were made of porcelain. The rifle gave a sharp report and a firm buck, and a puff of smoke dappled the center of the target.

"Nicely done," Bob said. He took a mat out of a cubbyhole and rolled it out. "Let's see how your eye is gauged after all this time."

Flint lay down on the mat and loaded another round. Sighting the three-hundred-yard target, he squeezed off another round. Plunk in the center. He reloaded and looked out at the five–hundred-yard target.

"Start to take the wind into account," Bob told him. "We're looking at eight knots from the right and downwind. I'd put it a quarter-right."

Flint shot. The round hit the target a good six inches high and three to the right. "I jerked the trigger on that one."

"Try it again," Bob said, unconcerned. As Flint reloaded and sighted the target, he told him, "We don't know what they want to hit this time; we just know it's in the Seattle area. We've been drilled in everything from dams to schools. There are half a dozen likely scenarios, and each has at least a dozen targets!" Crack-ow! The shot hit a quarter-inch high and an inch right. It was still in the kill zone. "There you go nice shot! Now, let's move out to seven hundred. We're starting to get into manly territory."

"Where do you think they'll hit?" Flint asked, slipping another copper-jacketed round in the chamber. He focused on the seven-hundred-yard target. Things were beginning to look small in the scope. "One up and three-eighths right," he whispered to himself.

Crack-ow! The rifle report had a distinct double shot due to the echo.

"If you ask me, the grub in the trenches, it smacks of diversion. All the attention's been on the East Coast. There you go, not bad, a little low. If it were a head shot, he'd lose his nose and jaw, probably a kill, though. You'd definitely smoke him with a chest shot."

"Why not have a few high-visibility attacks in the West before you go for something really dramatic on the East Coast again," Flint mused. "That makes sense. This is a good area to hit, too. People out here think any problem can be solved over a cappuccino."

"Right, like that'll keep those bastards from sailing a nuke into New York harbor in the belly of an oil tanker, or sending a Royal Saudi 747 into the White House," Bob nodded, tapping Flint on the shoulder. "Try a thousand just for shits and giggles. The thing is, for an East Coast thing to work, they have to get us looking elsewhere. They know our security is lax—too much red tape. Our SEAL teams have planted hundreds of these bastards without anything getting into CNN, all on foreign soil, of course. We're weak here because we have to react on U.S. soil. Overseas, we can take the initiative; in our own country, our hands are tied."

"Same reason the legions were never allowed in Rome, Bob, but I see your point." He studied the silhouette at a thousand yards. The crosshairs took up a large amount of the head, and he had a hard time keeping the sight steady. Two inches! The height of the kill zone behind the eyes—a narrow band in the brain that guaranteed an instantaneous kill.

"Are you going to shoot or what?"

Flint squeezed the trigger and watched for the impact.

Crack-ow-crack!

Just as he wondered where the third echo came from, Flint felt something tug at his sleeve. The unmistakably harsh whine of a ricochet stung his ears. He involuntarily followed the sound and sensation. Right between his elbows, a bullet ripped through the foam mat and ricocheted off the concrete, tearing through his left sleeve before exiting under his arm.

"Shit, sniper!" Bob shouted, diving to the dirt three yards from Flint.

Flint looked out to the fringe of trees, automatically following a line between where the bullet went through his sleeve and the groove in the mat. He searched the trees with the scope. Nothing. Then he saw an almost imperceptible puff of smoke.

The bullet whizzed by his ear and skipped off the concrete two yards behind him. The wind must've swirled. The sniper had the windage right before, but poor elevation. This time, he reversed his mistake.

"I got a bead on him at nine hundred and seventy-five yards!" Bob told him, instinctively filling the spotter role. "He's perched on the outcropping of rock, under the gnarled pine, to the left of the trunk. Quick, he's getting ready to take another shot!"

Wolfe saw him.

"Half right and three up!" Bob breathed.

Wolfe squeezed the trigger. A shower of splinters exploded right next to the shooter's head. He saw the white face pull away from the scope, blobs of red appearing across the blurry features, gloved hands reaching for the wounds.

"Come on!" Garner said, pulling out a 9mm pistol, jumping up and running for the tree line.

Wolfe followed, chambering another round in the rifle. They reached the edge of the range in short order, but it was over half a mile to the shooter. Garner slowed to a tactical trot in order not to get winded before they reached the target.

Crack-ow!

They stopped and looked at each other.

"That wasn't a rifle shot. Did he just off himself?" Garner asked.

"He may want us to think that," Wolfe replied, and they continued.

Four minutes later, they reached the outcropping. Garner motioned Wolfe to the right, and he crept deeper into the woods. Slinging the rifle over his shoulder, he pulled out the Walther—it was much more effective at close range than the sniper rifle. Slowly, carefully, Wolfe scaled the backside of the outcropping, working his way over a tangle of slippery moss-covered roots and basalt. It was twilight under the trees, but as he turned back to the cleared area of the firing range, the sunlight was dazzling, making it hard to see. Wolfe stayed low, shifting his head left and right to keep it out of the stabbing, blinding shafts of sunlight. He saw the rifle barrel too late—it was aiming right at him.

Garner's head and shoulders appeared above the barrel. His pistol pointed down at the ground. "All clear!"

Wolfe took a deep breath and climbed the rest of the way. The sniper was face-down a few feet away from his rifle. His right hand still gripped a pistol. The back of his head had a gaping wound that soiled his civilian shirt with dark-red blood and brains.

"Who are you?" Garner said, putting his boot on the man's shoulder and kicking him over. A young, white, bloody face lolled drunkenly to the side, its mouth hanging open and glazed blue eyes staring wide.

"Hubbard!" Wolfe exclaimed, and he was about to kneel next to the corpse when the left hand, which lay pinned under Hubbard's chest, flopped out. Something small and round rolled free.

"Grenade!"

Wolfe dove to his left toward the edge of the outcropping. He hit the ground on his belly and slithered behind a tree root.

Bam!

He felt a hot rush of air surge over his back and legs, followed by a rain of dirt and debris. Wolfe waited a moment, and then he lifted his head.

"Flint, are you alright?"

Wolfe checked himself over. He was unscathed. Standing up, he waved to Garner, who also appeared to be alright. Hubbard, however, was a mess. The grenade took care of the part of Hubbard's face not marred by the splinters from Flint's shot and the 9mm.

Garner walked up to the remains of his man. "Did you know him, Flint?"

"He staked out my house last night; that's how I got his wallet," Flint explained. "He said he was working for Dixie Dallas of the ACLU on the side. That made sense. She's been after me since 9/11."

"Why didn't you tell me?"

Flint shrugged and said, "It all seemed innocent enough, relatively speaking. All he had on him was a camera. I didn't think it was a big deal, and then he told me about his wife and kids—I thought I'd cut him a break."

"Hubbard didn't have a wife and kids," Garner told him. Flint handed him Hubbard's wallet, pointing to the picture of the woman and kids.

"That's what he showed me." Flint nodded.

"That's his sister," Garner said, shaking his head. He held the wallet out to Wolfe. "You want these?"

"For what?"

"I don't know; to do whatever you guys do with them, track his contacts?"

"I suppose," Flint replied, taking the wallet and dug through

Hubbard's clothes for his cell phone. "I think OSI will want them, though."

"Last time I checked, the Company trumps any OSI investigation—this was an assassination attempt, Flint. You need to figure out who Hubbard was working for and why."

The MPs arrived a few minutes later and cordoned off the site. Flint and Garner headed back to the range building, collected their things, and followed the MPs to their operations center. Flint expected to be there all day, but to his surprise, they ran his ID, took his statement, and sent him on his way. He was even given custody of Hubbard's things.

When he asked why, the petty officer told him, "Mr. Wolfe, when I swipe your ID, I get a security screen that says CIA, XSCI Clearance, Sensitive, GSX, and a statement telling me to cooperate fully, no questions asked. At the bottom is a telephone number I don't want to call. That's all I need to know, sir. Have a good day, sir!" He handed Flint Hubbard's things and saluted.

"Thank you," Flint said, but as he was leaving the building with Garner, the petty officer asked, "Sir, would you like me to sweep your car?"

"Excuse me?"

"Considering what happened, I'd like to have my team sweep your car for bombs, sir," he said seriously. "It's for your protection, sir. Five minutes and you'll be on your way. Don't worry, sir, my team covers the president when he's in the Pacific Northwest; they know what they're doing."

"Knock yourself out," Flint sighed, looking at his watch. "I've still got three hours before I have to get the kids—four if they hop on the bus."

"I'll give them a call, sir," the petty officer said, punching in a four-digit code on his desk phone.

That reminded Flint of Hubbard's phone. "I suppose I better take a look at this," he said aloud, though he was thinking, *What the hell am I looking for? Oh, well, I suppose I can't muck this up by looking.*

He keyed the menu to recent calls. It seemed the obvious place to go. Most of the numbers had innocent labels, like, "home," "work," "Lt. G," and the like, but the top one, the one most recently used, said,

"Wolfe." It wasn't his number. Curious, he highlighted the number and pressed, "Send."

Boom!

CHAPTER 26: The Meaning Hits Home

The minivan burst into flames. Flint ducked as debris smacked against the bulletproof windows of the security building.

Flint rushed outside, knowing he'd set off the bomb. The sweep team—had he just killed a bunch of sailors? At first glance, there were no bodies next to the carcass of the van, and then he saw the navy ordinance van fifty yards away. The men were collecting their gear, looking at Wolfe. Embarrassed, he sat in the corner and watched his van burn, relieved that his stupidity hadn't killed anyone.

"They teach you that in spy school?" Garner asked, joining him as the fire trucks screeched to a halt beside the burning vehicle.

Hubbard's cell phone rang.

Flint looked at Garner, who shrugged, and answered it.

"Hello?"

"Is your work finished, Mr. Hubbard," asked a raspy voice that sounded somewhat unnatural.

The sirens were wailing outside, so Wolfe said simply, "Listen for yourself."

There was a pause, and then the voice said, "That will be satisfactory, Mr. Hubbard, at least until we have confirmation."

"I expect you'll see it in the papers tomorrow," Flint said.

"If we get confirmation, you'll receive the remainder of your commission at the aforementioned location at twenty-one hundred hours."

"No," Wolfe told the voice, not knowing where that might be and knowing better than to ask. "I can't be seen there again. I need another location."

"Why is that?"

Wolfe thought furiously, and hoping he didn't take too long, blamed it on Dixie C. Dallas—after all, why not? "She followed me there; she knows about it. We need another spot."

"Where do you suggest?"

"Toy's Topless, same time," he said. "Everyone will be watching the dancers."

"How wonderfully seedy," said the voice. "Very well, Mr. Hubbard, we'll see you there." The line went dead.

"Who was that?" Garner asked.

"Whoever was behind Hubbard," Flint told him, "but it doesn't sound like a terrorist. Anyway, I'll find out tomorrow." He checked his watch. "I better get going; I've got to pick up the kids in a few hours."

"I don't think your van's going to get fixed in time," Garner told him. "Come on, let's give our statements to the MPs—again—and I'll run you out to the ferry!"

Garner dropped Flint off and he walked on with about a dozen other people. He climbed into the passenger cabin and watched the cars load. The ferry backed out and then turned around to head over to the island. He sighed with relief. If he could catch a ride, he'd still make it to the bus stop in time, and the kids would never have any idea about the day he had.

The trip was as short as it always was, but for some reason, he was impatient. Flint went back down to the car deck to wait. He stood at the safety rope, feeling the cold wind on his face, and watching the scenery of Puget Sound. The crowd going to Vashon, actually only a few dozen cars at this time of day, was always amusing. The one on his left was a beat-up VW van painted in traditional Vashon hippie flowers. It looked as though they'd been living out of it for the last thirty, no, forty years. Smoke drifted out of the half-opened windows. He shook his head. Stoners. On the right was a car more to his liking: a silver Crossfire coupe.

A man got out of the coupe. He was short, bald, except for his French-braided ponytail, and he wore small, wire-rimmed glasses.

With a very pretentious swagger, he walked quickly off the car deck and up the stairs. Wolfe drifted over to the car and glanced within. It was a six-speed with sleek, two-tone leather seats and a navigation system. Like a true islander, the man left the keys in the car—after all, who'd steal a car on a ferryboat?

Wolfe sighed as he realized there was no backseat for the kids.

The man was back.

"Oh, just admiring the car," Wolfe said.

"It's a real babe magnet," the guy said in a cheesy, conspiratorial way.

"I bet it is," Wolfe nodded, "but I have kids."

"More for me, then," he said, sporting a gap-toothed grin, and he slid into his car.

"Say, you wouldn't be able to give me a ride to town, would you?" Flint asked before he closed the door.

"Does the wife have the minivan today?" he asked with a smirk.

"No, an assassin blew it up," Flint said in a matter-of-fact voice.

"What happened to the assassin?"

"I shot him," Flint replied in mock surprise.

The guy laughed and said, "You'll have to come up with a better line than that if you want a ride, buddy!" Then he shut the door.

Flint grimaced and muttered, "Damn movies have jaded everyone!"

The ship docked, the ramp came down, and Wolfe stepped onto it.

He was halfway up the ramp when his phone rang. It was Orani.

"I was going to call; it's been rather a hectic day," he began, expecting to explain himself.

"Save it, Wolfe, where are you?"

"I'm on the ferry from Southworth to Vashon. We just docked, why?"

"Terrorists have taken over the Vashon Elementary School," she said tersely. "We just ascertained that off a live Web cast. There are at least three of them. Get there as soon as you can; we're trying to get a hold of a SEAL team on alert, but something's going on at Bangor and the base is locked down."

Wolfe didn't hear anything else. He ran back down to the ferry and

213

to the Crossfire. Yanking the door open, he yelled, "Out now! I need your car!"

"What, are you insane?"

Wolfe whipped out the Walther. "Sorry, buddy, it's a matter of life and death, literally. I wouldn't do this if I didn't mean it!" He reached for the man's arm.

"No! I won't let you have my car! Shoot me first; you can't have it!"

"I don't have time for this!" Wolfe shouted, but try as he might, he couldn't get the man out, and he couldn't shoot him. "Listen, buddy—"

"Bernie!"

"Bernie! I'm with the CIA, no shit, and terrorists have taken over the elementary school. I need your car. Kids' lives are at stake!"

"Is there a problem here?" It was one of the ferry parking attendants, not Toad, but a guy who was actually large enough to be a problem.

Wolfe was about to explode, but Bernie said, "No problem, sir, just a lover's spat! We're fine! Get in, Adrian!"

Wolfe got in the passenger side. Before he got the door closed, Bernie punched the accelerator and raced off the car deck. He careened off the docks and up the hill, passing cars and ignoring the blaring horns.

"I hope you weren't lying; what am I saying—don't get me wrong, I don't want to see any kids get hurt. But are you really with the CIA?"

"Actually, yes," Wolfe admitted, holding on tight as Bernie screamed around the tight corner opposite Vashon Realty. "I'd appreciate it if you don't spread it around."

"So there's really something going on at the school?"

"I'm afraid so," he said, trying to stay calm. "My two kids are there."

Bernie pushed the accelerator to the floor and skidded around the hard right-hand turn at the top of the hill. Somehow, the Crossfire stayed on the road. It hit the straightaway and the speedometer climbed through one hundred.

"How am I doing?"

"You're doing great, Bernie, better than I could do myself."

Bernie dodged the small downtown district by ducking left at the

Subway shop, cutting behind the Thriftway, and taking the back road to the school. He slid to a halt in the school parking lot.

"Thanks, Bernie, I owe you!" he said, patting the man on the shoulder.

"Good luck!" Bernie yelled.

The police were already there—both of them. Dozens of children and teachers were outside, but he didn't see Conner or Kathy among them—it didn't matter. Wolfe waded through the crowd of panic-stricken adults and children, heading for the front door.

"Sir! You can't go in there!" exclaimed an officer, running to cut him off.

Wolfe turned angrily on him, saying, "What the hell are you doing out here, waiting for gun shots? Don't you realize what's happening?"

"Sir, I understand you're upset, but we're waiting for reinforcements and a negotiating team," he put a hand on Wolfe's chest. "Now, step back, and leave this to us."

Wolfe took the officer's hand and, with a flick of the wrist, turned it. The officer whipped around, helpless in a wristlock. His partner rushed up, drawing his weapon. Wolfe let the first officer go and said, "I'm Flint Wolfe, CIA counterterrorism."

He took out his ID and held it for them to see.

"Now, it's up to you, if you want to sit on your ass like they did at Columbine and wait for the body count—fine! But get out of the way and let me do my job!" he said harshly. "Those jihadists will negotiate with you to release as many of their sick friends as they can, and then they'll kill the kids. They're here for body count, not for political gamesmanship."

"We're under orders to secure the perimeter, sir, not aggravate the situation," the officer said defensively.

"Then your chief is an idiot. We're at war, and there's no negotiating with this enemy," Wolfe told them through clenched teeth. "Now, I'm going in to get the kids out. You want to stop me, then join the terrorists and shoot me! If you want to help, then get everyone away from the parking lot."

He strode forward to the doors and entered without incident. Then he drew the Walther and screwed the silencer into place. There were at least three of them, so he didn't want to tip them off any sooner than he needed to. If he could down one or two before the others knew what hit them, he'd have the best chance of taking them all down before they triggered a bomb.

Wolfe ran silently through the hall, running on his toes, peering into each classroom. He made his way toward the gym—the most logical place the terrorists would herd the kids. He heard them before he saw them.

Kids were crying and screaming. Adult voices were shouting in thickly accented English to keep quiet. Wolfe reached the double doors to the gym. Glancing through the tall, narrow windows, he saw at least a hundred kids huddled on the floor with several teachers. Patrolling around them were three terrorists with AK-47s. On closer inspection, he saw three more. One stood on the stage with a cell phone, and another was laying a wire around the seated children. There were black backpacks strung at intervals around the kids. The third was in the back corner of the gym. He had a video camera. Wolfe could see the light for the camera falling on an irregular-shaped mass of objects in the corner. It took a moment for him to realize they were bodies.

"They've most likely killed all the men of the group, or anyone they felt was a threat—just like Chechnya," he breathed, trying to control his emotions.

To make matters worse, the terrorists were all wearing explosive vests.

Wolfe took a deep breath. It was a nightmare. Six targets, all heavily armed; it was going to be tough. He doubted he'd have the luxury of changing clips, and all it took was a single terrorist setting off his vest to cause mayhem.

Wolfe eased the door open, but it stopped after a half an inch. He didn't force it but looked through the gap between the doors: chained.

There had to be another way in.

There were two other doors to the outside. He could see they were chained as well. He took a deep breath, trying to calm himself. The gymnasium was also the assembly hall for the school. To his left was a low stage. There must be a door there as well, but he couldn't imagine the terrorists would disregard that. Still, the ceiling over the stage wasn't the high-raftered ceiling of the gym. It was like the rest of the school: a lowered ceiling with tiles in a metal grid.

He got up and padded down the hall. There was a door to the gym. Carefully, he tried it—locked.

Looking up, Wolfe noted the molded ceiling tiles. Silently, he slid a table to the wall. Standing on top of it allowed him to lift a tile and stick his head through. It was dark, but to his consternation, the cinderblock wall continued to the roof supports. He bit his lip in agonizing frustration, and then he caught sight of an air-conditioning duct. Wolfe got down and slid the table beneath the ducting. He climbed up, slid the tile aside. To his relief, there was a large gap in the cinderblock wall for the ducting and wiring bundles going into the gym. He stuffed his pistol in the back of his belt, and grabbed the edge of the cinderblock. With a single, fluid motion, he was up on the wall. Lying down on the wall, he carefully lifted the edge of a tile on the gym side. The lights were on in the room below, but it appeared empty. It was the long, narrow room behind the stage. Shelves and stacks of boxes filled the space. A door was open to the stage.

There was the sound of a crying child coming from the opening, followed by the harsh orders of an adult.

"Shut the child up now!" exclaimed a voice in a heavy accent.

The crying continued. There was a scream.

Wolfe dropped to the floor and ran to the door, gun in hand. He peered around the corner.

There were the three jihadists with their AK-47s behind the kids. One was on stage with his back to Wolfe, one was at the foot of the stage fiddling with a camera, and another was dragging a blonde little girl to the stage—the little girl was Katherine.

She fought the terrorist and screamed at him, tears rolling down her face, but he dragged her by the hair toward the stage. A slight boy leapt up and attacked the terrorist—it was Conner.

"Leave my sister alone!" he shouted.

The terrorist backhanded Conner across the face. The boy fell back, senseless, into the laps of his classmates.

Wolfe felt a surge of flame in his gut, but he repressed his urge to act. Taking quick stock of the locations of the terrorists, he counted down who to fire on first, second, third, and so on. He'd have one chance.

The terrorist was dragging Katherine on stage, and the one with the camera said, "Abdul—something—ready! The world is—something—Allah be praised!"

The man dragged Katherine to the man on stage, who grabbed her by the hair. Wolfe was about to step out when the man waved to his fellow terrorists. The other five terrorists joined him on stage, taking their places behind the ringleader. He turned Katherine to the camera and took out a long knife.

"Allahu Akbar!" said the five terrorists behind him.

The kids screamed.

Katherine covered her face.

Wolfe stepped out of the doorway.

Time slowed down. Wolfe's vision went to black and white, painfully stark in every detail. They didn't see him. The six terrorists lined up in a row of five, with the ringleader in front. They were like cardboard cutouts on a practice range. He raised his gun.

Calmly, coolly, with the passion of a sphinx, he put a bullet in the right temple of the ringleader. severing the center of his body's motor activity from his musculature. The terrorist's eyes grew round and vacant. The knife clattered to the stage. His hand released his daughter's hair. A fountain of bright-red blood spurted from his temple—the only color to Wolfe's eyes. His dead body stood there trembling for a moment, and then it collapsed, sliding down upon itself like some crumbling tower. Before the terrorist hit the stage, Wolfe moved his sights down the line. The black-hooded terrorists looked like target dummies but for the shocked expression in their black eyes. He aimed right between the whites, squeezing the trigger in a slow, steady, deliberate motion.

The pistol rocked soothingly in his hand. Even the shell casings leapt from the chamber in a strangely comforting fashion, as if each reveled in a job well-done. Each time a casing left his peripheral vision, a black-masked head would drop down beneath the barrel. He shot the ringleader, the back two, and now Wolfe worked his way back toward himself. The fourth fell, and still no reaction other than shock. The fifth twitched, he thought, but he spun around and dropped anyway. The last reached for his gun, not his vest.

Wolfe steadied himself and put two into his forehead.

The terrorists were all down.

Flint rushed forward and swept Kathy up in his arms. Then he leapt off stage and collected Conner.

"Daddy! Daddy!" she cried.

Flint carried them over to the gym doors and shot the lock off. He yanked the chains savagely from the doors and ushered the kids and teachers out the short hall, past the principal's office, and urged them through the double doors of the entrance.

There were news crews outside. Wolfe stopped abruptly and waited for Katherine's teacher. He put the kids down and told her, "Get everybody out and accounted for. I've got to go back and secure the gym. I don't know if they have timers on those satchels or not. Take care of my kids until I come out."

Conner and Katherine didn't want him to leave them, but Flint assured them, "It's over, kids, but my job's not done. I have to make sure the school's safe. Honest, I'll be right back!"

The kids filed out, and Wolfe returned to the gym, but his intent wasn't just to disarm the satchels. He understood all too well what the terrorists were planning, and he intended on completing their spectacle.

First things first, he disconnected the satchels from the initiator. Then he went to the back corner with a slim hope that someone in that tangle of bodies might be alive. There was a thick, congealing pool of blood coating the floor. It gave the place a sickly sweet smell with a faint tang of iron. Carefully, Wolfe pulled the men out one by one, until he had eleven lifeless bodies laid out on the wooden floor. It was useless. They'd all had their throats cut.

Wolfe stomped back to the camera; his jaw set forward, his teeth clenched in a merciless, cold rage. Bending over, he inspected the video screen. It was still recording, showing the stage where the children were to be executed, but where the six dead terrorists now lay. He inspected the camera more closely. It was hooked to small, thick antennae—a satellite relay.

"Direct to the pressrooms of al-Jihad, no doubt," he growled. "No doubt this is one of their most watched reality shows." The light was still red. It was on a live feed.

Borrowing one of the terrorist's bloody masks, he drew it over his head, sticky hole and all; there was no sense in giving the jihadist world his picture.

"Enjoying the show, my terrorist friends?" he asked sarcastically. "Well, don't leave yet, we're not done! This is what happens to the cowards you send to prey on children! First, they're executed with bullets dipped in the blood of pigs, and then they're sent to their maker thus!"

Wolfe stomped onto stage. Taking the ringleader's knife, he set about his grisly task. When he was finished, he took the camera and recorded each of the pallid, dead faces, for the terrorist audience—their cocks sticking out of their mouths in a signal of absolute and complete contempt.

Wolfe's message sent the needed information. He turned off the camera, his mind on the next necessity; specifically, he needed to know if anyone else was in on the plot, and he needed to know now, before they disappeared. Checking the body of the ringleader, he found a cell phone latched onto his belt. As he paged through the menu of recent calls, his own phone rang.

It was Orani.

"Have you been watching?" he asked.

"Yes, we watched the whole show."

"Well get someone over here pronto; all their stuff's still good."

"That's already done," she said, and then it sounded as if she were talking to someone else. There was some excitement, and then Orani came back, her voice shrill. "Wolfe, we're getting a feed from the local media; everyone's gathered in the parking lot—if the terrorists follow their MO, they're going to set off car bombs with the first responders! You've got to clear the area!"

CHAPTER 27: Ultimatum

Flint ran out of the school like a madman.

The entire student body gathered in the parking lot; they were literally surrounded by cars. The wailing sirens of fire trucks and cops meant there was little or no time. Then he saw the TV crew; they'd arrived before the cops.

The two uniforms on the scene came up to him, but he cut them off.

"Go over there and keep the TV cameras off the kids!" he said. "There are car bombs in the parking lot, and the terrorists will be watching the news report. As soon as they see the kids in the area, they'll set off the bombs!"

"What do you want us to do?"

"One of you interview with the reporter, I don't know, tell them how SWAT has the scene locked down. Tell them there are still hostages inside—whatever. And get that cameraman off the parking lot and onto you!"

The officers ran over to the TV crew. One whispered instructions in the cameraman's ear, and the other walked the reporter over to the side of the building, away from the parking lot, pretending to give her details on the tactical situation.

Flint ran toward the kids. Conner and Kathy met him halfway, hugging him tight.

"Hey, it's still dangerous here," he told them. "We need to get your

221

friends and the teachers out of the parking lot. You two run to the ball field. I'll get the teachers."

The kids ran, and Flint went to the teachers. They crowded around him.

"We need to get out of here, and we need to do it quickly and quietly," he urged. "There are probably bombs in some of these cars, and if the terrorists see the kids leaving, they'll set them off. The cops are giving us a moment, but they'll get wind of it eventually. We need to get them out now!"

The teachers were surprisingly calm. Several went to the forefront, waving the kids toward the soccer fields and baseball diamonds behind the school, holding their fingers to their lips for silence. The rest went to the farthest students and herded them out of the lot. The kids, already fearful but knowing the importance of following instructions, filed swiftly and silently out of the lot. The teachers followed them, staying between the kids and the deadly cars. When the last people were out of the area, Flint gave the all clear to the cops, who immediately went on their radios, telling all respondents to stay clear of the parking lot.

A huge boom shook the ground; another boom followed it, and then another. The concussion knocked Flint to the ground, and the sounds of whizzing glass cut the air above him. When the sound died away, he looked up to see three wrecks gushing smoke and flames. Many of the cars around them were on fire, but thankfully, everyone was far enough away from the blast to escape harm.

Sirens wailing, the fire trucks careened into the scene. The sound of helicopters roared over the treetops, and a SEAL team descended on ropes like deadly spiders onto the school roof. The TV crew was already up and filming again.

Flint ran to his kids.

They hugged him close.

The phone rang.

"What?"

"Get over to the mosque!"

"What are you talking about; I just got my kids!" he yelled, holding them in his arms and not in any mood to let them go.

"The blast! A cell phone triggered it. A call came from the mosque to one of our numbers of interest and set off the blast. Get there now and find out who it was; we'll divert the SEALs there as soon as we can!"

"Damn it, Orani! Let the SEALs arrest them!"

"We can't give up the info, or there's nothing to pin it on him. Go! Find him before the SEALs get there and eliminate him—that's an order!"

Wolfe slammed the phone down.

"Do you have to go get the bad guys, Dad?" Kathy asked.

"Get 'em, Dad, we'll be okay," Conner told him.

"That's my Spartans! I'll be back, kids. I love you. Stay with your teachers!" And he was off. Wolfe intended to commandeer a squad car, but a scorched Crossfire drove out of the smoke.

The window rolled down, and Bernie smiled. "You need a ride, Secret Agent Man?"

"The name's Flint Wolfe, Bernie, thanks."

"The kids all safe?"

"Thanks to you getting me here in time, yes."

"Wow!" Bernie exclaimed. "Say, where are we going?"

"That's what I'm finding out," Wolfe replied, punching in the information on his phone. The GPS unit searched and spit out directions in a matter of moments. He passed them on to Bernie, who drove appropriately fast.

"Say, you wouldn't mind coming to a hang-out of mine, I mean, my friends would never believe this!"

"Get me to the mosque, Bernie, and I'll go wherever you want."

Bernie pulled into the mosque with the same dramatic flair as the school.

Wolfe put a new clip in his gun and glanced at Bernie.

Bernie beamed.

Wolfe stuffed the gun under his jacket and jumped out of the car.

Two men were barring the entrance.

"You cannot come in here!" said one, and they sought to grab him.

Wolfe kicked the first man in the gut and then kneed him in the face. He went down, as Wolfe blocked the other man's punch and returned his own—crushing the man's nose and sending him to his knees, bleeding profusely.

He stormed through the entrance, through the hall and the prayer room, and to the cleric's office. The door was locked. He heard the people in the office ten paces from the door. Whatever was going on, it was heated, and the only intelligible words were the oft repeated, "Jihad!" and "Allahu Akbar!"

Wolfe kicked in the door, gun drawn.

About a dozen men were in the room. Everyone fell silent and stared at him in amazement. Only one man failed to note him. His headless body lay in a spreading pool of blood. The head sat in the corner, staring up at him as if in pain.

The imam, a middle-aged brown-bearded man in clerical robes, backed against the wall with five other men in robes and two men in civilian clothing. Standing in front of them were two men with AK-47s and one man holding a long, bloody knife. His hands and trousers were soaked with blood.

"Infidel, what are you doing here?" the man with the knife demanded.

The other two men raised their AKs. Wolfe shot them shown. He already knew where they stood. He wanted the one in charge.

That man approached Wolfe with crazy eyes, as if he hadn't seen Wolfe shoot down his two comrades. Wolfe pistol-whipped him across the temple, sending the bearded, perfumed ideologue tumbling back over the twitching bodies of his friends. The terrorist dropped his bloody knife and stared at Wolfe dumbly.

The cleric started to say something, but Wolfe put a finger to his lips. The TV was on the newscast. "Watching the drama, I see. Well, are you disappointed or relieved?"

"I don't know yet," he stammered.

"All the kids survived," Wolfe said carefully.

"Then I am greatly relieved—praise Allah's mercy! I called the police when I found out about the operation on the school, but too late to prevent it," the cleric told Wolfe. "That's when Ahdan attacked me. Mustafa sought to protect me, but you see how he's paid for Allah's work."

Wolfe shook his head and said, "I really, really wish I could trust you, but there your own people are against you. Stay where you are, the rest of you against the wall, please."

"You're going to shoot us, aren't you, Crusader dog!" wailed a white boy of eighteen or so. He was one of the civilians standing with the cleric.

"Is that what you people teach in Sunday school?" He stepped up to the boy and yanked him out of line by the collar. "Know what you're talking about before you condemn me!" He threw the boy onto the headless body in the corner. "That's what your faith has gotten you so far!" Screaming, the boy scrambled to get off the body but instead slipped and fell into the gore, knocking the head against the wall and out into the middle of the floor like a billiard ball. Wailing, he cowered next to the mullahs.

Wolfe turned to the cleric, saying viciously, "If that's all you think of your faith, I'll gladly shoot you where you stand. If you have a higher opinion of yourselves, then start talking. Who's responsible for the school operation, and how many are still at large?"

The door burst open and the two bruised guards rushed in.

"Die, Crusader dog!" shouted the first one.

"Suit yourself," Wolfe said, and he shot the man in the chest.

The other man skidded to a stop, his hands up, staring at Wolfe in horror.

"Do I have any other takers?" No one said a word. He waved the security guard inside the room, noting he headed automatically to the cleric. He pointed the Walther at the ringleader. He was still sitting on the floor between his two dead companions, cradling his head. "You have ten seconds to tell me if there's anything else going on, how many terrorists are still out there, and what they're up to."

The man said nothing, but the cleric did. Despite the venomous look of the man, the cleric exclaimed, "How can this be; how can this happen here? This isn't Afghanistan or Palestine or Chechnya; we are in the civilized world!" He turned angry eyes on the man sitting on the floor. Shaking his finger, he yelled, "You've brought violence to our community, to our children, to our sacred mosque!"

"We bring Islam here, true Islam! We bring it with the sword as the Prophet demands!" the man retorted, eyes wide with madness, spittle dribbling from his slack lips—more animal than human. "You are worse than the infidel; you forsake Islam!"

"You dare!" the cleric seethed, and he looked back and forth between the man and the security guard. "You are illiterate dolts! Who among you can read and interpret scripture—none of you! Who among you has the right to take the life of someone of the book, of children, of the innocent—none of you!"

The two men screamed incoherently at the imam, crouching like rabid dogs, teeth bared, hands shaking.

"Traitor to your race; you side with the Crusaders!" shouted the security guard, turning to his comrades and exhorting them in Arabic. The two men rushed Wolfe, but they had no chance. He shot them down without a second thought, and then he picked up the two AK-47s. Turning to the cleric, he shook his head.

"Now you're going to shoot us too!" the white boy wailed, interrupting, crawling into the corner like a wounded dog. "You won't stop until all Muslims are dead; this is your Crusader war against Islam!"

Wolfe looked at the boy in complete contempt. "This isn't my war, boy—it's yours. This isn't Christianity or Judaism against Islam; it's a war within Islam. I can fight it, but you're the only ones who can win it. If you truly love your faith, then you are the ones who must fight it; you must eradicate the destructive part of Islam so your faith can survive."

The cleric whispered a short prayer, muttering, "I don't understand such hatred, such fury. Where was that fury when Saddam stole people from their homes? Where is that fury when sheiks bath their hands in basins of gold while peasants wander the desert looking for scraps? Here we can worship as we please without fearing religious police, zealots, or dictators—and how do my people act? It is shameful!"

"Very shameful," Wolfe said, but not without a great deal of suspicion. "Someone made a call twenty minutes ago that triggered three car bombs in the elementary school parking lot."

"No one has made any such call from here," the cleric said flatly.

"We'll see," Wolfe replied, and he dialed the number. "The coward who triggered those bombs meant to kill the parents, first responders, and any children not already slaughtered by the six vermin in the school."

The phone rang, and on the third ring, a connection clicked on.

"Mr. Wolfe, is that you?" asked a voice without preamble.

"Hamdi!" Wolfe growled, recognizing the voice. "I should have known you'd be behind something this heinous!"

"All to a good cause, Mr. Wolfe. We're at war, remember?"

"I'm coming for you, Hamdi; I'm right behind you."

"Then come along, Mr. Wolfe, I'll be waiting," Hamdi told him. "And by the way, thank Imam Ramsi for me, and remind him that Allah will be avenged on traitors as well. Good-bye for now, Mr. Wolfe."

The line went dead.

"Where is Hamdi?" Wolfe asked harshly.

"He's the one who stirred up all this trouble!"

A black-bearded mullah to Ramsi's right interrupted. "Imam, stop, you must not help him; you must not aide a non-Muslim!"

"Jahdam, they are animals! They don't speak for Islam!"

"They are martyrs!" he cried. "Even if you do not sanction their actions, they still fight in the name of Allah. If you don't see that, you're blind! The Crusaders started this war, and we must finish it—even if it is to the death. This war will bring the world under the blanket of Islam!"

"You're mad!" Ramsi stammered. "Killing women and children is not the way to spread the word of the Prophet!"

"You are wrong; whether we spread the word by the sword, the gun, or by the word, we must spread the word—by any means we can!" He turned to Wolfe, his dark eyes wide and soulless. "You think you've foiled our righteous strikes for Allah this day, but you're wrong. Even now, another band of martyrs positions themselves to reap a harvest of infidels!"

"Where?" Wolfe asked, pointing his gun at the cleric's head.

"I will never tell you!"

Ramsi took out his cell phone and dialed a number, saying, "It has to be Hassan! How can I have been so blind to this madness?" He tore at his beard as he dialed, muttering, "I didn't believe it; I didn't want to believe they'd actually do this!"

"You can't give up another Muslim! It is sacrilege!" exclaimed Jahdam. "Hassan, Hassan, don't listen to him, accomplish your mission!"

Wolfe heard enough. He pulled the trigger. The hammer fell on an empty chamber.

"You see, you see, Allah protects me; it is Allah's will that the mission succeed!"

"We'll see about that!" Wolfe growled, covering the space between himself and Jahdam in two long strides. He struck the man across the temple with the butt of his gun. Jahdam's head snapped back, spraying Ramsi with a splash of blood and broken teeth, and the cleric stumbled back into the wall and slid, unconscious, to the floor.

Ramsi recoiled in shock, his shaking hand reaching for his cheek. His fingers came away wet with blood. The cleric stared at the stains in disbelief.

A voice came from his open cell phone. It said, "Who is it?" in Arabic.

"Answer it—where are they?" Wolfe whispered.

Ramsi answered in Arabic, his voice wavering. Wolfe's imperfect grasp of Arabic caught, "Hassan, it is Imam Ramsi, in the name of Allah, come back to the mosque!"

The voice replied, "I am on a mission, you can't ask this of me. We must avenge our brothers!"

"It is over, Hassan; there need be no more bloodshed! You don't understand what you're doing. In the name of Allah, I command you to come back!"

"Hah! I will see Allah before you! I understand, but you do not! Allahu Akbar!"

The line clicked dead, but before it did, Wolfe clearly heard a low horn in the background.

"The ferry!" he exclaimed, and he turned to go.

"Wait!" Ramsi said.

"I don't have the time!"

The cleric looked at him in distress, his eyes dead, and he said, "Kill me; I can't deal with this madness anymore! I can't harm or give up a Muslim, and yet Muslims behead Muslim women and children—it is our own people! We stone women for looking askance at a man of the wrong sect. We bomb sacred mosques during prayer, markets with innocents and pilgrims during holy times. We raped, tortured, and killed school children in Chechnya in the name of Allah!" The cleric was white, beaten, and drained of all life. "I cannot bear what we've done in the name of Allah. Kill me, for I do not want or deserve to live in this world anymore. Send me to Allah so that he can make me understand."

"Father, I don't have the answers for you," Wolfe said, sliding a full clip into his gun. "All I know is that someone needs to lead your people into the twenty-first century, and it's not going to be Jahdam there!" He threw the unconscious man over his shoulder. "You either stand for faith or you stand for blood!"

"The men you seek are in a black Suburban. That is Hassan's car," Ramsi said.

Wolfe nodded and hurried out of the room.

CHAPTER 28: You Got another Thing Coming

Wolfe needn't have hurried; they shut the ferries down.

Bernie slowed down, stopping behind a long line of vehicles snaking down the hill. The ferry wasn't visible, but Wolfe could tell where he was from experience. When they started loading again, the terrorists might get on the ferry depending on where they were, but he wouldn't. He couldn't take that chance.

"Pull into the parking lot of the Mexican restaurant, Bernie."

"What about him?" Bernie asked, meaning Jahdam in the hatchback trunk.

"You have any duct tape?"

"It's in my emergency kit in back."

Wolfe hopped out as soon as Bernie came to a stop. He dug through the back, which was remarkably well organized, and found the tape. In short order, he had Jahdam trussed up and gagged. By the time he was done, the former cleric woke up. Wolfe smiled viciously and patted him on the head. "You sit tight. When I get back, I'll introduce you to some of my friends. They enjoy talking. After that, I wouldn't be surprised if you get a vacation in the Caribbean."

He shut the hatchback and told Bernie, "Stay here, and if anyone gives you grief, anyone official, that is, tell them to call this number."

He took out his wallet and handed Bernie a card with the CIA logo emblazoned on the front.

Wolfe left the lot and jogged along the line of cars waiting to get on the ferry. He saw the Suburban at the head of the line. A squad of cops with dogs already worked their way past it and were going through a station wagon with camping gear, coolers, and scared kids.

A parking attendant waved the Suburban onto the car deck. It looked to be the last vehicle that would get onboard.

Wolfe ran to the bottom of the hill, but all the foot passengers were already onboard and the captain was revving his engines in preparation for departure. He reached the ferry terminal just as the attendant raised the ramp.

"Wait!" Wolfe shouted.

"Sorry, you'll have to catch the next one!" the man said, lowering the gate and turning back to the ferry terminal.

The water began to churn. The ferry shook and slowly moved out of the slip.

Wolfe looked desperately around. The ferry attendants milled around the ramps. He couldn't rush the ferry without causing a scene—and that might prompt the jihadists to come out firing. If they did, he'd be outgunned. Still, he had to get on that boat; otherwise, there'd be a massacre.

The Vashon ferry had three slips for car ferries and one for a smaller, passenger-only ferry. Maintenance ramps ran alongside the slips supported by steel pilings lined with shock-absorbing tires. Wolfe walked quickly back to the ferry terminal and ducked around the back of the building. A catwalk led around the building to the steel ramp going between the passenger ferry and the departing ferry. The ramp could be raised and lowered according to the tide, and at the moment, it was in the raised position. Wolfe looked quickly around and ducked under the chain and onto the ramp. Another ferry was coming in on the other side, and the attendants were already focusing on that ship. No one noticed him run up the ramp.

The captains always backed out of the ferry dock with care because of the strong currents, but today, the wind was from the south and gusty, and it was giving the captain fits. The ferry banged and scraped against the pilings. Wolfe reached the end of the ramp and jumped to the top of the swaying pilings.

He was five feet below the upper car deck, about ten feet above the lower car deck. The ship moved by with gathering speed. There was no way he'd make the jump up, but if he went down, he would be crushed by the pilings. The ship rumbled. Wolfe swung over the side and climbed quickly down the access ladder to the lower deck level. The ship went by, and white water bubbled dangerously thirty feet below. The ladder was slippery and cold, coated with the slime of seagulls, algae, and tar. The ship squealed against the piling, causing a shiver to run down his spine. The white hull was so close, he could touch it. He could reach the rail, really just an oval hole cut into the quarter-inch steel plates between the ship's ribs, but he couldn't get up and over it without getting ground into hamburger between the ship and the piling. Wolfe waited until the ship moved past. As it pulled away from the piling, he leapt for the rail.

His hands wrapped around the edge of the rail and his body slammed against the steel.

That hurt! he thought as he hit. His hands slid along the wet, cold steel, and he barely hung on. Wolfe regrouped and hauled himself up and over the rail, feeling the piling brush against his leg. Rolling over the top, he dropped onto the car deck with a thump.

"Ouch!" Wolfe landed on his right shoulder, and the sting went all the way to the tip of his fingers. He didn't have time for that. Wolfe ignored the stinger and got up, crouching behind the quarter panel of a blue SUV. Car doors began to open as people went upstairs to the observation deck. Wolfe stood up and lounged over the rail, looking at the wake of the ship as if he were just another passenger.

He placed himself so he could see the black Suburban, but he wasn't visible to the jihadists. People filed up the stairs, and soon, the car deck was empty of everything but cars. The doors to the Suburban opened and three men got out on his side. Another two got out on the other side. The two headed up the stairs with the rest of the passengers. One was definitely Hamdi, and the other one, whose face was turned, might've been Khallida. They looked around before heading up to the observation deck, but not carefully—the ship hit a wave and rocked hard, sending Hamdi reeling into the car next to the Suburban. He fell to the deck. The other man helped him up and, cursing, Hamdi continued up the stairs. The other three jihadists waited for the passengers to go upstairs. When the car deck was empty, one of them squatted down between the other two. Wolfe couldn't see what it was he was doing; the hood of a car blocked his view. He heard a muffled clang, and the sound of the engines grew louder. One of the two visible jihadists bent over and disappeared. The third jihadist bent over momentarily. The sound of the engines diminished. He appeared again and walked to the back of the SUV. He turned away from Wolfe and opened the rear gate.

Wolfe saw his opportunity. Running doubled over, he worked his way behind the jihadist. It wasn't difficult. The rocking of the ship was a distraction; the sound of the sea covered his approach, and the wind was cold—the jihadist was so distracted by the chill he forgot to do his job. Wolfe made his way to the van next to the Suburban without being seen, and peered around the end. The sound of Middle Eastern music came through the open gate—ripped ragged by the wind and the waves. Six feet away, the jihadist wrapped his arms around his chest and jumped up and down in an effort to stay warm, the muzzle of an AK-47 just peeking out from beneath his jacket, but Wolfe didn't need the sight of the hidden gun to know what they were up to. The back of the Suburban was crammed with automatic rifles, boxes of ammunition, some RPGs, and three SAM-9 tubes.

The guard didn't do anything, but was apparently satisfied to gloat over the arms cache, relishing the slaughter to come. Wolfe checked the observation deck and the wheelhouse. The only possible witnesses were the two people in the car opposite the Suburban, but they were napping. This was his chance. Their plan was clear: disable the ship and then go on a killing spree before help could arrive. He had to act now. Only one thing didn't make sense: what were Hamdi and Khallida doing on the boat? The other jihadists might be on a suicide mission, but surely they weren't.

"Screw it!" he breathed venomously. "I'll make it a suicide mission for you, Hamdi!"

He reached for his Walther, but the hatch to the engine room came open. Two jihadists appeared. The one at the rear gate asked, "Now?" Another pointed at his watch and shook his head. All three got back in the Suburban to get out of the wind and rain while they had a chance.

Wolfe had an idea.

He glanced at the Sound and then up at the observation deck. The wind whipped the Sound into frenzy and the ship rocked dangerously, but fortunately it was cold enough that no one was on the aft observation deck. He crept behind the Suburban and unhooked the yellow warning line. There was a safety net at the back of the ship meant to stop cars from rolling off into the Sound. The net was separated into two sections clipped together at the center. Wolfe unhooked them, lifted the post from its hole, and put it close at hand but off to the side. Running doubled over back to the Suburban, he removed the chocks under the rear wheels. Working his way to the front of the Suburban, he crawled underneath the front axle. Wolfe cut the brake lines with his knife. As the brake fluid leaked out onto the rain-slick deck, he found the transmission gearbox and the tie-rod to the gear shift. It took only a moment to remove the pin and disconnect the tie-rod. He put the car in neutral and crawled out under the front bumper.

Wolfe got on his cell phone and ran through the menus. There were certain things about his phone not found on regular cell phones, such as a menu for the automatic locks for cars and trucks. There were only a limited number of frequencies, so all he had to do was scroll down to the line that said "Chevrolet Suburban" and select "lock" or "unlock." He selected "lock." It scrolled through the frequencies automatically and locked the car. He kept his finger on the "lock" command, threw his shoulder against the grill, and shoved.

At first, the heavy truck wouldn't budge. He pushed with all his might, feeling his legs knot and bulge as if on a tackling sled. He had to hurry! He dug in, and the truck started to move. As he pushed, he glanced over the hood. The jihadists were staring at him, wide-eyed with surprise. Then their expressions turned angry. As soon as the Suburban started to roll, however, they glanced behind them and realized what he was doing. Fear took over, and they bolted for the doors. Wolfe kept pressing the "lock" command, so every time they hit their buttons inside, his command closed the door locks again. It wasn't until he was halfway that one of them tried to open the lock manually. It was too late.

The ship's bow hit a wave and rose. The truck rocketed out of his hands. Wolfe stumbled but regained his footing in time to see the jihadists' silent screams as they plunged off the pitching deck and into the cold waters of Puget Sound. He couldn't help but smile.

A muffled explosion went off; it seemed to come from right underneath him. The explosion bounced Wolfe ten feet into the air. As he started to come down, all he could see was the white, frothing wake of the Sound slowly swallowing the black Suburban. He caught sight of frantic hands and howling faces pressed against the unyielding glass. He was about to join them!

CHAPTER 29: Connecting the Dots

Imam Ramsi gazed at the corpses in shock. The glazed eyes, the hanging lips, the bodies collapsed in grotesque caricatures of sleep—it was overwhelming. He had fled Lebanon thirty years ago and found peace as an American; he'd happily forgotten such violence. It had hitherto been comfortably far away, but the arrival of foreigners into his mosque made him walk an increasingly uncomfortable line. Now it came to this, his own people, cajoled by foreign radicals, and men he'd known since their birth lay in pools of their own blood in his mosque. His eyes welled up with tears and he tore at his beard.

"They will be martyrs; we will avenge them," whispered Saman. He laid a hand on the imam's shoulder in an attempt to console him.

The tears dried up in the imam's eyes, and his face turned to stone. Anger welled up in him. "Martyrs, martyrs for what?" he demanded, brushing off Saman's overture and slapping the young man in the chest with the back of his hand. "These men should be marrying our young women, having children, and raising them under Allah's scrutiny in our mosque! What did they have to gain by this?"

"We have to fight," the cleric insisted. "How can we tolerate this disgrace and this oppression?"

"What oppression do you speak of?" the imam insisted, and he looked wildly at those who were spared the slaughter. "Has anyone ever prevented you from coming to the mosque to pray? Has anyone in America refused you work because you were Muslim? Do we pay higher taxes because we're Muslim? Are we refused anything, anything at all, because we're Muslim?"

"Our tax dollars go to support the Zionists who have invaded our land!" Saman retorted. "That alone is cause for our humiliation, for jihad!"

"Our land, are you sure of that, Saman?" the imam asked, advancing on the younger man. "Tell me what land you speak of; let's be clear about this if we are going to talk of jihad!"

"Palestine and Jerusalem, of course," he said.

"Palestine, yes, so these radicals say. The Palestinians must have a homeland, is that not so?" he replied in a biting tone laced with sarcasm. "Do you speak of the Israelite Kingdom of Saul, Judea under Alexander the Great or the Province of Iudaea under the Roman Empire? It was not a Muslim homeland, it was a province of the Empire—the Roman Empire. The Empire became Christian three hundred years before the birth of blessed Muhammad!" There was momentary silence in the room, and imam paced the room, glaring at his cleric. "Do you want to speak of Jerusalem, or are you as ignorant of that city as you are of Palestine? The city of Jerusalem goes back in history four thousand years before the birth of the Prophet. It was a Jewish city, not a Muslim city."

"But some of our holiest shrines and mosques are there!" the cleric protested.

"Yes, they are," Ramsi exclaimed, clapping his hands in mock glee. "Praise Allah, he sees the light! Tell me, oh wise cleric, can we pray at those mosques and shrines? Yes, yes we can. Can we even pray at the sacred Al-Aksar mosque? Why yes, we can. Yet I ask you, upon what foundations was that mosque built?"

"Upon the Zionist temple of David, which we threw down and destroyed!" the cleric said triumphantly. "Allahu Akbar!"

"Yes, we destroyed it, as we did many Christian churches," the imam lamented. "Take note of our recent history and the outcry of Muslims when the Christian pope visited the Hagia Sophia."

"It was blasphemy to do so!" the cleric interrupted. "We are righteous in our anger! It is proof that the West hates Muslims; why else would they support such a heinous crime and violation of all that is sacred! The West should perish in the flame of righteousness for such transgressions!"

The imam nodded and said, "That is an excellent question, Saman. Why indeed would the West support the pope's visit to the Hagia Sophia, one of the most holy sites in all of Islam? Perhaps he visited it because it was *his* church." Ramsi stepped up to the young cleric and looked him straight in the eye. "The Hagia Sophia was not built as a mosque, but as a glorious church, the Church of the Roman Empire. When Constantinople fell to Suleiman the Great, our clerics ripped out the crosses, the relics, and everything Christian. They made it a mosque."

"It was Allah's will to spread the word by the sword," the cleric replied defiantly.

"So it was, and yet to who?" Ramsi asked. He turned around and spread his arms wide, looking at the survivors of Wolfe's culling. Looking them over, he asked, "To whom did Allah wish to reveal himself—the unbelievers, of course, the ignorant?"

"The Zionists and the Christians," Saman said.

"Why, when we already believed in the same God if not the same Prophet?" he said evenly. "We say there is no God but Allah, but so do Jews and Christians. We are speaking, all of us, about God, Jehovah, Allah—they are one and the same. We are all people of the book, so it is written."

"There is no Prophet but Muhammad!" Saman insisted. "That is the word that must be spread around the globe, by the sword if necessary."

"As it is being spread in Afghanistan and Iraq, where Sunni kills Shia and Shia kills Sunni? Is this the word of God being spread?"

"That is only because the Americans are manipulating the passions of our people with their occupation!" Saman insisted.

"If that is what you truly believe, Saman, then there is no hope for you, or for our people," Ramsi said sadly, turning away from the younger cleric. "We will all end up like these poor, misguided souls lying on my carpet, spilling their hearts out in our mosque. If you do not see the gentle message of God in Muhammad's teachings, then you are blind to all but the sword—so shall you die."

"If that is true, then I will die a glorious martyr," Saman said stonily.

Ramsi turned around. Saman held an AK-47. It was pointing at his chest.

"So you will be a martyr, like the foreigners who took children hostage at our own school? Like the martyrs who tortured and murdered hundreds of children in Russia? You wish to be one of those martyrs?"

"They were soldiers in the jihad!"

"They were cowards!" Ramsi shouted. "Any man who makes war on women or on children is a coward! I don't care whether he is Muslim, Christian, or Jew, he is a coward!" He stepped right up to Saman, and he grabbed the barrel of the AK-47. "If you don't understand even that simple concept, then I have failed as imam. If Allah condones the wanton murder of children, then it is time for me to die as well!" He shoved the muzzle under his own chin, beneath his beard, a wild look in his eyes. Holding it there against Saman's efforts to pull it away, he exhorted his young cleric to pull the trigger. "Go ahead and finish me! Become a hero to your foreign jihadists. Slay the imam who dared call their war on children a war of cowards, and a war of deceivers! Do it! Do it now!"

Saman's eyes grew wild. Sweat popped from his dark brow. His white teeth clenched, and he took a deep breath. Bang! Ramsi jumped, but he felt nothing, no pain, nothing. Saman was still there, and Ramsi still felt the gun barrel under his chin. Saman's expression changed quite suddenly from maniacal to surprised and then to blank. He slid to the floor as if curling up for an impromptu nap, but beneath his head, a pool of dark red blood spread to mix with the other horrific stains on the carpet.

Lieutenant Garner stepped all the way into the room. "It's a good thing for you we got here in time, Padre. You mind telling me what's going on?"

Ramsi tried to ignore the fact that his mosque was filled with dead men and heavily armed infidels, and his story spilled out onto a surprised and increasingly troubled SEAL colonel. As a squad locked down the mosque, Garner was on the phone, running for the choppers. In short order, three Black Hawks were airborne and heading low toward the Sound.

***

Flint came crashing down, but fortunately the stern came rushing up to greet him. He hit hard, face down, with his feet hanging over the edge. Wolfe began to slide backward into the sea. Frantically, he clawed at the deck. It was painted with a rough, textured paint for traction, and that's the only thing that slowed him down, but it wasn't holding him.

The ship heeled to the left, and the steel pole that he'd removed, the one attached to the safety net, slid across the deck and smacked him in the forehead. Wolfe had just enough sense to grab it with one hand and wrap the fingers of his other hand through the stout netting. The ship heeled back the other way, swinging him around to the right and off the deck completely. He was out into space, hanging off the back of the boat over a pair of slashing propellers and a pitching sea.

The movement of the ship tossed him back and forth, but that actually helped. He swung with the rolling ship and got his left boot over the edge of the car deck. Pulling hand over hand on the net, he hauled himself up. He wanted to catch his breath, but there was no time. One crisis was over; now he moved on to the next. Taking the steel post, he set it back in the hole and connected the two halves of the net back together. Next, he attached the yellow safety line. Everything was as it should be—except for the pool of brake fluid on the deck, oh, and the smoke pouring out of the open hatch. As if divine providence approved of the necessity of his acts, it began to rain.

There was one more thing lying on the deck: a large billfold.

Hamdi must have dropped it when he fell. Wolfe snatched it up.

The sleeping couple was awakened by the blast. The man popped out of the car, asking, "What happened; where the hell did you come from?"

Wolfe shrugged and said, "I don't know, it sounds like they blew an engine out or something."

The man ran his hands through his hair, and his expression changed again. "Hey, what happened to the SUV next to us?"

Wolfe looked around innocently. "What SUV?"

"There was an SUV here, a black one, right there!" he said urgently, pointing excitedly to where Wolfe stood. He ducked his head into the car. "Honey, wasn't there a black SUV there?"

She shrugged.

Wolfe shook his head, saying, "One ferry ride blurs into the next for me." Then, for some reason, he glanced up to the aft portion of the observation deck, the part outside the cabin of the ferry. His eyes locked immediately with those of Hamdi. The terrorist was staring at the vacant spot where the Suburban used to sit.

Wolfe smiled and waved.

Hamdi disappeared into the crowd gathering to investigate the explosion.

Wolfe ducked behind the cars and vacated the scene. As everyone rushed aft to see what the commotion was all about, Wolfe made his way through the crowd toward the bow. After a few moments, it was clear the ferry would continue to Fauntleroy and dock, although from the sound of sirens along the shore, the captain had already radioed in for help.

Wolfe took the opportunity to call Orani.

"Do we have any salvage operations in the Company?" he asked cryptically.

"What do we need them for?" she asked.

"There's a Suburban at the bottom of the Sound between the Fauntleroy ferry terminal and Vashon Island. If I remember correctly, it's about four hundred feet deep here."

"We can get the navy to do it if necessary; there's a base in Bremerton. Why, what's so important about the Suburban?"

"It has four jihadists armed to the teeth in it. Listen, I got Hamdi and Khallida on board. It's time to do this. I have an opportunity in the confusion."

"No, Wolfe; we've been over this."

The ship's horn blew, and the captain started the approach to the Fauntleroy ferry dock. Fire trucks and police cars waited on the pier, lights flashing. Frustrated, he opened Hamdi's billfold. Inside was a passport, several thousand dollars in cash, credit cards, and airline tickets to Charles de Gaul, Paris, France. Flint stared at the contents—something wasn't right—Hamdi's passport was red. Weren't most of them blue or green? He took it out and paged through it. There it was. Hamdi was carrying a diplomatic passport.

"Hamdi planned on allowing the jihadists their mayhem and then escape using diplomatic papers—not very sporting. Orani, I think he's on the way to SEATAC trying to get on Air France flight 213, but I've got his fake passport and his tickets."

"How on earth did you get them?"

"He dropped them, but he knows I'm here. At least let me bring him in. We've got an international connection here; isn't that enough reason—I'll keep him alive, I promise!"

There was silence on the other end.

"Well?"

"No," Orani said at last.

"Why not?"

"We want to know who he's going to meet in Paris," she explained. "Remember, Wolfe, we still don't know where he thinks he'll get a hundred nukes."

"Bloody hell," he growled, as the ferry docked. The ramp went down and a team of firefighters rushed on board. Cops flanked them, clearing the people out of the way and directing the passengers off the boat in two orderly rows. Wolfe was near the head of the line, with people all around him. Orani kept talking. "Listen, we know what's going on; they're not going for small stuff, they want to make a big splash—literally. We know how they want to do it; we just don't know how they're going to make it work."

The captain met one of the cops on deck and said, "We need to get these people off; we still don't know what's going on down in the engine room. My chief says it's a mess down there, but nothing catastrophic. Still, we're dead in the water here—probably for the rest of the day." A parking attendant rushed up to the captain.

"Sir, we have a car missing—we think," she said, looking both sheepish and concerned.

"What was that, Orani?" Flint asked. He missed what she said, trying to listen to the captain's conversation. Now he was eager to hear what the parking attendant had to say.

"What the hell are you talking about?" the captain asked.

The cop stopped talking on his radio, his brows rising in surprise.

"Flint, are you listening?" she asked in a very spousal voice.

"Hold on, Orani," he told her, moving out of the way of the people behind who were trying to get off the ferry as fast as they could.

It started to rain harder. It was a miserable, cold, misting rain that permeated everything—in other words, a normal Seattle day.

"Sir, I don't know how to explain it, but we think there's a car missing," the parking attendant said.

"Were the nets broken?"

"No, everything was up and as it should be," she said, adding, "except for a pair of chocks sitting in the middle of the deck by the hatch."

Flint mentally struck his forehead. *I forgot to put them to the side!*

"So there's a pair of chocks sitting on the deck; if the net's still up, nothing could've rolled through—it's designed to hold a truck if it needs to."

"But the guys back there swear there was a black Suburban that was parked right there, only it wasn't there when we docked."

"Then there wasn't a black Suburban there," the captain replied incredulously.

"Flint, are you there? Answer me!"

"Sorry, Orani, they're saying they're missing a car, or they think so," he said, and both the captain and the attendant looked at him.

"Are you sure it was a black Suburban?" the cop asked. "I heard a call from the SWAT team on Vashon saying someone from the school incident might have escaped in a black Suburban. Did you get the plates?"

Wolfe didn't wait any longer; he ducked back into line and hurried off the ferry.

"Alright, sorry, Orani, I got a bunch of things going on at once," he apologized. Then, more emphatically, he said, "I think we need to get this guy now. If he gets to Europe, we'll lose him. We may never see him again until it's too late."

"Wolfe, how are they going to get that many weapons? Remember, they need at least a hundred. We'd know it; the Russians would know it; everyone would know it."

"I think Hamdi knows," Wolfe told her flatly.

"Then he'll lead us to it," she replied quickly. "If they think they can get their hands on that many devices, we need to know about it. Really, think about it. The only way is to crack a nuclear storage depot, and frankly, that's impossible."

Flint had to admit she had a point, but his gut told him something needed to be done. "I still think I should find him and finish this!"

"Wolfe, you've done a good job today," she said forcefully. "Go back home and spend the evening with the kids. I'm on my way. We'll interrogate Jahdam tomorrow, as well as Ramsi. Get packed and ready to go to Paris. You'll be flying the trip in four days. Good-bye."

Wolfe sighed and turned toward the ferry terminal, meaning to buy a passenger ticket and return to the island. He'd almost forgotten that as bad as his day was, his kids had it worse; they needed him. He walked more quickly to the ticket taker, but a hand gripped his shoulder.

Wolfe stopped suddenly. He almost drew his gun, but then he saw it was a cop.

"Sir, can we speak to you for a moment?" he asked. The request left no room for argument. His partner stepped up and put a hand on his holster. In the background, Wolfe saw Hamdi, grinning at him.

"Of course, officer, what can I do for you?" he asked in as pleasant a manner as possible.

"Follow me, please." The officer led him into the terminal building, followed by his partner. They escorted Flint to a corner, and the first officer asked, "Sir, are you alright?"

"Excuse me?"

"Sir, you're bleeding, covered with grease and God knows what else—and we just had an explosion in the ship's engine room. Some of the passengers saw you in that area when the blast occurred."

He daubed at the blood and looked at his fingers. The rain already soaked through the congealed blood. It turned his fingers pink. "I don't know about that," he said, "there's an awful lot of jostling going on getting off the ferry."

"Can I see some ID?"

"Certainly," he replied, reaching for his wallet with the CIA badge. It wasn't in his breast pocket. Had he lost it during his acrobatics, or, then he remembered—he took it out to give Bernie a business card and left it on the seat of the Crossfire. Now all he had was the ID and papers of a terrorist.

"I seem to have misplaced my wallet," he explained, knowing how lame he sounded.

"Actually, we have a complaint that you do have a wallet, one that's not yours." One officer drew his weapon while the other spread him against the wall.

"Officer, I can explain. I work for the government in counterterrorism—" Wolfe began to say.

"So does everybody who gets caught these days, buddy—here we go! Here's the wallet, and whoa! What's this, an auto with a silencer? That's five to ten right there, mister!" He handed those to the second officer and then cuffed Flint with no pretense at being gentle.

"Don't lose those!" Flint said quickly. "Believe me when I say they're important!"

"Right, buddy," the cop said. "It's obvious they're not yours. That'll tack on another couple of years. It's not your day."

Flint was about to retort when Hamdi and Khallida approached the officers.

"Excuse me, sir, but I've got a very important flight to catch, and as you can see, I am a diplomat." He smiled and was very pleasant. "Isn't it unfortunate what people will stoop to, even in your great country?"

"Sorry for the inconvenience, Mr. Hamdi," the officer said. "We don't need these." And he handed Hamdi his billfold and tickets. "We have enough on weapons charges to put this guy away for a long time!"

Hamdi thanked the officer and headed for a black limo. Wolfe ground his teeth in frustration, but there was nothing he could do.

The second officer, an older man, shook his head. "You sure look like you've had yourself a day, I mean, you should really take a look at yourself. Your clothes are covered with blood and tar; your face looks like you've been in a prizefight. Did you think we wouldn't notice? You're just a bit out of place and a lot suspicious—especially today."

"I can explain," Flint said.

"You can explain at the station. We've got a whole bunch of people who'll be just dying to talk to you!"

Flint wavered between being angry and laughing. "Listen, I've got a suspect in custody and I need to get him processed. I'm on your side, but I work for the government."

"Of course you do," the officer smiled. "Where is this suspect, then?"

"I left him with a friend," Flint said weakly.

"You're a laugh a minute."

Flint lowered his voice and said, "I'm Flint Wolfe, CIA. Hamdi is the man I was trailing. He was involved in the school takeover on Vashon."

"Oh, that's rich!" exclaimed the first officer.

"Really, if you'll just call the Company, they'll explain everything!"

"We will, Mr. whoever you are, we will."

"Maybe we should, Tom," said the older officer. "You know how the lieutenant hates surprises."

"Screw it, just read him his Miranda rights," Tom said.

"It'll save you a lot of paperwork," Flint told them, knowing the bureaucracy.

"You have a point there," Tom replied, and he stopped short of the squad car.

"I don't want to spend all night doing paperwork," the older officer said emphatically. "My son's got a ball game. Give me the number, buddy, and I'll call it. But if you're just stonewalling us, so help me I'll put you in a holding cell with a bunch of gang-bangers!"

Unfortunately, the cops stopped Flint exactly where the press gathered to film the stricken ferry. Seeing the cops had a suspect, a dozen cameras turned on him.

"This is just great!" he muttered to himself.

"That's him, that's the murderer!" screamed a shrill voice with an unmistakable Texas twang.

Flint and the officers looked up in surprise to see Dixie C. Dallas hopping up and down in a pink suit and a pink rain slicker and waving a pink umbrella.

"That's him; you've finally arrested him! It's about friggin time!"

"Dixie, give it a rest, will you?" Wolfe asked. This was the final straw.

She got up in his face and said, "No, Wolfe, I'll never rest. You trampled on my pink parade, and I'm going to see you pay for it."

"What are you talking about; what pink parade?"

"Yeah, what are you talking about, miss?" the first officer asked.

"He killed all those people on 9/11!"

Officer Tom blinked in surprise and said, "Ma'am, the Islamic terrorists killed all those people on 9/11."

"No, no, no, they tried to take over my airplane, the one *he* was flying, and he killed them—he murdered them!"

"What the hell is she talking about?" he asked, turning to Flint.

He shrugged. "I was the pilot. I killed the terrorists who tried to take my plane. I saved her life; now she's pissed at me."

"You're kidding."

"Oh, no, I'm not kidding," Dixie assured the officer. "I was on my way to Seattle to be at my son's bar mitzvah and instead of having a plate of cake and ice cream, I get a terrorist's blood and brains in my lap. Now I can't get the image of that split open melon-head out of my mind, and it's all your fault!"

"That's what this is all about?"

"Ma'am, we don't have time for this. If you want to make a statement, just follow us to the station."

"Why don't you save the taxpayers some time and money," she asked, suddenly looking very calm and rational, like she put on a new suit and mask. "Just take him behind the building here and shoot him. I'll pay for the bullet."

"She's a little unbalanced, don't you think?" Flint observed.

"That's the only thing you've said that makes any sense," he replied, and he hustled Wolfe toward the squad car.

"Where are you going?" Dixie flew into a pink fury, waving her umbrella and shaking her finger wildly. "Now you listen to me, flat-foot, I'm the head of the ACLU, so if you don't want to be marking tires the rest of your career, you better damn well listen to me!"

"I think I've heard about enough, ma'am," the older officer replied with a huff.

"Sorry, Dixie, your powers of persuasion seem to be fading," Flint chided, feeding the roaring pink flame. "Maybe you ought to wear a shorter skirt or a plunging neckline."

"Oh, you'd like that, wouldn't you?" she chided. "You're about to have the same problem. They'll love your lily-white ass in the lockup. By morning, you'll be farting bass."

"Go home, ma'am!" he shouted, then shook his head and muttered, "God, her voice just cuts you to the quick—it's worse than one of my wife's conniptions!"

"I'm not through with you; I want your badge number!" Dixie went to block his path up the jetty, but a rush of wind and noise interrupted everything.

CHAPTER 30: Bluff and Double Bluff

A black, unmarked chopper hovered over the pier, scattering the crowd. Dixie's umbrella turned inside out, and her pink Jackie Kennedy hat with the fake pink pearls blew off her head, rolled under the railing, and fell into the Sound.

The SEAL team rappelled out of the chopper to secure the ferry, sprinting through the gaps in the crowd. Flint sighed with relief as the cameras followed the SEALs and forgot about him. Bob Garner appeared out of the black-clad soldiery and ran straight to Flint, followed by two big—really big—SEALs.

The SEALs looked to be in a foul mood. It was probably because they'd missed out on the action. Garner confirmed it, saying tersely, "Goddamn it, Flint, did you save any for us?"

"Sorry, Bob."

"So you did a school, a mosque, and now a ferry?"

Flint nodded.

"Jesus, you're going to put us out of business. How did you carry that much ammo, or does the Company give you those Hollywood guns that never run out?" Garner motioned to Wolfe with his M-16 and told the officers, "Get those cuffs off him, for Christ's sake, didn't he tell you he was one of the good guys?"

"But, Colonel," the officer started to protest.

"Officer," Garner roared, "get those cuffs off now! The guy just saved the lives of about two hundred kids and who knows how many people on this ferry—why do you want to throw him in the clink?"

"Sorry, sir, I didn't know," Officer Tom said, opening the cuffs and handing Wolfe back his weapon.

"Don't worry about it," Flint said, and he patted the officer on the back. "You're going to have your hands full as it is."

"What do you mean?" he asked, and Dixie hit him over the head with the broken umbrella.

"What the hell are you doing? You're letting him go after all the murders he's committed!" she shrieked, and she went after him again. "We've got more than enough lawyers at the ACLU to put you away too."

The officer was more than willing to turn his embarrassment into rage. He grabbed the shaft of the umbrella and yanked it out of her hands. "You can have your commy ACLU comrades bail you out then. You've just won a one-way ticket downtown, lady!"

Each officer grabbed a flailing pink arm, and they dragged Dixie down the docks. At least three cameras followed her and got wonderful shots.

Garner looked on incredulously and said, "So that's who's protecting the rights of terrorists, illegals, and pedophiles. Heaven help us. How do we fight people like that while we're trying to fight a war?"

Flint holstered his weapon and said, "We put them in jail, that's how. Although, I have to tell you, I wouldn't mind having her spunk on our side for a change! Right now, I'll settle for getting back on the island. Is everything shut down?"

"Everything except that pretty baby." Garner smiled, pointing at his chopper. "Come on, let's get you home!"

C. J. doted on everybody that night, like a modern day Mrs. Cleaver. She listened to their stories of the terrorist attack, and then helped Flint put them to bed. Flint gave them each a few sips of wine to soothe them. He hoped to get them through the night without any nightmares. What the wine didn't do, C. J.'s mothering accomplished. Soon, they were sound asleep.

Flint went straight to the liquor cabinet, made himself a martini and C. J. an amaretto, and went out to the hot tub. C. J. joined him. She didn't ask about his second or third martini, and Flint didn't offer any information. When he got up for his fourth, wondering why the alcohol wasn't affecting him in the least, she finally said something.

"I think you've had enough, Wolfy," she said. "I wouldn't want certain parts of you to be down for the count. What if I want to fuck you tonight?"

Flint groaned, "Really, C. J.—"

"I'm serious."

"So am I," he told her, returning with the drink. He climbed into the tub, groaning as he did so. "Today was a bad day. I doubt that I could respond appropriately even if you were serious. In fact, I have to say that for the first time since I've known you, I'm just not in the mood. It's all I can do to keep from shaking."

He held up his glass, watching it narrowly. It trembled. It wasn't bad, but it wasn't steady either. Flint lifted the glass to his lips, but C. J. took it away from him. She set it aside and stood over him, breasts glistening in the light from the house. Normally, it would be an inspiring sight, but tonight, he felt all cold inside.

"You know how I get when I'm told I can't have something," she said, moving over to him like a panther stalking her prey.

C. J. was right. She made Flint forget about the day.

He woke up the next morning and C. J. was gone. What did he expect? Grumpy but satiated, he threw on a robe and went downstairs to make coffee. He got into the kitchen and reached for the coffeemaker, intending on dumping yesterday's java. It was still hot. That didn't register. He stared at the coffeepot. Finally, he took it out and sniffed. It smelled fresh. Still confused, he got a coffee mug. That's when he noticed the bacon.

"You're just in time for breakfast!" C. J. said, taking the mug from him and pouring out a healthy portion of steaming black brew. Before Flint could say anything, he was ushered to the table and served bacon and eggs. He found the sensation comforting. It was a nurturing side to her that he'd never experienced. He liked it.

C. J. agreed to stay until he got back from Paris. Yet, it wasn't exactly a wholesome thing. He thought he'd eat C. J.'s adoration like sweet, sticky candy, but the whole domestic scene of C. J. and kids was so at odds with the quantities of blood he spilled—was that why he felt so detached? Or was it something else? He didn't see the faces of the terrorists. He didn't mourn their deaths, deaths though they were. The faces that stuck in his mind were the teachers and staff at the school, the ones lying wide-eyed and gray with their throats slashed. He knew some of them. One of them went to the Catholic church and taught Faith Formation for his kids. That's not what bothered him. Somehow, Wolfe felt nothing, no grief, no anger, no mourning—nothing.

That wasn't right; it wasn't human. He was losing it.

"I've got to leave when you get back," she said, and just like that, the balloon burst. "It will be almost ten days, and I've got horses. Who'll look after them?"

He sighed and said, "At least let me pay for your gas and food."

"You're not mad?"

"I don't have any right to be mad," he told her, and he was being honest. Then he brought up the other side of the subject, the one he'd rehearsed. "It's fine for you to be popping in and out of my life when it's only me to think about," he told her, looking up at the dark sky because he couldn't look her in the eyes. "The kids have a hard time with it, though. You should take this as a compliment, a huge compliment, but they want you to stay."

"They have a real mom."

"In name only; she doesn't act like a mother—you've filled that void."

"I'm not trying to," she insisted.

"I know, but you did, and you did it naturally and very well. I hate to tell you this, C. J., but you make a great mom."

"I can't stay. I have a life in Idaho," she said defensively.

"That's your choice, and I'll respect that," he told her evenly. He took a deep breath. "Sometime in the near future, you'll have to decide which way to go. I can't offer you an easy life, or a life without worry or responsibility, all I can offer you is love, devotion—"

"Kids, teenagers, terrorists, you being gone all the time, and orgasms," she finished for him. "That's an awful big price to pay for sex. What if you get your dick shot off?"

"I still have the rest of me," he smiled, licking his lips.

"Stop it! I think you just gave me another one!" She stayed silent for a long time, but she finally said, "I'm leaving when you get back."

Flint nodded, but inside he was worried. He was handling it well, almost as if he wanted it that way. He knew why. He was feeling too guilty to allow himself to be happy.

CHAPTER 31: A New Conspiracy

Toy's Topless was an aged, lime-green building under a bridge in the thriving metropolis of Gorst. It was packed inside, filled with sailors, marines, and blue-collar workers having a beer and watching the girls. Flint paid his cover and found a table against the wall and away from the stage. He ordered a beer and waited.

He watched three dances and drank a third of his beer before Hubbard's phone rang.

"Yes?"

"Where are you?"

"I'm in the back."

Click.

A man approached his table. Wolfe pointed the Walther at him through the pocket of his coat.

"Hubbard?"

"You want a beer?"

"No," the man said, sitting next to him. He reached into his coat pocket and put a thick envelope on the table.

Wolfe took it and tucked it in his jacket.

The man got up to leave.

That was it?

The man left out the back.

Wolfe hurried out the front. Hopefully, he could get a license plate number or something. He passed the bouncer and headed out the door.

Waiting in the shadows, he looked around the corner for the next car. He heard a heavy step behind, turned to look, and—bam!

He woke up in a chair. The chair was upholstered, but it was threadbare, like an old, neglected antique. He tried to jump up, but an ample supply of duct tape held him in the chair. Momentarily defeated, he sat back and looked around. The room was like something out of a bad novel. A rickety table held a desk lamp. The shaded bulb pointed at him, so that he could see only what was around him, not what was behind the lamp. What he could see was spare, grimy, and old. The walls were a nondescript gray, but the molding was the same horrid green as the exterior of Toy's.

I must still be at the bar; surely no one else used that paint!

A door opened behind the light. Several pairs of feet entered the room. He heard the beeps of a cell phone. "He's here, sir."

The same gravelly voice from the day before spoke over a speaker. "Good evening, Mr. Wolfe. Do you remember me? We spoke yesterday; you masqueraded as Mr. Hubbard, and I was myself."

"Who would that be?"

"You've been busy over the past few days, very busy indeed."

Wolfe tried to make sense of the situation. He assumed Hubbard had been hired by terrorists—was he wrong. Who were these people? "I assume I've been a nuisance, then, and that's why you tried to have Hubbard kill me."

"You have it backwards, Mr. Wolfe," the voice replied. "You are only now becoming a nuisance, albeit a small one."

He noted the voice didn't deny hiring Hubbard to kill him. "And who are you?"

"Suffice it to say we're part of the international game of politics and economics."

"In other words, you're financing the terrorists."

"Not at all. They don't need our money, regardless. They have as much as they can spend through their family ties in Saudi Arabia, or through our own government grants—misused as they often are."

"I don't understand. What's your interest in me, then? Why am I trussed up in a chair when all I've done is kill a bunch of terrorists?"

"To kill is not enough, Mr. Wolfe," said the voice. "Taking a human life is insignificant. It's the idea behind that life that's important.

You're treading in perilous territory, and your blindness endangers us all. This isn't just Terrorists and Heroes. When you're in this war, there's a lot at stake. Just look at your position."

"I don't follow," Flint said, but he did. This was about money; it was the only thing more important than human life.

"Let me be as plain as I can. There are segments in the legislative and even the executive branches that have an interest in you. You've already made waves on the left-hand side of the aisle by rankling Ms. Dallas and the ACLU."

"You've got to be joking," he retorted.

"She has clout in Washington. That means money. Any time you are the nexus of money matters, you have to watch yourself, and the greater the pot at the end of the government rainbow, the more trouble you can get in."

"You don't strike me as being part of Dixie's crowd."

"You're very perceptive, Mr. Wolfe."

"So what is it you want of me?"

"I simply want to apprise you of your situation. You have the unique ability to control literally billions of dollars of federal money. People have disappeared for less."

"Is that a threat?"

"After yesterday, no one can afford to make idle threats against you, Mr. Wolfe. You don't yet understand your power. All we want, and all I expect, is to make you aware of the broader geo-economic and geo-political implications of your actions. You're an intelligent man. We simply ask that you fight this war of yours intelligently."

"Certainly this war is yours as well," Wolfe said. "If its money you're into, then nothing could be as devastating as a jihadist victory."

"There are opportunities around every door, Mr. Wolfe, but you are right—they must not be allowed to win this war. In the end, they must be exterminated."

"Then we're in agreement."

"On that note, I will say good-bye, Mr. Wolfe. I hope that we have a very profitable non-relationship. You have my apologies for this evening's inconvenience, and please accept Mr. Hubbard's retainer as compensation for your minivan—spies should drive something with a little more pizzazz, don't you think?"

The vanilla envelope fell out of the darkness and onto the table. The light went out.

Wolfe spent the next five minutes getting out of the chair. When he turned the light on, the room was empty but for the chair, the table, and the lamp. He opened the door. Beyond, he saw a shabby hallway and another door. He could hear music through the door. Upon opening it, Flint found himself backstage at Toy's.

"Hey, cutie, you're not supposed to be back here!" a tall, blonde girl told him, planting her gloved hands on her hips and sashaying her way up to him. She winked at him and said, "Now am I going to have to call a bouncer on you or what?"

"I was just leaving." He smiled.

"You're not even going to stay for a dance? I'm up next, you know," she pouted.

Flint took three bills out of the envelope. They turned out to be hundreds. He stuffed them down her top. "Maybe next time."

She took the bills out and gasped. "Jeez, you could've at least copped a feel for this!"

He obediently did so, she giggled, and he left the building and went home.

It was dark when he got to the house. The kids were already asleep, but he could see the light from the living room where C.J. was watching television. She turned and asked, "How was your night spying on people?"

"I got bonked on the head, uncovered the mythical military-industrial complex, and fondled a topless dancer."

"Were her boobs as good as mine?"

"I don't know, she had her top on."

"Then it doesn't count."

Flint checked on the kids and took some Advil for the lump on his head. "I have a few loose ends to tie up," he told C.J. and went to mix himself a drink. He opened the cabinet, but there was nothing there.

"You're going without. I'm not leaving you a lush Flint."

He started to protest, but she raised a finger.

"I'm serious, you go do what it is you have to do, but you do it without alcohol. I'll be right here watching my *Lifetime* movie when you're done. You can ravish me when it's over."

"Yes dear," he sighed and retreated into his office. He tried to put C.J.'s words out of his mind. It was hard, but the wad of money in the envelope helped. It amounted to fifty thousand dollars. They were new bills. What was more interesting was that they were consecutive.

"They were shipped directly from the mint to a financial institution and then given to me," Flint observed, turning on his laptop and logging in. He accessed the Treasury Department Web page and typed in his password. The Web site let him into the interagency pages, and from there, he wormed his way into the confidential informational files. In five minutes, he had what he was looking for.

"There it is, ten million in cash delivered to the Wartham International Bank, New York, last month," he said aloud. Tracing the particular bills through the bank involved busting the bank's protocols. It took his CIA software a full thirty-seven seconds to do it. "The bills come from a hundred and fifty thousand dollar withdrawal from the CEO and chairman of the board himself, Mr. Warren Delaney, for *Miscellaneous Contract Outsourcing*." Wolfe laughed. "Mr. Delaney, you probably make ten million a year, but you still skim 2 percent off the top."

He found a company posting for a stockholders' presentation. Delaney was the speaker. Wolfe played the video. Delaney was a fat, balding, white man of medium height and pasty complexion. His voice was the same that Flint listened to over the speakerphone at Toy's Topless.

"This is getting interesting," he murmured. Then his laptop chimed. He had a Company e-mail. He clicked on the CIA logo and the e-mail popped up.

> Retrieved cell phone microchips from two of the three bombed cars at the school. The call to detonate the bombs came from the number 265-532-6243. We surmise a text was sent to all three numbers simultaneously as a trigger. EOM.

Flint moved the e-mail to his secure electronic folder and returned to Delaney. It was a simple matter to pull up his cell phone transcripts. They were encrypted, of course, but the software from the Company broke through the firewall easily. Flint was interested in Hubbard's number. Did Delaney have personal contact with the Hubbard hit, or did he do it through underlings? Hubbard's number came up three times before the attempted hit, but where did Delaney get Hubbard's number from? He ran a standard Company scan on Delaney's phone records. The scan cross-checked the numbers with every phone book and cell phone database published. The names appeared next to the numbers, and most of them were employees, Delaney's wife, business partners, and, surprisingly, Dixie C. Dallas. There were a number of phone calls between Delaney and Dallas and Hubbard. It was intriguing, if nothing else. One number came up as unlisted. It appeared three times before Hubbard's number was ever called, and immediately after the final time. It looked familiar. In fact, he'd seen it only a moment before: the number that triggered the bombs.

Since it was unlisted, that meant one of two things: it was re-programmed, or it had a government encryption on it. He ran it through the Company's directory, not expecting anything, but almost immediately, a name popped up—Marwan Hamdi.

Things were taking a decidedly nasty turn. It was obvious to Wolfe that Hamdi had contacts in world finance—contacts that had no qualms killing him if necessary.

Flint had one more thing to investigate. He brought up the Company file on Delaney and Wartham. The file was damning. Wartham was simply the financial arm of a giant worldwide conglomerate. Its businesses in the United States ranged from infrastructure to hospital supply to transportation. In just the last month, they'd been awarded $17.3 billion worth of no-bid contracts from the Department of Homeland Security. He went through the list of projects. Every single one of them had to do with disaster preparedness on the East Coast.

Flint spent the rest of the night combing through the RFPs, request for proposals submitted to various corporations and entities for the no-bid contracts. The RFPs led him back to Homeland Security memos and reports that were in turn generated by CIA secret threat assessments that led back to Hamdi.

Wolfe shook his head, realizing just why Hamdi had such pull. Through his jihadist operatives, he'd been tipping off the Company about the attack on the East Coast, generating billions of dollars worth of defense preparation. So what did Hamdi get out of it? He checked Hamdi's bank accounts and, as expected, found nothing there. He hadn't expected Hamdi to be that stupid; Flint didn't keep his *liberated* cash in bank accounts—not under his real name, at least.

He went back to the phone logs of Hamdi and Delaney and cross-checked the calls with wire transfers from the bank—transfers of large sums in even denominations. He found several, and after tracing them, found deposits made into Islamic charities and directly into mosques. Several hundred thousand dollars went into the mosque in New York, and now presumably rested in Wolfe's secret accounts.

It was 4:37 AM by the time Flint put the entire picture together. Hamdi was playing the feds, and the industrialists were playing both sides. The feds paid the industry money through no-bid contracts to defend against a terrorist threat that the industrialists were helping to fund in order to get federal money. It was a perfect circle of greed, and Flint had been warned in no uncertain terms not to get in the way.

He had no doubt that Hamdi requested the hit on him through Hubbard, who'd already been hired by Dixie C. Dallas. When Hubbard's original surveillance operation was blown, Hubbard reported it to Dallas, who complained to Delaney, who, under pressure from Hamdi, upgraded the surveillance to a hit.

It made sense to Wolfe, who was now in everyone's way, but would anyone else listen to him? He didn't dare call Orani and tell her his suspicions. It would have to wait until their next face-to-face meeting.

Flint reached for his cell phone. It was almost 8:00 AM in DC. He might as well get the particulars of his trip to Paris and set up a meeting. His cell phone wasn't on his desk. He checked his pockets. It wasn't there either. It had to be in the rental. Wearily, he got up, tip-toed past a sleeping C.J., and went outside. The night was chilly and wet. He got the cell phone. He'd call Orani—naturally the kids didn't have school—and he'd go to bed.

Yawning, Flint reached for the front door, trying to purge his thoughts of the negativity of the day and night, when the cold steel of a rifle muzzle snapped him back to reality. It nuzzled against the back of his neck like one of his ex-wife's forced kisses.

"Do not move!" said a voice with a Middle Eastern accent. "If you move, you die. If you resist, I will kill your children as well as you!"

"What do you want?" Flint asked, seeing a partial reflection of the gunman in the glass of the door but not enough to identify him. This wasn't a normal terrorist. The muzzle of the gun trembled.

"I want revenge for our martyrs!" the man said.

"Oh yes, you mean the jihadists who would murder innocent children?"

"I will not listen to such raving from you or from Imam Ramsi!" he said, jamming the muzzle painfully into the back of his head. That was it, he was from the mosque.

"So did you kill Ramsi before coming here?"

"No, though he deserved it, I will not kill another Muslim!"

"Your friends didn't think that way! They were willing to kill their own imam without any remorse. That's quite a convenient faith you have there, friend."

"Shut up, pig!"

"I thought Jews were pigs and Christians dogs; you better get your rhetoric straight, Abdul," Wolfe chided.

"Shut up! Get down on your knees! I will humiliate you as you humiliated our martyrs!"

"Go fuck yourself, Abdul, or go fuck your fellow jihadists," Wolfe said, turning around to face the man, and staring down the barrel of an AK-47. The man was one of the clerics at the mosque, stepped back out of reach. This was going to be touchy. "That's what you guys do in your caves, isn't it? You plan how to blow up women and children and then fuck each other up the ass." He took a step toward the cleric. "You saw the pictures of your cowardly friends, didn't you? Did the cocks in their mouths turn you on? I'll bet it did!"

The cleric screamed incoherently and raised the AK to his shoulder, ready to fire. Wolfe leapt to the side into the darkness. The cleric's gun wavered, and he stumbled and fell to the sidewalk. He looked at Wolfe with vacant eyes. A black pool of blood spread beneath his beard.

Orani stepped out of the shadows. She had a 9mm in her hand with a silencer.

"You're getting good at that," Flint said, getting up. "I think he took offense to our little religious discussion, but I hope you didn't!"

Orani looked at him with unblinking eyes, but she didn't say a word. Then she turned and retched into the bushes.

Flint rushed over to her, holding her steady with one hand, and holding her hair back with the other. "I'm glad you're not getting used to this."

She nodded, spitting out the last of her dinner. "Does it get any easier?"

"It does. That's the nasty part of it."

She finished and wiped her eyes, saying, "That was sweet of you to hold my hair back, thank you."

Flint took her inside and guided Orani to a chair. C. J. heard him and came over. When she saw Orani, she ran into the kitchen and fetched a drink. Orani smiled weakly and said, "Sorry to disturb you, C. J., but something's come up. I needed to see Flint. I couldn't take a chance on calling him."

"See what I mean," C. J. said, glancing at Flint. "I don't know if orgasms are worth all this. Especially if you're getting some on the side."

Flint stiffened.

Orani patted C. J.'s arm and said, "Don't worry about that, C. J. We're not going to go there."

"Are you sure?" She planted her fists on her round hips and nodded to the CIA agent. "What if you have to do it for appearance's sake, Wolfy? I mean, how are you going to turn it off? It's not that I blame you; I'd do her if I were you."

Wolfe sighed, unable to deal with it, and went back outside. He still had work to do. He carried the cleric's body into the garage, stuffing his head and torso in one garbage bag and his legs in another. He wrapped the body in duct tape with two bars of pig iron. Then he threw the body into the trunk of the rental car. It was a ten-minute drive to Dockton harbor and after hotwiring a boat, another twenty minutes to the channel southeast of the island. The water was over four hundred feet deep here, and the currents were strong. The body of the cleric disappeared into the inky blackness. Wolfe hurried back.

When he got back in the house, he found the two women sitting and chatting. He felt like he was being set up. "Listen, girls, I'm no good at this. I'm not thinking of doing you both, if that's what you think I'm thinking about."

"Why not?" they said in unison.

Wolfe groaned, taking them seriously, but then C. J. got up and patted him on the cheek. "Not to worry, Wolfy, we've had a nice little talk. We have more in common than just you and orgasms. We both like horses."

"We both like Michael Savage," Orani said.

"Borders, language, culture!" They said together.

"No worries, Wolfy. You two talk business. I'll be in the bedroom waiting for you. I can't let you go to Paris without a proper send-off!" She giggled. "Hopefully that'll hold you until you get back."

She gave him a squeeze and waved goodnight to Orani.

"So, how did the meeting go?" Orani asked.

"You knew about that?" Flint said, popping three Advil. "That well?"

"Apparently, before yesterday's events, it was cost-effective to kill me, but now I'd cause too much consternation. I passed their dollar threshold. So, they let me go." He slumped into a chair, desperately wanting a drink but remembering his promise to C.J. He told her the story.

When he finished, she shook her head. "I was afraid of this. I have no idea who these people are, Wolfe, but you're going to have to be careful," she said, getting her laptop. She opened it up and logged on. "You're right, they're one the chief financiers for the jihad in the United States. We've got most of the overseas channels covered, but we haven't spent a lot of effort on U.S. companies; it didn't seem plausible." She pointed out the various charitable organization, Arabic companies, fronts, and royal families funneling millions of dollars in cash into the jihad. There were no American or European interests whatsoever. "They're not the sole source of income for these terrorist organizations, but they're supporting them enough to be considered viable threats."

Wolfe nodded and said, "Delaney insinuated they had a great deal of money at stake. They didn't want the jihad to succeed, but they didn't want to interfere with it either."

"Of course not. War is money." Orani sighed. "There are billions of dollars being spent on security, response, rebuilding, and planning. They don't want the jihad to succeed, but a few attacks here, a few attacks there and they keep rolling in the dough."

"But why am I all of a sudden too important to eliminate?"

"Government spending is through government contracts, Wolfe," she told him pointedly. "If you were assassinated after what happened yesterday, there would be an inquiry, no doubt about it. If that inquiry highlighted certain corporations in the military industrial complex, those contracts worth billions of dollars would evaporate—even if there was no proof." Orani went to the fridge and poured herself some juice. Wolfe shook his head when she offered him some. She came back to the table and after a moment of digging through files, she said, "Oh, and speaking of money, the money Delaney paid Hubbard, do you still have it?"

Wolfe gathered it up and gave her the envelope.

"I'll have the lab look it over and catalog it—in case we need it to nail Delaney."

"Bye, bye," Flint sighed. "I don't suppose we can charge him for blowing up my car?"

"Sorry," Orani smiled. Seeing his rather put-out expression, she explained, "It's evidence, but don't worry. Tomorrow, you'll have it all in your expense account. We just want the actual bills."

"I have an expense account?"

"Yes, you do. We don't expect you to do what you do without some financial safety net," she told him, taking out a cigarette. "Can I smoke in here?"

"Sure, C. J. does."

Orani lit a cigarette. "You'll get a deposit for each assignment, less taxes, of course."

"Of course."

"If you make a deposit, it is assumed to come from the assignment," she added. "For instance, if you deposited the cash you found in al-Bashri's office, the Company would automatically take the taxes out—the rest is your working account and eventually your pension. Check the Web site when you log in next time. Buy yourself a car, maybe a couple of them; after all, you don't want to leave the family car at the airport. I'd keep a family car and a dedicated spy car. And Wolfe, don't get a minivan."

He simply growled at her.

Orani got up. "I'll sleep in your study. Don't worry, Flint; I won't get in the way of you and C. J." She looked at him from under long lashes. "Our little thing in DC was—"

"Business, I know," Flint said quickly. "You were trying to teach me not to get emotionally involved through sex. I suppose that's just in case I have to bang someone before I blow her head off!" His voice betrayed his, what? Was he angry, irritated, guilty—all the above?

It didn't escape Orani, but she shook her head. "No, that's not what I was about to say, Flint." She looked at him for a long moment before continuing, but when she did, she betrayed some small hint of wistfulness and maybe even a tinge of regret. "You're never going to be an assassin in the true sense of the word, Flint. We can't send you to knock off some pretty young mother of two because she saw a senator strangle his mistress. You feel too much."

"I'm so sorry to disappoint you!"

"I would have been disappointed if you had that sense of detachment," she said. "You don't, but you are a warrior with a conscience. We have to be careful about how we use you. Even there, I'm sorry the Company needed to use you, Wolfe. You were right. You've fought your war, and you should be here raising your wonderful kids."

"What does this have to do with—" he started.

"Sex?" she smiled, and laughed. "Sorry, I owe you an apology. That had a professional side. I mean, you were all pent up with years of celibacy, and so was I. I needed the release as much as you did."

"How on earth does a woman like you go for five years, Orani?"

"It's a character flaw; in that respect, I'm much like you, Flint."

Flint had to say something. "Listen, Yasmina, I need to tell you something. DC wasn't all business to me." He paused. "C. J. and I had experimented, but we hadn't consummated."

"Flint, you don't have to tell me any of this."

"I do, because I didn't just do you to add another notch to my gun," he told her. "C. J. ran back to Idaho, scared to death that she enjoyed what we had, scared of commitment. I thought we were done. I want you to know that DC wasn't about getting back at her or being on the rebound—I want you to know it was because you're an incredibly beautiful woman." She stopped him, putting a finger to his lips.

"You really are amazing, Flint," she said, looking off into the darkness. He couldn't tell whether she was relieved, hurt, or felt nothing at all. Her mask was back on. "You don't have anything to apologize for, unless you need to go to confession. I knew about it. C. J. called me. We've become," she hesitated, "confidants in a way. We have a lot in common, actually, but one of those things is you, Flint Wolfe. We both have a stake in seeing you come out of this war alive." She stretched and said, "Sorry, I don't have the energy to do you tonight, and I know you don't feel comfortable doing two women at the same time, strange though that sounds for a guy." She patted him on the head. "You don't have to worry about having sex with me, that is, of course, unless we have to do it for appearances. In that case, as a professional, I'm going to require that you give it your all—just like in DC."

Flint sighed as Orani disappeared into the study. He took her glass into the kitchen, noticing Orani left her phone on the counter. Someone was calling her. The screen flashed with the number, and he couldn't help but read it. It struck him that somehow he'd seen it before. Shaking his head, he picked it up and took it to the study. He knocked on the door.

She opened the door. "Change your mind?" she said as she accepted the phone and flipped it open.

A man's muffled voice said hello, and Orani's entire demeanor changed. Her calm exterior evaporated into one of shock and, Wolfe couldn't help but think, fear. Orani looked at him and said quickly, "I can't talk. I'll call you back."

Orani literally slammed the door in his face.

Wolfe wondered whether to let it go and almost convinced himself that was indeed what he should do. "What do I care if she has a boyfriend or husband?" Finally, though, he gave into his gut and opened his laptop. He'd done extensive searches in the past tracking down phone numbers, and the Company software automatically cataloged and cross-referenced everything he'd done previously. In this case, the simple memory tricks the Company taught him came in handy. He entered the number he saw on Orani's phone.

The number came up with several entries. That same number had triggered the car bombs at the school. It had also called his phone. The number was for one Marwan Hamdi.

***

Hamdi stood outside his father's home silently. He didn't move for quite some time, but his face twisted constantly as if with some inner conflict. At length, he shook his head and turned to a younger man who stood patiently behind him. "As a dutiful son I must give him one more chance. Wait until I come out."

The younger man nodded and stepped back out of sight. Hamdi knocked on the door and after a moment his father opened it.

"My son, happy am I to see you!" the elder Hamdi said, hugging his son close. "This is a surprise. Why didn't you tell me you were coming?"

"Sorry, Father, I've been busy," Hamdi said, following his father into the house. Lufti heard him and rushed into his arms. She helped her grandfather set the table for dinner and afterward served them tea. Then she went to play in her room as father and son retired to the elder Hamdi's study.

The elder Hamdi closed the door. "So, you've been busy," he said, sitting in his upholstered chair, lighting his pipe. "I hope you've been putting your education to good use. It cost me twenty years of my life, you know. Where are you working?"

"There are more important things than money, Father," Hamdi said evenly.

The elder Hamdi scowled, his dark eyes disappearing under his bushy white brows. "Yes, there are," he said sternly, "like being a professional, raising a family, and carrying on the family name."

"I aspire to a higher calling, Father."

"What calling? You're not going into the clergy, are you?"

"No, Father."

"Then what is it?" the elder Hamdi asked, sipping his tea noisily and staring at the carpet, obviously perplexed and frustrated. "What on Earth could be more important than an honorable profession, a family, and your name?"

"I do not aspire to earthly pleasures or pride, but to heaven and Allah's will."

"Doesn't everybody?" His father got up and paced the small room. He was a tall, wiry man whose agitation made him seem to jump instead of walk. "You have responsibilities here on Earth, regardless of what awaits us in heaven—what about those? What about your debt to me as my son? I didn't labor so long and so hard to have my son become a ne'er-do-well—or worse. What have you done with this precious education you begged for, and I paid for?"

"It is going to serve Allah."

"Leave that aside. We both know everything goes to serve Allah in its own time, but that is no excuse for sloth!"

Hamdi stirred uncomfortably in his chair. His guilt tempered the flash of anger he felt at his father's ignorance. He had always told his father he wanted to become an engineer and to build things for this brave new world. It was an exciting prospect in his youth, before he found out how transparent all earthly things were. His father indulged him, working a second job in order to pay for college. Now, when it came time to make good, he couldn't do it. Surely, his father could understand his priorities.

"Father, I would fulfill your wishes, but you know as well as I that the jihad calls all able-bodied men—especially those educated in the West."

"What jihad?" his father snapped in obvious anger. "You're not listening to those worthless hate-mongers, those unrealistic zealots who only speak out because they have nothing to offer? You already have enough blood on your hands, Marwan; don't tell me you're compounding your sins by listening to those idiots."

"They are not idiots, Father," Hamdi said firmly. "If we are to fulfill Allah's will—"

"Allah's will?" the elder interrupted. "You are thirty-six years old. Who are you to tell me what Allah's will is?"

"But the imam, Bin Laden, and many other great men have tasked us as Muslims—"

"They tap into that ignorance you so easily wear as a hat!" his father snapped, running his hands through his sparse white hair. "What has Bin Laden taught people about Islam? Death, that what he's taught us; nothing but death! Well, I, for one, refuse to ascribe to that!"

"But the infidels are in the holy land! Can we as true Muslims allow this?"

The elder Hamdi glanced at him with piercing eyes and said, "Christians and Jews called those same lands holy long before blessed Mohammad walked them."

Hamdi fell silent.

His father walked over and put a hand on his shoulder.

"My son, there are seven billion people on this earth. Of those seven billion, six in seven are not Muslim. Do you really think that Allah the merciful would wish that they either convert or be slaughtered? That is an insane notion!" He turned away and walked to the small fireplace. "Your ideas make me cold," he said, and he built a fire.

"You didn't rejoice when the martyrs took down the towers?"

"I once worked in those towers!" The elder sighed.

"Yes, where the capitalists took advantage of you!"

"Where I earned an honest living in an honest profession!" his father replied angrily, banging the iron poker against the brick hearth. He got up and pointed the poker at Hamdi. "You of all people should appreciate the opportunity I had here—it paid for your education. Do you know what you'd be right now if we hadn't come here? You'd be growing poppies for a drug lord!"

"I'd be a martyr!" Hamdi retorted. "Don't you understand? We are in jihad! We are called to martyrdom; we are called to war! The world of the infidel must perish by the sword, in flame, so that Allah's glory may spread throughout the world!"

"So these deceivers tell you, spouting their endless lies!" his father spat, shaking the poker in anger. "They preach nothing but death—death and lies!"

"What about the slain children of Iraq and Palestine; they brought death when they invaded our lands!"

"And what have we done when we invaded theirs? Can you answer me that? We destroyed their churches and synagogues. We told them to convert or die! How much better are we than them? We're not any better, and that's the truth of the matter. We're all men, every one of us, and the greatest truth is that we have to all learn to live together!"

"We cannot live with the infidel," Hamdi said with finality.

"You owe your life to the civilization created by those you call infidels, my son. Your culture could give you nothing."

"I care nothing for their civilization; I see it for what it is—a house of straw ready to be set aflame." Hamdi stood up stiffly and approached his father.

His father met him, his eyes bright with emotion, and said, "Let me ask you a question before you leave in a cloud of self-righteous anger. Why do you hate them so? What have they ever done to you?"

"They've trodden upon our people."

"So has every culture in the history of the civilized world. The strong tread on the weak."

"They've killed our women and children. They are doing so even as we speak—you can't deny that."

"A few yes, but those who do so are imprisoned and dishonored; yet have we not done that to ourselves? Who bombs the markets in Baghdad? Who executed women and children in Afghanistan during the reign of the Taliban? I will not say Christians and Jews do not commit crimes against Muslims, but we commit many more against ourselves—too many for us to complain about another."

"I can't believe you would question the moral fiber of our people, that you would value the infidel over the Muslim!" Hamdi said, shaking with mounting rage. His father turned and shrugged his shoulders.

"I don't; of course, all I'm saying is that they're people too, and subject to the same mistakes that we are." He sat heavily in his chair, as if his spry, thin frame weighed as much as a man four times his size. "I do say, however, that before we find fault with another culture, we would do well to address our own. If we can't live by the same rules we expect of other people, then no one has any reason to listen to our complaints."

"It's that kind of attitude that will cost us our culture and all of Islam with it!" Hamdi retorted, feeling flush with anger in the face of his father's practical logic. "You are blind, Father—blind! All of Islam is at risk. They seek to destroy it; they seek to wipe us off the face of the Earth!"

His father turned up his hands, as if giving up, but he sighed and said, "If they wanted us all dead, they could do it tomorrow. They have the bomb and we don't. I wonder," and he cocked his head as if an unpleasant thought just occurred to him, "I wonder if we would do the same if the situation were reversed. What do you think?"

"They need our oil."

"They can drill through glass to get our oil."

"You're very clever, Father, but I've heard the same words from their assassins. It is a fool's argument and an unholy thought."

"What happened to the energetic young man who wanted to better the world? With your mind, you could make a great contribution to people all over the world, and yet from what I hear, you would rather be an executioner than a savior. Where did you lose your innocence, son?"

"In reality," Hamdi told him. He sighed and reached into his pocket, withdrawing a photograph. He handed it to his father. "I have tried to speak to you as a man, and as a Muslim. I can reach neither. I'm sorry." He went to the door and opened it. Three men and a woman in a burkha walked in. He told the woman, "My daughter is in her bedroom. Take her out through the back door."

"What are you doing?" the elder Hamdi asked, and then he looked at the picture. It was of Orani. He turned white.

"You answer my question without saying anything," Hamdi said. "So you've known all this time that Yasmina was still alive and you never told me. I'm disappointed, Father. Still, I will not raise my hand against you. However, these gentlemen are under no such constraints. Good-bye, Father. Sleep well in hell!"

"You will not find reality in the people you're listening to!" his father exclaimed. "Leave Lufti out of this! She doesn't deserve—" His voice was cut off by a heavy blow. Marwan closed the door.

"Good-bye, Father," he said. "Good-bye to you, and your world!"

CHAPTER 32: Paris

"Meet me at Buffalo Bill's after you land—alone," the e-mail read. Wolfe deleted the e-mail. They assigned him the San Francisco-Paris trip at the last minute, just as Orani promised. The flight was uneventful, but that simply meant all he could think about was the connection between Orani and Hamdi. He tried to find out about it on his own with no luck, and he hesitated to bring it up with anyone in the Company. He owed her something—he didn't know what, but he owed her.

They landed at Charles de Gaulle on a hazy day and somehow navigated the labyrinth of taxiways to the gate—it was the toughest part of the trip. The passengers deplaned and Wolfe hauled his roll-aboard and the forty-pound flight case down the stairs to the ramp where a bus waited for them. After the bus navigated the Parisian traffic and deposited them at the hotel, he showered, changed, and headed to Buffalo Bill's.

Buffalo Bill's was a western-style restaurant and bar in the heart of Paris. It was convenient, being across the roundabout from the hotel. As with most Parisian restaurants, it had plenty of sidewalk seating, which was perfect for a clandestine meeting; the hubbub of the Parisian street would make even the loudest, most animated discussion as secret as if they held it in a vault.

It was no problem to go off alone. Wolfe's crew went out to eat at Sergeant Recruiter's, a favorite hangout on Rue Saint Louis for dinner.

He begged off, using fatigue as an excuse. Wolfe found Orani waiting for him at a little table surrounded by chattering people. She looked like she hadn't slept in a week.

"Are you alright?"

"I'm fine, Wolfe, how was the flight?" Orani asked, flashing him a very strained smile and sitting back down to her tea. She didn't order a drink, but she'd ordered a Guinness for Wolfe when she saw him exit the hotel. The French waitress, a tall, busty brunette, flashed a set of European health care teeth in her smile, set down the Guinness, and winked at Wolfe. Although he was at least twenty years her senior, she flashed him a sassy smile before traipsing off through the crowd.

"How do you manage it?" Orani asked.

"Manage what?" Wolfe said flatly, sitting down and placing his black knapsack next to the matching black knapsack Orani brought.

Orani took a long drag from her cigarette.

Wolfe lit a cigar.

They sat there.

Wolfe ordered a burger. Orani ordered a salad.

"So do we know where he is?" Wolfe said at last.

"We know he's here," she said, and she flagged down the waitress. She ordered a bottle of wine.

"You're nervous. What's up, Orani?"

"Isn't a hundred nukes enough to make you nervous, Wolfe?"

"There isn't anything else you want to tell me?"

"Like what?" Her eyes flashed, and her voice was testy.

He shook his head and blew the cigar smoke through his lips in a long, thin stream. "It seems to me you've been chasing Hamdi a long time. You probably know him better than anyone. Do you have any insight as to his next move?"

"He's here in Paris to incite the Muslim community and solidify Al-Qaeda operations here, but that's really just a secondary tasking." Her voice was tightly controlled. Something was bothering her. Did she know he was onto her connection with Hamdi?

Orani took out her PDA, scrolled about, and punched a few keys. "I just sent the file to your PDA. You know the pastry shop to the right of the hotel?"

"Yes, I get my coffee and croissants there—a very cute blonde works there. She's the daughter of the owner."

"And you prefer blondes?"

"I prefer beautiful women, as you well know—can we change the subject?"

"While we're no closer to finding out where Hamdi and Khallida will get the nukes, there's something here they need. We think we know who it is."

"Let me guess—someone to make things go boom!"

"You know it won't be easy," Orani said, and a flash of concern showed in her dark eyes. "These people are like rats; they keep to themselves in deep, dark holes. You only see them once in a while at specific places—unfortunately, those places are sometimes public and therefore problematic. What we're interested in is the presence of a Syrian bomb maker, Isa Fawahdi. He is a computer guy whose specialty is codebreaking. We figure that even if Hamdi gets the nukes, he can't arm them. That's why he needs this man. Take him out of the picture and we slow them down for months."

"And Hamdi and Khallida?"

Orani sighed and admitted, "We're hoping the hit causes some chaos in their organization and highlights them. If this man disappears they'll be scrambling to replace him. That should expose them. Right now, we've no clue where they are, and we need to know."

"Is there anything else anything at all I should know about Yasmina?"

She hesitated but said no.

"You're sure?"

"Why do you ask?"

"You have my back," he reminded her.

She shook her head. The food arrived. The waitress set his plate down, brushing his shoulder with her breast as she did so.

"I love Paris," Wolfe said after she left.

Orani just shook her head and said, "Make sure you leave it the way you found it, on schedule, in one piece, and with the job done."

Wolfe didn't like the tone in her voice, and he realized that she didn't enjoy it either. He wolfed down his burger and paid the bill. He got up to leave but Orani's voice stopped him. He turned, and she stepped up to him, taking his arm. Was she going to tell him? Instead, she kissed him on the cheek and said, "We just had dinner together; you can't just leave. Now kiss me back, and good luck."

He did as he was told, but he wasn't happy, not at all.

Once in his room, he plugged his phone into his laptop and studied the file. What he saw brought a scowl on his face. Two men, a pastry shop, in the morning rush hour, in public. To make matters worse, the file noted that Fawahdi was always accompanied by a bodyguard.

He checked the knapsack he swapped with Orani. There was nothing special. A Walther with a silencer—short range, two clips, a knife, and several small charges of C-4 with detonators and a remote.

The phone rang. He put on his earpiece, noting it was from home.

"'ello, luv. I thought we broke up?"

"'ello, luv," C. J. said, and then she corrected him. "We did break up, but that was two days ago. You know I can't last that long without you. How is Paris today?"

"It stinks as usual."

"What are you doing?"

"Oh, just going over some work," he said, scrolling through the photos and maps supplied by Orani. "I had a beer and a burger with someone from the crew at Bill's, but now it's back to work."

"It wasn't a flight attendant, was it?"

"No, it wasn't a flight attendant, but I imagine your boy wishes it was," he said, meaning her boyfriend/housemate/person she had an "understanding" with. "I'm still confused as to why you should care, C. J. After all, you're in Idaho, on a farm with your horses, in a lovely eight-hundred-square-foot hovel, with no job and no responsibility. What more could you want?"

"Orgasms," she said flatly.

"I can see where this is going; isn't he home?"

"He's out back fixing the fence."

"There, but for the grace of God, go I."

"Hey, I gotta go, he's coming back in. I love you; I want to fuck you!"

Click.

Flint shook his head. It was much easier for him to sneak around

275

the world and take people's lives than it was to sneak around behind another man's back with his woman—even if she wasn't really his woman. *I mean, what the hell was an* understanding *anyway, but a way out?*

Wolfe stayed up later than usual that night, but he was up at 5:30 AM, and by 6:00 AM, he was at the pastry shop. He lounged about on the sidewalk, having a morning cigar. At 6:37 AM, a motorcycle turned the corner with two men on board. He put out his cigar and headed into the shop. Wolfe looked at the pastries in the cases, waiting for the men. The blonde with the cute, mousy face and blue eyes was still behind the counter, and she glanced at him.

"Looking for something different today, *monsieur?*"

"I can never make up my mind," he sighed.

"Then I'll get the usual for you!" she laughed.

She picked out two rolls with sugar crystals and a baguette of bread, and fetched a cup of coffee. As she handed him the bag of pastries, the motorcycle parked right outside the shop door.

"*Merde!*" she whispered, looking in that direction.

The two men got off the motorcycle, and Wolfe glanced their way—they were his marks. They wore Western clothes with red-checkered scarves and beards, and the big one had a surly attitude. Fawahdi was a small, thin man. He followed his bodyguard, who loudly cut past the other customers to the front of the line. Wolfe stepped in front of them, blocking the way, a five-frank note in his hand.

The bodyguard apparently took offense. He poked Wolfe in the shoulder and uttered something loudly in French.

"Sorry, I'm an American," he said with a smile. "American," he repeated loudly for emphasis, "*Je ne comprend pas!*"

The expression on his face changed to one of surprise and hatred. "American!" he said, and then he spat in Wolfe's coffee.

The girl behind the counter gasped in surprise, and the French patrons, who were shying away from the confrontational men, muttered and cursed at rude behavior, even by their standards.

Wolfe simply smiled and tossed the steaming coffee in the bodyguard's face.

The jihadist screamed in pain and anger and, cursing, he swung at Wolfe.

Wolfe easily stepped aside the punch and struck him across the jaw. The bodyguard fell into the glass counter, breaking the glass and falling into the pastries. Fawahdi reached into his jacket and pulled out a gun.

How convenient, Wolfe thought, as the patrons and employees screamed. He caught the gun hand with his left hand and pulled the smaller man sharply toward him. As Fawahdi stumbled forward, Wolfe smashed his elbow into his jaw. It gave way with an audible crunch! Fawahdi dropped the gun and fell to the floor.

The blonde girl screamed.

Wolfe scooped up the gun.

The bodyguard staggered out of the broken display case and drew his gun. Wolfe shot twice. The bodyguard stopped as if he hit a wall, knees shaking and mouth hanging open. Blood dribbled from his mouth, and he collapsed back into the shattered glass and pastries.

The shrill call of a gendarme's whistle came from down the block. He knelt next to Fawahdi, acting concerned. The jihadist was shaking uncontrollably. He clutched at Wolfe's jacket, but Wolfe took the opportunity to transfer one of his blocks of C-4 and a detonator to Fawahdi's pocket. He put the remote in his hand.

The whistle was closer, and a gendarme appeared at the door.

Wolfe leapt up, yelling, "Everybody out! Everybody out; there's a bomb! Bomb!"

Everyone understood and bolted for the door. The clerk was screaming, still behind the counter. Wolfe reached over the counter and grabbed her, lifting her over and carrying her outside. The gendarme was waving everyone away from the shop. Wolfe headed toward him. He put the girl down next to the gendarme, and after taking one last look to ensure everyone was clear, he pressed the switch of his other remote.

The shop blew up.

Chaos erupted, but after a few minutes the gendarme asked what had happened.

Wolfe turned to the cute clerk.

She started yelling at the gendarme, telling him about the two men who came to kill her patrons. Forty-five minutes later, Wolfe was sipping coffee at the police station. They allowed him to make a phone call to Orani at the consulate, and it appeared everything was going according to plan. The gendarmes and detectives were polite but thorough. They questioned him three times.

He told the same story each time. No, he didn't know either man. He'd just gone in to get his pastries, bread, and coffee—as he did every time he flew to Paris. After all, the clerk was extremely cute. The gendarmes nodded approvingly. The Arabs started the altercation. One pulled a gun. Then the other pulled a gun. He defended himself and the patrons of the shop; that was it.

They seemed satisfied that it was nothing but self-defense. In fact, after the explosion, they were convinced that Wolfe had saved Paris from a cruel act of terrorism.

Two men in suits joined the gendarmes. They introduced themselves as Jean Brueget and Gerard Pardeau from INTERPOL. Brueget was a tall, lanky man with a pronounced Gallic nose, baggy eyes, and short, cropped hair. He looked like he could be very unpleasant if he wanted to, but at the moment, he had a genuine smile on his face. He offered Wolfe a cigarette but warned, "They are strong enough to peel paint, and I don't use filters."

"Sure, I could use one," Wolfe said. Brueget lit it for him.

"You've earned it. I've been tracking Fawahdi for some time. I have to admit I'm surprised that a terrorist of his standing would think so much of a pastry shop. It is indeed a strange stroke of fortune for us that he met his demise in so convenient a manner. We should compare notes, *Monsieur* Wolfe."

"I don't know what I have to offer; I'm just an airline pilot."

"You are too modest," he laughed, taking a thick drag from his cigarette. He leaned forward and lowered his voice, saying, "You're *Monsieur* Flint Wolfe, who foiled the terrorist murder attempt on your aircraft on 9/11?"

Wolfe touched the thin, white scar running down his face and under his jaw. "I didn't get this souvenir flying dissidents to Cuba."

"Not all Europeans are so blind, *Monsieur* Wolfe," Brueget said. "After all, we have our own problems with radicals—as you can see. You apparently interrupted a nefarious terrorist attack, but I think there's more to it than that."

"How so?"

"I think it was an assassination attempt, Mr. Wolfe," Brueget told him firmly. He poked him in the shoulder. "I think they were after you, not the *patisserie!*"

Wolfe rubbed his temples, saying, "I do have a fatwa on my head, but who'd have thought I'd have to worry about it in Paris during the morning rush hour?"

"Ah, but that was the point," Brueget said. "They were clever, these assassins. They brought a small amount of plastic explosive and created a confrontation with you. They had every opportunity to secrete the explosive on your person or in the shop. It was obviously their intent to detonate it after leaving, thereby killing you and any innocent people nearby. Your aggressive manner must have infuriated them, and things got out of hand."

At that moment, a tall, heavy man with a razor thin mustache sauntered into the room, followed by two other men. He looked around the room, and when he saw Wolfe, his swarthy Mediterranean tan turned almost red. Striding angrily up to Wolfe, he began shouting in rapid-fire French.

"Speaking of radicals, meet our chief prosecutor, *Monsieur* Foncke!" Brueget sneered.

This seemed to incense the man further. He shook his fists wildly and raised his voice even higher. The other two men were of Middle Eastern ancestry. One was taking his picture while the other, a tall, good-looking fellow in an expensive cream-colored suit, was on his cell phone talking in Arabic.

Wolfe caught the words, "We have him. Let Hamdi know. No, they don't have him in jail yet—we're working on it."

Brueget shook his head and leaned down to Wolfe while his partner started arguing with the prosecutor.

"This is what you would call our district attorney; he wants to know why you aren't in handcuffs."

The hubbub attracted the attention of the chief of police, who immediately joined the fray. The circus would be amusing if it weren't so loud. The Middle Eastern man was still on his cell phone, and he wasn't concerned with what he was saying—obviously, he didn't expect any infidels to understand Arabic.

"What do you want with me?" Wolfe asked the prosecutor in English.

The interjection infuriated the man even more. He turned beet red and planted himself directly in front of Wolfe, shaking his finger at him. Wolfe took the man's belligerent stance as an excuse for standing up. As the district attorney advanced, he took a step to the side—closer to the Arab on the phone.

The Arab glanced at him with black, soulless eyes, curling his lip in apparent disgust. "Yes, I'm standing right next to the infidel," he said. "He's in—" something Wolfe couldn't catch, "Send someone big. Hajji was a wrestler; he can—"

"*Monsieur* Foncke wants you arrested for murder," Brueget told Wolfe, and then he turned on the prosecutor and said something angrily in French. As if to add poignancy to his irritation, Brueget grabbed the cameraman's camera and shoved it away. Complaining to Wolfe, he said, "Right now, the plight of our Arabic population gets the most press, so here he is with journalists from their jihadist rag in tow! *Mon Dieu*, you would think we were in Saudi Arabia and not in the heart of civilization and Paris!"

"Why does he want to charge me with murder? They're the ones who were armed!" Wolfe exclaimed.

"I know; I agree, it is madness! It is perfectly obvious: you were the target of an assassination attempt in the heart of our city, but they want to charge you with murder for defending yourself," Brueget said fervently. He thumped the prosecutor on the chest with the flat of his hand and shouted in English, "You are letting the terrorists run things because that's where the news is; that's where the money is!"

The prosecutor turned red, but instead of retorting, he turned to his assistant, who nodded. He pulled a sheaf of papers out of his breast pocket and handed them to the prosecutor. The prosecutor took them and slapped them on the chest of the chief of police.

The chief took them angrily and looked them over. He glanced at Wolfe and shrugged. "*C'est la guerre*," he sighed, and told Wolfe, "I am sorry. You are to be kept for the night and arraigned tomorrow morning. The chief prosecutor is charging you with two counts of murder."

Two gendarmes who'd followed the prosecutor flanked Wolfe.

"In other words, the terrorists win," Wolfe growled. "Western civilization as we know it is over."

"Do not lose heart, *Monsieur* Wolfe," the chief of police said. "Every witness corroborates your story. Every piece of evidence does as well. These terrorists had motive, means, and opportunity. By morning, I guarantee, you will be released; you have my word." The chief himself put Wolfe into handcuffs. He leaned close to him and muttered in his ear, "Even if you had shot those men in cold blood, you'd have done the French nation a favor; who knows what their bombing spree would have hit, schools, restaurants, Notre Dame—these devils have no conscience or morality."

The cuffs were cold on his skin, and despite all of his training and experience, Wolfe had to fight the sudden rush of adrenaline and the sense of fright that came when bound. He'd never gotten used to it.

Wolfe glanced at the Arab reporter. The devil was grinning.

The chief slapped him on the shoulder. "Get some rest and try not to worry. We'll have you out in a few hours and you can fly your airplane back home."

"I hate to miss my glass of wine by Notre Dame," Wolfe quipped. "Seven o'clock every evening in the summer—I'm a creature of habit."

"We'll make it happen," the chief said, and two gendarmes led him away.

They took him to an elevator, a cramped, dingy thing that rattled and squealed; it took an interminably long time to get where it was going.

"You're taking me to the deepest, darkest dungeon in all of France, I suppose—not the Chateau D'If, I hope?"

The gendarmes said nothing.

A cold chill crept up Wolfe's spine. His breast trembled with an electric flutter. He'd lost control of the situation, and he knew it.

The door opened.

They ushered him through a stained green corridor illuminated by naked bulbs. At the end was a barred door. A gendarme sat at a desk in a small office. He opened the barred door. His escorts signed him in on a clipboard, and the gendarme pushed a button. The steel door on the far side of the office buzzed—an irritating and final sound that grated against his nerves. They pushed him through.

Wolfe was in a darkened corridor. The walls were the same sickly green, but the wan yellow light was even worse, hiding the stains, dirt, and wear. Rows of cells about ten feet by ten feet square stood on either side separated by chipped, green cinderblock walls. The back walls were stone and looked to be the foundation of the building.

A few prisoners sulked in the first cells, looking like caricatures of forgotten souls, eyes sunken, unshaven, pallid gray skin against the corpse-colored walls. They took him to the end of the corridor—out of sight of the others. One of the gendarmes called out a number in French.

"*Tres!*"

Thirteen? Yes, that was the number on the placard above the cell. The electric buzzer sounded, the door opened, and they shoved him in.

Wolfe shook his head in wonderment. The gendarmes were much more brusque and rude than called for. He turned around and waited for them to unlock his handcuffs.

The cell was the standard size with four dirty bunks, two on either side of the cell. He was alone. There were no other prisoners. Then he understood. "Of course. Hajji needs his privacy."

One of the gendarmes smiled and pulled out a small knife. While the other gendarme held Wolfe steady, he went behind and started tugging and cutting at Wolfe's pants. Wolfe had a sinking feeling, and sure enough, the gendarme appeared again holding up a short, straight bit of wire.

He laughed, and the gendarmes closed the door and walked away.

"Wait! You haven't taken off the cuffs!" Wolfe called, stunned that they'd know where to look or that they'd even suspect he had the tool.

They turned and looked at him with vacuous gazes. One of them walked back to the cell and smiled ever so slightly. His Caucasian eyes had a note of mad glee in them, and he said, "You'll rest just as well with them on, infidel."

Wolfe was taken aback—fooled by the man's European appearance.

The gendarme simply smiled and walked away.

CHAPTER 33: Incarceration

Wolfe now knew what a cold sweat was like.

It was frigid.

He'd have next to no chance against a trained killer while in hand-cuffs. He had to get free. If he didn't, it was no more than an execution—he'd die here in this wretched cell deep under the streets of Paris. He tried to wriggle himself through his arms—at least the cuffs would be out front. But Wolfe's arms were too short, and no matter how hard he tried, he wasn't bendable enough to get through.

The only other alternative was to pick the lock. He'd done it before, though it was time-consuming, but he needed a tool. Unfortunately, he had nothing else secreted on his person, and they'd emptied his pockets.

"God, what I'd give for a bobby pin!"

Desperately, he searched the cell, looking for anything: a discarded toothpick, a splinter of wood, a bit of wire—anything. The cell was clean. His mind whirled in frantic haste, on the verge of panic. He tried to slow it down, to think, but he felt his grip on rationality loosening. Fear wrapped itself around him like a cold, wet blanket. He trembled, helpless.

"Damn it, I've no time for this; think, damn it, think!"

The buzz of a lock snapped Wolfe out of it.

Instantly, thankfully, the trembling cold settled into a chill in the pit of his stomach. The panic faded. Like a gladiator in the arena, he waited for his opponent.

The gendarmes led a man in handcuffs to his cell. Hajji was a beast. He was half a head taller than Wolfe was and must have outweighed him by fifty pounds. Wolfe backed away to the stone wall, the feeling of panic returning.

"*Tres!*"

The buzzer sounded, and they opened the door.

The gendarme unlocked Hajji's cuffs and backed away. Hajji stepped in and the door closed.

"Goodnight, infidel! Tonight you sleep in hell!"

They left, laughing. The other buzzer sounded. The steel door clanged shut.

They were alone.

Hajji grinned and rubbed his hands together. "Well, infidel dog," he said in thick English. "How do you say, shall we dance?"

He crouched, and with a feral roar, he bull-rushed Wolfe.

Wolfe set his left shoulder against the wall and lashed out with his right leg. He aimed the side-kick at Hajji's solar plexus. It connected, but Hajji was a big man, and his momentum carried him right through the force of the kick. Hajji slammed Wolfe against the stone. The assassin's hands reached for his throat.

Pinned against the wall, Wolfe tried to duck away, Hajji's fingers clawing at the skin on his neck. He straightened in a sudden, spasmodic jerk, butting the side of his head against Hajji's jaw. Hajji grunted, and Wolfe thrust himself away from the wall and out of his grasp.

Instantly, he turned and lashed out with a kick at Hajji's knee. The knee bent and took the blow without buckling, and though Hajji fell to the floor, he wasn't hurt. Wolfe kicked at Hajji's head, but his strike was off-balance and weak. The terrorist caught his foot and threw him back into the bars.

Wolfe's head clanged off the bars as he fell. His mind numbed and his sight grew dim.

Don't black out! Stay awake! Stay awake!

Hajji dragged him to his feet and slammed him into the rock wall once, twice, three times! Then he pinned Wolfe there, leaning against him. Putting his sweaty cheek against Wolfe, he whispered, "I want to take my time with you; I want to enjoy this!"

Wolfe struggled for breath. Hajji's shoulder was against his neck, crushing his head against the stone. A hairy arm wrapped around his throat. The other arm locked behind his head in a figure-four hold. Wolfe ducked his chin, but it was only a matter of time. He squirmed and struggled as Hajji tried to manhandle him with the chokehold. Back and forth they went, but Hajji's weight was telling. He forced Wolfe back against the stone wall, thrusting forward with his hips.

"You bastard, are you trying to fuck me and throttle me at the same time?" Wolfe wheezed, and a wave of revulsion hit him as he felt Hajji's cock against his manacled hands.

Wolfe, you idiot, these bastards don't play by the rules, so why should you? He cursed himself vehemently. With both hands, he found the soft privates of the terrorist, and he squeezed with every ounce of strength and fury he had.

Hajji screamed but didn't let go.

Wolfe dug his fingernails into Hajji's balls, wrenching his shoulders and hips back and forth, trying to tear Hajji's scrotum from his body.

Hajji let go and staggered back.

Wolfe didn't wait. As soon as Hajji's grip loosened, he twisted and head-butted the terrorist in the nose. Blood spurted from Hajji's nostrils, and the big jihadist sank to his knees. Wolfe struck him viciously with his right heel and then kicked him in the chest. The terrorist fell backward, still grabbing his crotch. Wolfe leapt. Hajji was screaming, his head thrown back, his Adam's apple standing out in the dark trunk of exposed neck—naked and vulnerable.

Wolfe had a split second; he had one chance.

Like a pouncing lion, Wolfe sprang at the downed terrorist and stomped on the protruding Adam's apple.

Hajji's eyes shot wide open in surprise. His hands went from his privates to his throat. Wolfe kicked again, trying to make sure he got in a mortal blow. Hajji rolled away and leapt up, gasping, choking, and staggering around the cell clutching at his throat, clutching at Wolfe.

Wolfe saw panic in the man's eyes. He stayed out of reach.

Hajji was turning blue.

Hajji stumbled and Wolfe stepped aside and tripped him, dumping him on his face. He tried to get up, but Wolfe swept a short, sharp crescent kick up, dropping it like an axe onto the back of his head. Hajji dropped like a sack and lay twitching on the concrete floor. Wolfe made sure he stayed down, dropping his knee on the back of the terrorist's neck. Hajji went into spasms. A minute went by and Hajji's struggling grew ever weaker. In another minute, he was dead.

Panting, Wolfe fell onto the lower bunk. The ordeal was over, but he now trembled uncontrollably. He'd been so close to certain death that the emotional trauma unleashed itself—the suppressed panic and fear threatened to overwhelm him. He fought it; he fought for self-control.

"It's over, you're through it, and it's done!" he told himself through chattering teeth. "Damn it, breathe, that's right, breathe. Calm. Breathe. Get a hold of yourself. It's finished." He fought for calm, and slowly calm returned. Then he realized, "No, it's not finished."

With difficulty, he rolled Hajji's corpse over and stripped off the man's belt. The prong of the belt allowed him to pick the lock of the handcuffs, but it took ten minutes to do so.

"I've got to practice this; I'm never going through this again!"

Now for the next dilemma; i.e., Wolfe was in the cell with a dead man and the chief prosecutor had to be behind this—he'd do anything to pin this on him. Only one thing came to mind, only a single way to throw off suspicion.

CHAPTER 34: Unexpected Allies

Wolfe wiped down Hajji's belt and put the dead man's prints on it. Climbing onto the top bunk and using a pillowcase as a glove, he tied the belt onto the electrical conduit between the bunks, using the buckle as a slipknot. It hung down in a wide loop. He turned to Hajji.

The man was bigger and heavier than he was; this was going to be hard. First, he sat Hajji up, and then he lifted him under the arms, dragging the dead man to his feet. Leaning him against the cell bars, Wolfe wrapped one arm around his waist and the other through his crotch, locking his hands around the dead man's belly. Grunting with effort, Wolfe lifted Hajji off the floor and labored back to the center of the room. He steadied himself, and with a mighty heave, he lifted the dead man as high as he could. Hajji's head popped through the noose, and Wolfe let him fall forward. Wolfe let go, and Hajji jerked to a stop. The conduit creaked and bent, pulling the screws partway out of the ceiling, but it held. Hajji dangled there, swinging slowly back and forth, a put-out expression on his darkening face.

Wolfe had no idea how thorough French forensics would be, but the prosecutor was after him, so had a few cosmetic issues to take care of. He scraped up the cuffs to mask the marks made by his picking the lock. Then, leaning from his perch on the bunk, he put Hajji's fingerprints on the conduit pipe.

Wolfe undid his pants. He pulled them most of the way up, but left the zipper and the button undone. Finally, Wolfe set himself against

287

the bed and put the unlocked cuffs back around his wrist. He grunted as the bracelet touched his cut and swollen flesh, but it was necessary for the illusion—he couldn't trust an explanation of self-defense. He didn't lock the cuff but kept the teeth just short of locking, just in case the jihadists had a back-up plan. Then he settled back and took a deep, shuddering breath.

There was nothing to do but wait.

About an hour later, he heard the buzz of the outer door.

A voice sounded stridently in English, saying, "You mean to tell me one of our citizens defends himself against an obvious assassination attempt by known terrorists—against whom we're all fighting, may I remind you—and you stick him down here?"

It was a familiar voice, an unbelievably familiar voice. He didn't know how or why he was here, but he immediately felt safe—at least until he found out about C. J.

Wolfe clicked the bracelet shut. It locked and it hurt like blazes.

"*Monsieur*, I couldn't agree with you more. Please know that IN-TERPOL had nothing to do with this outrage." It was the voice of Brueget.

"Nor did the Paris police, *Monsieur*," the chief said. "This was our chief prosecutor's idea."

"I have my constituency to worry about, *Monsieur* Ambassador. This is bound to inflame our Muslim immigrants. They are a very passionate people."

"As are my people when our rights are trodden on, *Monsieur* Prosecutor."

"*Oui*, we are all aware of the heavy-handed power of the United States, which you use at every opportunity."

"Be happy we used it for you—twice last century, if memory serves."

"That was before my time, *Monsieur*—now here is your precious *Monsieur* Wolfe, safe and sound, as you say—*mon Dieu!*"

"Sweet mother of God!"

Wolfe opened his eyes. A group of four men and the jailer stood with a single woman, Brueget, the chief of police, the prosecutor, and the ambassador—C. J.'s father. Wolfe hadn't seen Ted in ten years. The lone woman of the group was, not surprisingly, Orani, but Wolfe had no idea what she may or may not have had to do with any of this.

The chief shouted at the jailer in French, and the man hurriedly opened the cell door. Brueget rushed in and laid a hand on Wolfe's shoulder.

"*Mon Dieu, Monsieur*, are you alright? Blast it, you left him here in handcuffs! Outrageous; we treat condemned murderers with more respect."

"I gave no such order!" the prosecutor insisted.

"That's not what your boys said," Wolfe mumbled.

"Let me get those cuffs off," the chief said, pulling out a set of keys. "Those are nasty bruises—jailer, get the prison doctor down here at once!"

The ambassador came in. It was none other than Ted, C.J.'s dad. He was furious, which wasn't so unusual. Flint knew he was in the diplomatic corps, and that in itself was a contradiction in terms, but he never suspected he'd be in France. "Flint, what happened here? Who's this man?"

"Ask the jailer who just left," Wolfe said, standing up and rubbing his wrists. "I don't know. All I remember is after roughing me up a bit, the bastard tried to rape me. I got a hold of his balls, but he smashed my head against the stone there. I've been in and out ever since. That's about all I know."

"Did you say anything while he was trying to rape you?" Orani asked.

Flint had enough awareness remaining to recognize the bone Orani threw him. "I called him every politically incorrect name in the book and said that's how God and his family would remember him: as a faggot who enjoyed raping bound men. The police would investigate and know I'd been raped before he killed me. That would be in the papers for his family and friends to read. That's how he'd be remembered in heaven and on Earth."

"That explains the hanging," Orani said, taking the story and fleshing out Wolfe's alibi.

"What do you mean?" the chief asked.

"This man's a jihadist, a fundamentalist," Orani told them. "When confronted by the exposure of his homosexuality, he had no choice. Whether Wolfe lived or died, he'd be defiled and damned."

"He was obviously sent to kill *Monsieur* Wolfe, so why not finish the job?" Brueget asked.

Orani crossed her arms, as if giving a clinical lecture, and shrugged. "It's difficult to say. These are powerful and emotional drivers in these people—when the possibilities of exposure entered his mind, he probably didn't think about fulfilling his mission—just redemption through suicide."

"What mission?" the prosecutor asked.

"*Monsieur le Prosecutor*, do not be ignorant!" Brueget chided. "This was an obvious setup. Someone wants very badly to have *Monsieur* Wolfe dead, and they used your office to try and accomplish it!"

"There's no other reason to bring you here, *Monsieur* Wolfe," the chief added. "This place is used for only the most recalcitrant prisoners, and regardless, you should not have been with anyone—especially in handcuffs. No, this was another assassination attempt, clear and simple."

"It is the fatwa; it's the only explanation." Brueget nodded.

"You're mad, all of you," the prosecutor said. "He staged this, just like he did the murders in the pastry shop!"

Brueget laughed. "So now you have Mr. Wolfe supplying two known terrorists with weapons in front of a crowd of people, and then blowing up one of the terrorists. Fantastic—you should write American spy novels!"

The doctor arrived and told Wolfe to sit down on the bunk. He didn't take a second glance at the hanging man, as if he'd seen that sort of thing before, but sat down next to Wolfe and started examining him. The doctor looked up from Wolfe, and Wolfe took the opportunity to exchange glances with Orani. Orani understood.

The doctor stood up and said, "*Monsieur* Wolfe has multiple contusions and lacerations, and a serious concussion. *Monsieur le Prosecutor*, if it is your contention that he did anything except lie here unconscious after being beaten, you'll hear my rebuttal in court."

"You didn't have anything to do with this, did you, *Monsieur le Prosecutor*?" Brueget asked.

"How dare you!" the prosecutor exclaimed, turning beet red and confronting Brueget. He placed his face inches from the inspector. "I can have your job for that!"

Brueget simply smiled and lit up a cigarette. He took a puff, blowing it into the prosecutor's face. "Don't be absurd, *Monsieur le Prosecutor*, I am INTERPOL; you cannot touch me, and you know it." He handed the cigarette to Wolfe and continued. "On the other hand, I see a conspiracy with terrorists here, a conspiracy facilitated by the office of the prosecutor. Knowingly or unknowingly, it makes little difference to me."

Wolfe didn't much like cigarettes, but right now, he could use a pack. He accepted it gratefully, taking a long drag. The warm smoke curled into his mouth, soothing his frayed nerves.

The prosecutor looked frazzled, and Brueget took advantage of it. "*Monsieur*, we will be looking over everything about you, from your bank records to the restaurants you frequent, to the brand of mustache wax you so frequently use. I will see to it personally. Indeed, I will start this very moment. If *Monsieur* Wolfe is willing, I will commence to find the gendarmes who put him here in so precarious a situation— with the chief of police's kind permission, of course."

The chief was no less angry than Brueget. "I am at your disposal, Inspector, indeed I will also conduct my own investigation. Obviously, the jihadists are infiltrating le Commisionne de Police. If an assassination attempt can be set up in my own headquarters, the problem is of extreme severity."

"I have nothing to do with it, I assure you," the prosecutor said fervently.

"You'd better hope so," Brueget told him.

"*Monsieur le Prosecutor*, if you are indeed so innocent of complicity, then you will have no objections in having your own office pursue this vigorously?" the chief said.

"There will be riots in the streets," the prosecutor said.

"That is preferable to bombs in our cafes, don't you think?"

"You will have my full cooperation," the prosecutor sighed.

"Starting with the charges against Mr. Wolfe," the ambassador interjected.

"Of course, all charges will be dismissed immediately. *Monsieur* Wolfe is free to leave the country."

"Excellent." Brueget smiled. "Now, let's get *Monsieur* Wolfe out of this dungeon and back into Paris proper!"

Wolfe went to the infirmary with the doctor, and after getting a more thorough exam, he returned to the station, where he picked the two jihadist gendarmes out of a lineup of two men—namely themselves. French retribution could be swift and efficient, even if its justice was tardy. He gave his statement and then left with the ambassador and Orani.

Brueget and the chief apologized for his treatment and shook his hand warmly.

In the ambassador's limousine, Orani poured him a drink. Handing it to him, she said, "How on Earth did you manage that trick in the jail cell, Wolfe? You must have gotten out of the cuffs before they put Hajji in with you."

"Actually, I didn't," Wolfe said, drinking the entire martini in one long, smooth gulp and trying to hide the flush of adrenaline as he relived that moment. After taking a moment to compose himself, he asked, "How did you know about Hajji?"

"We intercepted the cell phone call of Anwar, the reporter for the local Arab paper, but it wasn't known what the call was about until after they reported it to me. We came right away."

"Anwar is one of the bad apples we keep track of," the ambassador told him. "In fact, he's responsible for bringing Hamdi, Khallida, and Fawahdi together. Anwar heads a network that provides fake passports, documentation, and money to the growing fundamentalist cause. It was only a matter of time before he started on the paramilitary side of the house. That's one of the little sidelines Hamdi and Khallida have been working on, though we still don't know where they're hidden. Thanks to you, we've foiled the first foray into Paris, but he's persistent and motivated. All of Europe is going to be a mess before this thing gets sorted out."

"Sorry, I don't have time to take care of him this trip, maybe next time," Wolfe said.

"You're too close to him to be of any use to us," the ambassador said sharply. "Don't be too pleased with yourself, Flint. You're resourceful, but you draw far too much attention to yourself. One slip-up and that prosecutor would have your head on a platter. I don't like being brought in on these things; I'd much rather read about them in the paper."

"It won't happen again, sir."

"See that it doesn't," the ambassador told him curtly. The limousine pulled up at Wolfe's hotel. The ambassador turned to Wolfe, and his expression softened. He held out his hand. "Here we are, Flint, it's good to see you again—though you've looked better. I'll tell C. J. I saw you, but I won't tell her what you're up to! Dinner tonight?"

Wolfe shook his hand and smiled. "Sure, Ted, whenever it's convenient."

"I'll pick you up at eight," the ambassador said.

"You want to debrief this afternoon?" Wolfe asked Orani.

She looked at her watch, and said, "We've moved your flight back a day. How about Buffalo Bill's at five, alright? I've got things to do until then."

Wolfe waved to Orani, and the door closed.

The doorman opened the hotel doors, muttering a question in French.

Wolfe stopped, shaking his head, "*Je ne comprend pas Francais, s'il vous plait.*"

"Pardon, *Monsieur*, can I get you anything? Are you alright?"

Wolfe realized he was a mess. He sighed and smiled weakly. "Could you have a bottle of Beaujolais sent up to my room, *s'il vous plait*? I could use some of your wonderful French wine."

"What label, Monsieur?"

"I leave it up to you," Wolfe said. "Order what you'd like to drink after a hard day, two bottles please, one for me and one for yourself."

"*Tout suite, Monsieur!*"

#

"Mr. Ambassador, excuse me, but I didn't realize you knew Wolfe," Orani said as they pulled away from the hotel.

"Almost thirty years," the ambassador said, lighting up a cigarette. He held up his lighter for Orani. "My daughter went to school with him. I always wanted them to get married, but she had other ideas. Now that he's divorced and she's divorced, I'm hoping she get her head on straight and they'll get together—not that I like this business he's in."

The ambassador's eyes narrowed and he looked at Orani in a different light.

She coughed; she hadn't made the connection between C.J. and the ambassador until now.

"You wouldn't have any designs on Wolfe, would you?"

The question was serious, pointed, and took Yasmina completely by surprise. "No, sir, I don't."

"You slept with him yet?"

"For God's sake, I'm his handler, not his *handler!*" She tried to make light out of it, because she was afraid he'd see through her. Thank God it worked. He nodded and breathed a sigh of relief.

"Sorry, I don't mean to pry, but I've known him a long time. He's what's best for my daughter, and you know how stubborn fathers can be. Let's hope the job doesn't require sleeping with him," the ambassador said. He looked at her with a troubled expression. "If there's one thing Wolfe's not good, at it is impropriety. He'll kill a thousand people, or get himself killed, before he does anything he considers dishonorable. That's why I hate this. You people are bound to put someone innocent in his way—I don't know how he'll handle that."

"I realize that. We're handling him differently. I'll try not to let that happen, sir."

"It's out of your hands, Orani," the ambassador told her pointedly. "You just try and keep him alive, and don't sleep with him—he's spoken for!"

"I understand, Mr. Ambassador." He dropped her off at her hotel. Yasmina walked up the stairs to her room. For some reason, she didn't feel like taking the elevator. The ambassador's assertions about her and Wolfe bothered her. Was she that transparent? Certainly, they had a sort of flirtatious relationship, but she didn't really want that unique, powerful, haunted man for herself—did she? Well, she admitted, maybe in her fantasies now and then.

Yasmina shoved those thoughts aside and returned to her real dilemma—Lufti. She knew Hamdi had her, but she had no idea where. In fact, it had been her search for Lufti that had caused her to be absent when Wolfe was brought in, and nearly resulted in his death. She tried not to blame herself—indeed, Wolfe wouldn't have blamed her—but she couldn't convince herself that it was time to bring him in on her secret. Still, that made her vulnerable, and that's how mistakes happened. She learned that in Spy 101.

She slipped the key card in the door, determined now that she'd tell Wolfe everything. After all, who would understand better than a devoted father, and who could be more valuable in returning her daughter than that amazingly adamant and resourceful man? The door opened, and to her surprise, there was Lufti, sitting in the chair, watching TV.

"Lufti, my darling!" she cried, rushing into the room.

Everything went dark.

CHAPTER 35: The Depth of Betrayal

Lieutenant General Vince Steinham looked over the reports on his desk. Strangely enough, none of the paperwork had anything to do with the business of the Air Transport Command, of which he was Commander in Chief. Rather, they were press clippings, bios of senators, summary reports on foreign policy issues, and political summaries.

A knock sounded at the door, and General Steinham raised his pale, vulture-thin head to see the strong, black features of his aide, Colonel Lionel Page. He closed the files with thinly veiled irritation.

"What is it, Colonel Page?"

Page saluted and put a manila folder on the general's desk. Opening it revealed the photos and records of eight men. "Sir, I've a problem with the 'Argos' tasking, the transfer of the nuclear artillery shells to Israel."

Steinham grimaced. "This better not be because you're Muslim, Colonel Page. We're blind to that sort of thing in the air force—I shouldn't have to remind you of that."

A flash of anger seemed to pass over Colonel Page's dark eyes, but he hid it immediately, shaking his head vigorously. "I'm blind to it, sir, but whoever wrote up this tasking isn't!"

"I wrote it up, Colonel," Steinham told him, and he hoped the tone of his voice conveyed no room for argument.

"You, sir?"

"Me, Colonel, do you have a problem with that?"

"Sir, I don't have a problem with the mission; I have a problem with the crew."

Steinham stirred uncomfortably in his seat. He'd hoped to avoid this, but he should've expected it. Page was a very capable man. No matter how carefully he covered his aspirations or intentions, Page always seemed to see through him. The man had an irritating disregard for the political realities of command. How the hell did he get talked into taking an independent thinker as an aide?

"I don't understand you, Colonel. Is there a problem with the records of any member of the crew?"

"None whatsoever, except that every one of them is Muslim."

"I just told you that we're blind to that, Colonel. You, above all officers, should be sensitive to that."

"If we're blind to it, then why did we solicit Muslim volunteers for the mission—and only Muslim volunteers?" The Colonel was angry and there was no hiding it.

"Watch your tone of voice, Colonel," Steinham said, and then he smiled, trying to disarm Page's anger. He switched on his wall viewer, and the one-hundred-inch plasma display glowed, showing the schematic of a long, needle-nosed projectile. The general got up and walked over to the display. "Colonel, I appreciate your sensitivity on this issue, but this baby is a tool for our Muslim friends as well as our Israeli friends. It's an entirely new concept in tactical nukes: high–yield, low-radiation artillery. I was on the engineering panel—this one, we got right!"

Steinham pointed out the particulars of the shell, tracing his long, bony fingers over the smooth curves of the diagram. "We designed the shell with a fundamentalist regime in mind, one that had low technology and mass troops."

"Such as Iran or a unified Persia?" Page asked, crossing his arms and nodding as if in agreement.

"Or China, or North Korea," Steinham added. "The problem with tactical nukes is always radiation in the form of fallout. What use is it if you're going to irradiate your own troops? We solved the problem by making the shell a penetrator, like the 'bunker-busters' we designed to take out communication and leadership targets." He felt himself get very animated as he discussed his pet project, and why shouldn't he?

This was his baby. Page's expression betrayed his doubt. "What this nuke does is bury itself deep enough so that the earth absorbs most of the radiation. It kills by shock wave, taking men, material, and equipment, but doesn't spread a radioactive cloud over the battlefield. It's the perfect tactical warhead.

"It would be especially useful if Israel or the Arabian Peninsula is attacked by a large army. We can stop the army in its tracks before any appreciable damage is done and not obliterate the Middle East."

"Sir, with all due respect, is this wise?"

"What do you mean? This is a quantum leap in nuclear weaponry."

"That's exactly my point, and a reason to be extra careful," Page noted, apparently biting back his anger, though for the life of him, Steinham had no idea why he should be angry. "Sir, we've already seen what young, impressionable Muslim troops are capable of. To put an all-Muslim crew in charge of hundreds of nukes on the way to Israel is tempting fate—there's no logical reason for it."

"There's every logical reason for it!" the general retorted, thinking to himself, *Damn it, I'm not going to let some half-bit colonel derail my bid for a seat on the joint chiefs of staff! This has to end here!* He returned to his non-regulation leather chair, leaned back into it, and said, as from a mentor to a wayward but much-loved student, "Lionel, you're looking at this through a straw. It's precisely because of the incident in Iraq that we need to dispel this myth of religious zeal in our military. Our soldiers, every one of them, devote themselves to the service of the United States—regardless of their faith."

"That's a very comforting ideology, General, but it's an enormous risk to take. If anything goes wrong—"

"Are you worried about your career, Colonel?"

"I'm worried about our country; I'm worried about our civilization!" Page said, thumping his fist on the general's desk.

"We have politicians who are better able to decide those issues, Colonel," Steinham said coldly. That was enough. He'd have to look into transferring this man. Who was the general here, anyway? "This subject is above our pay grade, Colonel. There are certain members of the administration and the Congress who are very desirous of putting this issue at rest. Let it alone."

"Would those people be the secretary of defense and the chairman of the Armed Services Committee?"

"Be careful where you tread, Colonel."

"I'm simply trying to be prudent, sir—these are nukes we're dealing with."

"If you're questioning the loyalty of our Muslim soldiers, you're out of line, Colonel—you're out of line."

"There's no reason to take this risk, General. At least allow me to replace the security detail."

"Colonel, I've heard enough about this," the general said tersely. "That will be all."

CHAPTER 36: Collateral Damage

Yasmina's first reaction was to blurt out, "Get your hands off me!" but someone shoved a stifling black hood over her head. An arm wrapped around her waist and dragged her somewhere. Lufti was screaming, and then her screams were cut short. Yasmina was thrown down on a bed, but strong hands held her down while others taped her spread-eagle to the bed.

The hood was removed. Hamdi stood smiling at the foot of the bed. Four other men, all of Middle Eastern descent, waited there as well. She recognized the reporter, Anwar.

"Welcome home, Yasmina!" Hamdi said pleasantly. "It's been a long time."

"Not long enough, Marwan! Where is Lufti?"

Hamdi smiled and snapped his fingers. Lufti was carried in by another man. She was gagged and bound. The man set her in a chair, and Hamdi went over to it, patting her head. "My daughter is going to get the lesson of her life from her mother—a lesson in the ramifications of being a poor Muslim wife."

"You wouldn't dare torture your own daughter! You can't be that evil; you can't be that inhuman!"

"I am my daughter's father, and it's my responsibility to teach her right from wrong." He walked over to Yasmina and stroked her surgically repaired cheek. "They really did a nice job. I didn't recognize you wallowing in carnal lust with Mr. Wolfe, but turnabout is fair play, as the Americans say. These men will brutalize you, ravage you, and degrade you. After they are done with you, they will dispatch you in a holy way. The mosque has been informed. The preparations have been made. The stones are already laid aside. Then, my dear faithless wife, you will go to hell."

"You are not going to allow Lufti to watch this—she's a child, for God's sake!"

"It is exactly for Allah's sake that I will force her to watch it!" He patted Yasmina's cheek and taped her mouth shut. "She shouldn't hear your cries of ecstasy, though, the cries of a whore mother!" He stopped by Lufti and kissed the crying child on the head. "Learn what is expected of you!"

Hamdi went to the door, and without glancing back, he left.

As soon as the door closed, they ripped her clothes off like starving beasts over a carcass. Yasmina tried to give Lufti a reassuring look through the tangle of bodies, but the sight of her daughter's suffering forced her to look away. Yasmina tried to detach herself from the moment. They'd told her this was one of the special dangers for a woman operative. They told her how to deal with it. They trained her thoroughly, working with decades of experience—it was wholly inadequate.

***

Wolfe checked his watch for the tenth time. It showed five fifteen. Orani was late. Orani was never late—not without calling. He tried her cell phone—no answer. He was about to get up and leave when Brueget appeared.

"Am I disturbing you?"

"Not at all." Wolfe forced a smile. "Please sit down. I was waiting for the ambassador's attaché, Ms. Orani. She was supposed to meet me here."

Brueget ordered a red wine.

"And she is late? That seems unusual. She strikes me as a very capable woman."

"She is."

Brueget's wine arrived, and he raised his glass to Wolfe. "To the defeat of the jihadists," he toasted, "and to the preservation of our enlightened civilization."

"I'll drink to that." Wolfe smiled, but his mind was on Orani.

"*Monsieur* Wolfe, we are both working for the same goal, but alas, here in Europe, we do not always have the sternness of will that you Americans or even the British display. Perhaps it is your Wild West culture that allows you to get your hands dirty, so to speak."

"That's an interesting way of putting it," Wolfe said carefully. "However, a large segment of our society is sympathetic to the altruistic European way of looking at things." He took a sip of his wine. What was Brueget's game? Was this another trap? But then why entrap him when they had him incarcerated before? He must be legit.

"Yes, but like our society, those people are blind to reality. We need to save them from themselves, and yet half the time, I have not the power to bring the guilty to justice. That, I guess, is your job."

"I fly airplanes."

"Of course." Brueget hesitated. Then he reached into his pocket and withdrew a card. He handed it to Wolfe. "*Monsieur* Wolfe, I, we, are desperate. The time is coming and we have eyes that see the storm but no will to fight it. You have already made a difference. I ask you, I beg you, to continue to make a difference."

"We all do what we can, Inspector, that won't change. I am, however, constrained by regulations from doing freelance work; I can't just fly for another airline if I want to."

"But if Air France got permission from your," he smiled, "your Company for you to do some work, you would do it?"

Wolfe raised his glass. "I honor the services of Lafayette and will gladly return his favor if I can."

Brueget smiled.

Wolfe glanced at his watch and shook his head. He tried Orani's cell phone again. Nothing.

"There is something wrong?"

Wolfe grimaced. "Something, perhaps, this isn't like her. I'll have to call the embassy to see where she's staying."

"I know her hotel. Come, we'll take my car."

They couldn't drive fast enough for Wolfe, but Brueget careened through Paris at breakneck speed. Twenty minutes later, they pulled into the alley behind Orani's hotel.

Brueget took out a Sig Sauer and a silencer and pressed them into

Wolfe's hands. "It is the same as the jihadist carried—that should give the prosecutor something to ponder! Take the fire escape. If something's amiss, they'll be watching the lifts. Orani's room is on the sixth floor, room six twenty-one, two rooms down and to the right. *Bon chance, mon ami!*"

Wolfe climbed on top of a dumpster and leapt for the first-floor landing. He caught the wrought-iron edge and pulled himself up and over the rail. He hit the landing running, taking three steps at a time. He didn't feel the wounds of his trials; just the fear of what he might find when he got to Yasmina's room. When he reached the fifth floor, he slowed down, treading softly and with care. Patrons accessed the fire escape via large windows set at the ends of the hotel corridors. The windows were always unlocked.

Wolfe reached the sixth floor landing and peered through the window. There were two men standing outside Yasmina's door. They were of Middle Eastern descent. He watched them, just to make sure they weren't innocent bystanders. They didn't move.

He went back down to the fifth floor and entered the corridor. Wolfe found the stairwell and walked up the stairs, pulling the Sig and hiding it in the pocket of his overcoat. He opened the door and entered the sixth-floor hall. Turning right, he headed down the corridor, checking the room numbers as the two jihadists watched suspiciously. He reached room six twenty-one. Wolfe looked at the room number, and then at the jihadists.

"*Mon fiancée!*" he stammered, pointing to the door.

One of the jihadists said something in French.

"*Ou est mon fiancée?*" he asked.

One of them reached for him. Wolfe put two bullets in his chest, firing through the hole in his pocket. The Arab slammed into the doorjamb and slid down the wall with a whimper.

The other man reached inside his jacket, but Wolfe kicked him in the chest. The terrorist flew up and landed hard on his back. He stared up at Wolfe with terror in his black eyes; Wolfe put a bullet right between them—leaving him with three dark, windowless holes in his head.

Wolfe tried the door. It was locked.

He rifled their pockets, but neither one had a key card. He had no choice. He couldn't wait. Wolfe shot the deadbolt and kicked the door open. It splintered loudly. He rushed in. Wolfe was in a small living room—it was empty. He sped to the bedroom door and threw his shoulder against it. It crashed open.

Orani was tied spread-eagle to the bed. A man was on top of her; his pants were pulled down around his ankles. Two other men hovered around her like vultures. Those two turned their heads to him, eyes wide in surprise. Wolfe didn't think; he fired. Round, red holes appeared in the first man's forehead. He slumped open-mouthed to the floor. The second man whirled around, threw his arms into the air, and fell on his face—his naked ass pointing awkwardly to the sky.

The rapist on top of Orani was just now turning to see what was happening. His eyes went wide as saucers when he saw Wolfe. It was Anwar. Wolfe pistol whipped him and wrenched the rapist off the bed, throwing him face-down on the floor. Grabbing a roll of duct tape from the nightstand, he wrapped the tape around Anwar's head and then around his arms and legs.

Wolfe leapt to Orani.

"Yasmina! Yasmina, can you hear me?"

Her eyes fluttered open, wide with fright. It took her a second to focus on Wolfe. Then she shut them, and tears started to run down her cheeks.

Wolfe took off her gag and began to release her, but her first word was "Lufti!"

"What?"

"My daughter; they made her watch!"

Wolfe whirled like a lion and saw to his horror a little girl bound to a chair, looking at him with wide eyes. "Oh, my sweet Lord how could anyone do that?" he asked aloud. He rushed to the girl, but she pulled away. Wolfe stopped and got down on his knees. "I'm a friend of your mother's, Lufti; I'm here to get you out of this and to bring you home, okay?"

She nodded, and Wolfe undid her bindings. Then he released Yasmina, picking her up like a child. She threw her arms around his neck, but he said, "We can't stay here." He took her into the living room and put her on the sofa. Grabbing a blanket from the closet, Wolfe tenderly but quickly swathed mother and daughter in the blanket.

"Are you going to be alright?"

"We'll be fine," she said with an effort.

"Good girl, this will only take a minute." He took out his empty clip and reloaded the Sig. After chambering a round, he gave the gun to Orani. She took it and nodded.

Wolfe ran to the front door and dragged the two bodies inside. Closing the door, he turned his attention to the bedroom again. Only one rapist was alive—Anwar. He lay moaning on the carpet, oozing blood. Wolfe picked Anwar up and threw him on the bed. Then he piled the bodies of the other rapists on top of him.

He went to the mini-bar and took out the liquor bottles. Opening them one by one, he emptied them over Anwar, the bodies, and all over the bloodstained carpet. Anwar's eyes were now open and frightful, staring at Wolfe from beneath the tangle of dead bodies. Wolfe smiled mirthlessly and emptied a bottle of gin over the rapist's oily hair.

Anwar struggled, but to no avail.

Wolfe surveyed the room. He found their jackets in a heap on a chair. In the jackets, he found three pistols and several extra clips of ammunition. He also found one cell phone. Wolfe emptied the ammunition clips and took them to the bed. He dumped them on the stained sheets in front of Anwar.

"This should make an interesting story for your rag," he said, and he took a bar of C-4 from his coat pocket. "Five jihadists accidentally detonate their own bomb during an orgy—of course; someone else is going to have to write it."

In front of Anwar's terrified eyes, he taped the clips of ammunition around the C-4 and then taped it to Anwar's shaking hands. He emptied one last battle of gin over the makeshift bomb and Anwar.

"You know, you really should refrain from the use of alcohol when making bombs."

Wolfe took Anwar's cell phone and looked up the last number. Pressing "Send," he waited. The phone rang twice and a voice answered in Arabic.

"Give me the imam," he said in Arabic.

After a moment, a voice answered.

"Your boys distinguished themselves as dogs. Let this be a warning;

the next time I'm in town, I'm coming for you. Now, listen and enjoy; Anwar, it's all yours!"

He put the open phone next to Anwar's face so the listener could hear the pitiful whimpers and sobs. Hanging up, he pocketed the phone and left Anwar to his fate.

Yasmina had composed herself, but she'd been badly beaten. Wolfe took the gun from her, explaining, "INTERPOL will need this more than us." He went back to the bedroom.

Going to where Anwar could see him, he threw the gun onto the pile of bodies. Then he removed the remote for the C-4 and flicked the toggle to "arm."

A red light came on at the end of the C-4 brick Anwar held in his hands. A scream escaped the rapist's taped mouth. Wolfe shook his head and said, "I thought you vermin all wanted to die. Well, I'll help you along as much as I possibly can. Believe me, there aren't going to be any virgins where you're going!"

Wolfe left and closed the door. He scooped up Yasmina and Lufti in his arms and headed out of the room. As he opened the door, he noticed her purse lying on the floor where she dropped it at the onslaught of the attack. He snatched it from the floor, turned the latch, looked both ways down the hall, and stepped out.

"I can walk!" she protested.

"Later—we need to get you out of here and to a hospital."

"No, we can't afford exposure," she said, the Company voice of his handler returning. "Take us back to your hotel; there's no safer place in Paris!"

Wolfe closed the door and hustled to the end of the hall. He threw up the window and stepped out onto the fire escape. Wolfe turned back to the corridor and dug the remote out of his pocket. Pointing it back toward the room, he said, "Good-bye Anwar!" and pressed the button.

A muffled explosion rattled the fire escape. Smoke billowed from underneath the door of the room, and in places, the plaster bulged and cracked, but the damage in the hall was minimal.

They made their way down the fire escape to where Brueget waited with the car still running. As soon as they were inside, he gunned the engine and peeled out of the alley and into the street.

"*Mon Dieu*, you have a wee waif in this horror? Are you alright, Ms. Orani? Do we need to go to a hospital?"

"Just take us back to my hotel, for now," Wolfe said, and he tossed Anwar's cell phone into the front seat. "Here's a present for you; it should tie together all the principals in this investigation."

"I see this relationship going places, *mon ami*." Brueget smiled, glancing back over his shoulder and seemingly dodging the motor scooters, mini-cars, and delivery vans by feel. In short order, they were at the hotel. Wolfe gave Orani his trench coat, and they got out on the curb.

"Thanks, Jean; you have my number." Wolfe held out his hand.

Brueget took it, but said, "No, *mon ami*, I would not sleep if I let you here alone. I will go to your room with you. I will have agents on either side of you, above and below until you leave. Your adventures in Paris are ended, I guarantee it!"

Wolfe nodded. He hurried Orani and Lufti to the elevator and his room. Once there, he carried her to the bedroom and laid her on the bed. Lufti snuggled right next to her mother, afraid to leave her. "Alright, let's get a look at you," he said, meaning her wounds. She had several nasty bruises on her face, and her wrists and ankles were red and swollen where they bound her. He reached for her hand.

"Don't touch me!" Orani ordered, pushing him away. "Don't touch me!"

Wolfe backed away, surprised at first, but then he understood. He didn't press it. "Listen, I'll start a shower. I want you to get in and get cleaned up. I'll call the embassy. I can either have them send over a doctor or they'll send a car to get you, whatever you want."

"There's no need," she said shortly. "There's nothing about this the embassy needs to know. I'll file a report when we get back. I'll stay here. I'm booked back on your flight anyway—I'll go to the airport with you."

"I don't think—"

"I'm staying here!" It was almost a scream, or a plea. He couldn't tell, but she was so agitated, she doubled up as if in pain. She bared her teeth, like an animal, daring him to argue.

"Whatever you need," he said, and he started the shower.

When he came out to tell her it was ready, she scurried by him like a rabbit. The door closed, but then it opened a crack. "Sorry, Flint, I didn't mean to snap at you so, it's just that I don't think I'd get a wink of sleep or peace if you weren't here. Please, I'll be fine when we get back to the States."

"No problem. I'll cancel my dinner with the ambassador."

"No, we'll go with you." She picked up the phone and began ordering things from the gift shop.

Wolfe turned to Lufti, making sure the girl was comfortable and felt safe. He turned on the TV and ordered a movie for her. He stood there for a moment, watching her, wondering what he could do to take the edge off her horrible ordeal. Lufti smiled and watched the movie, getting lost in it. He sighed and returned to the bathroom, listening at the door. He could hear Yasmina's voice over the shower—he couldn't tell if they were muffled sobs and gasps of anger. Steam poured from underneath the door.

He knocked.

There was no answer.

He knocked more urgently. "Yasmina, are you alright?"

Opening the door, he poked his head in. The inside of the bath was a mass of steam. He leapt to the shower and turned the hot water valve down. "Damn it, you're going to scald yourself!"

"Leave me alone!" She reached for the valve again.

"Yasmina!" He stopped her hand.

"Get out of here and leave me alone!"

"It's not going to make it go away!"

"Let me get clean!" she screamed.

He wouldn't let her turn the water back on.

"Leave me alone; don't you see how dirty I am?"

Lufti heard the commotion and ran into the bathroom. When she saw her mother, she began to sob. "Momma, what's wrong?"

Wolfe turned the water off entirely and grabbed her wrists. He lifted her out of the shower and swathed her in a big, white towel. She tried to fight it at first, but he was too strong.

She gave up.

"Come with me, Lufti, Mommy's going to be alright." He picked her up and carried her to the living room. "I know what you're feeling, Yasmina," he said softer than his grip.

"How would you know anything about it; you're a man!"

Wolfe sat her in one of the upholstered chairs and put her daughter next to her. Then he sat in a chair across the room—at a safe distance for her peace of mind. He read the look in her eyes; it was castigating. She needed his protection right now, but he was a man. He sighed.

"Petty Officer Gonzales."

"What? What are you talking about?"

"I'm talking about Petty Officer Gonzales of the U.S. Coast Guard. He was on Governor's Island Station in the spring of 1982. I was a sophomore in college then, and C. J. was in the Coast Guard. She was my best friend, and I was madly in love with her. I got a letter from her one evening. I was so excited to get it, I almost ran back to my dorm room. I tore it open, and there it was."

"She dumped you, again," Orani sneered.

"No," Wolfe said sadly, "there were the words, 'I've been raped.' It was like someone stuck a dull, rusty knife in my chest and twisted it. She'd been raped, and I wasn't there to protect her. But it was the next line that killed me. She was a virgin, and she was proud of it. She said, 'I'm not clean anymore. I'll understand if you don't ever want to see me again.' Well, I didn't bother to read anymore. I rushed to the phone and got her on the line. It was strange. She was already over it; she said, you know, no big deal—these things happen. She was in the 'Q' at Governor's Island and asleep. They didn't let them lock their doors. She woke up to find Petty Officer Gonzales already on top of her; he was already inside her. He finished raping her and left."

Wolfe took a cigarette out of Orani's purse and lit it. He handed it to Orani, and then he lit one for himself. "She reported it, of course, but the officers in charge didn't want to hear about it. Instead of doing their duty, they told her they'd make her life a living hell if she pressed it. She did, and they lived up to their promise. C. J. was raped several more times in the military; she was a target—once word gets around, it's tough."

He took a long drag on the cigarette. The coals crept back toward his lips. Then he exhaled, wreathing himself in the gray smoke.

"She talked about the showers," he told her. "She talked about how she could never get the water hot enough to scrape off the filth they left behind. I'll track down Petty Officer Gonzales one of these days, and I'm going to destroy him. Don't interfere with that, Orani."

She was silent, but she looked away.

He looked down at the cigarette. "Damn, I've smoked more of these things today than the rest of my life combined—I hope they're not addicting."

"Thanks for saving me, Flint. Thanks for saving Lufti. I know you weren't there for C. J., but you would have been if you could have. You were there for us. Thanks."

Flint nodded. "You're welcome."

"I suppose you're wondering why I haven't mentioned Lufti before." She smiled and tousled her daughter's hair. Lufti hugged her closer.

Wolfe was dying to ask the question, but he couldn't, not with Orani so vulnerable. He decided he really didn't care what side she was playing. He got up and dug out his pipe, filling it with tobacco. "We all have our secrets to keep. I always assumed you had a family in the background, but how did Hamdi's people find out?"

He turned back to her and reached up to light the pipe.

"Hamdi's her father," Orani said.

Wolfe almost dropped the lighter.

"By Islamic law, we're still married," she said weakly. She took a deep breath. "After I fled Iran, I enrolled in Boston College. We met and we married. I got pregnant with Lufti. After she was old enough to start preschool, I wanted to go back and finish my degree. Marwan disagreed. He'd begun to shift his opinions toward fundamentalist Islam. He forbade me to continue my education, to get a job—well, you know the drill. I took classes unbeknownst to him. When he found out I was going out into the world without even a headscarf, getting an education, trying to make something of myself—like a real human being—he beat me. He nearly killed me. In fact, he thought he had. My father-in-law saved me and took me to the hospital. That's when the Company approached me.

"I'd been majoring in international politics; I spoke Farsi, Persian, even some Kurdish, and French. They gave me a chance to rebuild my life and to fight the evil that Marwan and his friends embraced; they gave me a chance for Lufti to have a future without the threat of religious slavery."

"It must've been difficult to see Lufti with Hamdi thinking you dead."

Orani shook her head. "He fled overseas, leaving Lufti in his father's care. After my recuperation, I moved in as her 'aunt' to help raise her. No one recognized me; because of the beating, I pretty much had to have my face put back together. It wasn't until Marwan returned just prior to 9/11 that things got complicated."

Wolfe nodded, feeling the fool.

She looked at him severely. "Did you ever suspect anything, Wolfe? Did you ever doubt me?"

The buzzer for the door sounded. He got up, laughing dryly. "With those beautiful brown eyes, are you kidding?" He looked back at her before opening the door. "I've always had complete faith in you, and I always will."

Flint opened the door.

An Arab man stood outside dressed in a hotel uniform. He had a wide smile on his face and pearly white teeth. "For Mr. Wolfe, from Ms. Orani!"

There was the sound of a gunshot and something hit Flint in the forehead.

CHAPTER 37: The Catacombs of Paris

Wolfe jumped back and reached for his forehead with one hand and his gun with the other.

"Oh, monsieur, a thousand pardons!" the man said as champagne spilled out over his hand. "My, but that was a lively one, was it not? Are you alright?"

"Fine!" Wolfe said sharply, rubbing the spot on his forehead where the cork hit him after ricocheting off the ceiling. Orani was stifling a laugh.

"Sorry, I forgot. I ordered champagne."

"Do you remember *moi*, Armand the doorman? You were so gracious as to help me to the extra bottle of red wine this morning." He was quite animated and seemed eager to please, and now Flint did indeed recognize him. Armand smiled again and said, "Well, when you came through the door this afternoon, *mon Dieu*, you looked even worse! So, I took the liberty of bringing some champagne, seeing as you had a lady friend. This is one of our best; I guarantee it. It will make pain and memory disappear *tout suite!*" He motioned behind him to another steward who had a rack of clothes on a wheeled cart. "Here we have mademoiselle's clothing; if it does not suit her tastes, I will have more sent up—whatever monsieur wishes!"

"I'm speechless, Armand," Flint said, shaking his head.

Armand must have thought he was tallying the cost, for he patted Flint's arm and said, "Do not worry about the bill, monsieur Flint, my manager tells me that the chief of police, your American Embassy, and INTERPOL are all fighting over who's going to pay your tab. You're a hero of France, it's said!"

"I'm going to have to come to France more often." Wolfe smiled, and he opened the door. Armand rushed in with the champagne and proceeded to put it on ice. Flint motioned the man with the clothes in and closed the door.

"You do that, *Monsieur* Wolfe," Armand said, and he poured the champagne. He handed a glass to Flint. "France needs a—how do you say it—housecleaning, as does all of Europe."

"That is a rather unusual view, especially for a doorman, Armand," Flint smiled. "Maybe you should change your profession to politics—that's what's really needed."

Armand laughed and replied, "No, in politics I would get nothing done, but here I am where I can see and listen to much that is going on in the world. You may not know it, monsieur, but this hotel hosts the largest number of foreigners in all of Paris. Some are dignitaries, yet others are not. Often, it is those individuals we are interested in." Armand motioned to the window, taking the other glass of champagne with him. The other man went to the door without being asked and checked the hall. Armand drew the curtains and pointed down to the street where the lobby doors emptied onto a broad swath of stone.

"Look at that, monsieur; we have the world at our doorstep. Here, in the center of Paris, they come from all over the globe to make their plans—and we are here to serve and observe."

Flint looked at the crowd and eyed them, as Armand must see them. There must've been a dozen different nations represented in the lobby crowd alone, and all their baggage was right there at his beck and call.

"How many languages do you speak, Armand?"

"I am fluent in eight, and do tolerably well in another six."

That explained Armand to Flint—almost.

"You are a talented man, Armand," Flint said, closing the curtains and sipping the champagne. "I imagine Inspector Brueget would be very impressed with you."

"The Inspector is a man of great insight." Armand nodded; that was that. Armand worked for INTERPOL.

"I'll be back," Flint said, giving Armand his card. "If you're ever in the States, Armand, look me up. I would consider it a privilege to return your hospitality."

The phone rang.

Armand answered it. He turned to Flint and said, "It is the Inspector. He's here with a limousine. He will personally take you to your dinner appointment at the embassy. Let me know when you and mademoiselle are ready."

Flint plied Orani with champagne—it helped. In half an hour, they were in the back of a black Mercedes 600 with Brueget. He handed Flint a file folder. Flint opened it and found the pictures of Hamdi and Khallida.

"They departed on a Royal Saudi flight for Jeddah this afternoon," the Inspector said, shaking his head and smoking a cigarette. Orani wasn't smoking. She was scrunched into the corner of the seat with Lufti. Flint had tried to get her to stay with the INTERPOL agents, but she refused. So they followed behind in a very businesslike motorcade. She stared over his shoulder at the folder, but her eyes darted here and there as if she was having trouble focusing.

"They're gone?" Flint mused, by now used to the smoke. "Then that's it for their plans for the time being."

"We've been over that," Orani said flatly. "It's the stuff of dreams—literally. The only conceivable way of triggering that fault line is with hundreds of nuclear weapons triggered simultaneously along the fault. There's no way the jihad could get their hands on that many weapons, and even if they did, there's absolutely no way they could do it without our knowing about it."

"I suppose you're right, Orani," Wolfe replied, but he didn't believe it. Hamdi didn't seem like the type of man who believed in dreams.

***

Wolfe couldn't sleep, so he walked the evening streets of Paris. Orani and Lufti were asleep in the bedroom, and there were a dozen INTERPOL agents around them. That freed him up for the night. He fiddled with Anwar's phone; after downloading the pertinent data from its memory, Brueget gave it to Wolfe so that the Company could take a look at it.

He was curious.

Under the navigation menu, in "favorite places," there was a location labeled, "Oasis." He brought it up. It was barely half a mile from his hotel. He followed the prompting of the phone until he arrived in the center of the plaza before Notre Dame. To his consternation, the phone showed that he was fifty feet from his destination, but every time he moved from that spot, the arrow sent him back.

"The destination's not fifty feet left, right, back, or forward. Where in blazes is it?"

He searched the plaza for five minutes, and then he heard a voice in English coming from behind him.

"And now, if you'll follow me, ladies and gentlemen, this is the last part of tonight's tour, and my personal favorite: the Catacombs of Notre Dame. Situated fifty feet below the streets of Paris, they are a labyrinth of passages, chambers, halls, and tombs that date back to the Middle Ages!"

Flint watched the tour group pass him and head toward the doors of the cathedral. He melted in with the three dozen or so people following the lantern of the guide. They filed through the door, and the guide gave each one a flashlight.

"Now stay close and follow me," the guide told them. "If you get lost, it might take us days to find you. There are literally hundreds of miles of tunnels."

A girl turned to Flint, who stood at the end of the party, and said, "Isn't this exciting? I wonder if we'll find any rats down there."

"Oh, I'm counting on it!" he replied, and he fell into step behind everyone else. They entered a small door to the left of the cathedral's huge entry doors and descended a winding stone stair. Flint heard a door open. A breath of cool, moist air welled up from below.

"Stay close now; we're entering the catacombs."

Flint followed the party, watching their progress on the cell phone's map. After about fifty meters, it was apparent they were going the wrong way. He turned off his flashlight and stopped. The party continued without him. Soon, they were out of earshot. Flint turned his flashlight back on and turned around. Quickly, he worked his way back.

The tunnels of the catacombs were lined with brick and slick with moisture. In places, the water gathered into puddles. It was a dank, musty place, with passages going every which way. He worried about losing his signal but every time it grew weak, he ran into an air vent to the surface and it got stronger. Flint walked carefully along slippery passages, his flashlight stabbing through the thick darkness. When he got within fifty feet of the destination, he heard voices. He switched off the flashlight and listened.

The voices were so soft and bounced around the tunnels so many times, he couldn't catch the words, but they were definitely speaking in Arabic. Flint crept forward through the darkness. After ten steps, he started to notice the darkness in front of him wasn't quite as dark as that behind him. After another few steps, there could be no doubt— there was a light in front of him. He came to a branching passage where it appeared the catacomb passage emptied into a wide brick sewer. The smell was old, but it was obviously not a heavily used sewer—probably an abandoned line. Water flowed down the center of the sewer line toward the Seine. On either side of the tunnel were stone catwalks. The light came from the right, and Flint peered carefully around the corner.

Fifteen feet down the line was an old iron hatch. Standing in front of the hatch were two men and a lantern. Although he couldn't make out their features, it was plain that they had AK-47s over their shoulders.

Flint tucked away Anwar's cell phone and drew his gun. Quietly, he screwed the silencer in place. He took a deep breath and stepped halfway around the corner.

Ping-ping! Ping-ping!

One of the guards slumped against the wall of the sewer and slid down to a sitting position. The other fell back, his arms hanging over the edge of the catwalk.

Flint hurried over. He stripped the guards of their rifles and took a green military jacket and black kaffiyeh off the closest man. Then he pushed the bodies over the side. They hit the water with soft splashes and floated slowly out toward the Seine.

Wolfe turned back to the hatch. They kept it closed, but not all the way. Some of the light in the sewer came from a half-inch crack. Peering through, Flint could see shadows moving in the distance, but not much else. He could hear voices speaking in Arabic, however. Slowly, gun ready, he opened the hatch another few inches. It was a large, well-lit chamber maybe twenty feet high and twice that wide. Someone went to an awful lot of time and trouble to transform it into a command center. At the far end of the room, there were a dozen large LCD-screen TVs displaying maps, data, al Jazeera, and CNBC. Beneath them were rows of desks and computers. Each desk had a laptop, and most of the desks had at least one operator. Other jihadists wandered around the room, talking on phones and going about their business. Many of them wore their kaffiyehs over the lower parts of their faces. Whether this was a comforting connection to their homelands or because the room was cold, he didn't know, but it helped him out.

Their business was obvious. On either side of the workstations were banners of jihad. On the left of the chamber, closest to where Wolfe spied on them, was a veritable armory of weapons. He saw racks of AK-47s, rocket launchers, boxes of rockets, and hand grenades.

Wolfe looked longingly at the grenades, and then a face caught his attention. Two men were speaking. Their backs were toward him, but one turned, gesturing to the other as he talked on the cell phone. It was Hamdi.

"So they didn't bug out. The show's still on. If the secret to those nukes is anywhere, it has to be here," he told himself. "Orani is right; I can't just blow it up. Not yet, at least." Seeing that everyone was dressed like the guards, he shrugged on the jacket and fitted the kaffiyeh over his head. He covered his face with the scarf and slung one of the AK-47s over his shoulder. Then he tucked his pistol inside the jacket, set his shoulder against the hatch, and entered the jihadist command center.

Thirty pairs of dark eyes glanced his way.

Fortunately, he was but one of many wearing a kaffiyeh and a green field jacket.

He muttered, "God be with you" in Arabic and went to a section of vacant desks to the left of the chamber, moving purposefully, as if he knew where he was going. Several of the desks had family photos taped to the surface, as if to remind the jihadists whom they were betraying. It seemed especially sick when he saw pictures of smiling women, wives, sisters, daughters, and mothers. Did they realize what kind of world their loved ones could expect under a Taliban-type rule? Chances were that the jihadist's brave new world would execute many of the women pictured for straying from the most obscenely restrictive laws on personal dignity ever devised by twisted human brains.

Wolfe saw a station with a European family photo and sat down. The jihadists went back to work. He moved the mouse and a sign-in page appeared. As he expected, it came up in Arabic. He put on his reading glasses with the camera and OCR projection program, thinking, *Now we'll see if they work in the field.* They did. He had a clear view of the bright green screen with the pseudo-Saudi flag and writing, which read, "Allah is the one Great God." Below was the standard entry for a personal ID and password.

He slipped this key fob into his left hand and plugged it into the left side USB port, being careful to hide it with his hand. A small icon appeared in the lower left of the window. It was in English, but easily overlooked.

Someone was moving over to see what he was working on. Wolfe moved the mouse to the login prompt, typed in his personal ID and password, and pressed enter. The computer whirred and clicked and logged him on. He quickly went to the start page and opened the most recent application.

"What are you working on today, brother?" asked the jihadist, or something similar to that, laying a dark hand on his shoulder. Wolfe tried to stifle a sneeze after the sudden assault of perfume and unwashed body. He coughed and cleared his throat.

The application opened, and Wolfe simply pointed to the first image that came up. It was self-explanatory. There was no mistaking the "Chunnel," or what the jihadists had in mind. It was typically despicable.

"Ah, yes, didn't you just leave two days ago?"

He needed an audio translator, his Arabic was so bad, but he caught the just of it. Wolfe took out his cell phone and tapped the camera. "The train made it simple, by Allah's will," he replied, not really knowing whether he said what he meant, or something more like, "The trains are simpletons, by Allah's will."

The jihadist laughed and patted him on the shoulder, perhaps amused by his imperfect Arabic—expected amongst homegrown foreign recruits. The jihadist moved away.

Wolfe had the moment he needed.

The USB key fob was like many of the memory devices you could buy off the shelf, but the Company made various improvements. It carried software on it allowing Wolfe to crack the security firewall, and it provided storage capacity. It had an interesting feature in that it was automatically smart. When plugged into a computer, the fob had three jobs: one) get in; two) copy everything on the computer; and three) it would data link everything to the Company via Wolfe's cell phone. The fob immediately started to download the computer's hard drive without any visible indication it was working, while at the same time transmitting the information to Wolfe's cell phone. The only limitation of the system was the satellite signal. Still, the phone would retransmit any data collected as soon as it got a signal. It was a pretty slick system.

Wolfe allowed the fob to do its job. To keep up appearances, he took out the cell phone and acted as if he were downloading pictures to the laptop, doing everything except actually plugging it into the USB port. The illusion set, he went surfing. As he expected, the computer linked to a network with firewalls. He suspected that his laptop had information about this terrorist operation alone. That concerned him. If that were true, the fob would get everything from this computer before moving on to the firewalls, and then on to the other computers of the network. It could well run out of memory before he got what he wanted.

Wolfe thought furiously. He found a dozen network connections— one carried the name "Oasis." He clicked it. A new access page appeared on the screen. He couldn't get in it without interrupting the fob's operation.

The "Chunnel" will have to wait, he decided. Pressing the escape key stopped the operation. As soon as he typed in his ID and password, the fob tackled the new pathway. The entire process started over again.

Wolfe growled to himself. He could've been out by now; the masquerade would only work for so long.

He hit another firewall. This time, a list of two dozen paths opened up, and each had its own access code. Which one? He scanned them with increasing agitation. There was the "Chunnel," fortunately labeled, "Chunnel." The other operations were self-explanatory, except for one that translated into roughly, "Wave of Allah."

It wouldn't have made sense to anyone else, but it did to Wolfe. He clicked on it. The fob started to download the data.

Someone came up behind him and said something about a vest. It caught him off guard, and he automatically asked the jihadist to repeat his request, turning as he did so. It was Hamdi. Fortunately, he had the scarf over the lower part of his face, and he had sense enough to stop short of facing the terrorist.

"Where is your vest?" Hamdi asked again.

Wolfe minimized the screen and selected a "Chunnel" picture, hoping Hamdi hadn't noticed where he was on their network. "My vest?" he asked sheepishly, as if surprised by the question, which he was.

"Your vest," Hamdi said earnestly, thumping his own.

Wolfe saw what he meant. Hamdi and everyone else wore an explosive vest. They were serious. If INTERPOL raided this place, they'd find only body parts and smashed equipment. He glanced around and saw the vests along the left wall by the grenades.

To Hamdi, he mumbled simply, "I'm sorry, I forgot," and leapt up to get a vest. He was picking one up when he heard a curse behind him. He turned to see Hamdi looking at his laptop, his black eyes seething. He said something unintelligible in Arabic and snatched the fob out of the computer. Hamdi held it up and turned toward Wolfe.

The stunned recognition was plain to see.

"You!"

Wolfe flung the vest at Hamdi and brought up the AK-47, firing at the jihadist in one smooth motion.

The vest struck Hamdi in the face and he fell back, tripping over a jihadist behind him. A stream of bullets meant for the bomb maker struck the other terrorist in the chest, and he fell back with a piercing cry.

The fob flew out of Hamdi's hand and clattered to the floor.

Wolfe fired the AK-47 blindly as he dove for the fob. Suddenly everyone else started firing too. He hit the floor close to an open box of grenades. The AK stopped barking, it's clip emptied. Wolfe grabbed a grenade, pulled the pin, and tossed it into the far end of the chamber.

Boom!

Screams, smoke, and debris—the command center erupted into pandemonium. Wounded jihadists cried out in pain, wailing like little children. A fire started at the far end of the room behind the three smashed LCD screens. AK-47's fired blindly into the gloom, and someone else was shouting for it all to stop.

Wolfe had only a moment. He saw the fob in the smoke and snatched it up. Grabbing a grenade with the other hand, he got up and ran to the hatch.

"Stop, Wolfe, don't move!" ordered the voice of Hamdi.

He ignored the order, until a stream of bullets hit the floor in front of him. Wolfe came to an abrupt halt. He turned around. Hamdi had an AK-47 on him. He was only four yards away.

"You're bold, Mr. Wolfe, to come here in the heart of the jihad. Was the information worth your life?"

"Is it worth yours?" Wolfe asked, holding up the grenade with the pin pulled. "Shoot me, and you become a martyr—you may not give a damn, but your 'Wave of Allah' scheme dies with you. Tell me how you plan on getting the nukes, or we both die."

Hamdi laughed. "Our societies have different views on death, Mr. Wolfe. Although I'd like to be the one to trigger Allah's wave of wrath, I will be content to see it from heaven if I must. You Westerners, however, cling to life at all costs."

"Tell that to the Spartans at Thermopylae," Wolfe replied.

"Dog! You would rather subvert the will of Allah and live a single extra day than to follow the path of the prophet and live in everlasting bliss," Hamdi spat angrily. Then he calmed down and laughed. "I've lived in the West. I understand that. You have kids. You will see them again. Now, give me that device and I promise to let you live. After the operation, I will release you into a new world. You're an intelligent man. I'm certain you'll see the light after all you hold dear washes away. Give me that memory chip, and I give you life; you have my word on that."

"Your word isn't worth a boatload of camel dung," Wolfe told him evenly.

"Then I'll take my chances, but you die, Mr. Wolfe," Hamdi said with a broad, yellow grin, and Wolfe saw his finger tighten on the AK-47's trigger.

CHAPTER 38: All This for a Key Fob

It was 1100 hours at McCord AFB Operations, Washington, United States.

Major Kashan of the USAF stepped up to the thick glass window and showed his ID.

"Kashmir!" he said, giving the airman inside his password.

"That's one of my favorite Zeppelin tracks," the airman said, and he buzzed the door for the major and saluted.

Kashan entered, and Captain Jones stepped up.

"Louisville!"

The door buzzed and he stepped inside.

Lieutenant Colonel Jacobs stepped up.

"Karen!"

Staff Sergeant Ashwani checked in last.

"Suleiman!" he said.

"Yes, sir, that's it," the airman said. As he saluted the captain, he asked, "Where's that from?"

"A reggae song," Ashwani said.

The airman opened the inner door to the vault for them and then closed it behind them.

The OIC met them there and ushered them into the briefing room. He handed the major a yellow satchel stuffed with navigational books and charts. Then he handed each officer a set of documents. They sat down, and he went to the overhead projector.

"This is a special, gentlemen," he said, throwing up the first slide. "Recent intelligence points to a possible mass attack by Arab states against Israel. The Israelis have their own stockpiles of nukes, of course, but since the alliance between a Shia-controlled Iraq and Iran is an increased possibility, the Israelis are facing a possible invasion by millions of ground troops at once. The Israelis are not equipped to repel that sort of mass assault either conventionally or with nukes; thus, your mission. You will be stopping in Colorado Springs to upload five hundred nuclear artillery shells. These will enable the Israelis to stop the rag heads in their tracks if it comes down to blows.

"Your call sign will be Crusader 99. Here's your route of flight over the CONUS. You'll stop to refuel and at Andrews; air refueling is deemed too risky with this cargo. Upon exit of the ADIZ, you're filed due regard. The navy will pick you up with fighter escort 200 NM from Gibraltar and escort you all the way to Israel. It's pretty straightforward. Any questions?

"Good, now standard procedure: your cargo is subject to the two-officer policy, and you will be armed at all times. Major, you'll relinquish control of the cargo to Andrews AFB security for the overnight and sign for it at Base Ops. Is everything clear? Fly safe."

***

Wolfe gathered for a desperate leap, but there was no avoiding the AK-47's lethal fire, not at that range. As Hamdi squeezed the trigger, one of his wounded jihadists, apparently wanting to fulfill his vow of self-destruction, triggered his vest. The explosion sent body parts flying everywhere amidst a rain of warm blood. The explosion blew Hamdi off his feet. He flew past Wolfe and onto the boxes of grenades.

Wolfe tossed his grenade between Hamdi's outstretched legs and ran for the hatch. He squeezed outside as a hail of gunfire rattled against the iron door. Without hesitation, he dove into the water at the bottom of the sewer.

As the water closed over his head, Wolfe heard a huge, rumbling boom. The hatch flew off its hinges, bounced off the far wall, and landed in the oily water next to him. The tunnel filled with smoke and Wolfe couldn't see anything. He struck out, half-crawling and half-swimming through the debris-strewn waters. Here and there, he ran into a soft, yielding body in the fetid stream, but he ignored it, fighting his way to cleaner air.

A light appeared in the tunnel ahead. It was dim, followed by the acrid smell of smoke. Voices followed it, shouting voices speaking in Arabic. Flashlights cut into the darkness, searching the turbid water all around him. Wolfe caught sight of at least three men with AK-47s on the catwalk. The lights were getting closer. He ducked into the inky water just as a flashlight swept over him. He thought he escaped, but the sound of automatic rifle fire corrected him. The bubble trails of several rounds swirled around him, and he felt the dull thud of one hitting him on the hip. His hand instinctively went to his hip, but there was no pain, and no bullet hole—he was lucky.

He stayed on the bottom, listening to the scattered bubble trails of more bullets. None came close, but it was only a matter of time. Then his right hand, which was trailing along the rounded bottom of the sewer, felt the bricks disappear. In their place was a sluggish current coming from his right. It must be a branch of the sewer joining the main way. Without waiting, he struck out into the darkness. Swimming blind, using the walls to guide his course, Wolfe didn't stop until his lungs burned for air; then he carefully stuck his head out. There were flashes like lightning back in the main tunnel. The sound of automatic gunfire echoed endlessly, blurring one shot into the last, so that all he could hear was a long, rolling blast.

Wolfe swam on another twenty yards and then climbed onto the catwalk. It was nice to get out of the cold water, but the air in the sewers wasn't much better. Now that he was wet, the cool air turned frigid. He sloshed along the catwalk, breaking into a trot to keep warm and to put as much distance between himself and the jihadists as he could. A ladder to the surface was what he needed, but it was dark, almost pitch black. The only illumination was from the sporadic gunfire behind him, and it was fading. So with his right hand on the sewer wall, he made his way farther and farther from the jihadists, or so he thought. After a few hundred yards, he got the impression that the tunnel was making a loop back whence it came. A sickening sensation gripped his stomach. Of course! Notre Dame was on an island. The sewers didn't connect to the city sewers. As if to confirm his suspicions, he smelled smoke in front of him. The darkness brightened perceptibly. He'd come almost full circle.

The sound of shuffling feet attracted his attention. Up ahead and to the right, flashlights cut the thick air, bouncing off the sewer walls from a side tunnel. Wolfe was about to get back in the water when he noticed the smaller, rectangular catacomb to his left. He splashed into the water and crossed the sewer line, pulling himself into the tunnel. He ducked inside just in time, as automatic fire ricocheted off the brick behind him, showering him with clay splinters.

"Where the hell is the Paris police? Didn't my explosion attract anyone's attention?" he cursed to himself. "It's a helluva step backward when terrorists can shoot AK-47s whenever they want!"

He ran down the catacombs. Arabic shouting followed close behind. He didn't worry about his direction but simply tried to lose his pursuers in the dark, winding way. Wolfe ran along more by feel than sight. That changed when he heard voices and saw flashlights ahead of him. It was the tour group. The Arabic shouting closed in. A dozen faces turned toward him in alarm.

He waved his gun in the air, shouting, "Get out of here and get to the surface, now!"

They seemed to freeze at the unexpected interruption and just stared at him.

The sound of running feet grew louder and Wolfe turned around to see two jihadists run around the dark corner, flashlights in one hand, AK-47s in the other. They saw him and skidded to a halt. Wolfe raised his gun and fired four shots, two for each. The jihadists fell back against the wall. He ran to the closest one, scooped up the AK-47, and fired at the flashlights in the tunnel behind.

That was apparently enough.

The tourists screamed and tried to catch up to the terrified guides.

Wolfe, having momentarily stopped the jihadist advance, followed them. The tour group, despite their terror, was none too quick. The jihadists soon caught up again, this time from several tunnels. *How many rats do they have in this maze?* he thought, ducking into a side tunnel. He waited in the darkness, and a group of jihadists rushed by the opening. With cold, ruthless efficiency, Wolfe stepped out and sprayed automatic fire into their backs. He heard their cries and the sound of bodies thudding to the wet brick floor, but the barking from his AK-47 stopped. He was out of ammo.

He was about to retrieve another weapon, but a number of jihadists were following. He ducked back into the tunnel, hoping he'd given the tour group the time they needed. Wolfe didn't really have any idea where he was or where he was heading. He guessed that the tour group was heading back toward the cathedral, and that would put him somewhere under the broad, paved plaza in front of Notre Dame.

He trotted along after them until his right hand ran into the rusted rungs of a ladder climbing the side of the passage. Wolfe took it, and after fifteen or twenty feet, he bumped into a concrete roof. He took out his waterproof Company-issue cell phone and flipped it open. The small LCD screen gave him enough light to make out his surroundings. He was in a hollow concrete box. A metal plate with a push-button latch was directly in front of him. He pressed the button and a two-foot-by-two-foot door swung open. Wolfe climbed out and swung the doorway shut, only then noticing that the door was actually a plaque. Looking around, he saw he was in the plaza before Notre Dame. He'd emerged from the base of the statue of Charlemagne.

"Thank you, Your Highness," he said, sheathing his gun and dusting his jacket off.

He looked around at the beehive of activity that was the cathedral grounds. Gendarmes had indeed arrived, and they tried to maintain order, but the plaza was crammed with people. Everyone on the district it seemed to have congregated at the cathedral, and no wonder. There was a gaping hole in the plaza. Flames illuminated the cathedral in a flickering red light. It looked as though Lucifer was assaulting Notre Dame from a fissure leading directly to hell.

Wolfe dialed up Orani on his cell phone and worked his way at the edge of the crowd toward the bridge. All he wanted to do was get back to the hotel and data link the information in his key fob to the Company. He might even be able to catch some sleep before his flight tomorrow.

"Wolfe, what is it? It's 2:00 AM. Where are you?" announced her irritated voice.

"I'm at Notre Dame, where I've just blown up what appears to be the al-Qaeda rat hole in Paris," he explained. "I was just taking a walk and getting some air when, well, you can guess the rest. I've down-loaded some data from their network. Maybe you can find something on it."

He walked quickly but casually toward the bridge. He was happy to see the tour group gathered around a pair of flustered gendarmes, who were apparently trying to make sense out of their babbling.

"Alright, plug it in and I'll download it," she said.

He stopped prior to the bridge. A half dozen gendarmes and an ambulance blocked the way. He turned toward a closed food stand, taking out the fob and plugging it into his phone. He looked down to select the "send" cue, but as he did, he caught sight of two black eyes staring at him. It was Hamdi.

The jihadist sat on the back of the ambulance. His face was swollen and bloody. The paramedics were daubing his wounds. Suddenly, Hamdi smiled. He felt the cold barrel of a gun against his neck.

"Don't move, Mr. Wolfe," said the smooth voice of Khallida from behind. Someone plucked his cell phone from his hand. Another hand relieved him of his Walther.

Khallida appeared at his side, along with a smaller, rat-faced man with a straggly black beard and glasses. Khallida handed the rat-faced jihadist the phone and the fob. "We certainly appreciate your help on such short notice."

"You're paying me enough for it," he smiled, speaking with a thick French accent. Flipping open the phone, he scrolled through the menu. "Standard CIA, no surprises here, but this," and he held the key fob up to the light. "I've heard of you, *mon petite cheri*, but I've never seen one." He put them both in his pocket. "It'll take time, but we can see what's on the drive. We don't need him to open it."

Khallida smiled and spread his arms wide, saying, "I'm sorry, Mr. Wolfe, but we don't need you anymore." He nodded to the river and said, "You like touring the less-frequented attractions in Paris, Mr. Wolfe. Let us show you the bottom of the Seine. Take him where he won't trouble us any longer."

Khallida and the rat-faced jihadist turned and headed toward the cathedral. Hamdi, sporting stitches on his cheek and chin, joined them, grinning. He waved to Wolfe.

"Come on, Crusader dog!" growled a voice behind him, shoving

327

the muzzle of the gun painfully into his neck and grabbing him by the arm. He yanked Wolfe roughly into the shadows, out of sight of the gendarmes on the bridge.

Wolfe spun around, using the jihadist's hold on his right arm as a pivot. He ducked away from the muzzle of the gun and then exploded upward into the jihadist. The sudden move surprised his opponent, and the other jihadist tried to grab Wolfe's left arm but was too slow. He lashed out with a vicious sidekick to the ribs, propelling the second jihadist into the food stand. The first jihadist didn't fall, but he stumbled back. Wolfe kicked the pistol out of his hand. The jihadist regained his footing and rushed him, trying to tackle him around the waist. The attempt was awkward, and the jihadist had his head down. Wolfe caught his right shoulder with his left hand and shoved down hard on the back of the jihadist's neck with his right. As the jihadist's momentum carried him down to the cobblestones, Wolfe slipped his right arm under the jihadist's right arm and grabbed the man's bicep. Using his right elbow on the back of the jihadist's neck as a lever, Wolfe pulled up on the arm and threw all of his weight down on the neck. A sharp, hard crunch and a stifled cry were the only sounds of the kill, easily drowned out by the hubbub in the plaza.

The other jihadist was on Wolfe almost instantly. He had a knife in his right hand. He slashed at Wolfe's face and neck. Wolfe stepped back, guiding the knife arm away with his left forearm and clutching the wrist in a vice-like grip with his right hand. The jihadist instinctively punched with his left hand, crossing his extended right arm. It seemed awkward and unnatural, but it was a reaction on his part, and almost completely automatic. Wolfe blocked the punch with his left forearm and rolled his own hand down to another wristlock. Wolfe now had the jihadist's arms crossed left over right, and he cranked the right arm up hard, folding it over the left. The jihadist flipped, landing hard on the cobblestones. Wolfe struck down hard with his knee in the jihadist's throat. The jihadist gasped, and Wolfe disarmed him of the knife. Covering the man's mouth, he put an end to him with one swift stab through the ribs.

He tossed the knife into the Seine, retrieved his gun, and headed back into the plaza, straightening his coat as he did so. Looking around, he caught sight of Hamdi, Khallida, and the rat-faced jihadist at the statue of Charlemagne. They disappeared behind it. Wolfe walked as quickly as he could to the statue. It took what seemed like an eternity to find the button releasing the plaque, but when he did, he slithered through the hole and back down the ladder.

It was pitch dark in the catacombs, but he heard footsteps. He followed them, padding as quickly as he dared. In a few minutes, the light of a flashlight rewarded his boldness. The jihadists talked amongst themselves in Arabic, but he couldn't keep up with the speed of the conversation or the muffled voices. Then he heard the sound of running water, and soon he saw the sewer in front of them. The three jihadists exited the catacombs and turned right down the sewer, toward the river. Hamdi appeared to be talking to someone on his cell phone, but all he caught amidst the echoes and the noise outside was something about, "Meet us with three—something—the Seine."

He came to the edge of the catacombs and peered around the corner. The light in the sewer came from above. The roof over the jihadist command center caved in and Wolfe could see the truncated spires of Notre Dame. To his right, the jihadists continued down the catwalk to the end of the sewer. Wolfe slipped back into the inky water like a crocodile. He followed them, steadily gaining. Hamdi lead Khallida; the rat-faced jihadist brought up the rear.

Hamdi stopped and looked back. Maybe he heard something, or maybe he just felt Wolfe's presence. Wolfe submerged and stayed still. When he raised his head, the three continued. He caught back up. The end of the sewer loomed. Wolfe thought he could see a pair of armed men waiting at the exit.

Creeping up behind the jihadists, Wolfe slowly emerged from the water. He gripped the dripping stone at the edge of the catwalk and reached for the rat-faced jihadist. His hands grabbed a handful of his jacket and he pulled the smaller man into the black water. Wolfe thrust him under, wrapping his left arm around the jihadist's throat and searching for his jacket pocket with his right hand. The panic-stricken jihadist gulped a mouthful of water almost immediately, and his struggling weakened. Wolfe found the pocket; the phone and the key fob were still there. He took them out and let the jihadist go. The rat-faced jihadist burst toward the surface, but Wolfe struck out, holding his breath, and swam toward the exit. He took the time to put the phone and the fob in his jacket pocket and stuck his head up to grab a lungful of air.

Hamdi and Khallida were dragging the rat-faced jihadist out of the water and trying to find out what happened. He was scrambling up the slick bricks and coughing the water from his lungs—too wretched to relay the particulars of Wolfe's attack.

Ahead, the gaslights from the far bank glinted on the barrels of the guards' AK-47s. The guards were trying to find out what the excitement was all about, and their flashlights stabbed into the darkness. Wolfe turned onto his back and stuck his feet out in front of him, drifting along with the current. The heels of his boots scraped along the bottom. A flashlight beam began to search the tunnel. He was only a few yards away when the jihadist's light found him. Wolfe slammed his heels into the bricks and gathered his legs under him. He exploded out of the water, arms outstretched, and clotheslined the jihadists, tumbling them both outside and into the river with him.

The shock of the cold Seine drove the air out of the jihadists' lungs, and he could hear their surprised screams, even underwater. He grappled one of them, using his body to climb for the surface. His head surged into the air and he gathered a breath. Wolfe wrestled behind the flailing jihadist, holding his head under by keeping a hand gripped on each shoulder. The jihadist didn't try to get away, but struggled wildly in a mad panic.

Flashlights stabbed at the river from the mouth of the sewer, searching for Wolfe. The light was dazzling against the gas lamps on the river walk of the Seine. There was yelling, and then the water to his right erupted. The unmistakable sound of automatic gunfire rolled across the river, budda-budda-budda! Wolfe yanked the jihadist out of the water, and he came up sputtering and gasping. He whirled the flailing terrorist around, placing him between himself and the gunfire. Budda-budda-budda! This time, the jihadist on shore aimed true. There was the soft but heavy sound of bullets thudding into flesh, and Wolfe felt his human shield jerk at the impacts. Wolfe swam away from the gunner, dragging the twitching body of the jihadist with him. Peering around the dead jihadist's lolling head, he saw the gunner scramble up the bank to the river walk and follow him downstream. He kept his flashlight on Wolfe and aimed the AK-47 from his hip with his other hand. His aim wasn't great, but it didn't need to be. Bullets thwacked into the body and splashed in the water all around Wolfe. It was only a matter of time before they hit him.

He struck out for the far shore, trying to at least gain some distance from the gunner, and in the process of re-gripping his human shield, Wolfe felt something smooth and bulbous hanging from the jihadist's vest. He grabbed it. It was a grenade. Without further thought, he pulled the pin with his teeth and flung it across the water. The grenade hit behind the jihadist and to the right of Wolfe's target, but it didn't matter; the jihadist never saw it.

The grenade flared in the darkness, exploding in a sharp, popping sound, and as he ducked into the water, Wolfe saw the gunner briefly silhouetted in the red-orange flash. When he bobbed up, there was no sign of the gunner except for a still-shining flashlight spinning slowly round and round in the river.

Things grew eerily quiet, with only the sounds of the flowing river and the now-distant sirens. Wolfe pushed the corpse away after relieving it of three more grenades and a knife, thinking he couldn't leave them there for a civilian to find. He tucked them in his jacket. Wolfe was about to strike out for the riverbank when he heard the low growl of a motor behind him. He turned quickly around to see a dinner barge bearing down on him. People were crowded on the flat bows, apparently wondering what all the noise was about. Wolfe had to swim energetically to keep from being run over, but as the bows swept by, white faces staring down at him, he saw a rope hanging over the side. He grabbed it and clambered out of the water. Up and over the rail he climbed, dripping. He stood on the deck, running his hands through his hair and rubbing the water from his eyes. A group of a dozen people stood around him, mouths agape, as if he were some terrible apparition.

Wolfe couldn't help but grimace at their expressions. He took a glass of red wine from one of the frozen patrons, saying, "Excuse me; it's damn cold in there. I need this more than you." He drained the glass in one gulp. It was smooth and warmed his sodden limbs. "Thanks; now, don't let me disturb your dinner any further," he said, handing the glass back and making his way through them toward the pilothouse. The captain met him halfway.

He let go a fountain of angry French, but Wolfe fixated on a new sound on the river: the whine of high-pitched motors. He left the captain and looked aft. Three speedboats left the Isle de Notre Dame about a hundred yards behind them. He took the captain by the shoulders, turned him around, and hustled him back to the pilothouse. The captain protested vehemently, but he couldn't resist Wolfe's forced guidance. He sputtered, cursed, and shouted, but Wolfe shoved him back in front of his wheel and threw the throttles forward. The barge lurched forward, and the captain tried to pull the throttles back, until Wolfe drew his gun. The captain threw his hands up.

Wolfe pointed behind to the approaching speedboats. Even the dim light of the river was enough to highlight the jihadists crowding the bows. The captain cursed again and tried to shove the throttles further still.

Running to the aft end of the barge, Wolfe took out the grenades and started lobbing them down the river. The jihadists opened up as the first grenade sent a geyser high into the night sky. It blew between two boats but otherwise did no damage. Wolfe lobbed the second one higher. It burst between the same two boats, but this time it blew in the air. There were screams from both boats, and three jihadists toppled into the Seine. One of the boats veered suddenly to the left, skipped up the bank, and slid into the intersection, coming to a stop exactly in the middle and effectively blocking traffic from each direction. A single dead jihadist leaned over the side, his arms flung out, his mouth and eyes wide open as if arguing with the angry motorists.

His third grenade exploded in the water beneath the third speedboat, starting a fire in the engine bay. Although stricken, the boat had enough momentum to catch up to the chugging barge. The jihadists on the bow scurried onto the barge like a pack of rats.

Wolfe shot the first two before they could fire a shot, but three more were on the deck and they opened up on him. He ducked back to the bow, the wood cabin of the barge splintering behind him. As he ran up front, the last remaining speedboat pulled alongside with two jihadists up front and one driving the boat. Their AK-47s barked, tearing up the heavily varnished wood and shattering the glass windows. There was nowhere to go. Wolfe jumped.

He landed on the boat's deck and rammed the jihadist at the helm with his shoulder. The blow drove the jihadist into the gunwale, and

Wolfe followed up, pummeling the man in the face with the butt of his gun. The jihadist fell half over the gunwale, bleeding from his forehead, so Wolfe helped him the rest of the way, dumping him into the Seine.

The two jihadists on the front turned to fire at Wolfe, but he grabbed the wheel and yanked it hard to the right, back to the left, and then back viciously to the right. Both jihadists fell and slid across the slick bows. One of them lost his AK-47 in the river. A burst of gunfire from the barge hit the boat and shattered the windshield. Wolfe threw the throttle forward. The boat jumped, dumping one of the jihadists into the river. The other tried to regain his feet and fire, but Wolfe jerked the wheel back and forth, spilling him with each maneuver.

The fire from the barge stopped as Wolfe pulled ahead. He dodged to the left to avoid the piling of a bridge and shot through the other side. The jihadist was on all fours, his teeth bared like a dog with rabies and his black eyes wide with fear. Wolfe cut the throttle. The boat's nose dug into the water. With a cry, the jihadist flew into the Seine.

As the jihadist slid into the water, Wolfe gunned the motor. He heard a thump, and then the propellers ground and shook for a few seconds before rotating free. The jihadist popped to the surface, his face bloodied, his arms flailing weakly. He shook his fist at Wolfe, yelling and screaming. Wolfe saluted him as the huge, blunt, black bow bore down on him. The jihadist turned, screamed, and disappeared.

A burst of AK-47 fire drew his attention back to the bow of the barge.

The three jihadists had taken the barge, herding the dinner guests into a huddled knot of frightened cattle ready for slaughter. One of them walked to the prow and stood exposed, waving at Wolfe. It was Hamdi. "Give me the data fob, Mr. Wolfe, and I'll spare these people; otherwise, they will all die!"

Again, Wolfe acted without thinking, letting his anger guide him. He gunned the motor and spun the boat around to face the barge. He shoved the throttle up to the stop. The bow rose. Wolfe shoved a fresh clip into the Walther. The boat picked up speed. Wolfe rushed toward the barge. Thirty yards, twenty yards and then ten yards. Wolfe climbed the dash, putting his boot on the windshield frame. Hamdi's brows rose in surprise. At the last moment, Wolfe drove against the frame and launched into the air.

CHAPTER 39: Diversion

The crisp river air flew by his face, and he brought his right leg up and his left followed, leading his flight with his boots. Wolfe's left boot struck Hamdi's stomach. His right thumped into his chest a split second later. The impact ran through Wolfe's shins, knees, and hips. He heard the breath leave Hamdi's lungs, and his chin hit his chest with an audible thump. The jihadist lost his AK-47. It spun into the crowd of dinner guests as Wolfe rode his foe down to the deck as if he were a surfboard.

He launched off Hamdi's body and rolled up to his feet.

"Get down on the deck!" he shouted. He couldn't see both the remaining jihadists, but the one on the right began to fire blindly. Three civilians went down, and Wolfe brought the barrel of the Walther in line with the bearded face. He fired twice. Pop-pop! The jihadist fell back off the barge and into the darkness.

Wolfe looked around for the other jihadist, but it was tough to see anything through the chaos. The only light came from the dim gas lamps and the strings of Christmas lights over the dinner area. Out of the corner of his eye, he saw a dark shape duck into the pilothouse. Picking his way through the panicky crowd, he headed that direction. By the time he got to the other side of the dinner area and broke into the clear, the jihadist dragged the captain out and held a gun to his head.

Sweat beaded on his shining forehead. His white teeth stood out;

his lips pulled back in a frozen snarl. The jihadist looked more terrified than the captain, who looked more angry than scared and let loose a torrent of French curses. The jihadist shook the captain by the collar, yelling incoherently at Wolfe.

Wolfe was too angry to listen. He'd gone into that cold, cold rage, and everything slowed down. He saw the jihadist as if on a movie screen, his face sharp and distorted, spit flying from his wet mouth. Wolfe stopped, raised his Walther, and shot. He swore he could see the bullet whiz three inches left of the captain's cheek and tunnel through the black hole of the jihadist's left pupil. A splash of blood and retinal fluid doused the captain, who squinted against the spray as if a sailor in a storm. The jihadist's head flew back as if yanked by a puppeteer, but his hands went instantly limp as the bullet tore through the motor center of the brain. He crumpled down to the deck.

Wolfe turned back toward Hamdi, but to his surprise, the dinner patrons took care of him themselves. Hamdi wasn't dead. Wolfe could see his face. He was moaning in pain and clutching his torso, but the civilians had him off the deck and in their arms. They dragged him to the rail, and with a chorus of shouts, they threw the wounded jihadist overboard. He ran to the rail, but the Seine was empty. The dark surface roiled for a few seconds as the barge churned away, and then grew still and black.

CHAPTER 40: Treason

"Crusader nine-nine, Mayday, repeat, Mayday," Major Mustafa Kashan called over the HF radio. He repeated the message until Santa Maria radio answered.

"We copy, Crusader nine-nine; state the nature of your emergency." The voice wavered and crackled, barely readable, but that wasn't uncommon for the HF radio.

"We've lost two engines and are unable to put the fire out. We are going down; repeat, we are going down. Our coordinates are zero-two-one-two-decimal-three-north, and zero-zero-one-three-five-decimal-six-west. We are—" Kashan stopped and released the microphone switch. He looked at Lieutenant Colonel Jacobs in the left seat. "Are we ready?"

"We are," the colonel said and keyed the plane's intercom. "Colonel to crew, we have a problem and are performing an emergency descent. Take your seats; we are starting our descent now." He clicked off the autopilot and pulled back all four throttles on the C-17. The engine instruments, all of which read normal with no indications of fire, retreated to idle. The nose of the cargo airplane dropped and the deck angle decreased to negative twenty-five degrees. The attitude indicator pitched down. The airspeed indicator wound up toward the barber pole, and the noise of the slipstream grew louder.

"Crusader nine-nine, how copy?" crackled the radio.

Kashan laughed.

"Crusader nine-nine, how copy?" They could hear the concern of the controller through the static. "Crusader nine-nine, please respond!"

"They've bought it, the fools!" Kashan chuckled.

The cockpit door burst open and Tech Sergeant Ashwani ran in. He wore his battle gear, as per regulations, with his Glock in its shoulder holster and his M-16 in his hand. As the senior MP, his charge was the nuclear cargo, a charge he obviously took very seriously.

"Colonel, what's the problem? What's this about a descent?"

"We've lost two engines, Sergeant. They exploded, and we can't hold altitude!" Kashan told him excitedly.

"I didn't hear anything!" the sergeant said, his dark complexion contracting into a look of surprise and suspicion. "What's going on here?"

"We're going through our procedures," Kashan told him pointedly.

"Go strap yourself in!" the colonel ordered.

The sergeant straightened and looked like he was about to follow the orders and leave, but his eyes strayed to the instrument panel. "If an engine exploded, shouldn't there be red lights, alarms, or something to show you what's wrong?" he asked, as if to himself. Suddenly, he pulled his Glock out of its holster and pointed it at the colonel.

"Airman Khamadi to the cockpit on the double with your weapon!" he shouted over his shoulder. "You two get to the cargo and secure the area! Go! Go! Go!" He turned to the colonel, his dark eyes serious, hand pointing the gun at the pilot's head. "Now, sir, you'll level this plane and tell me what's going on here. Now!"

There was a sharp crack!

Blood spattered the cockpit as a bullet penetrated the back of Ashwani's skull and exited out the top. The sergeant's dead hand went into spasms, squeezing the trigger of his Glock three times in mortal heroism. He fell, betrayed, to the aluminum deck—dead.

The colonel screamed as a bullet tore into his ear and cheek.

As the sergeant fell against the center instrument pedestal, his right arm hit the metal edge, sending one bullet into the forward windscreen and the next into the HF radio. The Plexiglas windscreen exploded, blowing the colonel back into his seat and cutting his flight suit and face to ribbons. Kashan instinctively covered his face as a hurricane of Plexiglas and wind howled through the cockpit. The air sucked out of his lungs by the lack of air pressure, and he fumbled for the lifesaving oxygen mask. His fingers, already cold from the plummeting temperature, tried to squeeze the dual triggers that would release the mask, but panic took hold, and he started to black out. Something was wrong; he couldn't get his fingers to work. His breath came in ragged gasps, and his lungs hurt.

Kashan fought his rising panic, but it was too much for him. He gave up, whispering to himself, "Allah has the airplane." Everything went black.

***

Flint checked with Orani before she boarded his flight from Paris to Washington, DC. She would be sitting in first class with Lufti, but otherwise, there was nothing to the business. They both carried scars from their ordeals, but beyond that was the frustration of having lost Khallida. Hamdi's body was never recovered.

"Did Khallida make it out of Paris?" Flint asked, sipping his coffee as he waited for the cleaners to finish working on the airplane.

"No one has any idea; he's disappeared," she replied, adjusting the dark glasses that hid her blackened eyes. "None of the bodies recovered from the Seine were Khallida or Hamdi's, but we're pretty sure Hamdi's fish food."

"That's only one out of two; in this game, that's not good."

"The fob was full of information we already had. Unfortunately, the transmission stream was interrupted before the details of the nukes came through. All we got was a reference to something called 99 Crusader—nothing else. We don't know what that might mean. As long as the terrorists don't have a weapon, we can lay low and wait for Khallida to pop up."

"Alright, you're the boss," Flint sighed. "I've got to get back to work. You relax and get some rest; I'll make sure the flight attendants take good care of you."

They took off, and an hour later, they entered the NATS, the North Atlantic Track System. It was south of where they usually flew, but the Canadians were charging heinous fees for crossing their airspace and it was cheaper to burn gas than to pay for kindergarten hockey programs. The bunky's, or relief pilots, were already on break, and the ship was settling down to the routine of a thirteen-hour flight. Wolfe was glad of it. His body ached despite the number of Advil in his system. He wanted to get home and sleep for a month. Let someone else worry about saving the world from jihad.

He had one last thing to do before sitting back and relaxing; he had to check the HF radios. He dialed in Shanwick's frequency and called, "Shanwick, Shanwick, United seven-five-one, how copy?"

"United seven-five-one, you're on Santa Maria. Stand by, please."

"Santa Maria! How the hell did I get them?" Wolfe asked, irritated with himself. When he checked his chart, though, there was no mistake. He was on frequency eight-nine-zero-six, and it was a shared frequency between the centers. Wolfe realized Shanwick must be on a lower frequency, but as he put his hand on the selector to change it, the Santa Maria controller called another aircraft.

"Crusader 99, Crusader 99 please state the nature of emergency. Crusader 99, how do you copy Santa Maria?"

99 Crusader was an aircraft call sign! Wolfe had a sinking feeling.

Wolfe asked, "Santa Maria United, can you give me the position of Crusader nine-nine? We'll try and get him on the VHF radio."

"Thanks, United, but he's fifteen hundred miles south of you between the Azores and the Canary Islands," the controller told him.

Flint gripped his armrest so hard his muscles stood out in his forearm. "Where's his destination?"

"Israel, now please stand by; I have to alert Air Sea Rescue."

Suddenly he had a sinking feeling, and things began to make perfect sense. There was just one more thing to check. He took out his PDA and signed in to his Internet account.

"What's going on, Flint?" asked the captain. He wasn't listening to the HF radio, which was normal; no one wanted to listen to the crackling, hard-to-hear HF unless they absolutely had to—Air Force Electronic Warfare officers had been know to go mad after listening to it hour after hour.

"In a minute, George, we may not be going to San Fran. Punch Tenerife, La Palma into the Fix page, will you?"

"Are you serious?"

"Just do it, I'll be right back with you; the company is sending us an ACARS. They're insane!"

The accusation of airline corporate insanity was instantly understandable to the captain—he started punching the airport into the computer.

Flint had a good satellite signal, and he logged into his CIA account. He had a feeling of helplessness, making it hard to stay calm—thank God, the Company used a retinal scanner on his PDA and not a password he had to type! He was in, and using a shaking finger, he navigated to the "Active Mission" page, and then to "Analyst Support." Typing as fast as he could, Flint requested the "Flight plan and cargo of Crusader 99? Urgent!"

Funny, he thought, how he could be completely calm when he had something he could physically do. Sitting here trying to get information was worse than waiting and doing nothing.

Flint's PDA flashed a message seemingly too quickly, the analyst as obviously far more comfortable and capable than Wolfe at this. "Crusader 99 Andrews AFB to Ben Gurion with military cargo-N."

"What's the cargo?"

A moment later, it came through. "500 nuke artillery shells."

"Shit!"

Wolfe thought furiously. He typed in the ACARS message he wanted the Company to send their aircraft—he couldn't just turn the airplane south without permission from center, the Company, and the captain, not without hijacking the plane and blowing his cover forever more. He made up the message as he went, finishing it with the authorization code, and the urgency code. The Company would take care of the rest.

He was downloading the newest satellite photos of the Canary Islands when the ACARS printer whirred, and the captain let out a harsh stream of curses.

Ripping the paper off the printer, the captain read the message aloud. "To United 751, new flight plan to follow, you are cleared to the Canary Islands TFS Reina Sofia as 'Lifeguard Nine.' Pax Ms. Orani in 2A has a heart waiting for her in the hospital. Shanwick and Santa Maria have already been notified. Customer service will brief Pax on arrival." He looked down, and sure enough, a new flight plan was sliding out of the computer. "I've never heard of anything like this!"

Wolfe would have smiled, if the prospects of Armageddon weren't so real.

"Shanwick to United seven-five-one, you are now Lifeguard United seven-five, how copy?"

"Lifeguard United seven-five-one loud and clear, go ahead."

Center turned them south, approving the new route of flight. They were eager to help.

The captain punched in the new course and then briefed the purser. "Tell Ms. Orani we're flying her to her new heart courtesy of United Airlines, the company that cares! I'll make an announcement to the passengers."

For the next hour, they each dealt with the complicated business of diverting the flight to a new destination. The captain sent Flint back to check on Orani, after a little subtle prodding, and he was able to inform her of the emergency. Yasmina skillfully played the part of a critically ill patient, and considering the past few days, that wasn't difficult.

"You aren't trying to make a point with me, are you, with this heart business, I mean?" she asked.

He patted her on the head and told her, "They'll have an ambulance waiting for us, and I'm going to get the flight attendants to watch Lufti, but there's not much else in the way of help." He'd gotten several messages on his PDA since his initial message, and it seemed to him that the only plan of action was the one in his head.

Orani said as much. "Wolfe, you're the lead on this; go with your instincts. What do they tell you?"

"Nothing good," Wolfe said, thinking furiously.

She turned on the reading light and opened up her laptop. Plugging in a headset, handed it to him and explained, "This is a transmission from the Air Force C-17 that went down in the Atlantic—at least that's what we initially thought. Now we're not so sure. The reception's not great, but our people cleaned it up a bit. There's a formal radio call followed by background noise in the cockpit—apparently, the first officer's mike stuck in transmit. I want your take on it."

Flint listened to the transmission of Crusader 99. His frown deepened as he went further into the tape. "Were those gunshots I heard at the end?"

"Two shots, maybe three, fired from a Glock nine-millimeter. After that, the transmission goes dead."

"Who shot who?" Flint asked. "It sounds like the pilot's faked an emergency, but someone broke into the cockpit—who?"

"We think that was Tech Sergeant Ashwani. He was the head of the security detail for the flight."

Flint squirmed upright in his seat. "They're hauling five hundred nukes, Orani—five hundred."

Orani shook her head and said, "Sometimes I really, really hate it when you're right."

***

When Kashan came to, he slumped forward in his straps. The wind still howled in the cockpit. The lights were on, but it was still dark outside.

"I didn't imagine paradise was like this," he mumbled to himself, sitting up straight and looking around. As his eyes began to focus, they snapped to the only sign of movement. The standby altimeter spun counterclockwise, winding down through nine thousand feet. His training caused him to react before his mind was fully awake, and he found himself pulling back on the stick, leveling the airplane off in the darkness by using his instruments. Still groggy, he put the autopilot on at three thousand feet, automatically picking the altitude they'd planned on in the briefing. The C-17 stabilized, and Kashan scanned the cockpit.

The colonel leaned to his left, a bloody mess. Kashan reached over and grabbed his shoulder. The colonel stirred, turning his chewed-up face toward Kashan. One eye was completely cut out by the flying Plexiglas, and half his face was torn off—his bloody teeth could be seen through his cheek.

The squeamish copilot pulled away from the colonel, whose tattered, three-fingered hand reached for him. The colonel's mouth opened as if to scream, but Kashan couldn't hear anything over the wind. The bloody figure collapsed over the prostrate form of the sergeant, who laid face up, his mouth open in protest at the treason.

Kashan puked all over the instrument display. He sat there heaving until his stomach emptied. Exhausted, panting, he stared straight ahead. Something grabbed him by the shoulder, and he jumped. Terrified, he turned around.

"What are you doing?" Airman Khamadi, the one who'd murdered the sergeant, shouted at him. He was bleeding from shrapnel cuts, bruised, and disheveled, but his eyes were hard-set.

"The colonel's injured," Kashan complained, looking behind Khamadi. Through the open cockpit door, he could see the other two MPs. They had the loadmaster, who along with the sergeant wasn't part of the plot, on his knees with his hands on his head. One of the MPs took his Glock and shot the man in the forehead. The loadmaster fell to the deck. He rolled over on his back, his eyes staring blankly, a short, pulsing fountain of blood bubbling out of the bullet hole.

"Continue with the mission!" Khamadi insisted, pounding Kashan on the shoulder. "Come on, that's why there's two of you!"

Kashan nodded sheepishly, gladly turning away from the execution. He punched in the prearranged coordinates into the flight management computer. He moved the coordinates to the top of the navigation page and executed the command. The airplane rolled right and took up a southeast heading. He set the speed at two hundred and eighty knots and reset the altitude to one thousand feet. Then Kashan leaned back and took a deep breath. If everything worked as planned, they'd reach the island airfield by morning.

CHAPTER 41: Reality Check

Morning came and the Canary Islands came into view.

The colonel was still alive, but the others dragged him into the back and out of the slipstream. They took the sergeant out of the cockpit as well, but despite the wind, the place still smelled like blood and death.

Kashan maneuvered the cargo plane around the northern tip of the island, staying low under the radar coverage. There was a small dirt strip on the north end of the island. He lined the plane up and set it down. The C-17 made easy work of the unimproved airfield, despite its size. Kashan taxied it between some trees where a group of men waited with camouflage netting. He shut the engines down and unstrapped, glad to be back on the ground.

Quickly, he went to the back. The MP opened the exterior hatch, and a group of men rushed in. The first thing they went for was the cargo. They seemed quite anxious until they'd opened up one of the crates and verified that they had what they wanted. Shouts of, "Allahu Akbar!" resounded through the plane. The excitement was infectious, but the colonel's groans reminded him of the price they'd already paid. He went to the man directing the offloading of the shells.

"Excuse me, but we need some medical help. Is there a hospital we can get the colonel to?"

The man looked concerned, and he followed Kashan to the bunk where the colonel lay. "What happened?"

Kashan explained, and when he finished, the man turned to the colonel and asked, "Can you walk; can you move?"

The colonel groaned and shook his head.

"Very well," the man said, and without hesitation, he took out his pistol and shot the colonel in the head.

Kashan stared at quivering body of the colonel in shock and stammered, "What did you do that for? He was one of us; there was no need to kill him."

The man turned to him, pointing his gun at Kashan's chest.

"You Americans are soft. We can't bring attention to the operation by bringing him to a hospital, and we don't have a doctor. He's a martyr now. Do you have anything else to say?"

"No, I don't," Kashan replied.

"Good, now help get those boxes unloaded—move it, before I decide you're as useless as the other pilot!"

Kashan jumped to it, feeling more like a prisoner of war than a compatriot in their jihad. Before long, he realized he wasn't alone in those feelings. The jihadists treated the other Americans with the same level of distrust as they treated him. One of the MPs had more guts than he did. When they'd loaded all the shells, they all moved to the back of the truck to get on with the rest of the men.

"No, you four stay here with your plane. Someone will have instructions for you later."

"But we've got no food, water, or lodging," the MP complained. Then he added, "I've had about enough of this! This is our jihad too, and we sacrificed a lot to get you this stuff!"

The man pulled out a knife and held it at the MP's throat, saying, "Then be happy with that! You've done your part, Westerner, but we can't trust you. You're not a true Muslim born of the holy land. At most, you'll be allowed to live as a convert in the subjugated countries, but you'll never be a true warrior like us."

"Oh, you mean like the Afghanis and Iraqis we've been kicking up and down the Middle East over the last couple of years?" the MP retorted, and unwisely so.

"Western dog!" the man barked, and he slid the knife across the MP's throat, releasing a torrent of red blood.

The MP fell to his knees, clutching his throat, blood spurting through his fingers.

The man kicked him in the chest, knocking the MP to the ground. He then waved to his men and told them something in Arabic. They fell upon the still-living MP, despoiling him of his body armor, weapons, and even his boots while he was still alive.

The man turned to Kashan and asked, "Do I need to cut your throat as well?"

Kashan shook his head vigorously.

"Then give us your stuff."

Kashan and the remaining two MPs stripped. Ten minutes later, they watched the truck pull away, standing in their underwear next to a plane with dead people on board and dead people outside. They had no country, no friends, and no fuel.

"What do we do now?" asked the MP.

"Hell if I know," Kashan replied, and he meant it.

Kashan and the MP waited for hours. They had no choice but to strip the dead of their clothes. As evening fell, a four-wheel drive vehicle approached them loaded with jihadists.

The MPs almost collapsed, sobbing, "They're going to finish us off!"

Kashan shook his head and pointed to the fuel truck behind the jihadists. "I don't think so; why else would they bring us gas?"

Sure enough, a jihadist armed with an AK-47 jumped out and approached Kashan. "We have need of you after all, it seems. We have too many warheads for this operation, so you will fly the rest to Morocco. There, they'll be distributed around the world," he said, and he pointed the AK-47 at Kashan's stomach. "That is, unless you have objections."

"Not at all," Kashan said enthusiastically.

"Good, then you can fuel the airplane, and you two," he pointed the gun at the MPs, "you can help load it. Be quick!"

Kashan and the MP's hopped to work, and he had an inkling of hope.

***

The captain landed the triple-seven expertly, and he pulled off the runway onto the tarmac of Tenerife. As they stopped, Wolfe saw a truck pulling up alongside with air stairs. Wolfe cut the engines and put his jacket on. Before he left, he slipped the Walther and four clips out of the secret compartment of his flight bag. Then he left the cockpit. The medics already had Orani on a litter with an IV plugged into her arm. They carried her down the stairs and into the waiting ambulance with Wolfe following. He hopped in the back and closed the doors.

"Take us to the Nuevo Maria airfield as fast as you can!" Wolfe told them through the small partition window between the cab and the back.

"Right, sir, it'll be almost an hour," he informed Wolfe, and he closed the window.

Orani sat up, but they both had to hold on as the ambulance driver peeled out of the airport. "How do you know where the nukes are?" she asked, grabbing the rack of medical equipment for support.

"They came in on a C-17," Wolfe told her, taking out his PDA and accessing a series of satellite photos. He chose one showing the main islands in the Canaries. The International Airport was easy to see, but Wolfe had to zoom in on the northern end of the island to see a small dirt strip on the coast. "This is where they came in, and there's the C-17. No one would notice it unless they were looking for it. From there, they'll have to take the nukes by boat to La Palma—it's the only way." He touched his finger to the image and scrolled over to an island to the northwest. He pointed along a white ribbon of road along the eastern edge of a long, crescent-shaped ridge. "This is where the University of Colorado drilled their instrumentation shafts, with Mr. Delaney's grant money, mind you. That's where the nukes are headed."

Wolfe had to hold on as the ambulance careened around a corner. Orani fell off the gurney, and he had to catch her. "Now then, no time for that!" he joked, setting her down.

"Very funny," she grimaced. "How much longer did he say?"

"I can tell you," Wolfe said, getting their current position from the GPS in his PDA and having it calculate the most direct route to the field. It took a moment for the GPS to synch up, but then it showed a map.

"Turn left on the Natividad Highway in zero-point-three kilometers," it said. Wolfe glanced up through the window, but to his consternation, the driver pulled the curtain.

That's strange, he wondered. *He should be slowing down.* Looking through the side window, they both saw the exit for the highway pass on the left.

"Recalculating route," the PDA announced.

"Maybe they're taking the back route," Orani suggested.

"If they are, they're going the wrong way," Wolfe said, after consulting the GPS position on his PDA. He jumped up and rapped on the window. "Driver! Driver! Where are we going?"

There was no answer, but the ambulance slowed down. He gazed out the side windows. On the left was a high, barren ridge of rock. On the right, he saw the ocean. They appeared to be climbing a steep hill. The road suddenly leveled off, and the ambulance came to a stop. They heard the doors open on either side, but the ambulance engine kept running.

Wolfe drew his gun.

"Stay down, Orani," he told her, moving her below the window.

The passenger door closed. The driver's door slammed closed. The ambulance rolled forward and started down a hill. Wolfe saw the driver and the other man wave at him from outside the ambulance. He leapt to the back door, but it was locked. He threw his shoulder against it. It didn't budge.

The ambulance started to gain speed.

Orani jumped for the pass-through window, but it too was locked.

"What are we going to do?"

Wolfe shot the lock, but the doors wouldn't open. He could see a plastic-coated cable wound around the handles. He glanced back into the ambulance. There were saws and knives, but they'd take far too long. Then he saw the two oxygen cylinders. He ran over and threw one of them down, aiming the blunt green base at the doors. Without waiting, he shot the valve and hoped the tank didn't explode.

Whoosh! The tank discharged its oxygen, turning into a rocket. It launched at the doors, tearing the right-hand door off its hinges. The gray ribbon of the narrow road showed behind them. The ambulance lurched as it scraped against the guardrail, but it still picked up speed.

"On the gurney," he shouted, pulling Orani onto her stomach and then pushing it out of the ambulance. At the last second, he leapt on top of her, and out they went. They hit the pavement with a thump, but the gurney didn't roll over. Instead, it began to roll down the hill at breakneck speed. To make matters worse, the road turned hard to the left at the bottom of the hill. Straight ahead was a cliff with a drop of several hundred feet to the ocean.

"It can't get much worse," he muttered over the wind.

"Really? Look behind us!" Orani yelled.

Wolfe looked over his shoulder. There was a black sedan coming down the hill after them. He looked in front. They were picking up speed and gaining on the ambulance as it was scraping against the guardrail. Wolfe leaned to the right, and the gurney turned toward the ambulance.

"You can't steer this thing around that corner!" Orani protested.

"Hang on tight and get ready to grab the ambulance!" Wolfe told her.

A shot whizzed by, and then another. A staccato of automatic fire sprayed the pavement and the ambulance.

Wolfe steered for the driver's side door, and with nothing to slow it down, the gurney thumped against the side of the ambulance. Wolfe got a hold of the door handle, but he couldn't open it; the gurney was in the way. He pulled the gurney forward and grabbed the mirror, nearly falling off as the ambulance bumped against the guardrail. Orani screamed and grabbed the door handle as the gurney's wheels started to shred and it started to swerve. He couldn't wait. Wolfe lifted himself off the gurney, using the mirror as support. The steel tubing held. He got one foot on the running board and looped his free arm around Orani just as the gurney's front legs collapsed.

Orani screamed, but he lifted her clear of the tumbling wreck and set her on the running board.

"We're back where we started!" she protested, her brown eyes wide with terror. Two more shots plinked against the side of the ambulance.

Wolfe broke the driver's side window with the butt of his gun and cleared away the shards from the frame. "Get in and drive!" he told Orani, and without waiting for her to answer, Wolfe heaved her up and through the window with his free arm. That got her halfway through. He put his hand on her buns and shoved her the rest of the way. Orani slithered around in the seat and grabbed the wheel. She immediately stood on the brakes, almost throwing Wolfe off.

"I don't think we're going to make it!" she screamed.

"You don't have a choice!" he replied, taking a couple of shots at their pursuers. The rounds bounced off the windshield, but it was enough to drive the shooter back inside the car.

The tires squealed, and the force of the turn plastered Wolfe into the driver's side door. He stared over his shoulder. They were in the turn, and the only thing keeping them out of the ocean was the guardrail. He held on. Orani gritted her large, white teeth, grimacing like an Olympian as they scraped, screeched, and clawed their way around the hairpin turn. Somehow, she made it.

"We did it!"

"We're not out of the woods yet; keep driving!"

"What are you going to do?"

"Ask me when it's over!" Wolfe replied, and he clambered onto the roof of the cab and then slid over the emergency lights to the flat surface of the ambulance bay. He could see the right door flapping in the slipstream and the black sedan in pursuit. A man popped out of the passenger-side window, an AK-47 in his hands. Wolfe took the time to fire two shots at him, but Orani's driving made it doubly difficult to aim. In her quest to shake the pursuers, she used every bit of the narrow mountain road. It wasn't making it any easier for Wolfe to hold on. Fortunately, the ambulance was a Mercedes, and the Germans used a raised ridge on either side of the cab and bay to keep the rain off the windows. It came in handy when Orani swerved, as she did now, cutting to the left to avoid a burst of automatic gunfire, and then coming back hard to the right to avoid the mountainside.

The action tossed him like a rag doll, and his boots lost their grip. He slid off the right-hand side of the ambulance bay, grabbing the ridge at the last moment. His legs flew off the roof and into space, hanging out over a hundred-meter gulf that ended in the ocean. Wolfe's obvious concern over falling was interrupted by his more immediate concern of losing his legs. Orani's maneuvers brought the ambulance against the guardrail again, and he had to lift his feet to keep from losing them. Then the ambulance banged against the rail, almost tossing him over the edge. He flew out over the gulf, fingers desperately gripping the ridge. Looking down, all he could see was the wash of the surf against the rocks, and then he crashed back against the flat side of the ambulance. He couldn't help but steal a glance at the passenger-side mirror, where he could see Orani's shocked expression. She mouthed the word, "Sorry!"

"Woman driver!"

She eased the ambulance away from the guardrail and mouthed something like, "You're the man; get rid of them!"

He worked his way to the back of the ambulance, shuffling his left hand along the ridge and leveraging the butt of his pistol against it with his right. When he got to the right rear corner of the ambulance, the passenger with the AK-47 caught sight of him and immediately began to fire short bursts. The bullets hit uncomfortably close by. With a heave spurred on by the jihadist, Wolfe clambered on top of the ambulance and slid to the back where a convenient rail gave him something to hold. Lifting his feet up, he allowed his legs to slide off the back and he swung into the open bay.

"Well, we're right back where we started!" he gasped, safely inside the ambulance again. He started swimming his way into the ambulance, tossing everything he could get his hands on out the back. Soon the sedan was swerving to avoid test equipment, boxes, blankets, and everything else one might find in an ambulance. The last item was what brought him in the back in the first place: the remaining oxygen cylinder. He steadied it with his foot against the ambulance wall and aimed his pistol at the valve. Stealing a single glance at the sedan, he saw the questioning expression on the driver's bearded face.

"Sweet dreams!" he smiled, and shot. The second oxygen cylinder went out like the first, flying through the driver's-side front windshield of the sedan. The eyes of the passenger with the AK-47 grew as wide and round as his mouth, and he stared with horror at the headless thing sitting next to him.

Funny, Wolfe thought, *how those who are so willing to dish out terror can't take their own medicine!*

The sedan swerved once to the left, bounced off the rocky embankment, and then turned ninety degrees to the right, crashed through the guardrail, and launched over the cliff. Wolfe thought he heard a long, drawn-out wail of despair.

CHAPTER 42: La Palma

Orani slowed to a stop and Wolfe climbed back into the cab. He caught his breath and pulled out his PDA. In a second, he had directions. The route was thirty miles and it went over twisting mountain roads that were often narrow. As they drew closer to the northern end of the island, the asphalt gave way to gravel and dirt. They came to a *T* intersection and Orani had to slam on the brakes to avoid a truck loaded with men.

"Where do you think they're going?" Orani asked.

"The docks," Wolfe said. "I saw a small harbor in the analysts' briefing; it's an old fishing village."

"Should we follow them?"

"Go to the airfield. If there's a chance of stopping them before they can offload the nukes, we've got to take it."

Orani spun the tires and turned left. In ten minutes, they were at the airfield. The C-17 sat at the end with its ramp down. Orani drove up to it.

"Park next to the entry door on the left," he told her. "You do the talking. Make them think you're part of the plot. I'll go around back."

Orani did as he directed, pulling up to the aircraft as if she were supposed to. She tied a scarf around her head as three men stepped out of the aircraft. They weren't armed. She rolled down the window.

"They told us they didn't have any doctors," said the older of the two men. He wore a torn, green flight suit—stains that looked suspiciously like fresh blood stood out on the neck and shoulders. "You're too late; anyway, the rest of the crew is dead."

"You don't look like you're in very good shape yourselves," she told him.

"The operation has had some difficult moments," the pilot admitted.

"It's about to get worse, trust me," Orani said.

"What do you mean?" asked the pilot.

"She means you have to deal with me now," Wolfe told him. He'd moved around the back of the ambulance and now stood behind the men. "Hands up, all of you. Now face down on the ground, legs crossed, with your hands behind your head."

They did as he ordered.

Wolfe trussed them up in duct tape and ran into the C-17. He found the nukes, but much to his chagrin, there were a hundred missing. He gathered up the crash axe and ran back outside and rolled the pilot over on his back.

"Where are the rest of the nukes?"

The pilot clamped his mouth shut.

Wolfe took out his gun and shot the pilot in each knee.

"Alright, Major Kashan, I've had about as much of you as I can stand," Wolfe growled. "I hate traitors—a lot. Now, I'm not going to waste any more ammo on you." He took out his knife and held it up to Kashan's face. "I'd rather you tell me everything I want to know so that I can deliver you back to the U.S. military for the hangman, but if you're not going to talk, then I'm going to deliver you to Allah in pieces. Do you understand?"

"I don't have anything to say!" he groaned. "Allahu Akbar!"

"Have it your way," Wolfe said evenly, and he slit the flight suit at the crotch. He set the edge of the knife under Kashan's balls and told him, "You're going to meet Allah as a eunuch; good luck with those seventy virgins, pal; you'll have to be satisfied with the little boys!"

"No! No, wait, they took them. I don't know where, but they took them," Kashan wailed. "We were supposed to fly these to Morocco. I don't know any more, I swear it!"

Wolfe brandished the crash axe. Kashan screamed, as did the other jihadists, obviously expecting him to brain them with it. Instead, Wolfe dragged the pilot's hands over his head and pierced them with the pick of the crash axe. Then he did the same to the other two jihadist's hands and took the edge to their knees. By the time he finished, their pitiful wailing made him wish he'd shot them—but no, that was too good for traitors.

"I'm leaving them with you, Orani," he said, "but this should ensure they don't give you any trouble." He taped their mouths shut and tossed them in the back of the ambulance like firewood. "Take them back into town. They deserve to go through the humiliation of a court martial and the hangman—it's better than they deserve." He shut the door.

"Where are you going?"

"La Palma!"

"How are you going to get there?"

"I'm going to fly!"

Wolfe ran back to the C-17, climbed in and closed the hatch. The heat in the cargo jet was stifling, and it baked the already putrid concoction of vomit, shit, and blood. Fortunately, Wolfe's experience with the B-52's forty-year collection of stinks made him nearly immune to the olfactory assault. Ignoring the stench, he slid into the stained co-pilot's seat—it still had a window—turned on the battery, and started the auxiliary power unit. That took a minute to wind up, but when it did, he closed the contact for the generator and the jet came to life. He opened the air valves to the starter manifolds and the big fans started to turn. He was guessing at the start RPM, and he was in a desperate hurry, but he didn't dare put fuel into the engine too soon. It would take longer to have to restart an engine from a hot start than it would to be patient. He waited until the RPMs stabilized and added fuel to each engine. Obediently, they rasped to life, emitting a steadily climbing whine until they stabilized at an irritating pitch.

Although unfamiliar with the C-17, Wolfe knew jets. He went across the panels turning on generators, hydraulic pumps, and air-conditioning packs, lowering the flaps, and the like. When most of the red and amber lights went out, he released the parking brake by pumping the top of the rudder pedal. He pushed the throttles up. A tiller on his right controlled the nose wheel. He taxied out of the trees and onto the grass runway, kicking up dust in huge clouds. He straightened the jet, grabbed the stick, and shoved the throttles forward. The jet gathered speed slowly at first, and then it accelerated rapidly. He held slight nose-down pressure on the stick until, passing 120 knots, he felt the nose want to rise. Decreasing the forward pressure slightly made the jet spring from the runway and into the sky. He raised the gear and flaps as he banked to the right, angling through a gap into the hills and heading north over the ocean.

The first thing he saw was the dock on the coast. A fishing boat was pulling away. The men in the stern were covering up a batch of large boxes—obviously not fishing gear. A quick glance told him the pallets on the docks were empty.

Some of the men on the docks looked up at him as he flew low over their heads, pointing their AK-47s into the sky and firing in celebration. Wolfe started a wide left-hand turn, searching the overhead panel for the fuel controls. Once he found them, he armed the jettison pumps and uncovered the safety for the jettison valves. Picking up the boat about halfway through his turn, Wolfe stayed low, and when they were half a mile in front of him, he slowed and lowered the flaps full down. As the huge jet decelerated, he threw the jettison switch. A red message reading, "Fuel dump in progress," flashed on the electronic display. He flew with the ship just off his right shoulder so the nozzle would dump the fuel directly on the boat. Once past, he shut off the jettison pumps and closed the nozzles and pulled up and around for another pass. As he horsed the airplane in a tight bank to the right, Wolfe found the panel he'd glanced at when he got into the plane: the electronic countermeasures and defense panel.

He armed the flare dispenser and switched it from active mode, meaning it would dispense flares automatically on sensing a threat, to manual mode. Then he turned the selector knob from "two" through "eight" to "continuous."

The dispenser switch glowed amber.

He picked up the boat three-quarters of the way through the turn and close enough to see the crew. One man swung his AK-47 at him, but another stopped him from firing—the jet fuel must've soaked the boat. Good.

"Time to say good-bye, boys," he said, and he crept lower and slowed. The men on the boat all turned to look at him. Wolfe slowed down as much as he could and punched the flare dispenser. Even from a couple hundred yards, he could see their eyes grow wide with alarm, and several men jumped overboard in sudden panic. Then he eased up on the stick just a bit. The boat disappeared beneath the bulbous nose, and then it shook as if it went through a wave of turbulence. Wolfe banked to the left and saw the pyre of the ship trailing a growing black cloud. There were a couple of secondary explosions, and then it sank into the waters, leaving an oily slick and a field of charred wood and body parts.

Wolfe set course for the island. Twenty minutes later, its dry, rocky ridges popped over the horizon, rising thousands of feet over the blue waters. The concave curve of the crater faced ominously to the northwest. He could soon make out a pier and a pale ribbon of road climbing through the scrub forest along the eastern side of the ridge. Three trucks climbed the ridge, smaller than deuce-and-a-half's, but larger than pickup trucks. Wolfe banked to the right, paralleled the trucks, and surveyed the road. The trucks were coming out of a sharp right turn and faced another switchback before joining onto a straight section of road atop a long, gradual incline.

The trucks in front and behind carried men with AK-47s. The middle truck had a canvas topper over the bed. All at once, the men in the front truck started firing in his direction. They must've heard about the boat over the radio. He banked sharply away, hearing a few plinks as he did so, but nothing more. He made it a tight turn, lowering the flaps to full down and slowing to 120 knots. The road came into view, and the men started firing. Bullets ricocheted off the Plexiglas and penetrated the radome. He could hear the high-pitched zing of metal on metal, but he stayed on course. Wolfe threw the landing gear down, and the big airplane started to rumble. He fixed his aim point on the center truck. More bullets smacked into the fuselage in rapid succession. A panel blew out on the first officer's side. The red and amber warning messages popped up on the electronic displays. The first truck was coming close. Boom! His number-two engine exploded, and Wolfe instinctively kicked in right rudder as the jet yawed to the left. He didn't consider shutting it down; let it burn! The first truck was about to disappear beneath the nose when the middle truck hit its brakes. Wolfe punched the nose down and felt the crunch of metal underneath. The

C-17 veered to the left as it settled on the road; hopefully, he had two of the three trucks beneath it. The front truck was full of jihadists. Their white-rimmed eyes were a testament to his success and their surprise; but the shock was short-lived, and they fired a hail of bullets his way. The Plexiglas panels of the windscreens shattered, showering Wolfe with chunks of glass. He ducked low but steered toward the truck. The aircraft heaved in protest, and the scream of ripping metal reverberated through the fuselage punctuated by a rising shudder, as if he were careening over a terribly rutted road.

The aircraft started to slow, and the truck pulled away, peppering him with a deluge of fire. Through the shattered window, he saw a jihadist wrestling with a shoulder-mounted rocket. Wolfe shoved the power up. The engines whined, and the vibrations grew exponentially. Wolfe could no longer focus on the truck, so violent was the shaking, but he saw the dark blur pass under the nose and felt the crunch of the impact. A dull explosion lifted the nose of the airplane. Fire rolled up and around the nose, and Wolfe smelled burned metal, smoke, and gasoline.

He pulled the power back and the nose fell precipitously. The shaking grew even more violent as the nose dug into the roadway. The jet swerved side to side, but as it slowed, the rudder offered less and less control. He hit the brakes. Nothing. A tongue of rock projected to the edge of the roadway to the left. There was no way to avoid it. More to the point, the road curved to the left around the rock. Straight ahead was a low, wooden guardrail. Beyond was a gulf dropping five hundred feet to the clear, blue ocean. Bang! The rock sheared the left wing and engines off, igniting a cloud of fuel. The jet spun to the left, screeching sideways along the road and then backward.

Wolfe unbuckled his straps and clawed for the shot-up window. The force of the deceleration made it hard to move, and he had to climb hand-over-hand to the window frame. He pulled himself through and swung his legs over the nose. He was going to slide down the nose, but the airplane groaned and the nose suddenly rose. He leapt to his feet as the nose pulled away beneath him and staggered to the bullet-ridden fiberglass point. His boot touched the apex and he shoved off, jumping with all his might. As the C-17 pitched over the cliff, he hit the edge of the road with his chest. It knocked the breath from his lungs, and he began to slide, but at the last second, he caught hold of the asphalt lip of the road.

Wolfe hung there as the C-17 slid down the cliff and exploded on the rocks below. The cliff was almost shear, and the toes of his boots scrambled against the crumbling stone, but there wasn't a ledge or stone to support his weight. A few feet to his right was a wooden post for the now-destroyed guardrail. Enough of it remained to offer a better hold than the hot asphalt. He worked his way over to it and hugged it close, pulling himself up high enough to peer over the roadway.

A truck was coming down from above. He found a lip of concrete, left from pouring the base for the post, and he rested on that, peering over the lip of the roadway. The truck stopped and Hamdi got out, cursing.

"What the devil happened?" Hamdi shouted, limping toward the wreckage. One of his arms was in a sling.

"The devil has nothing to do with it," Wolfe muttered, reaching into his shoulder holster and pulling his gun. It was time to finish this madman here and now.

"The cargo plane, they say the cargo plane attacked them; the pilot is a traitor!"

Hamdi shook his head and pulled at his beard. He turned and jogged to the broken guardrail. As Wolfe pulled back under the edge, Hamdi looked down at the flaming wreckage of the C-17. "May Allah curse him to hell. Come, there's nothing more to be done; there's nothing left here." He turned away and headed back to the truck. Wolfe followed him with his eyes. As Hamdi approached the door, he whipped the pistol over the edge and rested it on the hot pavement. The terrorist was only ten yards away. He centered the sights on the back of his head, right in the center of the sweaty, black mat of hair. Wolfe couldn't miss.

"Good-bye, asshole," he breathed, and his finger tightened on the trigger.

"It's no matter, we have enough warheads to trigger the tsunami," Hamdi said. "As soon as I set the program, we'll leave. Our work is all but done."

Wolfe froze, his finger already depressing the trigger a fraction of an inch. Hamdi was going to wherever the triggering mechanism for the bomb was. The terrorist turned and headed back to the truck. Wolfe holstered the gun and rolled up onto the pavement. Running doubled over, Wolfe sprinted to the back of the pickup and rolled into the bed, hiding beneath the back window. The truck started. The driver released the brake and gunned the motor, heading back up the hill. The road switched back to the left and led straight in the opposite direction he'd come. Looking through the open back of the truck, he got a clear view of the devastation on the road below. The remains of the three trucks were strewn across the road, half hidden by columns of thick, oily smoke. Over the edge of the cliff, another column of smoke twisted high into the clear, blue sky.

After another series of turns, the truck entered a scrub forest. The pavement gave way to dirt, and the truck kicked up clouds of dust. After five minutes of bone-jarring bounces, the truck skidded to a halt in a small clearing next to several other trucks. The chunky basalt ridge formed a natural wall to the left. On the right was a copse of trees, and beyond that a flat area where a helicopter was parked. Men in Arabic garb wearing red scarves milled around. All were heavily armed. Several approached the truck. Wolfe slithered out the back of the truck and underneath the bed. Hamdi got out; he could see his booted feet. Two pairs of boots approached him.

"What happened?" someone asked.

"It doesn't matter; it's over with. Are the warheads all wired?"

"All the ones we have, that is eighty—one every two hundred fifty meters," replied the voice. "We're ready for the next batch. Everything will be wired by sundown."

"We don't need the last weapons," Hamdi told them. "What we have is enough. We'll arm the weapons presently and then leave. Tell the rest to get to the boats. By the time the authorities get here to investigate the trouble, we'll be gone and they'll be met with the fire of jihad!"

There were shouts and fired weapons, and the boots followed Hamdi to a steel door set in the stone of the ridge. He entered followed by four men. The rest went to the trucks and drove away. *Now, that helps!* Wolfe thought, and he waited for them all to leave. All that remained between him and the door were two guards. Wolfe screwed on his silencer.

It was an afterthought, killing those two men, and not worth remembrance—unless it was the callousness of the act that unconsciously made his gut twist just a little.

Wolfe ran to the downed jihadists, dragging them out of sight and stripping one of his jacket, kaffiyeh, bandolier, clips, grenades, and AK-47. After arming himself more thoroughly, he carefully opened the door and looked inside. Within was a long, rough-hewn rock corridor illuminated by naked bulbs hanging from a spliced wire fixed to the roof. There was no attempt to make the corridor comfortable except to smooth the floor with a layer of concrete. It was cool, almost cold. Wolfe slipped inside. Voices echoed along the corridor from his left. He closed the door and started in that direction, but a hole in the floor attracted his attention. It was close to the inner wall of the corridor and slanted away from the corridor, down into the heart of the crater rim. The hole was about eighteen inches in diameter. Two yellow sixteen-gauge wires ran from a newly poured section of concrete about two feet wide. Whoever poured it was in a hurry, or they didn't care about aesthetics, as it wasn't even skimmed smooth. They'd shoveled the concrete into what looked to be a channel that housed whatever the wires went to.

"They've covered the main wire bundle for the detonation sequence to the artillery shells," Wolfe murmured, remembering the professor's comments on the exactitude of the detonation sequence. It all made perfect sense. In the hole was a nuclear artillery shell. An electrical impulse would trigger it from some central point. The shells would be sequenced to explode simultaneously along the crater rim, thus triggering the enormous landslide and consequently the "Wave of Allah."

"Ingeniously simple," he sighed, realizing he could easily sever the wires to this particular shell, but it would be impossible to get them all. He'd need a jackhammer to get through what looked to be at least eighteen inches of concrete in order to get to the main bundle. He needed to find the central control for the sequence and shut it down from there. That, however, could be anywhere. The whole thing could be run from a laptop or even a PDA.

"Sahib, what are you doing?" asked a voice in Arabic.

Wolfe glanced to his left. Coming back along the dimly lit corridor were Hamdi and five others. Their guns were at their sides, and Hamdi's expression was more perplexed than hostile.

"The Wave of Allah! My pardon!" he replied reverently, standing quickly and making his way back to the steel door, as would any underling caught absent from his post.

Hamdi laughed and told another man something about the helicopter. A man separated from the group and headed toward the door. Hamdi turned his attention back to the silver PDA in his hand. Wolfe eyed it narrowly. That was it. All he had to do is take care of these men and interrupt the firing sequence.

The man going to the helicopter had stopped just as Wolfe held the door open for him. Wolfe's face was covered by the jihadist scarf, and it was too dim to see how pale his skin was. What was the man stopping for? The jihadist was staring at his boots—his glossy, black *Ropers*, his flying boots shining in the sunlight of the open door. They didn't fit at all with the common jihadist wardrobe.

But the jihadist was merely confused, not suspicious, and he asked, "Where did you get those boots?"

The jihadist stood there dumbly, but Hamdi looked up, stared at Wolfe, stared at his boots, and stared back at Wolfe.

"Wolfe!"

Wolfe slammed the door into the jihadist, sending him stumbling outside, but then he pulled the door back in front of him as a hail of AK-47 fire came his way. Dropping to his knees, he whipped the AK out, firing blindly from behind the door. Several yelps and screams welcomed his volley.

There was a momentary silence, and then Hamdi's voice came through the cloud of cordite. "You have an irritating knack for staying alive, Mr. Wolfe, but it is time you gave up; the game is over."

"By that you mean I'm blocking your only way out; we're at an impasse," Wolfe replied.

"Not at all, I'm willing to die—but are you so keen to lay your life down for your God? Remember, you have your children to think about."

Wolfe fished a grenade out of his pocket and said, "I'll make you a deal, Hamdi. You shut down the detonation sequence and give me the

PDA, and we both walk out of here alive. I see my family and you get to go back and raise your daughter. Everybody wins."

"My daughter has left the path of Islam, thanks to the perversions of your Western world; I shall correct that and many other falsehoods when the Wave of Allah washes over your shores," Hamdi said sharply. "Dying doesn't frighten me as it does you; I have seventy-two virgins awaiting me in paradise."

"Don't forget the twenty-eight prepubescent boys they've promised you—I've read your scripture, you sick bastard!" Wolfe retorted, shifting the AK-47 to his left hand and placing his ring finger through the ring of the pin.

"You Western dog; how dare you blaspheme the scriptures!"

"You're doing that all by yourself, Hamdi!"

"We shall see if your faith is as strong, Crusader. My soul is ready for glorious death!"

"Then don't let me keep you from it!" Wolfe replied, and he got ready to pop around the door with the AK. At the same moment, a grenade skidded past the door. Without thinking, Wolfe flicked his grenade past the door and dove for it—like a third baseman laying out for a stinger down the line. He clutched it in mid-bounce with his right hand and threw it back down the corridor from whence it came. A second later, the explosion filled the tunnel with a blast of sound and heat. More screams. Shrapnel rattled against the rock walls and tugged at his jacket. Smoke filled the cavern. His ears rang and he staggered up, almost falling. He fell into the corridor wall, shooting blindly into the smoke. There was no return fire. The smoke started to clear, and the first thing he saw was the shaft of light coming from the open door. Slowly, it revealed three huddled bodies—Hamdi wasn't among them.

"What do I have to do to kill that bastard?" Wolfe rushed to the door. Through the high-pitched throbbing in his ears, he discerned something else: shouting and the whine of a helicopter engine. He ran outside, but he wasn't two strides from the door when there was another blast. It knocked him flat. He glanced behind to see smoke and dust billowing from the door to the tunnel; the sound of rock falling inside made it all to clear there was no way to reach the bombs anymore.

He was up and running toward the chopper, and as soon as he was out of the dust cloud, he saw Hamdi limping for it as well, but with a forty-meter head start. Hamdi limped through the copse of trees, and it was the trees that saved him. Wolfe fired the AK-47 as he ran, and what he lost in accuracy the weapon made up for in quantity. Still, the shells meant for Hamdi were swallowed by the trees.

Hamdi reached the open door of the helicopter and tumbled in. Wolfe held his fire; if he hit the chopper's fuel tank, it would explode, taking the PDA with it. He put his head down and sprinted as the pilot applied power. The chopper lifted off, albeit slightly wobbly—the pilot might be wounded. The nose turned to the right and dipped, and then it steadied and began to rise. Wolfe whipped the AK-47 onto his back and hit the prop-wash. It almost knocked him down, but with two lunging strides, he leapt for the skid. He caught it with the crook of his right arm, slinging his right leg up and hooking it around the skid. The toe of his boot hooked on the aft brace. The chopper roared away from the ground. Wolfe reached for the deck, but just as he got a handhold, Hamdi slammed the door shut, catching his hand painfully and losing his grip. Wolfe's weight was already on the hand and he fell back, also losing his grip on the skid. He swung off the skid, and a sharp pain hit his right knee as he swung upside-down. Suddenly, all he could see was water two thousand feet below. Desperately, he hooked his other leg over the skid, improving his precarious hold. Then the helicopter pilot started to yank and bank in an effort to throw him off. Wolfe whipped this way and that, but when the pilot punched the nose down momentarily, it brought the skid within reach of his right arm. Like a striking cobra, he whipped the arm around the skid. There was a sound of gunfire over the chopper motor, and shards of Plexiglas flew from the side of the chopper. A boot kicked out the rest, and then the muzzle of an AK-47 appeared out of the opening. An arm, a shoulder, and finally Hamdi's leering face followed. He smiled as he mouthed the words, "Good-bye, Crusader; I'll see you in hell!"

Wolfe swung the AK-47 around, and as Hamdi gloated, he fired through the floor of the chopper. Hamdi winced in surprise and fell away from the window, dropping his AK. Taking advantage of the momentary respite, Wolfe scrambled up the skid and got a hold of the window's frame. Hamdi was struggling, trying to get his gun up, and blocking Wolfe's entry. Blood was dribbling from his mouth and his eyes were clouded with pain. Wolfe grabbed him by his greasy hair and pulled his head and shoulders through the window. Wedging Hamdi into the bottom of the frame with his left elbow, Wolfe reached by the weakly flailing jihadist and found the leather holster for his PDA. He yanked the instrument free and checked the screen.

It was counting down from one minute and thirty-seven seconds.

He braced himself against the window frame with his right arm and raised Hamdi's head with his left hand. The jihadist winced and gazed at him in horror.

"Don't let me keep you from your date with hell!" he shouted in the jihadist's ear. He let his head go and grabbed the back of his belt. With a mighty heave, he jerked the jihadist through the window and let him slip into the turbulent air. Hamdi left with a high-pitched wail, gyrating like a bad Hollywood stuntman against the deep azure of the ocean far below.

Wolfe slithered into the helicopter and checked the screen.

One minute and sixteen seconds.

The pilot glanced back and saw Hamdi was gone. His mouth was a huge round *O*, and his eyes darted back and forth. Wolfe whipped his gun up and pointed it at the jihadist's forehead. The jihadist swallowed, then turned away, set his teeth in a grimace, and punched the stick down. Wolfe flew to the top of the cabin and hit the roof. The ocean filled the view screen. Wolfe fired. A half-dozen shots left his gun and they seemed to hit everything but their mark, so violently did the pilot stir his stick, but finally, a bullet hit him in the shoulder. He let go of the stick and Wolfe crashed to the deck. He fired twice more from his belly, and the pilot slumped to the side. Wolfe clawed his way up and slid into the other seat.

He'd flown the V-22 simulator fifteen years or so ago, but he'd never flown a helicopter, and he didn't have time to learn. First things first, he pulled back on the stick until he was nearly level—there wasn't any time to mess with the collective. The chopper somewhat under control, he glanced at the PDA.

Thirty-one seconds.

Enough flying. Wolfe clamped on the stick with his knees.

He took out the pen and hit the back arrow. A menu appeared. It was in Arabic. He saw a list of macros. He selected the top one. It looked like the arming sequence. There was a red macro button and a green macro button. The green one was selected. He selected the red one. A flashing red message popped up and the green button remained active. He hit it again, and then again. There was no change. It was too late to disable the bombs. He had to alter the sequence. He hit the back button.

Twenty seconds.

He selected the next macro. Strangely, instead of his hand shaking, everything slowed down. He saw the numbers in the upper right-hand corner, and he thought, *Seventeen seconds, alright, I've got time.* He couldn't believe the thought, but he rolled with it.

The next macro was obvious: it was the firing sequence. All the bombs were spaced at equidistant intervals, so in order for them to fire simultaneously, it was a simple progressive equation based on the speed of the electrical impulse through the wire and the distance to each successive bomb. The equation was right there. He highlighted it with the pen.

Twelve seconds.

What to change it to?

"I don't have the time to figure that out!" he realized. "Keep it simple, stupid; if it worked without a progressive firing sequence, they wouldn't have used one."

He hit the delete icon.

"Are you sure you want to delete?" the idiotic box asked him in Arabic.

"Yes!" he shouted, hitting the "OK" icon.

The equation changed to a simple equation, "f=0.00 sec."

The prompt asked, "Do you wish to institute the change?"

He hit "send."

"Sending," it said in Arabic, and the bars crossed the screen with agonizing sloth.

"Sent."

Three seconds.

Wolfe looked out across the bloody pilot to the crater. Three—two—one, a dozen, two dozen geysers of rock, dust, and smoke flew high into the air from the center of the crater. That was it, just those. Wolfe understood why. Since the detonation sequence went out to all the bombs at once, only the bombs closest to the impulse generator went off. The blasts vaporized the electrical cables before the electrical impulses could detonate the remaining weapons. Wolfe banked to the left and flew over the ocean to the left of the plumes. The center of the ridge slid into the sea, and then as the shock waves spread, the landslides progressed outward. Huge columns of water shot hundreds of feet into the air. The blue water turned into spray-lashed foam. The west side of the island became a boiling cauldron; a series of waves emanated from the center—but then the interference patterns Doctor Kadir warned of became evident. Dissonant waves cancelled out the main force of the energy, making the water chaotic instead of focused. The Wave of Allah was no longer the cataclysm it was intended to be, but an irritating symbol of twisted impotence.

Having done what he could, Wolfe turned back toward the main island.

"Flying this isn't so bad," he muttered to himself, "but landing is the real trick. Please, God; give me just a bit more luck—after all this, I don't want to check out because I can't land a chopper!"

CHAPTER 43: Return to New York

Wolfe knocked on the door of the apartment.

Orani opened the door. She smiled and showed all of her large, white teeth. It was a relaxed smile; it was a sincere smile. "Wolfe, come in, please come in!" She grabbed his arm and led him into her home. Lufti was there. She said hello and gave him a big hug. There was one more person there, a spry, elderly man. He approached Wolfe and held out his hand.

"Mr. Wolfe, it is a pleasure to meet you; I've heard so much about you!"

"It's nice to meet you too, Mr. Hamdi," Wolfe said, feeling strange that he was shaking the hand of a father whose son he'd just killed. They made sure of it this time, finding Hamdi's body floating in the surf. Khallida, however, was unaccounted for.

Hamdi led them into the small living room, where the TV was on. "It really is rather funny when you think of it," he chuckled. The news reports were still centered on the cataclysmic landslide on the remote island in the Canaries. The shot switched to a bearded cleric pounding on the podium with a sword, telling the world about the impending wrath of Allah.

He bent over and kissed Lufti on the head. "Go wash up for dinner, granddaughter."

When she'd left, he said, "The jihadists wanted a prophetic coup; they wanted to show their power by predicting it before it happened—

then it would seem as if they had divine support. You made fools out of them and my son. He is dead, I expect."

"He is," Wolfe told him. "I'm sorry for your loss."

"Don't be," the old man said. "I didn't know him the last time I saw him; he'd have had me killed that day. Thank God Yasmina told me to pray." He smiled at her and went to their corner nook. "If ever you're in trouble, Papa, pray here and someone will hear." He pointed to a small relic on the table. Wolfe knew Yasmina had it wired. It was a panic button. When the elder Hamdi touched it, it triggered a microphone that relayed everything to the Company. By the time Hamdi finished his prayers, a dozen men broke into the townhouse and arrested his would-be assassins.

As for his son, "I lost him a long time ago; better that he died with his mad scheme in ruination than to bring ruination on us all." He shook his head. "Where does such madness spring? Certainly not from scripture." He sighed and sounded truly relieved. Picking up a picture of a smiling young man, he stroked it. "You saved him, Mr. Wolfe. You saved him from a terrible crime. Now instead of remembering him as a mass murderer, I can remember my son as he was, as a child, as a curious boy, and as a young man insatiable for knowledge."

Then he laughed and pointed to the TV. "There is the real brilliance!" The image of a Catholic cardinal, a Protestant minister, a Jewish rabbi, and a Muslim imam praying together for God to avert the jihadists' "Wave of Allah." Hamdi pointed at the screen, saying, "So he did, or so you did," he added, pointing at Wolfe.

The TV showed the waves rolling in on the Eastern Seaboard. They were large, thirty to forty feet, but not the monsters promised by the jihad. The cameraman zoomed in. There was one final and well-deserved insult to the terrorists: surfers. Surfers poured in from all over the country to catch the waves. The TV displayed a well-tanned, scraggly blond boy giving the hang-loose sign to the world.

"Thanks for the waves, man! Hey, Allah rocks!"

Hamdi shook his head and said, "You've humiliated their leadership in front of their young men. I hope they take this righteously and renounce their violent ways. The world is a hard enough place to live in without jihad; there are better ways to spend the gift of life."

"Amen to that," Wolfe said.

CHAPTER 44: To Kill Is Not Enough

Orani dropped him a line. It was friendly, curious, and even a little concerned over his welfare. It was also full of information concerning some of the seedier aspects Flint uncovered in the military-industrial complex—and how certain people still had their eye on him. She finished with the cryptic words, "These people are operating outside the boundaries of government and need to be reeled in—take your pick."

He took the hint.

His work over the next few weeks culminated in a conference call with the six most powerful groups of people in the world. It didn't include the White House or the Congress. After all, these people controlled the money in every election, and if they didn't choose you, you didn't get elected.

"Gentlemen, excuse me for breaking into your teleconference, but as you see, I'm beginning to get the hang of this business," Wolfe told the assembled audience. He studied the faces of the six screens of people, each a separate boardroom. "I congratulate you on your cold-blooded capitalism—I'd never dreamed that so few could control the fates of so many, or that you could agree to be so ruthless in the pursuit of the almighty dollar."

"Trillions of dollars, Mr. Wolfe, let's not be so trite," laughed Delaney, who looked like he might run a carnival in his spare time. "While none of us would be accused of having an altruistic bone in our bodies, even we would not sacrifice millions of people if the profit were not several thousand per head!"

"That's nefariously cold," Wolfe told them.

"Not at all," the man retorted. "Who do you think took the threat seriously? If it weren't for our combined efforts, no evacuation would take place if the terrorists made good on their threat. As it was, men and material were ready for the greatest evacuation humanity has ever known."

"That's an interesting choice of words," Wolfe said.

"Think of it what you will, Mr. Wolfe. The fact remains we did everything in our power to prepare for the worst," the man said gruffly.

"And you did everything in your power to ensure it was a credible threat," Wolfe said. "You played both sides, all of you, capitalizing on fear to make a killing before the event, while guaranteeing you had the exclusive contracts for reconstruction."

"There's no crime in making money, Mr. Wolfe, even if it is a great deal of money."

"But there is in facilitating terrorism, which you did, and by trying to have me killed. I take that personally."

"There's nothing you can do about that, Mr. Wolfe," the man said. "The past is the past, and there's no profit in revisiting it. We've cancelled our contract on you. Take that as a sign of respect and admiration, if you will. I congratulate you on survival. Let's leave it at that."

"I'm afraid I can't do that," Wolfe smiled. "Though you've cancelled your contract on me, I haven't cancelled mine on you."

"You must be joking; you can't touch us!" the man said angrily. "Each of us can place a call this moment to the White House and have you removed. That's all it would take, Wolfe!"

Wolfe held up his remote and said, "There will be no phone call, gentlemen. I have your number. The first one of you to disconnect this line or pick up a phone is dead."

"You're bluffing!"

"I want to make a point, gentlemen," Wolfe said slowly and with relish. "In fact, as you know, I'm not a rogue operator. I'm a Company man, and you've made the Company nervous. You've put millions of people at risk, all for your own self-gratification. However, you have an equal potential for doing good work. It's up to you how you use your power. I warn you, however; I'm watching."

"And this is your threat? You're watching?"

"Yes, but to show you I'm serious, I'll let you in on a little secret."

"What?"

"Every person in one of your boardrooms is already dead."

"Bullshit!"

"No really, but as I'm a merciful man, I'll give you a few seconds to make your peace with God." He took a deep breath, coldly relishing the darting eyes and nervous gasps of the dozens of players who but a moment before felt themselves in complete control of absolutely everything. "Time's up, good-bye!" He pressed the button.

A table exploded. The charges molded into the table's edging exploded outward, gutting the people around the table, but sparing the camera. Everyone saw the carnage. There was no doubt whatsoever.

Delaney was gone.

"Have I made myself clear?" Wolfe asked.

"You bastard, you've become a terrorist yourself now!"

Wolfe laughed and said, "You're at risk now, just like everyone else. How does that feel? I'll be interested to see whether that changes your way of doing business. The powers that be want you to reevaluate your positions. If you don't, well, my employers know where you live."

"You're just a cold-blooded killer!"

"As the late Mr. Delaney once told me, to kill is not enough."

EPILOGUE

Wolfe drove down the Idaho road, a cloud of dust spreading out behind. It was early evening, and the Palouse hills were turning golden from the setting sun. As he drove, he thought of everything Father Richard had said to him. Specifically, the priest's response to a singular question, "Do I deserve to love and be loved in return?"

Father Richard said softly, "That is what Christ tried to tell everyone, including those who nailed him to the cross. If they were acceptable for God's love, then certainly you are. You've born a terrible burden for so many others; why should you not love? After all, isn't that God's ultimate way of healing even the most heinous sins?"

With that thought in mind, Wolfe pulled into the driveway of a little cabin tucked in the Palouse hills. The sound of horses whinnying drifted through the cool Idaho evening.